KEY
OF
ARCANDUS

• CARVING LEGACIES •

KEY
OF
ARCANDUS

BOOK 1

LAUREN N SEFCHIK

*This book is dedicated to my mother, Michelle,
whose unconditional love and support has never
wavered throughout my journey to becoming
an author.*

I love you!

PREFACE

The concept for the *Carving Legacies* series started with a song, an idea, and a long work commute. Over a decade ago I decided to build a world that I wanted to play within and tells stories. Stories about people, both mortal and immortal alike, who struggle to find their place in their world as we do in ours. My hope is that this book is the beginning of a new journey for you, with the start of many more to come.

A NOTE TO THE READER

The world of Clayne has a variety of languages which differ between the races and regions. The most common of these world languages belong to the Adami. For this book, whenever you see dialogue in "standard text," you may safely assume it is the Adami common tongue. If the dialogue is in *"italics,"* then a different language is being spoken. The narration will typically indicate which language the character has swapped to, and you might see some dialect or sentence variations based on a character's individualized fluency between one language and the next.

The only exception to this rule is in the instance of sound effects. Things like chopping, ripping, or someone's drunken hiccups through their dialogue will also be in italics, but this does not mean they're in another language.

the world of

Clayne

Fi

Seda

Vasile

Ysil

Balforem

The Hive

Sek'hithis
The Sand Gates

Libstravad

Pustelia Crest

Niravad

astas
el Kingdom

Caspia

Finnlock

Mortis Gordia

Map created by: Lauren Sefchik for *Carving Legacies* copyright © 2020

PART I

Niravad

1

$\mathcal{E}$VERYTHING TOOK PRECISION, and this task was no exception. Her vertical pupils constricted into slits as she honed in on the exact angle needed to keep the fabric seamless. The needle slid through the red linen, and Siroun reached over and pulled the thread through to complete the ladder stitch. With a soft tug, she brought the edges together to make the seam disappear. She gave it one last tug to ensure the stitch was perfect, then paused and admired her handiwork.

"*Beautiful,*" she said to herself, then tied the string off with a knot and snipped it with her teeth.

"*Siroun,*" called a male voice from downstairs in the throaty Drakish language of her homeland, "*are you ready to go?*"

Panic struck her hazel eyes as she looked out of the window and toward the sun to find the day was slipping into the late afternoon. She shook the jacket with a snap of her wrists and said to herself, "*Shoot!*"

She hopped off of her bed and ran over to the tiny,

hand-carved dresser with a mirror as old as she was and found her favorite hair comb resting in front of her. A flurry of hands worked to pull up her wavy silver locks into a hap-hazard bun that cascaded down the back of her head, before plucking a hair clip and pinning the mess into place. Several tendrils floated around her face, and she blew at one that rested just over her right eye.

"Siroun!" the male voice said again in agitation. *"I can't be late today."*

"I know, brother, I know!" she shouted back in a hurry as she put on her light sweater and jammed a nearby book into her satchel. With a last look around the room, she took the coat with her bag, and rushed downstairs. When she reached the bottom floor, Siroun witnessed her brother pacing back and forth, repeatedly checking the sun through a window.

When he saw her arrive he sighed in relief, *"Finally."*

The tone wasn't sarcastic, but it wasn't pleased. However, Siroun had the remedy to his dour mood. With pride, she presented the coat and replied, *"Ta-dah!"*

It took him a minute to realize what she had done, but when his reptilian eyes finished scanning the garment, they widened. His claw reached out and touched the location where the tear had once been.

"You mended it?" he said.

"Yep!" Siroun said with glee. *"I couldn't just let you stand before the council with nothing but your civilian tunic."*

A smile crept along his scaled lips before taking it from her hands and draped it around himself. The regal jacket fit with perfection around his arched back, leaving room for his long tail. Siroun watched the stress in his eyes fade away.

He gave her an appreciative nod. *"Thank you. I can't believe you did this in such a short time."*

She grinned. *"Let's go, before we're late."*

They made their way to the front door and said in unison, *"Goodbye, father!"*

In return, an elderly Dragomyr called to them from the kitchen, *"Be safe."*

The two of them traversed along the only road that passed through the mountain village of Pustelia Crest. Once they approached the busier part of town, Siroun pulled the long sleeves of her tunic over her iridescent scales.

Her brother glanced at her a few times before saying, *"I don't understand why you insist on wearing such conservative clothing in the summer."*

She tucked a lock of silver hair behind her tipped ear. *"I don't like to attract attention."*

He sighed. *"Your entire physique attracts attention, Siroun. I don't think a scant sweater to hide the scales on your arms is benefiting you."*

"Perhaps." The ruefulness clear in her voice. *"I guess I try to do what I can to offend no one."*

Her skin was a blend of flesh and scale. A taboo to the village, and a defiance of The Great Three according to the council. Yet, it seemed her brother found her efforts to remain a wallflower within her homeland moot. She could see it in his eyes he didn't agree with her response, but he nodded anyway and continued walking.

As they made their way through the crowds, other villagers glanced at Siroun and turned away or curled their upper lip at her. Siroun wasn't blind to their behavior. Instead, she learned to ignore them as they scowled and sneered with their distaste. She couldn't help but pity the contempt they felt for a single, insignificant individual who did little to disrupt their world. At least, that's how she saw it in the grand scheme of life.

However, one villager came up from behind and yanked sideways on Siroun's small tail, tugging her off-balance against her brother. The satchel on her shoulder slipped off and hit the ground, spilling her belongings.

"Whoops, better watch it, half-breed," they chortled while passing by.

Her brother helped to stabilize her while his neck turned, and he hissed, *"That was deliberate."*

"Yeah, yeah…" the other Dragomyr said, waving him off. *"Go cry to the councilmen about it, Vasylvad. You're so damn good at it."*

Vasylvad clicked his tongue and muttered, *"Spiteful cur."*

During this exchange, Siroun collected her things and hoisted the satchel over her shoulder. Dust stamped the side of her clothing, unnoticed. Before she took a step, however, Vasylvad reached out and halted her to brush off the dirt.

"Whoops," she said.

Her brother's sigh sounded exhausted. *"Let's just get you to work."*

It didn't take much longer to reach the library. Today seemed busy as Dragomyr came in and out in droves, most of them farmers. Among them, a familiar Dragomyr stepped out from the double doors and checked the time.

"Nik," Vasylvad called out to the other male, and the Dragomyr turned toward them and smiled.

"Vas! Escorting Siroun to work, are you?" He then shifted his gaze to Siroun and said, *"I see you mended your brother's coat. Well done."*

Siroun gave him the biggest of smiles. Out of all the villagers in Pustelia Crest, Nikostraz treated her with kindness and without prejudice toward her racial origins. He was a Dragomyr of the world. Intelligent, well-read, and handsome with his rugged plume of emerald-black feathers that rested along his collar. He moved to the village several years ago, and she grew to consider him a best friend. Whether the sentiments were mutual, she couldn't tell. Nikostraz interacted more with her brother for business reasons. However, he always spent time with her when he came to visit, and she felt that counted for something.

"Did you find anything of interest, Nik?" she asked him.

"Not this time," he said with dismay, forcing a smile. *"Lilistraz kept eyeing me whenever I tried searching for information on the back shelves. If I had to guess, I don't think the Head Librarian likes me much."*

To that, Siroun laughed and replied, *"Lilistraz doesn't like anyone as far as I can tell."*

Nikostraz chuckled. *"You might be right."*

Vasylvad interjected with, *"Was there something in particular you needed to find?"*

The Dragomyr shook his head. *"It's nothing that can't wait another day."*

"You are way more patient than me, my friend." Vasylvad then diverted his attention back to Siroun. *"What time am I to pick you up?"*

"Oh?" Nikostraz raised a brow. "Are we working late?"

Siroun nodded at her brother and said, "We should be done before the third moon rises."

Then she turned to Nikostraz and answered with, "We're re-organizing the library, and I believe I have to scribe a new copy of a book a farmer lost. I'm hoping it's not a thick one. They always make my hand cramp."

"Interesting," Nikostraz murmured.

Siroun tilted her head at him. "Is something wrong?"

"Ah, no," he said, clearing his throat. "I'm just thinking how unfortunate it must be for you to have to work so late."

"I like it," she said. "There aren't as many people around. It's peaceful."

"Very well," Vasylvad interjected while taking a furtive look at the sun. A quickness came to his next statement, "I'll return later tonight. Remember your mantra."

The both of them recited together, "Hear the words, but don't listen. Acknowledge the action, but don't dwell on it. Reject the pain and don't show it."

Nikostraz remained reticent on the little ritual the siblings shared. Instead, he waited for the two to finish up by taking several steps away to allow them a moment of privacy. When Siroun finished, she took a deep breath and exhaled slowly. The meaning behind the words might have sounded strange to others. To Siroun they helped her visualize a protective barrier that kept her sane against the prejudices of the other villagers. She alone bore this burden, but Vasylvad constructed this mantra when she was a child to give her strength during times he could not be there to protect her.

He nodded with confidence. "Have a good day at work."

"You too," said Siroun, and as her brother and best friend left, she walked through the double doors to the haven of literary pages that took her far from this world and into many others.

.

2

*S*IROUN'S MUSCLES TREMBLED as she finished the last few letters of the text and set the quill into its holder. She massaged her right hand as she double-checked the words to make sure that everything was as she remembered. The Almanac of Summer Crops wasn't the most thrilling of reads, but the tome was essential to apprentice farmers.

A few feet away Lilistraz sorted books while Siroun blew on the last page to dry the ink. It didn't take long before the Dragomyr paused and looked toward her, saying in Drakish, *"Are you done yet?"*

Siroun nodded, placing the last page upon the pile for the librarians to bind in the morning.

"Good, then clean up and leave."

She raised a brow at Lilistraz and replied in kind, *"Don't you need help?"*

Lilistraz snorted and turned up her muzzle. *"I don't need some half-breed like you doing my job."*

Siroun balled up her fists but held her tongue. She had

been working at the library for almost six years, and just when she thought she had proven her worth, they were quick to remind her she was not one of their own. Instead of furthering the argument, she swallowed her frustration and started cleaning up her station.

Other librarians were with them that night. Four with two in the back to organize the Archives while Siroun and Lilistraz sorted and copied books upfront. By now, the second moon had risen and it wouldn't be long until her brother came to collect her. Siroun placed the ink bottles into their respective container when both women heard a muffled thud in the distance. While Siroun paid no attention to the noise, her supervisor halted in response.

After several seconds passed, Siroun sighed and said, *"I'm sure it's nothing. Those two are probably goofing off again."*

There was a slight edge of annoyance in Siroun's voice because Lilistraz didn't allow her to go into the Archives to help. Siroun's physiological differences from her peers barred her from a slew of tasks and privileges. Having access to the Archives was one of them.

Lilistraz shook her head in disdain as the Dragomyr loaded the last book onto the cart and went to fetch another. *"Honestly, would it kill the councilmen to hire some decent help around here?"*

Siroun ignored the comment as she plucked a discarded book from a nearby table and trudged over to the shelf where it belonged. No sooner had she lifted her fingers off of the leather spine when a crash, followed by a gurgling yelp of pain, echoed from the Archives. Then silence.

Both she and Lilistraz wondered what was transpiring.

Their male colleagues caused grief with their antics from time to time, but this sounded different from their usual antics. Lilistraz abandoned her current task. Her long, reptilian physique made quick work navigating around the carts as the Dragomyr tilted her head and listened for any declaration that they were all right, but none came. When she was sure there was trouble afoot, her neck arched over and locked eyes with Siroun.

"Don't follow me," Lilistraz hissed before making her way towards the Archives.

Siroun raised a brow in curiosity, but stayed put. The last thing she wanted was to get fired for not obeying instructions. Minutes passed as Siroun listened for any sign of caution or clearance by the Head Librarian. None came. However, the front door opened and she turned to find an elderly Dragomyr take a step inside.

"Lily?" said the woman's crackled voice.

Siroun recognized her as one of Lilistraz's favorite patrons who was always sweet and endearing to the Head Librarian, but a disgruntled wretch to everyone else.

The moment they saw each other the elderly woman wrinkled her snout and hissed, *"Where's Lily?"*

Siroun waved her hand before whispering, *"Shh."*

Yet, the Dragomyr narrowed her eyes and snapped back with, *"Don't 'shush' me, village reject. Now, where's Lily?"*

With restraint in her voice, she whispered back, *"The library has been closed for over an hour, and Lilistraz is very busy. She'll help you tomorrow."*

"How dare you sass me like that!"

Siroun went to retort when Lilistraz's muffled shouting echoed up ahead.

"No, stop!" said Lilistraz's panicked voice as she fled.

Chairs scraped along the floor as the female Dragomyr bashed through them to flee from her invisible assailant. Lilistraz looked over her shoulder several times as a shadow descended upon her. Siroun stepped forward to help when the figure obscured the Head Librarian from sight, and a blast of cold air rushed through the main hall. The wall sconces around the library extinguished, leaving Siroun in darkness with only the moonlight for guidance. In the distance, echoes of the patron from earlier screamed for the guards as she exited the library.

Smaller books, papers, and other loose objects scattered everywhere along with the familiar creaking of the shelves and rafters that spoke to the building's age. Though she heard nearby books shifting around her, she missed one that flopped at a precarious angle before tilting off the shelf and plummeting to the floor. The corner of the spine landed on her, and she yelped in pain before the loud slap-sound landing echoed throughout the main hall.

Clutching her left shoulder, Siroun sucked the air in through her teeth while her fingertips tingled. She looked around and bemoaned the mess, but before she could worry any further, her eyes caught sight of Lilistraz upon the floor.

Her breath hitched in her throat, *"Lilistraz?"*

Siroun rushed down next to the fallen Dragomyr, not paying attention to the puddle beneath her knees. When her fingers touched Lilistraz's throat to find a pulse, Siroun's hand became coated in something slick. Her body tensed as she brought her fingertips to her nose to catch a faint waft of iron from the blood that coated them. She screamed and scurried to her feet while turning to flee from the lifeless body, only to slam into the figure that stood before her. Her chest tightened, and her breath grew short and rapid. Meanwhile, the shadowy figure remained still with an unnerving calm.

"I can hear your heart racing," said the voice with a rich lyric tenor and a hint of mirth to it. He wasn't a Dragomyr, and the words he spoke belonged to the Adami. A race of humanoid beings that inhabited much of the world outside of the continent of Niravad. It was the only other language she knew, by textbook standards, due to it being so prevalent in multiple kingdoms. She forced her eyes to get a glimpse of the individual, but the dark surroundings didn't help. Only a sliver of the moon's radiance peered through a nearby window and reflected against his cloaked face. The illumination showed nothing more than a gaunt jawline. Her stomach lurched when she smelled putrid flesh wafting from his bulky robes, fresh blood compounding the odorous combination.

With what scant courage she could muster, Siroun swallowed and replied in his native tongue, "How did you get into this country? What happened to the others? Why did you kill Lilistraz?"

To those questions, the man chuckled. "I'm surprised you're so offended, given how—," a withered hand reached out and snatched Siroun by the wrist. She tried wrenching herself free, only to have his grip tighten as he pulled back her sleeve revealing the glistening reptilian scales along her arm. He ended his statement with, "… different you are."

He released her, and continued, "I figured I was doing you a favor."

"A favor?" Siroun scoffed. By now her eyes adjusted to the lack of light as she said, "You're deranged."

During their exchange, Siroun glimpsed his other hand and found a rolled-up parchment. The edges somewhat damaged, showing he ripped it from its frame.

Siroun's eyes widened. "What have you done?"

"I am borrowing something," he said, sounding proud of himself. "Isn't that what a library is for?"

"You have no right to be here, much less take from us as you please." Siroun attempted to snatch the item away from him, but his reflexes outmatched her own. Her fingers clamped on a corner fragment of the unidentified document. Growling, she gave it a light tug and said through gritted teeth, "Give it back."

The intruder couldn't help but chuckle. "This is very entertaining, but I'm afraid you're wasting your ti—."

Riiiiip!

The sound made Siroun wince and her muscles tense. Slowly, she opened one eye and saw that a small piece was now in her possession. A corner partition with strange markings she had never seen before, yet they felt familiar. As she thumbed the weathered paper, Siroun's eyes widened to saucers.

The man clicked his tongue at her with mock pity as he said, "Poor little bookkeeper. Have we committed a grave sin?"

Compelled to do something, Siroun returned her gaze to the larger partition and noticed faint lettering, and artwork, shifting around as though it were alive. The fragmented words lifted off the paper and swirled around her with streams of light. Her lips moved to read the symbols as though she had known them her entire life. The two pieces of parchment pulsed as more symbols converged to produce partial glimpses of a desert landscape. This display lasted only a few seconds before the guards burst through the entrance and interrupted the spell. The cloaked Adami lunged forward to snatch Siroun's piece, but she held on tight hoping to stall the criminal long enough for the guards to catch him.

"Let go!" He snarled.

"No!" said Siroun, while a deathly odor drifted into her nostrils making her fight the urge to vomit. She slammed her body against him, attempting to knock him off balance. Though unsuccessful, the commotion led the guards toward them, and the man grunted before shoving Siroun to the ground and tucking the larger parchment into his robes. Before Siroun could blink, his form changed into a massive black hawk that ascended to the rafters with the stolen item somewhere in tow.

She rushed to her feet and tried to give chase, but a wall of guardsmen blocked her path as the sconces were re-lit. When Siroun moved around them, they took another step to pervade her once more. Confused, she saw the bird making its escape through the main entrance and pointed while switching back to Drakish, *"He's getting away!"*

"Restrain her!" barked the commanding officer.

"Yes, Lieutenant," said the guards, then grabbed and folded Siroun's arms behind her back with their claws.

The officer in charge snatched the paper fragment from her fingers. She gaped at him. *"W-what are you doing?"*

To that question, they turned her around and forced her to take in the scene laid out in front of her. Though she had felt Lilistraz's blood on her hands, seeing it smearing the ground and leading to a trail of gore toward the Archives made Siroun turn pale.

Behind her, she overheard the Lieutenant issue his orders, *"Deliver the suspect to her father and set-up a perimeter around the house until the councilmen arrive in the morning. They'll decide her fate."*

"Suspect?" Siroun couldn't believe what they were saying.

A guard jabbed her between the shoulders with his muzzle and hissed, *"Walk."*

Siroun's feet stumbled along as she made her way out of the library in front of a mob of villagers. Many of them gasped as they saw Siroun smeared with blood. Gossip buzzed while as she marched through the crowd and up the road toward her two-story home. She didn't dare look anyone in the eyes as she trudged onward with her arms secured behind her back. When she cleared the last group of Dragomyr, one spat in her direction just missing her face. Her nose wrinkled in disgust, but she didn't dare speak. Meanwhile, the Lieutenant commanded the other half of the guardsmen to coax people back to their homes while assessing the carnage. Despite the cries of protest, the villagers scattered.

Pustelia Crest had no prison to jail criminals since the village was too small to waste precious land toward that affair. Instead, house arrest was a favored method until the council decided their fate. As they approached the door to her home, one of the Dragomyr shifted to the front and knocked on the door.

Tears filled her eyes as she looked over her shoulder. *"I swear, I didn't do it."*

"Hush!" the guards hissed in unison.

Their intimidation tactics didn't still her tongue this time around, and she shouted back, *"An Adami is here in the village! I saw it with my own eyes!"*

"Silence!"

As front door opened, Siroun felt a claw thump her behind the skull. It wasn't hard enough to knock her unconscious, but the pain made her see stars.

"What is the meaning of this?" said an elderly Dragomyr as he came outside and stood as tall as he could muster to appear larger. *"Take your claws off of my daughter!"*

The guards remained unmoved, and the one holding Siroun responded with, *"Olekstraz, your daughter is under house arrest."*

Siroun watched as her father furrowed his scaled brows before looking in her direction. Streaks of tears rolled down her cheeks as he studied her current condition. He saw the blood smeared over her knees and lower legs causing him to pull his long neck back in shock, but he composed himself enough to ask, *"Under what charges?"*

"You can get the details from Lieutenant Alekstrad, but I would start with murder."

"Murder?" Olekstraz scoffed. *"Preposterous."*

"Is the blood not enough evidence for you, old man?" said another guardsman.

To this, Siroun said to her father, *"There's an Adami in the village, father. I tried to stop him, but he turned into a bird and flew away after he murdered my colleagues and stole something from the Archives."*

"*Stop spouting lies,*" said the guard holding her in place.

"*I'm not lying!*" Siroun wasn't taking the fall for a crime she didn't commit. She knew the punishment she would endure if they found her guilty. "*Why is there a shape-shifting foreigner in our country? We need to find him before it's too late!*"

"*I said quiet half-breed!*" shouted the guard one last time. He raised a fist to strike Siroun again when Olekstraz wrested her from the other Dragomyr's grip and brought her inside. Vasylvad stared at her with bewilderment since they forbade her to traverse the village without an escort. In fact, she could see he was in the middle of changing coats to come fetch her when the two locked eyes inside their home.

While the other guards bellowed in protest, Olekstraz slammed the door in their faces and clicked the locks, muttering, "*Disgraceful.*"

3

CHOP-CHOP, CHOP-CHOP, CHOP...

Siroun's eyes fluttered open as the smell of Yaso stew roused her. That salty, meaty flavor accented with root vegetables made her stomach growl. It felt like forever since she had last eaten. The yelling back and forth between her and Vasylvad took too much of a toll on her emotions, and she retreated to her room and cried until she passed out. Even now, she didn't believe the reality she faced.

She rolled out of bed and trudged toward the window to see the posted guards around the house. It was a matter of time before the council summoned her to recall the events. At least, that was her hope. When the Yaso stew tickled her nose again, she took a deep breath and meandered her way out of the bedroom to face her family.

As she suspected, her father was cooking, while Vasylvad and Nikostraz sat at the table conversing with one another in low whispers. Both of them looked concerned, and Siroun interrupted by clearing her throat. All three Dragomyr stopped what they were doing, and Olekstraz wore a look of relief, saying, *"I wondered how long it would take before you'd come out of there."*

He adjusted the pot, so that nothing boiled over, before making his way to embrace her. She relished being in her father's arms. Her cheek brushed up against the bright plumage that adorned his neckline, and his hug helped wash away the recent ordeal.

When they pulled away from each other, her father beckoned her to take a seat. *"I'm just finishing up with lunch. Come, join your brother and Nikostraz. We can talk about what happened."*

Siroun found a spot at the massive hand-carved table while Vasylvad's eyes kept glancing over and looking away. His twitchy disposition made her antsy.

She could endure his nervous looks no longer, and finally said, *"What?"*

This must have been the opening he was looking for, because he wasted no time with his reply, *"They asked me to inform you that your presence is no longer welcome at the library."*

Siroun's eyes widened as she digested the news before responding with, *"Wha—, why?"*

"Isn't it obvious? They're accusing you of murder and theft of a sacred item from the Archives." He gave a heavy sigh and pinched the bridge of his muzzle with his claws. Every muscle in his body looked tense as he continued, *"I always said that getting a job was a bad idea."*

"Are you kidding me right now?" She just lost a job she loved, only to have her brother scold her. *"So you think it's better I stay holed up and hidden for the rest of my life?"*

"I'm just trying to be pragmatic, Siroun," said Vasylvad.

"*You know this village is looking for a reason, any reason, to get rid of you.*"

Instinctively, she stood upright and Nikostraz tried to assuage her with a gentle claw upon her shoulder. In that same moment, Olekstraz conveyed his displeasure with a firm, "*Vas!*"

Nikostraz chided Vasylvad with, "*Is now the best time?*"

Vasylvad's eyes remained stern as he spoke to his younger sister, "*I'm not saying this to be cruel, Siroun. I'm just trying to explain the gravity of the situation. You need to face the facts and realize that our people don't recognize you as one of them, and they never will. No matter how many times father and I declare otherwise. What worries me most is that I don't think I can save you this time.*"

It took every ounce of self-control for Siroun to sit still. Given that he donned his council tunic again, she had to assume that he met with them this morning. It explained his nervous disposition and straightforward warning. With naïve hope, Siroun asked, "*I know Lilistraz didn't make it. What about my other two colleagues?*"

"*They're dead too.*"

Now the room enveloped silence with only their father's delivery of food to break the tension. "*Enough of this unpleasant conversation. Let's eat.*"

Siroun's eyes were wide and glassy, horrified by the news to where she had to take a deep breath to calm herself. As they passed plates around, Siroun grabbed her utensil to help her eat while the others leaned in and took a few bites of their meals. Too many questions flooded her mind over what happened last night. Though the stew enticed her, she replayed the memory in her head again and suddenly the food tasted rancid in her mouth. Between the death of her work colleagues and getting banned from the one place she loved the most, Siroun had little appetite. A knot developed in the pit of her stomach, and she set aside the spoon before pushing the dish away. The soft splash of a tear hit the top of her hand, and she wiped at it in haste.

Everyone stared at her, and she felt compelled to say something. *"I know I should have done more to protect Lilistraz from that intruder, but I—."*

Vasylvad cut her off, *"You don't get it do you, Siroun?"*

"Vas, please. Don't do this," said their father.

It seemed moot for Olekstraz to scold his son further, but he tried. Nikostraz observed in silence, likely out of respect to the current conversation between family members. Meanwhile, Vasylvad paced side-to-side in the kitchen looking distraught, even angry. The way he glared at her spoke volumes on its own.

"No, father," he replied. *"I won't stay silent over something of this caliber. You knew the risk, Siroun. Something like this was bound to happen."*

"What are you saying, brother?" Siroun balled her hands into fists. *"Are you blaming me for what happened last night, is that it?"*

"They told me that the item the intruder stole is an ancient map leads to a dangerous artifact. One that our Regent Lord swore to guard with utmost secrecy. The council believes you assisted the foreigner in coming to take it."

Siroun slammed her fist on the table. *"That's absurd! I didn't help him take it. You can't possibly think I would risk my entire livelihood to steal an old document from a place I love and respect."*

Vasylvad snorted in frustration. *"They found you with a*

piece of the map, Siroun. They assume you were an accomplice and intend to carry out a full investigation of our family. Even if it wasn't your fault, none of that matters now!"

Siroun balked at that information. *"T-they can't do that. Besides, how did that Adami foreigner get into Niravad without being noticed?"*

"They have already determined you're guilty."

"There's no way they can prove that."

"There's no way you can prove your side either!" Vasylvad bellowed and assumed an imposing stance. The brilliant collar of orange feathers around his upper neck fanned out in distress. His eight-foot reptilian frame dwarfed hers. The two of them squared off, but Olekstraz stepped between them to subdue the argument.

"I will not stand by and bear witness to my children insulting each other," their father said in a soothing voice. *"Our priority is deciding the next step."*

Vasylvad went to protest but was interrupted by the sound of knocking at the front door. It was the reprieve they needed, although Siroun worried who was here. Her brother begrudgingly volunteered himself to get the door from the opposite side of the house. His clawed feet thudded along the wooden floor before transitioning to the sound of stone.

Siroun let out a sigh before saying to Nikostraz, *"I'm glad you came."*

He returned her words with a warm smile. *"When Vas told me what happened this morning I came as fast as I could. How are you feeling?"*

Despite wanting to tell him she was afraid, she compelled herself to stay resolute over the matter. Bringing a hand upon her chest, she forced a smile. *"Much better, thank you."*

Indiscernible voices echoed across the house. It sounded as if multiple people had arrived to pay a visit, and Siroun wondered if it was the guards coming to take her away. A wave of anxiety washed over her, and she heard her pulse echoing in her eardrums. This information was beyond overwhelming, and the fear of an unknown future did nothing to calm her nerves. While her brother came off as insensitive, she knew his reaction was out of concern. Had Siroun been a pure-blooded Dragomyr they would have given her a chance to tell her side of the story.

Olekstraz noticed her muttering to herself. *"Beskonerynth, stop."*

Hearing that forbidden name made her look up and reply, *"Father, you know you're not allowed to call me by that name."*

"I said stop," Olekstraz said with love in his voice. *"Everything will work out, you'll see."*

Siroun wanted to believe him. Nibbling on her bottom lip, she nodded in response, but it didn't help the feelings go away. Perhaps these thoughts of self-deprecation would never subside. However, she suppressed them when she heard the entourage tromping toward the kitchen. Her brother returned first and Siroun's eyes widened with surprise.

Vasylvad did not look pleased with the individuals who followed behind him. Transitioning to the Adami common tongue, he grunted, "We have visitors."

Siroun had only known her brother to use the Adami tongue once in her life, and that was when they took a single trip to the western region of Kalstravad as a family many years ago.

Three foreigners shuffled their way in, each one of them appearing physically different from the other. But they wore a silver and gold badge etched with burnished-black letters upon their chests that showed they were from the same organization. The only exception being another Dragomyr that stood behind them decked out in a military uniform from Libstravad. Siroun assumed that the regal-looking Dragomyr was the escort since Niravad upheld many restrictions against outsiders. This group appeared to be the rare exception for reasons beyond her understanding.

The two males were Adami, but the third shorter member of their party with the long ears and animal stripes on their skin was a Skivat. Siroun couldn't tell if they were male or female. She read stories of their deceptive appearances. Many of them wild tales of shape-shifting into both men and women to fool others. Siroun tilted her head to the side in contemplation, only to have her focus dashed when the eldest Adami stepped forward. A hint of color even came to her cheeks as she looked upon his face.

Vasylvad pointed to the regal-looking gentleman with his claw. "This is Lord Valter Flynn."

"Good afternoon," he said before catching a glance at Siroun and gave a slow blink afterward.

She frowned. "What's wrong?"

"My apologies, My Lady." Lord Valter cleared his throat and followed up with, "I noticed your eyes. They are most striking."

"Oh…" Siroun's skin flushed as she mumbled, "Thank you."

Lord Valter appeared to be in his forties with clean-cut silvering hair and a door knocker styled beard where the facial hair ran along the lower jawline and around his mouth. His build was tall and strong, with fair eyes, chestnut skin and strange branching scars that crept up his neck from underneath the collar and over part of the left side of his jaw. Of the three, he was the most regally dressed to match his title. She could tell by looking at the fabric, despite it being dirty from extensive traveling, that it was handwoven silk and linen, embroidered by accomplished tailors. He exuded a sense of calm collectedness she found to be most intriguing. Siroun caught herself stealing a glance at him as the introductions continued.

"Next," said Vasylvad with a twitch from his lip, "is Zikky."

Already the second individual was making a two-fingered salute as a method of greeting. They wore a medium-length coat over semi-revealing armor that showed off their toned abdomen and trim muscles. Based on where Zikky's head lined up next to Vasylvad's shoulders, the Skivat was similar in height as Siroun. Unlike the Adami, however, Skivat ears were elongated and rotatable, allowing Zikky to pivot them at whim. Animal striped tattoos ran down their cheeks, under the clothing, and along their bronze-skinned body. If what Siroun read about the Skivat was correct, the tattoos were birthmarks and gave a hazy glow under the moonlight. Skivat were also the least welcomed among the Dragomyr.

The Skivat hopped forward. "Hiya!"

When Siroun heard the voice, it gave a clearer distinction that this Skivat was most likely female. The shock of their short, spiky, tri-toned locks of reds, oranges and golds faded out in streaks with silver tones bounced as she moved. Zikky looked to be in her later thirties, with a cheery demeanor that made Siroun smile. Secretly, she was glad to meet with total strangers instead of any council members coming to judge her recent crimes.

Vasylvad gestured toward the last individual, and Siroun noticed his saturnine disposition. Unlike Lord Valter's regal clothing or Zikky's spunky personality, the last man appeared mundane by comparison. His unruly brown hair with smatterings of silver, fair skin and unkempt facial stubble didn't age him well. From his disheveled clothes to his semi-slumped posture, there was a cantankerous air surrounding him. The only anomaly from his aged visage was his bright aqua eyes that reflected a youthfulness lost to time.

"And this is Colin Lockwood," said Vasylvad, and Colin nodded as the introductions finished and the conversation moved on to the next topic. "They are ambassadors from the Vanis Aer Æther Guild in Anastas."

"Mages," Nikostraz snorted in Drakish. Siroun's sense of calm turned to worry. She wondered if she should be on guard with these individuals if Nikostraz suspected them.

Leaning next to Nikostraz, she asked, *"Is being a mage a bad thing?"*

Zikky overheard the strange whispers going on between the two of them and interjected by clearing her throat. "We're here to capture Felthane."

The words meant nothing to Siroun and her family.

They sat there, dumbfounded, trying to gather what the mage meant. Shaking her head in confusion, Siroun replied, "I'm sorry, what is a Felthane?" When she noticed that, once again, Lord Valter was staring at her, she glared at him. "What now?"

Zikky went to open their mouth when Lord Valter rested a hand upon their shoulder and tugged them back. The two exchanged glances before Zikky conceded the floor to their superior and folded their arms.

"I must apologize for my unusual behavior. It is a rare occasion where I hear perfect Drakish spoken by an individual who does not appear to be a Dragomyr. Even though I can see that you share similar qualities."

As much as Siroun wanted to take offense to Lord Valter's words, she knew he spoke the truth. She pointed to her throat and said, "It's because I have the dual vocal chords that my people possess."

"That is most fascinating, My Lady. Again, please accept my utmost apologies for any reaction that you perceive rude while I further acquaint myself with you." The nobleman then looked to Olekstraz and gestured to the chair in front of him. "May I sit?"

The elderly Dragomyr nodded in response, but made no further attempts to offer any refreshments or local comforts to the strangers. Siroun observed every movement as the nobleman sat upon the plush cushion. The mage's hands stroked the grain of the wooden table as a smile crossed his lips. "This is exquisite craftsmanship."

Olekstraz beamed with pride. "Thank you. I constructed it myself along with the rest of the furniture in the house."

"Ah, so you are a woodcarver by trade?"

"Carpenter, yes. I constructed this house in my younger years."

"You have remarkable talent, Master—?"

"My name is Olekstraz. I appreciate your kind words, but let's return to the purpose of your arrival."

"You are right, my apologies."

Everything about the man was so elegant that it was hard for Siroun to imagine the nobleman being outside a castle's walls in this manner.

Folding his hands upon the table, he glanced over to Siroun and gave her a sympathetic smile. "You are Siroun Fatima, correct?"

"Yes, that is correct." Even though the home belonged to her father, all the attention focused on her. It was a new sensation. She was so used to being ignored whenever they received visitors that this change unnerved her.

"Forgive us for intruding," he said. "My condolences for what transpired last night. I realize it must have been a traumatic experience for you."

She looked over to her father with a slack expression. When Olekstraz shook his head and shrugged, Siroun returned her gaze to Lord Valter. "Thank you, I guess. But can you please get to the heart of your visit? It's been hectic, and I still have much to discuss with my family once you leave."

"Of course," Lord Valter replied amiably. "As my colleague has indicated, we are here on a particular mission to find and bring a wanted criminal, Felthane, to justice."

"This is the second time you've mentioned this Felthane person," said Siroun, and then her gaze hardened. "Is that the Adami who murdered Lilistraz and the rest of my colleagues? And what kind of name is Felthane, anyway?"

The nobleman straightened his posture the moment Siroun started firing off question at him. With a heavy sigh, he replied, "He claims it symbolizes him as a Fallen Thane. It is not atypical for an infamous criminal to adopt a new name when they ascend to power in the manner of which he did."

Siroun couldn't help but scoff. "You mean he gave himself that name? Does he fancy himself a ruler or something?"

Lord Valter shrugged. "Perhaps. The main concern is that he practices a school of magic that is taboo within our world. An art that feeds on the living as fuel known as necromancy."

The description went over her head, but her family knew what the nobleman was referencing. Vasylvad's features were grim, "A warlock."

"Indeed," said Lord Valter. "Last night he acquired an item known as the Map of Selvarethon. They found you holding a piece."

"I didn't help him steal it," Siroun blurted out.

"Calm down gel-gel," said Zikky, waving a hand at her with at a slowed speed. "We ain't accusin' ya of anythin'."

"Gel-gel?" Nikostraz raised a scaled brow in confusion.

Zikky responded to his question with a playful wink before Lord Valter tapped her on the arm as a signal to pull back again. The Skivat rolled her eyes, but said nothing further. The atmosphere shifted once more when Vasylvad checked the time.

"I need to go," he hissed to his family in the Drakish

tongue. *"Hopefully, I can mitigate the severity of your punishment. I'll return in a few hours. Don't wait up for me."*

"I will join you once we wrap things up here," said Nikostraz, and Vasylvad nodded in approval.

From what Siroun gathered, the Vanis Aer were performing their investigation separately from the council since there was no mention of Vasylvad's meeting being postponed for this foreign arrival. Vasylvad was quick to collect his bag and head out the door, and Siroun realized the direness of her situation. Feeling lost and confused, she fidgeted with her skirts and stared at her lap. She wanted nothing more than to hide under a rock and live there forever. Shame and disgrace now plagued the family because of her. To think the council might do something extreme made her fear a severe punishment.

Lord Valter continued the conversation, "Lady Siroun, my intent in coming here was not to accuse you of any wrongdoing. It is the opposite. I am looking for answers, and everyone who can help us is dead except for you."

"Please don't remind me," she could feel the lurch in her stomach returning.

Zikky quirked her head to the side and raised a brow. "Why ain't ya grateful that he didn't make a meat pie outta ya?"

Given that the Vanis Aer mages weren't familiar with Dragomyr customs, Siroun bit her tongue. She wasn't the only one doing it either. Lord Valter seemed perturbed as he stared at the Skivat until she realized her faux pas.

"Oh yeah," said Zikky, snapping her fingers as her eyes lit up. "Y'all are into that whole 'dyin' with honor' and whatnot. Whoops, my bad."

Siroun suspected that this was a common occurrence with Zikky.

"Again, my sincerest apologies," said Lord Valter, trying to stifle the grimace on his face. "My colleague's choice in words are often outlandish. That aside, what transpired between you two last night? There must have been some specific reason he overlooked you after a confrontation."

Siroun grew impatient with this conversation. Her fingers tapping upon her lap as she forced herself to answer, "Why do you think anything I did had any special bearing on why I'm alive?"

"Because he's not the type to leave survivors," said a voice that remained unheard until now.

Everyone's attention turned toward Colin. The mage didn't return eye contact with any of them, preferring to feign interest in staring at the walls.

"Oh," was all Siroun said in response.

She had no clue why this Felthane person had spared her life, if she could even call it that. She didn't think he was attempting to keep her around. The second the map started acting up, Felthane seemed to improvise the rest of the way. Chewing on the inside of her cheek, Siroun thought long and hard on the matter. Her father and Nikostraz kept a watchful eye as she tried to recall the interaction in her mind to remember any important details.

"Everything was dark. It was hard to make out any physical features other than I think he was Adami-born. I tried to grab the map from him knowing how important it was to our library. "Siroun reached up and tucked a lock of hair behind her ear. "The only reason I had a corner in my hands was that I somehow tore a piece of it away when I was struggling to take it back. I didn't steal it from the library, I don't even have access to the Archives. My coworkers enjoy throwing my favorite books in that room because they know it's restricted to me."

Olekstraz wrapped an arm around his daughter to comfort her. "You're not on trial here. Take a deep breath."

Lord Valter nodded. "I only wish to know what happened, My Lady. Nothing more."

Being addressed as a Lady was a first for Siroun. Yet, she continued, "Something strange happened when I read the words from the map."

The moment she said those words, she saw the mages' eyes go wide with disbelief.

The shock of that information appeared to shift the Skivat's words to her native Vat'tu tongue. *Well I'll be a Skyhawk's uncle.*"

"Excuse me?" Siroun blinked in response to the quirky language change.

Lord Valter gave Zikky a sideways glance. "That better not have been vulgar."

Zikky patted him on the shoulder. "No worries, Boss."

With that out of the way, Colin and Lord Valter exchanged uncomfortable glances before the nobleman looked back over to Siroun. "You can read the Map of Selvarethon?"

"If that's what you call it," said Siroun, "then yes. I suppose so."

"That can't be the map, can it?" Zikky poked Lord Valter a few times, causing him to sweep her hand away only for them to follow up with, "If we're chasin' the wrong guy it'll be our heads."

Olekstraz's curiosity piqued. "Do you even know what this Map of Sal-whatever-you-call-it even looks like?"

"The Map of Selvarethon is written in a deity's language," Lord Valter said. "We do not know whom, but many from the guild believed it belongs to our patron god, the Archmage Arcandus. Selvarethon was a mortal name he went by in a previous era. We believe he may have drafted it during that time-frame. At least, that is what we suspect regarding its name and history."

"We're dealing with something that belongs to a deity?" Nikostraz's scaled brow raised in suspicious interest. "What kind of artifact does this map lead to?"

"Unfortunately, that is official guild business," said Lord Valter.

"Oh?" A wry smirk inched along Nikostraz's lips. "I believe that translates to 'we don't know' in most of my political conversations."

"Ya wanna get political?" Zikky cracked her knuckles twice but soon found her hands frozen together in a block of ice. The Skivat's brown eyes darted over to find Colin fanning out his hand and looking more interested in his nails than the fact he had just welded his colleague's hands together with magic without speaking a single incantation.

As Lord Valter closed his eyes and sighed, Olekstraz could only chuckle. "My, my. It's been a long time since I've had guests that were this amusing. However, I would appreciate it if your subordinates didn't threaten a friend to our family."

The exchange of conversation continued back and forth for the next several minutes as Siroun clutched her skirts, staring at the table. Her breathing escalated to a point where everyone halted what they were doing and noticed her hyperventilating. She didn't often succumb to bouts of anxiety. Yet, the overwhelming amount of information she absorbed in the last twenty-four hours brought her to a breaking point, and now she needed a place to escape.

"Besk?" Her father's soothing voice tried to bring her calm. When she felt his claw upon her hand, she jumped out of her chair and pushed past Colin.

"I'm sorry, I can't!" she said in Drakish.

Siroun fled up the stairs and slammed her bedroom door shut, leaving everyone behind in stunned silence. She couldn't catch her breath while her heart raced. Every gasp felt like she had run a marathon. To counteract the panic attack, she closed her eyes and focused on taking slower breaths. All the while, she heard muffled conversation with the scraping of chairs and the shuffling of boots. Siroun could only assume that the Vanis Aer mages left now that she was no longer taking part in the discussion. She noted the Skivat mage speaking with a tone of protest. When Siroun heard the door shut, the tightness in her chest subsided.

"Calm down," she murmured to herself. *"You need to calm down."*

Eventually, she heard the mages chattering outside of the house. Curious, she crept to her window and peeked around the edge so that the mages wouldn't see her. Several feet down, the three conversed back and forth among one another while their escort lurked behind. The two Adami focused on the Skivat as she made wild gestures. Siroun maintained the utmost silence while unlocking the latch of her window and cracking it open ever-so-slightly.

Zikky's voice came blaring into her bedroom. "I coulda given her a relaxin' massage or somethin' to chill her out—huh?"'

Siroun watched the Skivat's ears twitch before turning to look up toward Siroun's window, forcing her to dodge to the side to avoid being seen. After a few seconds passed, the three mages continued their conversation. Siroun peeked once more from the side to see how they interacted with one another.

"The last thing you should do is touch people who already think you're a maniac," Colin chuckled only to eat dirt afterward when he tripped over Zikky's carefully placed foot.

Siroun put a hand over her mouth to stop herself from giggling. When Colin recovered, he balled up his fists intending to retaliate, but Lord Valter stepped between them with an admonishing look on his face.

"Come," said Lord Valter. "We need to gather more information and hope we are not too far behind."

The team of mages were about to step away, then paused. Siroun held her breath thinking they noticed her again, but Colin shook his head as they untethered their mounts. "First we find a bite to eat."

"Yeah, good luck with us tryin' to find service in the middle of this *soul-sucking* part of the country," said Zikky sarcastically, only to have their escort snort into her face. The Skivat reached up and wiped her cheek and replied with, "Ugh, lizard snot."

The guardsman nodded in satisfaction before climbing onto one of the massive hard-skinned Tremlisks and led the group toward the center of town. The beast sauntered one flat-foot after another as the soft thud of its heavy body left behind prints in the dirt.

Exasperated, Lord Valter gave Zikky another disapproving look. "How many times do I have to tell you to watch your language?"

"Ya don't even know what I'm sayin'."

"It is the context that gives it away."

The nobleman turned to follow their escort while Zikky made mocking facial expressions at him. Once again, Siroun forced herself to not laugh lest the Skivat's ears picked up on her eavesdropping. When they appeared well out of ear-shot, she closed the window and went to collapse face-first onto her bed. Siroun had been awake for less than an hour and already fell back asleep.

4

"ANOTHER! *-HIC!*" ZIKKY slammed her empty mug on the table and flagged her hand at the bartender again. Lord Valter and Colin stared in disbelief as they watched their shorter member of the team chug her way through half of the establishment's ale.

True to form, Pustelia Crest was not friendly to them with acquiring supplies and information. Despite wearing the insignia of the Grand Regent of Libstravad, and a Niravad guard as an escort, it only granted them the courtesy of not being thrown out of the village. The other problem for the Vanis Aer mages was the language barrier. Only a handful of the locals knew other languages beyond the native Drakish tongue, and their Dragomyr associate preferred silence, making him of little use to their endeavors.

After poking their heads into each business within the quaint village, the three of them found a tavern that tolerated them enough to provide food and drink while the group planned their next move. Their escort chose a seat at the far end of the bar, likely to disassociate himself with those of whom he had to guard. That left the three mages to take a small circular table on the opposite side. They stood out like a sore thumb, with most of the Dragomyr around them keeping their voices low as they kept their eyes on the foreigners that occupied the establishment.

"You think that girl gets stared at as much as us?" said Colin, returning a few of the suspicious glares that the natives were giving him.

"The heart of Dragomyr society values its traditions and culture," said Lord Valter. "We must respect their laws while we are here. I recommend savoring this moment. It is a rare opportunity for us."

A light scoff came from the younger mage's lips, "I'm not here to savor anything other than to capture our target. You can cherish the art and architecture. I'll pass."

During that time Zikky helped herself to more ale, making it harder to keep quiet. No amount of scolding subdued her, so the three of them remained tucked in the corner as their colleague chugged away.

"Don't you think twelve is enough?" Colin arched a brow. "How can a Skivat pack away so much alcohol in that small frame of yours?"

"Hey… thish is mah firsht an onny time here. I gotta live it up." Another hiccup later, Zikky rested her head upon her palm as she looked over to Lord Valter and smiled drunkenly. "Ya hash purdy eyes."

"Consider this your last drink for the evening," said Lord Valter while he surveyed the room.

The direct order elicited a chuckle from Colin. His laughter didn't go unpunished as Zikky gripped his drink and incanted a quick-fire spell.

"Hey!" Colin tried to pull his mug away, but it was too late. The beverage heated to the point of boiling, and a drunken smirk greeted him in response. He growled at Zikky, "Knock it off!"

Lord Valter raised a brow at the both of them before clearing his throat, grabbing Colin's attention. Pulling out the scrap of map which they had collected from the local enforcement earlier that day, he scrutinized the few bits of artistry that were fragments of foreign symbols. "Hmm, vexing."

Colin rubbed at his lower lip and nodded. "It has a different fluidity compared to Arcandus's scripture. See this jagged part here?"

Lord Valter could only shake his head in disapproval. "This small piece of the map is not enough to tell us what direction Felthane may have gone. Even if it did, we are at a loss in being able to read it."

Colin paused before making his suggestion, "Have the girl read it for us."

"You are speaking of the Lady Siroun?"

Zikky pursed her lips into a pout and interrupted with, "Hey, how come ya never -hic- call me a Lady?"

"Because you do not behave like one," Lord Valter replied before returning his attention to Colin. "Considering the panic attack she had earlier, do you think she would oblige to the request?"

Colin gestured with his thumb in Zikky's direction. "Sure, just don't bring loud-mouth with you and you'll be fine."

Zikky might have been drunk, but she wasn't deaf. Reaching across the table, she grabbed the younger mage's cheek between her fingers. Colin yelped in pain as she jiggled him side to side, muttering, "Ya may -*hic*- look like a man but yous shtill jush a sheventeen year old -*hic*- boy, sho dun talk back to those who are more 'sperienced than…-*hic*-… ya."

The struggle lasted a few more seconds before she released him, instigating a silent stare-down while Colin rubbed at his cheek. Lord Valter concluded that if the mission was to succeed, they would need to overcome their discourse.

Several more patrons filed in as others left, and Lord Valter observed the transitions. Colin and Zikky continued to bicker with each other as he honed in on one Dragomyr in particular. The creature hunched over the bar, wheezing each time it drew a breath. There was no drink in front of him, and the bartender didn't appear inclined to serve him either. Before he inspected the newer patrons entering the establishment, a loud thunk and a splash occurred. Ale poured over the side of the table and spilled into Lord Valter's lap. He launched to his feet, and swiped away the liquid, but it had already soaked into his pants in the most unflattering of places.

"Blast it, Zikky!" he said.

"Sorrweeee," her mad giggles showing no remorse in the matter. However, her eyes shifted toward the same suspicious patron Lord Valter had been watching before going back to her usual exploits of harassing Colin. While his subordinates continued bickering, Lord Valter patted at the stain with a kerchief and shot Zikky a vile glare.

There was no point in reprimanding her further, so he headed over to the bar and lingered near the hunched over patron. "Bartender, may I trouble you for a pint of that Sivftrum you poured me earlier?"

The Dragomyr nodded, being one of the few who knew enough of the Adami common tongue to complete the request. In the meantime, Lord Valter peered over at the unserved patron. The closer range allowed him to notice a heinous smell coming from them. No wonder the bartender wanted nothing to do with the individual, they reeked. A putrid mix of week-old meat and excrement wafted in the air. As much as Lord Valter tried to conceal his displeasure, he couldn't help but frown. Perhaps this Dragomyr was a gravedigger to the nearby cemetery.

The door behind him opened again, and more sickly-looking Dragomyr wandered into the establishment. They didn't appear any better than the guy next to Lord Valter, and other patrons recoiled when they sniffed the air. Others were nudging one another as they recognized the garments the suspicious Dragomyr were wearing. Something felt wrong, but Lord Valter couldn't figure out what was giving him the chills. He didn't pick up on the significance of the dirty garments and weird swaddling, but the patrons understood.

"Um, Milord?" A distressed tone came from Colin, and Lord Valter turned to their table to see one of the macabre Dragomyr lumbering over his colleagues. The younger mage tried to stay calm, but the nervousness reflected in his eyes as he maintained his stance. Meanwhile, the bartender appeared transfixed at one of the intruding figures.

"Ixanostraz?" the bartender whispered to the creature in front of him, their presence unexpected.

A wave of frost magic fluttered by, and Lord Valter

looked back to find Zikky clapping at the display. The figure that had closed in on the two earlier stood frozen as Colin maneuvered himself out of the corner, dragging his teammate along.

"We need to leave," said Colin.

"Ooh, are we -*hic*- fightin'?" she replied.

Slipping from Colin's grip, Zikky turned and round-house kicked the frozen creature, shattering it to pieces and littering the floor. A fit of laughter belted out of her as Colin attempted to get her to stand, but she swatted at him in refusal. Plucking the undead Dragomyr's head from the floor, she stuffed her hand into its skull and used it as a puppet. The jaw clanked open and shut while Zikky spoke through it via some haphazard ventriloquism, "Hi, I'm Zikky! Kicker of butts. -*hic*- Flee my wrath!"

"Are you kidding me right now?" griped Colin, but she had already gestured the skull to nibble on his shoulder with playful abandon. Despite the chaos and panic ensuing all around them, the two mages exchanged a moment of pause before he muttered, "I really hate you."

Pulling the skull away, she smiled at him. "No ya don't, but I 'preciate the shentiment."

Meanwhile, Lord Valter found himself sandwiched between two creatures imbued with necromantic magic. These reanimated bodies explained the horrid scent, which meant Felthane wasn't too far away. On the one hand, he was grateful that they found him. On the other, it meant facing the warlock and a ton of minions.

As the undead Ixanostraz climbed over the bar to get to the owner, Lord Valter murmured a series of words under his breath. The arithmancy that rolled off of his tongue summoned a set of equations to come together. The letters and numbers gave off a faint glow before transforming into the element he commanded. Static filled the air, and his right hand crackled with electricity. Before the cretin leapt forward, Lord Valter reached over and placed his palm on its face. The Dragomyr shrieked and recoiled from the rough shove that came after the spell. It continued to writhe and hiss which caught the attention of several others who lunged at Lord Valter in a coordinated formation. They were mere inches away from reaching their target when a wave of fire struck them. Cries of rage pierced the nobleman's ears as the flames consumed them to smoldering ash.

Zikky stood among the rubble and leaned her head back, belting out a laugh of victory. "Bwahaha! Gotsha! -*hic-*"

Most of the patrons already fled. However, the mages' efforts halted when they noticed what awaited them beyond the tavern walls. Once they regrouped, they noticed more undead meandering outside of the tavern. Only a handful had trickled into the bar to cause the initial trouble, but the majority were out in the main street ambling like cattle in a single direction. Among the undead hordes were the village guardsmen trying to take action while appearing confused by this whole event.

"Any idea where they are going?" Lord Valter looked to Colin who gave him a non-committal shrug.

The continued sounds of maniacal laughter and bones being kicked around resounded in the background. The fruits of Zikky's antics gifted them with burning flesh to add to the other nauseating smells. Lord Valter lifted part of his tunic to cover his face and filter out the polluted air. He stepped toward the bartender and looked over the table where the Dragomyr crouched low, looking shaken.

"You, sir. Shut the doors and windows after we leave. Keep everyone inside and out of sight. Do you understand?"

The bartender nodded but didn't budge, making it pointless for Lord Valter to repeat himself. Right now he had to figure out the source of the necromantic power. He rejoined his colleagues and moved to the front of the tavern, keeping a low profile by the window and waiting for an opportune moment to make their escape.

Colin halted and said, "What about our escort?"

They both looked to the other side of the bar where the Dragomyr was shepherding patrons out through another escape route. Even though Lord Valter knew they might suffer consequences for abandoning the Regent guards, time was of the essence. He wasn't compelled to chase after an individual whose priority was not in protecting the interests of the Vanis Aer Æther Guild.

With that in mind, Lord Valter looked at Colin and replied, "Our priority is the mission at hand."

"Shouldn't we leave Zikky here since she's not exactly fit for a fight?" The ice mage pointed over to their other colleague in the throes of wrestling a living patron before being tackled by an undead one.

Lord Valter groaned while rubbing at his forehead. "No, she might set the tavern ablaze."

"Better the tavern than us."

Once again, Zikky's pristine hearing kicked in, and an undead arm came sailing across the bar, hitting Colin in the back.

"Ow, cut it out!" Colin shouted back.

"Yous a verwy wude boy!" she said.

It took every ounce of patience for Lord Valter not to knock some sense into them. Sometimes he questioned the guild's wisdom with the selection process of the field agents. However, with the sounds of outside screams capturing his attention, he snapped his fingers at Zikky and gestured for her to rejoin the group.

With one last punch, she brushed herself off then skipped over to Colin to drape herself over his back. "Carry me, teammate!"

This action caught Colin by surprise, and he almost collapsed to the ground if he hadn't reacted in time. Zikky's hands started wandering, and he clutched her arms so she couldn't grope him further. Giving their leader Lord Valter a pleading look, Colin whined, "Why do I have to always drag her around every time she gets hammered?"

Lord Valter ignored the question and focused on the undead masses that limped along the road. When he saw the opening he was looking for, Lord Valter gestured for the two to follow and they shuffled their way out of a side window then tucked around the building. Lord Valter counted his blessings that no one noticed them. The water barrels acted as their look-out point as they observed the direction of the horde. They meandered toward a particular path as death wafted in the air from the years of rotting flesh now exhumed. It abused the senses in such a foul manner that the Vanis Aer mages paused to calm their stomachs.

Zikky was not as successful as the other two. A burp passed her lips before she muttered, "By the shands, I zink I'm gunna be shick—!"

Panic struck Colin as he reached up and clapped a hand over her mouth. "Don't you dare!"

Lord Valter winced and tried to pretend he didn't hear, or smell, the vile remnants of ale that poured from the Skivat's mouth. Even worse, Colin received a shower he didn't deserve. Cries of anger came from the ice mage as he dumped her limp body to the ground. Mortified could not describe the expression on Colin's face, and Lord Valter felt sympathetic to his plight.

"Lovely, now we are both wet," he said. "She spilled ale on me and relieved herself upon you."

Colin shot him a look of contempt. "I would have preferred the ale!"

Zikky sighed, contented. "Ah, that feels sho much betta."

It took a moment for Colin to analyze the damages rendered to his uniform. He forced himself to overcome his sense of smell and summoned a solution for his soiled jacket. He spoke no words. Instead, the spelled formed from thin air as glowing blue numbers floated over his palm. With a snap of his wrist, the magic froze everything firmly in place before he slipped out of his jacket. A firm shake shattered pieces of Zikky's drinking exploits off his coat and into the air. Flecks of moonlight glistened off of their repulsive fragments as most of the contents fell to the ground. Only the stain remained.

Lord Valter knew it was none of his business, but he couldn't help see the spell and furrow his brows. "Should you be doing that?"

He was met with apathy as Colin put his coat on

and brushed past Lord Valter. "You deal with your arcane issues, and I'll deal with mine."

The nobleman's hand reached out to halt the ice mage. "I do not wish to see you squander your life on spells that do not require urgency. Your affinity to magic is not aligned toward offensive techni—."

Colin shook himself free. "I didn't join this team to play it safe. I know what I'm doing."

"You need not go to this extreme."

"Yes, I do," his voice sharp before it softened. His aqua eyes shifted back to Zikky who attempted to stand again. "We all do."

For now, Lord Valter respected his opinion on the matter. Their fiery cohort ambled her way to standing before raising a finger. "How 'bout I shacrifice a sock? *-hic-*"

A sigh came from Lord Valter as he trudged forward. "Come, we need to intercept the Lady Siroun."

"Yeshsir!" Zikky saluted before pulling back an arm and reciting a slurry of arithmancy incantations designed to summon her battle armor. Both men noticed this and turned to stop her. Instead, the fire spell leapt off her arm and onto a nearby building. Flames licked the wall, consuming the ancient wooden beams. Before things got out of hand, a lance of ice struck the heart of the fire, snuffing it out.

"Dammit, Zikky!" said Colin as he flicked the remaining frost from his fingertips.

Though Zikky seemed thoroughly impressed, she turned to find both of her comrades glaring at her.

Lord Valter said, "I ban you from using Æther in your inebriated state."

"Aww, but it was only a little fire," Zikky whined, but Lord Valter ignored her simpering. When he didn't hear a third pair of feet following, he glanced over his shoulder to find Zikky flailing her arms and legs at the undead.

"Zikky, hurry!" Lord Valter's voice barked at her.

Zikky blew a raspberry in his direction out of sheer insubordination, then maneuvered away from the mess of bodies left in her wake. With every clumsy step, Lord Valter heard Zikky swearing at him in her native language at the top of her lungs.

5

"*T*HEY'VE BEEN GONE *for hours,*" Siroun grunted in frustration, sweeping away the sawdust from the porch as her father finished up lacquering the new table.

Pride reflected off of Olekstraz's aged features before he got up and stretched. *"They can run five to six hours long depending on the discussion."*

Seeing her father happy with another commissioned piece made her smile, but the conversation caused her to regain the look of dissatisfaction. *"I guess I never paid attention to their length until now."*

He gave her a sympathetic smile. Everything hung in the balance of Vasylvad being able to convince the council she had nothing to do with the warlock's activities within the library. The building was on lock-down and new librarians hired to replace the ones lost. Oddly, a full investigation did not transpire after the initial sweep through the building.

Her father's gaze drifted, and she spoke up, *"Father."*

Olekstraz tilted his head in her direction. *"Hmm?"*

She ran her fingers along a dried portion of the intricate table and stared past it. *"Where will I go?"*

He ruminated on the question. They were a small family with few connections to the rest of Niravad, let alone the outside world. Siroun had lived the whole of her life in Pustelia Crest. She did not understand what the world was like and only had Nikostraz as a glimpse into its possibilities.

Her father reached an arm around her and placed a small lick upon her left cheek in reassurance. *"Everything will be just fine."*

"But what if it isn't? What then?" Her hazel eyes reflected concern knowing they were both helpless to the upcoming decision by the village council.

"I don't know, Besk. I will speak with Nikostraz over this. He is better versed in these matters. Perhaps he knows of some places where you can settle in if the worst should happen."

Of the available options, that was the most favorable. She wouldn't be alone, but she wondered how long she would be bereft of her family. As she mulled these thoughts over something tickled at her sense of smell, and not in a good way. Siroun wasn't the only one to notice either. Her father's muzzle twitched before he perked up and looked around. Night crept upon the small village, and a warm breeze brought forth the putrid scent of rot.

"That's strange," he murmured.

The scent gained strength at an alarming speed, and they heard sounds of panicked shouting and fighting in the distance. Stepping to the edge of the porch which overlooked the main path into town, Siroun found the road flooded with Dragomyr sauntering toward their home. Never had this many gathered in the village, unless it was for a festival. The other peculiar aspects were their shambling steps, and what they were wearing. It was a mixed medley of fashions from different eras, but they were wrapped in the same swath of burial cloth that alarmed Siroun.

"Father?" Her voice trembled as she backed away. The ambling bodies coming closer while Siroun felt her father tug at the back of her clothes.

"Inside!" he said.

"What about your table—?"

"Besk, get inside!"

Without further delay, she followed her father into the house before shutting and bolting the back door. It wasn't long before a loud slam resounded, along with a series of raspy screeching. Neither of them had witnessed anything like it.

"What are they?" Siroun asked in a high-pitched voice. Fear gripped her senses. The slam against the door made her jump back as the Dragomyr on the other side clawed, screamed, and banged themselves against the house trying to get in. *"What's going on?"*

Olekstraz grimaced. *"Those mages are in luck. They were looking for a warlock, yes? I guess he's still in town."*

"Ha, ha. Very funny, father," said Siroun when the door pounded behind her again. The wooden barricade bent under the external stress while more undead gathered outside. Frantic, she pressed herself against the door as a countermeasure while looking to her father for guidance. *"What do we do?"*

"You're the librarian, dear."

"Former librarian, and what does that have to do with anything?"

"Think, Besk," said Olekstraz as pounding echoed from the front door. He rushed to the other side to prevent it from caving inward. His voice shouted from the other room. *"In that entire library; did you ever read up on anything that involved warlocks or necromancy that those mages were talking about?"*

"You know that topic is taboo," said Siroun. *"Our village doesn't have that information."*

"Nothing? Not even in a children's story?"

The door slammed again, and the wood ebbed as Siroun pushed back. She understood where her father was going with the suggestion, but her mind struggled to recall the information from memory.

"Um, I think perhaps—." When the door pounded again, she squeaked and shut her eyes, trying to drown out the noises. Several books surfaced from the library within her mind. She honed in on one in particular; an old Dragomyr myth that hearkened back to the ancient era where gods and monsters fought. It had a necromancer mentioned as a side-kick in the tale, and they commanded the forces of the undead with limitless power. One by one her mind focused on the pages, recalling as though she were opening the book in person sifting through the text. Bang after bang struck the door, but she remained fixated on her task in finding the weakness to this character's power.

The words filled her mind, and she opened her eyes when she found the answer. *"It's possible the power is being channeled by something, like a talisman. Breaking the talisman releases them from this curse."*

"That's all well and good," Olekstraz grunted, *"but how do we find it?"*

Heavy thumping pounded the upstairs by her room. Someone broke into the home and tears flooded Siroun's eyes. Despite flipping through more pages in her head, the book was of little use. The character abandoned the protagonist to chase glory and power elsewhere, leaving no further suggestions on any weaknesses to the undead horde she commanded. They were out of time, however, the upstairs noise had not come from any of the shrieking creatures. Instead, the two muzzles of her brother and Nikostraz came into view as they descended the stairs.

"Siroun!" said Vasylvad.

Hearing her brother's voice brought Siroun relief, and she called back, *"Vas!"*

She nodded toward the front door where their father was keeping it blockaded. While her brother assisted him, Nikostraz came to her rescue and held the door in place.

"I think they're dead… but not," said Siroun with uncertainty. Stuff like this only happened in fables and fairy tales, not real life.

"We know," Nikostraz pressed his shoulder harder against the bending door. *"We saw them coming up the street and took a different route. Climbing the house to get into your room wasn't easy."*

Siroun couldn't help but blush in embarrassment at the mention of him going through her room to get inside. The feeling didn't last long as she overheard her father ask, *"Do you think this could have something to do with that person the mages were after? Perhaps they're doing this from outside the village."*

Nikostraz shook his head before replying, *"It should be impossible to reanimate an army from far away. I imagine that whoever is controlling these things is nearby. It appears they're coming for you, Siroun."*

A chill surged through her body. *"Why are they after me?"*

"It might have something to do with that map you can read," he replied.

"How do we stop them?"

Glass from a nearby window shattered open, and Siroun screamed as she saw one of them fumbled along the broken window as they pushed their way inside.

Vasylvad looked over to his friend. *"Nik, have any ideas? You seem better versed at this than we are."*

After some deliberation, Nikostraz answered, *"Fire. Fire might stop them!"*

"I'll see what I can do," Siroun pulled away from the door and searched the woodpile in the kitchen. Logs and kindling were grabbed by the armfuls and chucked into the fireplace. She grabbed the flint that laid next to the hearth, and her fingers fumbled as she banged the spark stones. Several times her sweaty hands dropped the rocks on the floor, and every part of her body shook before her father swooped in to assist.

Together the two of them created enough sparks to get a small flame going. During this time, Vasylvad barricaded the door with a propped-up chair to deal with the window intruder who dangled from the narrow entryway. A severed arm wiggled its way into the house past Vasylvad through one of the broken windows, and Siroun caught sight of it at the corner of her eye. However, she kept her focus on stoking the flames.

Nikostraz grunted against the crumbling door. *"This is not looking good."*

Another window shattered, and the sound of glass clattered to the floor causing Siroun to look up and find that more slipped into the house. By now the undead barraged every avenue of escape. The situation was surreal, but Nikostraz's voice broke through her fear. *"How's that fire coming along?"*

A stray claw punched through part of Nikostraz's door and grasped at anything on the other side. When Siroun turned to her father, he handed over a piece of wood engulfed by flame. *"Help him."*

With her new weapon in tow, she sprang into action, extinguishing the fiery element into the wandering claw. The creature screamed and retreated, giving Nikostraz a moment of reprieve. Several more claws burst in from the broken opening to replace the first. Out of instinct she grabbed the closest thing, which was a fire poker, and swung at the appendages with violent abandon. Nikostraz yelped in surprise as he dodged her wrath from the first swing. Bones snapped apart, scattering pieces of limbs and sinew everywhere. The adrenaline coursed through her veins leaving a numbing sensation as she clobbered anything that tried to force its way through the semi-broken door.

Nikostraz gaped in shock as he stared at the remnants first, then turned his gaze to Siroun with a slight crack in his voice, *"W-well done."*

"Thank you," she replied through belabored breaths.

With that moment over, Nikostraz cleared his throat. *"Your father needs help with the fire. I'll take it from here."*

She handed Nikostraz the poker and made her way back to her father to ensure the hearth remained well-fed with wood, but the effort was futile. The undead screamed and tore into the structural integrity of their home. It wouldn't be long before they made their way through. Even as those thoughts crossed her mind, her ears caught the sound of more wood breaking apart. The undead Dragomyr demolished the front door, and now Vasylvad was fighting a losing battle. To Siroun, time slowed as their resistance fell apart before her eyes. Her father, brother, and best friend fought the odds only to fall back to the numbers that overwhelmed them. Soon the doors gave way, and the flood of undead Dragomyr squeezed inside the home. Siroun watched in disbelief as she recognized they failed.

Suddenly, Siroun's lungs felt crisp. The air chilled, movement slowed, and sheets of ice crept along the door frames and into the house. Siroun saw her breath in puffs of condensation as her body shivered. Even the fire that she and her father put together subsided from this wintry grasp.

She held out her hand to the small flakes of white dust falling inside the home. *"Snow? At this time of year?"*

It wasn't a common occurrence to see snowfall, even less so with it being the middle of summer. Niravad was a continent that didn't experience freezing temperatures, let alone snow. The foreign substance hit her skin and turned to water in her palm. First, there was animating the dead, and now it was snowing. She wondered what other oddities were destined to come into her life before the night expired. A bright flash of light became the answer to her question, followed by the nearby sound of rolling thunder. Siroun shut her eyes and plugged her ears. Whatever creatures blockaded them from the front door vanished. Their remains nothing more than an obliterated mess littering the ground. A minute passed after the thunder subsided, and Siroun glanced toward the door to see a mage standing at the entrance. Colin, if she recalled correctly, made his way inside to scout the home.

His face still reflecting that dour expression from before as he spoke in the Adami tongue, "Good. You're still alive."

They came back.

Pulling her hands away from her tipped ears, Siroun blinked as she took his offered hand and stood. Any impending danger seemed to be at a standstill for the moment. Her father and brother were catching their breaths, but Nikostraz still monitored his side of the house, the semi-frozen arms welded together in a hole through the damaged door.

"You came back for us?" said Siroun with hesitation in her voice.

"We came back for you," said Colin.

She bit back the urge to snap at him since they went out of their way to help, even if it was only for her sake. Before long she heard the steps of another individual enter through the obliterated front door.

The leader of the trio, Lord Valter, checked on Olekstraz and Vasylvad with a polite nod of his head. "Are you all right?"

The old Dragomyr sighed, "I'm not cut out for this

kind of trouble. I assume this chaotic mess is because your warlock is still hanging around?"

"Most certainly, and based on what we have observed, the Lady Siroun is in danger."

As everyone looked at Siroun, her attention was upon Vasylvad who wore a pensive look on his face. In their Drakish language she spoke with a tremble in her voice, *"Brother?"*

He ignored her and looked over to Lord Valter and Colin, "What are you planning on doing with Siroun after you save her?"

"Brother!" she protested.

"Still your tongue!" he hissed back in Drakish before returning his glare to the two mages.

Lord Valter blinked at the exchange, but it wasn't long before he deliberated on the matter. Clearing his throat, he said, "If the Lady Siroun can translate the Map of Selvarethon, then we need her aid in stopping Felthane from getting a hold of the artifact toward which it leads."

Siroun shifted her gaze at the pile of extinguished wood that had once been their fire and folded her arms.

"I understand this is overwhelming," Lord Valter replied. "If my assumptions are correct, the Lady Siroun is a target. Perhaps Felthane changed his mind about leaving her alive. Either way, she is in danger along with the rest of the village. With your permission, I need her to be my charge as we complete our mission."

"I refuse," said Siroun. Though Lord Valter's presence put color on her cheeks and a strange flutter in her stomach, he was still a stranger trying to take her away from home. "I'm not leaving my family behind. You can't make me."

"My Lady, I—."

"I said I refuse!"

"They have banished you," said Vasylvad in their native tongue. His words cut through the tension, piercing Siroun in the heart. Her eyes widened. At first, she thought she misheard him. It had to be a joke. However, Siroun knew better. Her brother wasn't the sort that told jokes.

Swallowing the lump that formed in her throat, Siroun looked at Vasylvad. *"What?"*

"They don't want you here anymore, Siroun." Vasylvad's jaw tightened as he added, *"I just came back from the council meeting. They made their decision. They're giving you two choices: Stay and they will execute you for murder, or leave and never come back to Niravad again."*

The air left Siroun's lungs and her vision dimmed. Through the shock she murmured, *"But I... I didn't kill anyone. It wasn't me. It wasn't—. I have to fix this. I have to clear my name."*

Throughout the conversation, the spell that kept so many of the creatures at bay started thawing. Colin's spell, having finite power behind it, could not keep them encased forever. The screeching and howling that had invaded the house earlier roused back to life. The kitchen door began to buckle against the pressure. Nikostraz grabbed a nearby chair to jam it against what they had left of the wood before retreating into the living room.

"We're out of time." Nikostraz's gaze bored into Siroun who was focused on Vasylvad gathering her coat and stuffing some meager belongings into the large pockets. He wrapped it around her only to have her twist away, causing

him to miss. Instead, he settled for tying the sleeves around her hips before shoving her toward the nobleman.

"No!" Siroun turned away from Lord Valter. *"I won't leave you behind!"*

Her hand reached toward her father, tears welling up in her eyes. Siroun tried believing that this was a bad dream, but she knew she could not fight against this change. As the two mages took their positions to stop the barrage from the back room, Olekstraz gave his daughter a reassuring smile.

He pressed his claw to her cheek. *"We'll see each other again, Beskonerynth."*

"No!" The word repeated over and over from Siroun's lips as Nikostraz exchanged nods with Vasylvad and pulled her away.

Tears streaked down her cheeks. Colin and Lord Valter carved a path to help everyone find a way out of the surrounded abode. All sound transformed into loud ringing in her ears as she cried out, heartbroken, while her father and brother retreated in another direction, away from the undead hordes. The creatures honed in on Siroun and followed her path, ignoring her family.

Nikostraz hoisted her onto his back. *"Hang on."*

With no other choice than to comply, Siroun wound her fingers into his clothing and buried her face into his back while Nikostraz navigated through the chaos. As far as she knew, this was last time she would ever see her home and family again.

Nikostraz forced himself through the masses, enduring the endless ambushes from every direction. It wasn't long before he bypassed the Skivat, who punched her way to victory with two other Dragomyr guards. Siroun's hysterical fits subsided, and she heard the mages drag their drunk cohort along.

Locked arm-in-arm with Lord Valter and Colin, Zikky hiccuped and said, "Weee'rrre retreatin'?"

Both men did their best to keep a decent sprint going, but they couldn't do this forever. The mages struggled to keep up with Nikostraz given the long-legged physique that allowed the Dragomyr to take greater strides. By now Siroun had wiped the tears from her eyes as the village drifted further away from her sight. The swarms of undead kept coming.

"We will have to do something about the source," Lord Valter's voice huffed and puffed. "We cannot keep trying to outrun them until dawn."

The nobleman found himself the recipient of a giggling Skivat as Colin shoved the fire mage into Lord Valter's arms and stopped to face the impending crowd. "Go. I will handle this."

"Colin, you've already—."

"We don't have the time, Milord. Find the Tremlisks and retreat into the mountain pass. I will catch up. Go!"

Lord Valter hesitated, but took Zikky and headed up the left path in the fork out of Pustelia Crest. Meanwhile, Nikostraz veered right since he was several paces ahead of them.

"Where are you going?" Siroun whined in Drakish. *"They went the other way."*

Nikostraz snorted in frustration as he turned himself around and chased after the nobleman who was hobbling along with the Skivat in tow. He almost made it when Siroun jumped off of his back and tumbled to the ground.

The dirt skidded across her skirts and along her palms, but she dusted herself off and stood.

"*Siroun, we need to leave. Now!*" Nikostraz snapped.

"*I want to watch,*" she murmured.

He reached out and grabbed her arm. "*We don't have time!*"

She glared at him with a fury in her eyes and yanked her arm away. "*I said I want to watch!*"

He shook his head in surprise, and she averted her gaze after snapping at him. Never had she spoken in such a tone to Nikostraz before.

She bit her lower lip before replying, "*I'm sorry, Nik. Just this once, please?*"

Siroun realized the urgency involved. She watched him deliberate as his gaze darted back and forth between her and the oncoming undead. With the ice mage preparing to counterattack, Nikostraz sighed and said, "*Fine, but only for a minute.*"

Satisfied, Siroun turned her attention to the undead horde and the lone mage who faced them. Lord Valter didn't notice that they weren't following him because Zikky kept his hands full.

Meanwhile, Colin faced his opponents and cracked his knuckles. Æther tingled along his fingers and glowing numbers materialized in mid-air before swirling around his arms. As he summoned the spell through a series of gestures, Siroun saw a pleasurable smirk reflecting on his face. Colin crouched and wrote out a line of runic text on the ground. Ribbons of ice mixed in with the sun-soaked dirt and hummed with power. When he finished scrawling out the incantation, he took a step back and performed another sequence of gestures with his fingers to aid in conjuring the next spell. With preparations completed, he opened his stance and waited for his prey. "All right, you bastards. Try to get past this."

He didn't have to wait long, and when the first undead Dragomyr took a step over the line in pursuit of Siroun, Colin's eyes narrowed at them. "Got you."

The runic spell exploded in a line of frost and snow, blasting the front lines of undead into the masses behind them. The backlash from the first spell allowed Colin to gather up extra Æther to bolster his next move as he throttled his hands forward. Needles of ice sprayed out into the crowd, then pillars of icicles spiked out of the ground, impaling over half of the undead masses. Colin's next set of gestures sent a pulse of magic to course through each icicle, exploding not only the spike but shattering the undead creatures in its wake.

Colin summoned one last swirl of ice magic that danced around his hands and into his lungs. Slow exhaling summoned mists of cold down the path, sending sheets of ice to freeze any remaining undead lucky enough to miss being impaled. Sources of nearby water, along with the edges of homes and windows, also fell prey to the creeping frost along their surfaces, locking everything in place. Villagers cooped up in nearby homes pressed their faces against the windows to take a peek at the unusual abilities Colin displayed.

As the last of his breath expelled, droplets hit the ground. Siroun watched as Colin looked at the red puddle underneath him, and touched the slick warmth just above his lip. His fingers traced his mouth and pulled away to show them coated in blood. Even Siroun swallowed hard as she wondered what caused his sudden condition. With his jacket already soiled from Zikky's earlier exploits, Colin wiped his face along the sleeve of his guild uniform and made a quick retreat out of the village. He paused when he found Siroun and Nikostraz staring at him from afar.

"Don't just stand there," he growled, making a sweeping motion with his arm. "Get out of here!"

Siroun continued to stare in shock at the blood smeared on Colin's face and coat. Nikostraz pulled her onto his back and ran while Colin followed from behind.

6

*S*IROUN CLICKED HER tongue in frustration as she attempted, yet again, to get enough of a spark to start up their campfire. After the men finished tethering the Tremlisks to nearby boulders, they scouted their immediate surroundings while searching for firewood before it grew too dark. Colin returned first with an armload of timber, his dour mood unchanged since they had first met.

"I told you," he grumbled, "if you wait for Zikky she'll finish."

"Zikky's still hunting, and I know how to build a fire, thank you very much," said Siroun.

Colin rolled his eyes at her. "I don't understand why you're trying to prove you're not useless. You need to leave that to our fire expert and try something else."

She averted her eyes and smashed the flint harder together which caused a small spark to light up and land into the kindling. With a smug look of satisfaction, she encouraged the flicker of heat to grow by blowing carefully upon the embers. Despite the methodical efforts, it wasn't long before Zikky strolled up with a wide grin on her face. The Skivat fanned her palm at the wood, and a burst of heat radiated from the center of the pile. Siroun recoiled and shrieked in surprise.

When the fire blast subsided, she turned to the Skivat, "You could have given me a warning!"

Meanwhile, Colin was curt with Zikky for a different reason. "And you scold me for using my spells without their incantations."

"Because you are reckless with them," Lord Valter chimed in as he and Nikostraz returned with more wood in tow.

The Skivat shrugged off Colin's hostility and started constructing the spit. "Sorry gel-gel, I thought Colin told you I'd start the fire when I got back."

"I did," he muttered. "She's great at disobeying orders."

Once again Siroun shot him a glare that he ignored.

Zikky continued, "As for my spell-craftin', I know what spells that cause me the most harm. On that note, anyone wanna skin our dinner while I get this goin'?"

None of the men jumped on the opportunity in getting their hands dirty. Nikostraz looked at the dead creature and snarled in disgust. "I have no expertise in that unsavory task."

Given that the fire was alight and there was nothing further for Siroun to do, she plucked the hunt up off the ground. "I'll do it. Did anyone bring a knife?"

With Zikky hacking away at branches with a hand blade, borrowing hers was out of the question. Siroun's gaze shifted toward rest of the group, and Lord Valter's eyebrow raised at her before opening his coat pocket and offering a jeweled knife. She hesitated at touching such a gorgeous piece of artistry; the sheath decorated in gold and handset gemstones in red hues. It was far too extravagant for use on something as mundane as skinning an animal.

However, the Lord gestured for her to accept it. "I believe this is the only thing sharp enough to skin the animal."

"But, it—," she halted her words and collected the knife from his hands.

A flush of pink rushed to Siroun's cheeks, but she forced herself to stay focused while finding a suitable surface to start the meticulous task. Meanwhile, Lord Valter unfolded a parchment from his coat and started reading. Siroun recognized it as a map of the central region, Libstravad. While her fingers toiled over their dinner, she snuck another glance to absorb the artwork on the map. Something appeared out of place. She finished the last bit of cleaning and set the skinned creature next to Zikky.

"Yer fast!" A big grin spread along the Skivat's face.

Siroun took the bottom part of her skirts and wiped the blood off of the knife to clean it the best she could. "It's a common skill in my village."

"I take it yer family and ya do a lot of housework together?"

"I suppose. Pustelia Crest is a small village. We have small farmlands that we take turns working throughout the seasons. More often than not I'm stuck with the unsavory tasks when it's my family's turn to help."

"That's a bummer."

Turning her attention back to the nobleman, Siroun

kept her hands tucked to the side realizing she needed to find a place to clean them.

"By the way," said Siroun, "you have an outdated map. The road that goes through Tin's Pass collapsed years ago. The Regent had a new route built that connects to the upper highway that the merchants take called the Mondoro Path."

This news led to the Lord's brows to furrow as he folded the map and returned it to his pocket. "That would have been nice for our escort to have divulged in the beginning."

Nikostraz couldn't help but chuckle. "Who supplied you with that map?"

Lord Valter was embarrassed to say, but cleared his throat and straightened his posture. "The guild provided it to us knowing that the natives would refuse."

Nikostraz burst into laughter, and even Colin scoffed at the misfortune. With a sardonic tone in his voice, the ice mage quipped back, "Even our 'diplomatic relationships' can't get us a proper map of this place."

"I didn't think they even let foreigners into Niravad until now," said Siroun, looking equally perplexed at Lord Valter. "How were any of you even allowed in here?"

"It is a most tedious process, My Lady," said Lord Valter. "One that can take months. Even then, entry is often a fruitless attempt."

"Then why now?"

"I assume the Dragomyr are knowledgeable of the artifact that Felthane is chasing, and may have their reasons for allowing us to make this visit unimpeded. What those reasons are, I cannot say. Only that we are on a deadline to return to Ysile Marden the moment we have concluded our business."

"I have a question," said Nikostraz. "How did you know Felthane was here? It seems unlikely you knew exactly where to be at the time this individual was committing his crime. Either you have impeccable luck, or one of you is clairvoyant."

By now Zikky finished mounting the cleaned creature on the spit and listened. She didn't appear concerned with the exchange in conversation as she gave an audible yawn. Siroun was not willing to be as apathetic to Nikostraz's curiosity. She, too, wanted to understand; and since Zikky remained preoccupied with cooking their dinner, Siroun looked to the mages for a response.

When eyes first fell on Colin, the ice mage rolled his own before deferring to Lord Valter with, "I'm not allowed to say anything."

Siroun's gaze shifted to Lord Valter next. The bouncing back and forth on who had authority to speak on the matter confused her. Nikostraz must have predicted the answer would come from Lord Valter's lips since he spent no time looking in Colin's direction.

"Yes, well—," Lord Valter fidgeted with a cufflink as he shifted his sitting position. "Please understand that I speak of this information in the strictest of confidence. Anastas is a proud nation. Nothing is too great that our people cannot achieve, including the works of the gods themselves."

Siroun was the only one whose facial expression looked horrified. "That's blasphemous."

"That's Anastas," said Colin.

"Our goal," Lord Valter continued, "is to act as a beacon of reason and knowledge. The royal family supports many schools of thought whom bring wealth and prosperity to the kingdom whether mundane or magical in form. However, the one thing that we consider verboten in the realm is the art of sooth-saying."

Nikostraz curled his lip. "You're implying—."

"Oracles came to consult with the King in secret over this matter, and it sent us here to investigate," Lord Valter's jaw tightened slightly, but he forced a smile despite his discomfort.

Colin waved his hand dismissively. "What do you expect when the renegade Isle of Vasile is part of our kingdom? That region still operates as a sovereign state despite their downgraded titles and forced allegiances. It shouldn't be surprising that the King will use whatever resources he has to gain the upper hand in his affairs."

"Yes, but relying on fortune telling brings ruin instead of reward. Visions get misinterpreted, and prophecies are vague riddles. I thought His Highness felt secure in that decision."

"Yer just angry 'cause he's consultin' Duke Rovani in trade affairs more than ya like," said Zikky with amusement. "And now ya gotta square with the fact that his oracles were right about where Felthane was, and when he'd act."

That hit a nerve because the nobleman stood up and started walking away. "I will make another round to ensure our location is safe."

Siroun and Nikostraz exchanged glances while the other two mages snickered and went about their business.

"Duke Rovani?" inquired Siroun as she quirked her brow.

"Don't worry 'bout it, gel-gel." Zikky waved her hand nonchalantly. "Just another high-to-do that likes to cause Lord Sparkles grief, that's all."

"I see," she nodded before noticing the gore coating her hands had dried and made her skin sticky. "I need to wash up."

"There's a spring not too far from here," Colin gestured toward the small thicket behind them.

"Ah, thank you, Colin," Siroun smiled, wondering if the mage decided to be cordial for once.

"Don't take too long," he said. "I planned on taking a bath first, but I guess you need it more than me."

Balling up her fist, she clenched her teeth and growled, "Don't worry, I won't."

7

THE WARM SUMMER water felt good against her bare skin and scales. It helped wash away the grime and soothe the nerves. Despite Colin telling her not to take too long, she lingered for a while to spite the curmudgeon. The first moon glowed in the night sky while her skin started to prune. Siroun sifted her fingers through the lake and dunked her body once more into its depths. Her wavy locks of silver hair suspended in slow animation, drifting around her face in the underwater silence. In this moment of stasis, she meditated on the events that transpired to calm her nerves.

"You've been banished." Vasylvad's voice echoed in her mind, and Siroun winced while her heart ached.

Then her father's words pierced through the negative thoughts. *"We'll see each other again, Beskonerynth."*

His warm voice gave her hope, and made her heart stop fluttering. Soon the watery silence took hold once more. As her muscles began to relax, the sound of another body jumped in, triggering a sense of urgency to surface.

Siroun's natural inclination was to cover her chest with her hands before looking over to identify the intruder. While she figured the worst, her surprise turned to shock when she came face-to-face with Zikky.

This awkward intrusion allowed Siroun the chance to analyze the woman's physique. Every toned muscle in the woman's body flexed under the assorted scars from previous battles. The most interesting part were the feline-like stripes along the sides of her body. The markings gave off a soft glow as the day turned into dusk, another oddity that Siroun never encountered before. Though many questions came to mind, Siroun didn't want to ask just yet. Instead, she watched as Zikky made herself comfortable with her elbows tacked along the edge to keep her in place.

"Ah, this is the life," Zikky sighed, acting as though there was nothing wrong with the unannounced intrusion.

Siroun flustered. "W-what? Can't y-you see I'm bathing?"

"Hmm?" Zikky blinked a few times before replying, "Well, yeah that's why I joined ya. Figured ya could use a bathin' buddy, and to clear up my head. That Sivftrum's gotta kick to it."

Siroun raised a brow at Zikky. "How did you sober up so quickly after drinking Sivftrum?"

"Eh…" Zikky waved her hand in a carefree manner. "Booze and I go way back. I can recover from almost any drink on a dime given the right tools."

The explanation made no sense, and Siroun decided not to inquire further. On a positive note, having this conversation between them started piecing together the differences between each mage in the trio. The jury was still out on Colin, but Siroun appreciated Lord Valter's pleasantries and Zikky's confidence despite its indiscretions.

Zikky acted indifferent to the social constructs of indecency as the Skivat patted her breasts and replied, "It's not like ya got anythin' I don't, save maybe the tail an' scales. It's just us girls for now."

"Wh-what do you mean 'for now'?" Siroun sunk deeper into the water so that only her face was above the surface. She felt too exposed, and Zikky's implication didn't sit well with her.

Zikky shoved her pinkie finger inside her ear canal and wiggled it around. Whatever came out she discarded with a quick flick. "The boys might want their baths next. Lord Fancy Pants ain't used to slummin' it out in the wild. He gets grumpy when there's too much dirt under his nails. Not to mention I kinda puked on Colin." She ruminated on that memory a moment before continuing, "We haven't had a decent place to stay since we got here. Dragomyr ain't exactly the paragons of hospitality in their homeland." After the words slipped from her mouth, Zikky back-peddled with, "What I meant is that they're too cautious with strangers. I ain't used to that."

Siroun rolled her eyes, but let the comment slide. "Dragomyr culture is founded on principles of tradition, honor, and loyalty. Many of our traditions were stripped away over time due to wars and trade routes with other kingdoms. The country decided that it was best to close our borders to foreign kingdoms to rebuild our way of life and rediscover the things that identified us as a people. I'm sure it's not lost on you that the Skivat pillaged most of our books and artifacts that gave us insight into our ancient heritage."

Zikky looked taken aback by those words before saying, "Yeah well, our people were fightin' their battles too, mainly enslavement by the Dragomyr if yer books failed to mention that. If it's any consolation, I'm no thief. Well, not in that sense."

An awkward pause followed. They knew so little of one another, and finding common ground to build a friendship proved challenging.

Zikky tapped her fingertips upon the water. "So, how'd yer dad come up with the name Siroun?"

Siroun combed her fingers through her hair as she reflected on that question and answered with, "My father gave me the name Beskonerynth. However, the Regents didn't want me using a name meant only for Dragomyr. Siroun was the name of a famous Adami singer he admired when he was a whelpling, and Fatima is short for Fatima-vas, who was my father's deceased mate."

"Yikes, that's awkward."

"I try not to use the surname around my brother if I can help it. It bothers him a lot, plus it doesn't uphold traditional standards. A Dragomyr only has one name. Once taken, they record the name within a Prime Dossier so it permits no one else to share it until several generations have passed."

"What about the ones I've met outside of yer borders? Some of 'em have titles beyond their first names. Not all of 'em, but some."

Siroun frowned at that information. "They abandon the traditional precepts of their heritage, which is a shame. They should be proud of who they are."

"Yeah, well, everyone has their reasons," said Zikky, before noticing Siroun's drifting gaze and followed up with, "Ya okay?"

"Do you think I'm okay?"

"No, that's why I'm asking," Zikky muttered to herself in Vat'tu. After a few more sidelong glances, she said, "Sorry. I know it's rough bein' away from yer family, but we'll figure out how to get ya back there. Lord Sparkles makes good on his word when he says he'll take care of ya. Try thinkin' of this as an adventure?"

"Adventure? I don't know a thing outside of the place I've left behind."

Zikky's right eye twitched at Siroun in disbelief. "That's the point of an adventure. That aside, ya never left Pustelia Crest?"

"I went on a family trip when I was three or four, but other than that, no. Niravad shuns foreign-looking people such as myself, whether or not I am native born. I was lucky they let me live with my father and brother for as long as I have. Now, I fear there's no way they'll let me come back." The words tasted bitter in her mouth, "The only reason I'm tagging along with you guys is beca—."

"You had no choice?"

Siroun frowned. "No. If I help you capture Felthane, I can prove my innocence and perhaps they'll reconsider my banishment."

"Not to be blind to yer plight, believe me, I ain't. I understand ya love yer father and brother, but let me shed some perspective on yer opportunity." Zikky's offer was greeted not with enthusiasm but with a scrunching of the face from Siroun's disgust. To that, she forced a smile and continued, "Yer the bookish sort, yeah? Ya like readin'?"

Siroun nodded with hesitation. "You have a horrible way of motivating people, assuming that is what you're attempting right now."

"Just hear me out, gel-gel."

"Ugh. That pet name again," Siroun muttered.

Zikky kept going, "Ya ended up readin' how many books from that library, several hundred?"

"Around five-hundred; give or take."

Zikky calculated the sheer quantity in her head. "Ya've read that many in your life already?"

"One month. Some had fewer pages than others."

"One month—? *Wow, you are a freak!*" The slip back into the Vat'tu language elicited a raised brow from Siroun. Zikky replied, "Ya don't understand, gel-gel. That dwarfs the amount I had to read by years. Do ya even absorb any of it?"

"Yes, why? I don't lie about those things. And why do you call me gel-gel? Can't you at least translate that for me?"

"Uh—," pressing a finger to her left temple, Zikky thought hard on how to best respond. "It's kinda like… uh… a fond nickname for someone."

"Why do I feel you're hiding something?"

"Back to the point," Zikky eyed Siroun like she was trying to solve a mystery and just couldn't wrap her head around the evidence provided. "I'm not callin' ya a liar, but ya gotta understand that's not normal."

"Well, what's normal in this day and age anyway?" Siroun couldn't understand why Zikky was so taken aback by her speed-reading capabilities. She soon followed up with, "I don't know why I can do it, I just can."

"Ah, got it."

When Zikky made no further comment for the unusual talent, Siroun changed the subject and asked, "So where are we going next?"

The Skivat scratched the back of her head. "Not sure at this point. We gotta return to Libstravad to validate we left within our allotted deadline. We've got some potential hunches, but now that Felthane has the map I don't know what our next step is. I leave that to our fearless leader. Would help if the King gave us more details than rumor and hearsay."

"So the King sends you three on a blind mission by oracles, yet can't give you any actual details on your target? I find that hard to believe."

When they had first met, the only thing the three of them divulged was that the Map of Selvarethon led to something that was dangerous and relegated as guild business. Zikky's slip of the tongue revealed more of the mission, and the Skivat looked disappointed in herself. "Uh, I wasn't supposed to tell ya that."

"Oops," Siroun replied with sarcasm in her voice as she closed the distance between the two of them and gave the older woman a scrutinizing eye. "What do a King and a warlock want with this dangerous artifact once they find it? What is their connection to each other?"

Zikky hesitated for a second as her eyes flicked downward a couple of times with flushed cheeks before sighing, and said, "I guess if yer gonna tag along its best ya understand who we're huntin' and why." With that out of the way, Zikky continued, "Ya heard of the Archmage Arcandus, right?"

Siroun shrugged and kept listening.

"In the Hanmel Kingdom, he's kinda a big deal. The creator of the arcane arts, some people say. He ain't the only one in the pack. I know ya've lived under a rock for yer entire life but have ya at least heard of any other deities besides the ones you worship?"

Siroun pursed her lips before replying, "There's very little literature on lesser beings since we Dragomyr only recognize The Great Three as legitimate divinity."

"Lesser—? Ah, I see. The Titanians have their pantheons too. I guess I shouldn't be surprised by what the Dragomyr canonize as deities. Anyway, the Archmage Arcandus is infamous for his extensive research on Æther and the arcane arts. We have always known him to tinker with different magical artifacts. One of such toys might be a book called the Sinefine Bible. The Vanis Aer Æther Guild has minimal understanding of its existence with the King's recent request involving Felthane." Zikky tilted her hand side-to-side. "I'm not sure how long the artifact has been around. The only thing I'm told is that it's dangerous and might even be Arcandus's collar."

Blinking a few times, Siroun shook her head. "Collar? What is he, a dog?"

"A collar is a weapon. It amplifies a god's powers by incalculable standards."

"Oh."

"It's too bad we only have a small corner of that map. Not much good it'll do us without the rest."

Those words resonated with Siroun. She thought

back to her encounter with the warlock in the library and recalled how the Map of Selvarethon reacted to her words. If Arcandus was a scholar of all things arcane, then perhaps the map was also a magical tool of sorts.

Water flew in droplets off her scaled skin as Siroun shimmied out of the lake. As she slicked the excess water away from her body, she could feel Zikky's eyes lingering on her.

She raised a brow at the fire mage while covering strategic parts of her body with her hands. "Do you mind?"

"Nope," Zikky grinned, but Siroun didn't find the Skivat's response cute. Instead, she plucked her clothes and walked away while trying to dress at the same time.

"Ah, where are ya goin' gel-gel?"

"I need to see that map piece," said Siroun, pulling her wet hair from the neckline of her tunic. She tried shoving her arms through the sleeves only to have them stick to her skin like glue. This forced her to halt for a minute while she struggled with her outfit. After a couple minutes of struggling, she buttoned up the top and jammed her feet into the boots.

Zikky wasted no time and followed suit, leaping out of the water and scurrying to put on her clothes to keep pace with her newfound friend, only to encounter the same issue. In Vat'tu, Zikky cursed, *"Blast the sands and its infestations!"*

When Zikky saw that Siroun wasn't spending any time waiting for her, the Skivat stuck to just putting on the crop top and shorts and bunched up the rest of her uniform into her arms to follow along. In a sing-song voice, she said, "Ya thinkin' ya can do somethin' with it?"

"Not sure. Maybe."

Shuffling their way through the trees and bushes, it didn't take long to find the rest of the men sitting around the campfire eating. The atmosphere felt tense, with Colin and Nikostraz looking dour at one another. When both of the women came into view, the ice mage stood up and passed them in a huff. "Finally!"

There was no time to ask what was wrong or to see if he would stay and engage in this next bit of conversation. Siroun blinked at Nikostraz, but he didn't appear to want to reciprocate any response.

At least Lord Valter appeared agreeable and greeted them both with a smile despite the tension. "Lady Siroun, did you enjoy your bath?"

"She needs the map piece, Fancy Fingers," blurted Zikky.

Siroun shot the other woman an incredulous look. She should have known by now that Zikky's mannerisms were lackluster. It still didn't stop her from being jarred by the shock value of the other's approach.

"Yes, Milord," Siroun's response was toward Lord Valter's question about the bath before she moved on to the other topic. "I was wondering if I could see that small piece again? I want to try something."

A brow raised on his handsome face, but Lord Valter reached into his coat to grab the small piece of parchment and handed it to her. Siroun felt the map between her fingers, and it brought back the memory of that night. Anxiety throbbed in her chest. She remembered the experience, and holding that bit of map brought forth that same familiarity of power it exuded the last time.

Instincts told Siroun this map was made for her. While the others looked at the thing perplexed, she looked upon the strange scrawling with fluent appreciation. The fragmented letters came alive, and the world around her became insignificant. Though there was only a minimal amount of letters to work with, Siroun felt confident that she could make out something with what they acquired. Her lips moved as a language foreign to all but her spilled from her mouth. Breezes kicked up around the campsite, and all three observers looked on in awe as swirls of light and power danced.

"Whoa!" whispered Zikky in Vat'tu.

They watched the parchment emanate a golden hue of kaleidoscopic light around Siroun's hands. Even though the spell was jerking and twitching from the damage, the map tried to function in some capacity.

A hand tapped Lord Valter in the arm as the Skivat grinned. "This could be entertainin'."

He nodded, catching a brief glimpse at Nikostraz whose expression was grim. The glittering light and elegant displays captivated them all as Siroun tried to strengthen her connection to the magic held within the map piece. Symbols and patterns jittered and fizzled. She tried making sense of the partial information that flooded her subconsciousness. Images flashed at her in rapid waves and, when it conveyed all it could, knocked the wind out of her.

8

*S*IROUN'S EYES FLUTTERED open, and she took in a deep breath of air. She jolted upright and bashed foreheads with her medic, causing both of them to yelp in pain as they clutched their faces.

When the throbbing subsided, she pulled her hand away. "What just happened?"

"You're tapping into things you have no business touching," Colin growled, still smarting from the head-ache. He capped the empty vial and pocketed it, then pressed the back of his hand to her forehead. With things returning to normal, he walked toward the spring. "I'm resuming my bath."

Zikky was about to give Colin a cheerful pat on the back, but he pointed at her and growled, "Don't touch me."

The fire mage responded with a mischievous grin but complied to his wishes, allowing him to saunter away in peace. Siroun tilted her head at Colin's perplexing behavior as she watched him leave. For a guy who appeared to be in his thirties, he behaved like a child. The other two paid little attention to his reactions. Instead, they made themselves comfortable while Nikostraz sat beside Siroun.

"Are you all right?" said Nikostraz.

"My lungs are a little chilled, but otherwise I'm okay." She realized what had transpired, and she placed a hand on Nikostraz's claw before looking over to Zikky and Lord Valter. "I think I know where we need to go."

Lord Valter looked impressed. "You found the artifact?"

"No, but I know where the map is going. The bit I tore away wants to reconnect itself. At first, I didn't understand what it was showing, but I could see a few flashes of a giant mountain in the distance as it's crossing an ocean."

"Is it kinda rounded?" Zikky asked as she gestured the shape with her hands.

"Yes," said Siroun. "The map was saying something to the effect of 'land of thieves'?"

"Treasure hunters." Zikky corrected with an annoyed tone before looking to Lord Valter and grinning. "We're goin' to The Hive!"

While Zikky looked thrilled, Lord Valter seemed less than enthusiastic about the news. Not understanding, Siroun chimed in, "The Hive?"

Zikky started celebrating by pumping her fists and cheering, while Lord Valter clarified, "The Hive is in the desert lands of Fi'ro and homeland to the Skivat people."

"Oh!" said Siroun as she realized this meant leaving Niravad. The opportunity to explore another country did, however, pique her interest, thanks in part to the recent conversation with Zikky. The strange vision given to her by the map, and that only she could read it, gave her a sense of purpose in all of this madness. Siroun knew very little about the Skivat and their culture. The few tomes available to her in the library of Pustelia Crest painted them all from a negative perspective. This would be her chance to see for herself on whether the claims were true.

"I guess it couldn't hurt to expand my horizons a bit?" said Siroun as she looked to Nikostraz for validation.

She caught a slight twitching of his scales near his eye, but he relented with a sigh. "I believe there is little choice in the matter. Even if you and I were to head to elsewhere, the warlock will follow you anyway. I agree that it is in our best interest to continue traveling with the Vanis Aer while I send letters out to my connections and see where I can find a safe place for you to re-establish yourself."

An arm reached out from nowhere and squeezed Nikostraz from the side. The unexpected gesture caused him to grunt in surprise as Zikky shoved her head between them and chimed in, "That's the spirit!"

The Dragomyr wasn't pleased having his personal space invaded, but it made Siroun giggle while she watched the interactions unfold. She enjoyed the frivolity. These strangers, who had come into her life out of nowhere, accepted her without question of heritage or bloodline. It confused her why they didn't care that she was a half-breed, and it made her curious to find out how Niravad differed from the other realms.

Nikostraz wrenched himself free from the lively fire mage and waited for a moment of respite before leaning toward Siroun. She saw him pull a small trinket from his pocket and discreetly hand it to her.

"Keep this with you," he murmured in Drakish.

"What is it?" She wanted to lift it to see it better, but Nikostraz pushed it towards her bosom so it stayed out of sight.

"It's a protection reliquary. In case that warlock returns."

She cupped the reliquary in her hands like a tiny bird, her eyes flicking back over to Lord Valter and Zikky who ate while discussing methods of travel to The Hive. They were too preoccupied to notice Nikostraz's conversation with her.

"Why the secret?" said Siroun.

"It's an ancient relic given to me of great sentimental value, but the Vanis Aer Guild regulates magic of this caliber. I don't want a family heirloom being confiscated by these people."

She blinked. *"Do you think they would do that?"*

"I don't want to find out."

"Good point," she said, and pocketed the relic before wandering eyes caught the exchange. Though the mages were pleasant enough, she still did not know them. It made her appreciate Nikostraz's presence through this journey.

"I'm so sorry to have involved you, Nik."

He gave her a toothy smile. *"Don't worry about it. I already discussed this situation with your brother on the way back to your house. My job adapts to this kind of thing, whereas your brother needs to stay with the council. It keeps him close to the ones that marked you for exile. With any luck he can exonerate you."*

"Mm," Siroun nodded, then fell quiet. Staring at the palm of her hands, the edges of her opalescent scales cuffing just along her wrists before skin and flesh exposed the rest of that area. Every part of her looked like a biological

experiment, and that scared people in Niravad. A pang of remorse tugged at her heart knowing that she dragged Nikostraz into being a bodyguard despite him volunteering. He was her only friend outside of her immediate family since he, like the Vanis Aer, didn't judge her based on physical appearances alone. Maybe there were more people out there who accepted her without conditions. One could dream.

"What do you think of them so far?" she asked.

"I don't trust them." There was no hesitation in his answer. It followed a measured shrug before adding, *"However, it is in my nature not to trust the Vanis Aer Guild due to my experiences with them. I have never seen these three before, although I'm sure I've met Lord Valter in the past since he is blue of blood."*

"You're familiar with the Hanmel Kingdom?"

"I've been to court before if that's what you're asking." A slight smirk twitched at the corner of his mouth, and Siroun couldn't help but smile back.

"What about this Hive place?" she said. *"Have you been there too?"*

"Briefly," he replied. *"No one knows how to get in except the Skivat. I recall witnessing where I entered and exited the place, but every time I try to remember the exact method, my mind draws a blank. The routes also change a lot, so trying to remember them is moot. Stay close to me when we get there. It's not a place for tourists. The Hive has a black market for many unscrupulous folks. It is best that you do not wander around without an escort."*

Siroun's eyes widened with fear, and she clutched at her chest before an arm wrapped around her upper body.

The fluffy locks of colorful hair pressed against her face and tickled her ear as Zikky mashed up against her. "Whatcha talkin' about?"

Caught by surprise, Siroun tilted away at the sudden intrusion. "N-nothing!"

"Didn't sound like nothin'."

"I was telling her to be careful once we reach The Hive," said Nikostraz. His face devoid of emotion. "Given the unscrupulous nature of the area, and that this is her first time outside of her home."

"Oh, don't ya worry about any of that nonsense. Those claims are scare tactics. We'll keep ya safe! I know that place like the back of my hand!"

To prove her point, Zikky fanned out her hand and admired it. The confidence she exuded didn't last long as she scrutinized a dark spot on her palm and furrowed her brows. "Wait a minute. How'd that show up outta nowhere?"

As Zikky inspected further signs of aging, Siroun pushed herself free and made some distance between them. "I'm sure I'll be fine."

Siroun nodded with faux assurance before glancing to Nikostraz with a half-hearted smile. Despite her curiosity of The Hive, the constant flux of emotions from realizing she was walking away from her home made her waffle with both trepidation and excitement. Before she could stop it, a tear ran down her cheek and splashed upon her hand. Surprise struck Siroun as she wiped away the rest from her eyes.

Lord Valter glimpsed the change in moods and offered her a kerchief from his jacket. "Here, My Lady."

Without further words, she retrieved it from his fingers and dabbed her face. The softness of the handwoven linen dressed in colorful embroidery caught her attention only after she had given it a thorough use.

She asked, "What does the 'R' stand for?"

A smile twitched on his handsome face. "It is the emblem of the family in which I serve."

"It's lovely," she murmured. Her fingertips stroked the fabric, having never owned or seen anything this nice before.

Nikostraz analyzed the kerchief before saying, "That's vague, given how many families in the Hanmel Kingdom boast that letter."

The nobleman chuckled. "One must use caution when divulging information these days."

"I guess cleaning up a civil war after fifty-plus years does that to a kingdom," quipped Nikostraz.

Both men narrowed their eyes at each other but said nothing further as they prepared to sleep for the night. Siroun noticed the tension building but said nothing. She realized there were subtle undertones to the brief exchange between the two men. However, she had limited knowledge about Anastas. While she was well-versed with Dragomyr history, Pustelia Crest held only a handful of texts with information outside of Niravad. Knowing that Nikostraz didn't trust the guild, she assumed he was testing their motives. Despite her growing fondness of the trio, they were still strangers.

With a giant yawn, Siroun retired for the night. She rolled her jacket into a pillow and tucked it under her neck as she looked up at the stars in the sky. Luckily the summer nights in these regions didn't require any further coverings. The fire was more than sufficient in keeping the area well-lit and warm. As she drifted off to sleep, she overheard Zikky offering to take the first watch. The sounds of the night animals calling in the distance lulled her down the dreamer's path.

9

"**W**ELL, THAT SUCKS. How are we gonna get to The Hive without a nearby sailing port? Swim?"

Lord Valter shook his head as he handed his mount over to the stableman, and said to her, "I believe you are forgetting where we are heading, Zikky."

"Oh yeah—," she mused. "I forgot."

"How convenient," quipped Colin, only to find himself on the receiving end of a flick behind his left ear by her fingers. He clapped a hand over where she struck. "Ow!"

Since the two mages were quarreling, Siroun and Lord Valter handed over the other Tremlisks to the livery. With the borrowed mounts returned, the group waded through the crowds of Dragomyr citizens, receiving multiple stares along the way. The city rested atop a steep mountain range where they constructed every building with angled pillars or cut into the terrain to adapt to the geography.

The ancient structures of Libstravad stretched to the skies, with curved tile rooftops and lacquered wooden eaves topping every building. Every home and shop displayed exterior embellishments painted in complimentary color combinations, or statues crafted from stone or marble. Much of the art resembled three menacing-looking dragons, or other figures within Dragomyr history. These intricate buildings took over every square inch of the bustling city with a population that dwarfed Pustelia Crest by comparison.

Tapping Siroun upon the shoulder, Lord Valter waited for her to turn around. "Lady Siroun. Might I inquire about the prominent depictions displayed on the larger buildings?"

Siroun blinked and replied, "The Great Three? You've never heard of them in your country?"

"We memorize arcane equations, not foreign historical myths," said Colin as he didn't spare a glance at the architecture. It never ceased to amaze Siroun on how Colin's actions reflected kindness, but his choice in words left something to be desired. Even though Zikky and Lord Valter always apologized on their colleague's behalf, she had to wonder if there wasn't an underlying issue with the guy that Siroun wasn't seeing.

"Well, I'm sorry if you think your work is more important than mine; but remember that if it weren't for The Great Three, your immortal scholar would cease to exist. Everyone in Niravad knows they are the creators of this world and its creatures. Stick that little nugget of wisdom in your spellbook."

Flicking a stray piece of hair out of her face, Siroun hastened her steps to create distance between her and the mages, squashing any motivation she had in answering

Lord Valter's questions. Meanwhile, Zikky swatted a hand upside the back of Colin's head then whistled a happy tune. The yelp of surprise from Colin gave both women a sense of smug satisfaction as Zikky caught up to Siroun and looped an arm around hers.

"Ignore the moody teenager back there," she said. "A toddler has better social skills than him."

Siroun's eyes flashed wide as she glanced over her shoulder to Colin whose defined features had long lost any boyish aspects to his physique.

Blinking, she looked back to Zikky. "Teenager?"

"Ya don't know?" Her tone reflecting amusement. "I'm guessin' none of those books mentioned the arcane arts then?"

Siroun shook her head. "No, nothing."

With a soft nudge against her arm, Zikky took advantage of this moment, "Allow me to give ya a crash course. Clayne harbors many sources of magical energies, and they ebb and flow through every inch of this world. Over time, mortal races started discoverin' that they could tap into these different energies and do extraordinary things with 'em. Different theories opened up different abilities, and now we are where we are today."

"That makes sense given that The Great Three were so powerful," said Siroun in agreement as she continued to listen.

Zikky raised a brow at Siroun but carried on, "Anyhoodle, one type of energy source is called Æther. It can change form into fire, ice, lightnin', or stay in its neutral state. It depends on the person's affinity to an element."

"So that's what you manipulate?"

"Yeah!" There was an extra pluckiness to Zikky's response. "Bein' an individual who practices an art form of supernatural schoolin', there's always a price for usin' one's skills. It differs based on the school of magic a person uses. Druids gotta balance themselves with the energies of nature. Shamans are at the mercy of the spirits they serve. Ya get the idea. We use arithmancy as the basis of our craft."

"Arithmancy?"

"Semi-complicated math magic. We manipulate the elements through a form of mathematical equations to bend 'em to our will. Forcin' Æther to take shape against its current nature with no kinda catalyst requires lots of focus and personal energy. Over time, it takes a toll on the body."

Nothing arcane-related resided at the Pustelia Crest library to reference, but Siroun had an inkling of what Zikky was insinuating. "It prematurely ages you?"

"Ya got it!" Forcibly turning Siroun's head toward the rest of the group, Zikky gestured to her companions. "Lord Sparkles is thirty, and Ice-Master Angry Face is seventeen. Yers truly is twenty-seven, but I've aged better and have way more skills. Not to mention I'm the strongest of the group."

Zikky winked at that last sentence, and shock riddled Siroun's face. "It's hard to believe everyone is so much younger than they look. I thought Lord Valter was in his forties or fifties. I can't believe he's only six years older than me."

"Yeah, he really pulls off that silver fox look, don't he?" A wry smile crossed Zikky's lips.

"So why aren't you affected?" said Siroun. "And why is Colin's change so drastic compared to the rest of you?"

"I recite my spells in full since they're used to augment my natural fightin' skills. As I said before, manipulatin' Æther is a dangerous business. The safest way involves usin' reagents, spellbooks, and incantin' the spell's full-length of equations. For us field agents, that takes too long and ain't realistic for our line of work, so we use shortcuts. We use our life force as the reagent, recite abridged versions, and try to stick to spells we have a higher affinity with when we can. These methods come at a cost. The more we deviate from the safer routes, the higher chance we have at activatin' the Hemophæther State, which is bad news."

"Hemophæther State?"

"Yeah. It's like havin' a magical aneurysm. We start bleedin' from the nose, ears, mouth, or other places. It's our bodies warnin' us to back off, or suffer the consequence."

"Which is?"

"Death."

Siroun tried not to leave her mouth agape, but she averted her eyes elsewhere when she realized the other two men made eye contact with her. Tucking a stray piece of hair behind her tipped ear, she was at a loss for words on the situation. At least she knew why everyone appeared to age at a different pace. But her thoughts drifted to Colin and how much further he appeared to age by comparison to the others. It explained his bloody nose after the fight with the undead in Pustelia Crest.

Zikky nudged Siroun in the arm again before saying, "Buck up, gel-gel. These dangers are common knowledge for us. We accept our fate as part of the job. Not to mention we have ways to help mitigate things a little, see—?" The Skivat held up her left hand and wiggled her forefinger. On it rested a silver ring with small orange-colored crystals laid within. "It's not much, but we draw power from these Æther-packed crystals so we're not burnin' ourselves out too fast. When they crack though, we're on our own. Our badges are also infused with Æther which we use as a back-up conduit."

While Siroun nodded in passive acceptance, the group halted at a tall building blocked by merchants selling their wares along the front. The merchants lacked any respect for space as they pushed their goods to other Dragomyr, leaving no opening to enter the building behind them. Despite how fervent they were with making a sale, there was a particular level of blindness towards the four of them, save Nikostraz.

Colin scowled in disapproval. "They don't to want to sell to us."

As Nikostraz rejected an assertive merchant in his native tongue for the third time, he gave the other a sideways glance. "It's because they don't sell to foreigners."

"Ah. I had almost forgotten the unfounded xenophobia of this country," Colin curled his lip at a nearby merchant.

"What of the Lady Siroun?" Lord Valter said as he wove through the blockade of bodies to reach the door.

"Unfortunately, she looks just as foreign as the rest of you," said Nikostraz with sympathy in his voice. "Not to mention she's never left Pustelia Crest. As far as they are concerned, she's not a native."

Siroun realized she was just as out of place here as the

mages, and her fingers combed through her hair to calm her anxiety. When she saw Lord Valter gesture for her to come inside she spared no hesitation. The rest of the group followed with Nikostraz tailing them last as he scolded the merchants with impatience at their persistence.

"Tch! This atmosphere's killin' me," Zikky muttered as they passed through the entrance and looked around. The building already looked big from the outside, but it was nothing compared to the inside.

"Whoa," said Siroun under her breath. She had to stop herself from looking like a fish again. Her teeth clicked when she remembered to close her mouth. Never had she seen such a place before, but the others appeared nonchalant.

They stood within the great hall, occupied by individuals walking back and forth in pairs or groups. Many of them were Dragomyr, but sometimes she saw an occasional foreigner traversing side-by-side and conversing in languages she hadn't yet learned, as if it were of no consequence to the social climate just outside the doors. The ceiling was the tallest thing she had ever seen, even beyond that of the library in Pustelia Crest. Stained glass windows depicting The Great Three decorated the higher portions of the walls, and greenery draped off of them to give the interior a sense of organic sophistication. The tapered ceiling displayed every square inch with calligraphy-styled murals painted in colors that shimmered and moved as they walked. As if the rooftops weren't a sight to behold, Siroun drifted her focus to the ground and saw that the marble floors swirled with ocean blue colors and traces of gold and silver. Hand-crafted statues acted as pillars that weren't of anyone she recognized.

Then her eyes saw something that told her what she needed to know of this place. A large emblem fortified with magic hovered at the center of the grand hall. It matched the symbol that the three mages wore on their uniforms, which meant the building acted as a hub for the Vanis Aer Æther Guild here in Libstravad. The group walked toward a service desk stationed underneath the massive floating symbol, and a middle-aged Dragomyr presiding over it. If Siroun had to guess, her physical appearance didn't match her actual age. She was in the middle of scribing notes when she acknowledged their arrival.

"I take it you found what you were looking for?" said the desk clerk.

"Yes, and no," Lord Valter replied. "As promised, we have returned within the designated deadline."

She nodded to the nobleman's vague response before eyeing the group one more time. Siroun's heart skipped a beat when the woman scrutinized her face. But the clerk turned her attention to Lord Valter next and asked, "Where's your escort?"

Siroun's gaze drifted in the nobleman's direction when she heard the hesitation in his next set of words.

"There was an incident in Pustelia Crest unrelated to us. He stayed behind to assist the Lieutenant since they were a little short-staffed," replied Lord Valter and then cleared his throat afterward.

Though it wasn't a lie, Siroun couldn't help but raise a brow at him in response to the answer. But the reason still stretched the truth to where the desk clerk gave Lord Valter a slow blink, and replied with an unconvinced, "Uh-huh."

Nevertheless, the clerk carried on with her processing duties and said, "Very well, I'll check your references on that reason. In the meantime, I'll need your identification."

The three mages opened up their coats and grabbed an insignia from the inside of their garments. When they pulled their emblems off the fabric, the badges revealed threads of blue energy disconnecting from the lining, and Siroun's jaw went slack again.

"Nexus Floss," Zikky whispered in Siroun's ear after flashed her badge to the clerk. "Only the owner of the garment can manipulate it once a tailor crafts it."

Siroun blinked. "There are mage tailors?"

"Skills involvin' magic ain't limited to just bein' a field agent, y'know. We can use our talents for all sorts of work."

"Does it age them too?"

"Not if ya take the right precautions. Like I said before, usin' spell components and recitin' full equations ain't practical out in the field, but that don't mean it's a hindrance to everyone. For example, Spellweave Tailors are rare and make tons of money."

"Have you ever considered being a Spellweave Tailor?"

"Nope."

"Why not?"

Zikky gave Siroun a sly grin. "I ain't the artsy type."

A plethora of questions swirled through Siroun's mind, but she thought it was best to ask at a more opportune time. She observed the receptionist take everyone's sigil and run them through a bizarre magical identification contraption. After the sound of whirling, a sharp chirp came from the machine, and the receptionist returned the items

"Left hall, all the way to the back," the clerk gestured with her right claw over her shoulder and returned to her work.

With Lord Valter leading the way, Siroun wondered why they were here. She kept stride with Nikostraz while gesturing that she wished to speak with him, of which he leaned into oblige.

"Did you know that the Vanis Aer had a base here?" she said in Drakish.

His responded with a shrug. *"I knew the Vanis Aer had a headquarters somewhere in Niravad, but I didn't know it was here."*

While they walked the hall, Siroun took in the sights and sounds. Her thoughts halted when a short Sylvani raced past her to join up with another group to the left. They shared some light banter, laughed, and headed toward another part of the building.

"I don't understand," said Siroun as she returned to the Adami language while rubbing at her forehead. "I didn't know foreigners were allowed in Niravad. How come this is the first time I'm hearing of this?"

"The guild is neutral territory, and this is the last remaining embassy before Niravad closed its borders to outsiders," said Lord Valter as they reached the left hallway and proceeded onward. "The Vanis Aer Æther Guild recruits members from every kingdom. Its ideology encourages working together to foster peaceful relations and leaving political agendas to the wayside. Well, most of them."

"Wouldn't that mean abandoning your duties back home, My Lord?"

Lord Valter acted accustomed to this question with minor hesitation in how he answered, "Somewhat. My designation within the guild is a complicated affair. Think of me as an ambassador to my country under the Vanis Aer banner rather than a Lord sitting around collecting taxes every day."

To his last sentiment, she smiled. She enjoyed the way the nobleman conversed with her, and he presented himself as a decent person from what she could gather. It was unfortunate that Nikostraz did not agree with her on that thought. Maybe someday that would change.

"Here we are," said Lord Valter interrupting her thoughts.

They made their way into a dark room, its source of illumination coming from a huge mechanical contraption in the center. Its construction was like a globe with the center being hollow. Large rings spun and rotated around the empty center-point as light bounced off the walls in waves reminiscent of water reflections. A thrum resounded from the power source that kept it in motion. The metal plates beneath them acted as a foundation and surrounded the mechanical wonder with glowing runic symbols that she didn't recognize.

"Wh-what is it?" Siroun asked in amazement.

"We call it the Orpheum Compass," Lord Valter replied as he, too, marveled at its design.

"The Orpheum Compass," the name repeated from her lips as she found herself unable to take her eyes off of it. Upon further observation, the architects of the compass bolted the machine through the flooring and into the ground. Even Siroun could sense that this room held a massive amount of raw energy and assumed the mechanical contraption sat on a font of power. None of the books she read in the library had prepared her for this.

"Nowhere in Dragomyr literature does it say this compass exists in Libstravad," said Siroun.

Zikky closed in and whispered in Siroun's ear, "Not everythin' ya learn comes from books, gel-gel."

Flicking Zikky away with a hand, Siroun thought back on everything she read in Pustelia Crest and realized the limitations. A sizable chunk of those books were repetitive tomes of poetry, myths, and Dragomyr tales. Siroun wondered, in the thousands of books she read, how much of the information was of practical use.

The room held a few other guild members, and most of them kept to their research while one female Dragomyr greeted them. She had a slender build with a long neck and smaller muzzle. Her brilliant yellow-and-green feathers around her neckline made Siroun jealous. The researcher used a lithe claw to adjust her glasses and analyze the group before addressing them in the Adami's tongue, "I'm sorry, but do I know you?"

Lord Valter stepped forward and gave a nod of respect in line with the social custom. The Dragomyr responded in kind before he spoke to answer her question, "Forgive our intrusion. My name is Lord Valter Flynn, and you are?"

"Katyazfina," she said in a cordial tone. "You may call me Katya. I am the acting Chief Engineer for the Orpheum Compass."

"A pleasure meeting you, Katya. Might I inquire

about the other engineer that assisted us several days ago? I believe her name was Urania."

"They rerouted her to Seda. I am her replacement. She debriefed me on your impending return, and my assistants can prepare the compass for Ysile Marden."

"Actually," Zikky interrupted, "we need to teleport to The Hive."

This news jarred Katya, as her glasses slid down her muzzle when her neck recoiled at the request. "The Hive is not accessible to us via the leylines."

"There's an old transport pad located to the southeast in the Sek'hithis region just off the coastline," said Zikky. "If I give ya the coordinates, think ya can land us near it?"

Katya paused to consider the request before answering with, "Should I be concerned that a Skivat is asking me to drop a group into a desert death trap?"

Zikky smiled and tilted her head. "Better a Skivat than someone else."

The Chief Engineer didn't look amused by the cheeky response, but since Lord Valter did not object to the suggestion, she relented, "Very well. If you give me the exact coordinates, I assure you my team will do their best to get you there. Assuming everything is functioning on the receiving end. Also, I only recall three being in your party."

Lord Valter raised a brow. "Will the larger capacity be an issue?"

"Not if you have the proper catalyst to boost the power levels high enough."

Without hesitation, Colin removed his sigil from his jacket and handed it over to Katya. When Lord Valter raised a brow at the gesture, the younger one said, "The guild can always craft me another one. I trust you'll vouch for my identity if it ever comes into question?"

"Of course," said the nobleman.

Colin nodded to the researcher in final approval and watched her take it to the grand machine in the center of the room. When Katya opened up a panel, Siroun caught a glance of the interior power core to find nothing more than a void of darkness and crackling electricity. Katya stuck her claw into the portal-like receptacle, the sigil reacted to the energy with a pulsing glow before floating off of her palm and into the abyss.

The researcher retracted her claw from the machine and pushed her glasses along her muzzle, looking at her guests expectantly. "I hope this is enough to get everyone there in one piece. However, I recommend buffering the compass more to be on the safe side."

Just as Colin was ready to offer himself up again, an arm reached across and halted him. Lord Valter gave the youth a shake of his head. "I will do this."

Katya interjected, "It is less taxing if the three of you share the load, Grigonstraz will prepare the platform for you. Make sure to tuck anything loose someplace snug."

A large, burly Dragomyr sauntered over to the Orpheum Compass and fiddled with a few levers and buttons. While the oscillating rings slowed, the Vanis Aer mages discussed which spell equations to use with Katya. After a few minutes the machine came to a full stop, and Siroun's eyes widened as Grigonstraz approached her.

"Get in," he grunted in Drakish, forcing Siroun and Nikostraz to shuffle up the small platform and into the center of the compass. It took her friend a minute or two

to find the most comfortable position given that his tail was too long for the inner diameter of the mechanism.

The engineers gave instructions to the mages as they latched solid metal bands to their right wrists. When they were ready to move out, Lord Valter led the pack towards the compass. Before stepping inside, they each placed their wrist into the panel that contained Colin's sigil. A vibration pulsed through the enormous machine each time one of them placed the specialized wristband into the receiving portal. Katya observed and dialed in adjustments before completing the syncing process to their elemental energies.

"Are you okay?" Nikostraz asked her.

At first, she didn't hear him addressing her. When Siroun felt his claw touch her shoulder and repeated the question, it brought her back into the present moment. *"Oh, yes! I'm just nervous."*

"You let me know if you don't want to do this."

"No. If this gives us a chance to get to The Hive before Felthane, then we need to go. I need to prove that I didn't help him kill the others and run off with that map. If this helps me get home, then I must do it. Even if it scares me."

She placed her hand upon Nikostraz's claw and squeezed it. Knowing he was here with her helped ease the anxiety. When the others stepped inside, Zikky gave Siroun a wink. "Ready to experience somethin' awesome?"

Siroun stared at the large device. "Is this safe?"

"About as safe as jumpin' off a cliff," she replied with a giggle, causing Siroun to gasp in slight horror. "Don't worry, gel-gel. We've done this before. Ya don't earn these sigils by bein' incompetent."

"Just reckless," Colin chimed in from the side as he

and Lord Valter stood in an incomplete triangle position and put out their right hands, palms facing toward each other. "Are you going to join us?"

"Oh! Right," Zikky bumped Siroun on the arm before she took her position and completed the formation.

Katya and Grigonstraz fired up the compass. The rings gyrated as both Dragomyr observed the energy waves and made adjustments. Lord Valter and Zikky spurred the compass faster by speeding up their incantation, yet Colin's lips never moved. Glowing equations appeared in mid-air before transforming into their respective elements and absorbing into the machine.

When the Orpheum Compass revved up to full capacity, Siroun's body started feeling weightless. Electricity crackled around the outer shell of the compass as the oscillating rings moved at a speed that made them a blur. Looking down, she saw that her feet no longer touched the ground. All five of them floated in the center sphere as light blinded and engulfed her vision.

Siroun shouted out in a panic, "Nik!"

The silence unnerved her, and what started as a bout of worry turned into an anxiety attack. Her chest tightened, her breathing labored, and the uncertainty of whether she was alive or dead flooded her mind. When she reached out into the white oblivion nothing was there to anchor her fears. In a flurry of movement, Siroun tumbled around in the blinding abyss. Her stomach lurched from every motion no matter how slight, and she felt grateful that she didn't eat much that day. Eventually, the sensation ended with an intense pressure on her chest that shoved her backward, hitting the ground. The light vanished, and she found herself sprawled out on the dirt looking up at the sky with the sun blazing down. Intense heat warmed her body as she came to her senses and rolled over to stand. Her mouth watered as she tasted sugar on her tongue.

"Why—," Siroun smacked her lips as she continued to register the intense flavor that wasn't there before. "Why do I taste something sweet in my mouth?"

Though she struggled with standing, she soon made it to her feet only for a wave of vertigo to hit her. A pair of strong arms wrapped around her to keep from falling as Zikky's voice said, "Gotcha!"

"I think I'm going to be sick," Siroun mumbled as her head titled sideways.

"Yeah, first time's always the roughest. We shoulda warned ya," said Zikky, giving Siroun a moment to regain her balance. "The sweetness in your mouth is normal. Happens every time ya ride a leyline."

Lord Valter pressed a palm to Siroun's forehead, bringing calm to her frazzled nerves. However, her chest remained sore from the earlier panic attack. Zikky brought Siroun over to a nearby boulder to sit and collect herself.

The mage giggled while reaching out and straightening the stray hairs. "Ya got tossed about pretty badly."

Siroun's pallor subsided, but her stomach kept churning. "Are we alive?"

"Alive an' well, gel-gel. No worries 'bout that. Congrats on survivin' your first teleport! Nicely done if I say so myself." Zikky gave Siroun a wink and a pat on the cheek, then made her way over to Lord Valter.

Colin finished checking on Nikostraz who seemed in better shape than Siroun but still jumbled. Bursts of wind whistled through the desolate area as the three of them took a minute to survey their surroundings. Ocean waves echoed from a distance, but the land they stood on was desert with a tiny smattering of trees. Northward, huge mountains blockaded the peninsula they were standing upon. A wall of rock as high and wide as the eye could see acted as the barrier between them and the rest of Fi'ro.

"Well, navigator, what secret Skivat voodoo gets us to The Hive?" Colin said while crossing his arms and tapping his fingers. His eyes squinted at the intense sunlight as beads of sweat were trickled down his face.

"Pfft! Please, it's so easy that even gel-gel here could get in," Zikky goaded. "Ya just have to close your eyes tight, like this!"

Enacting out her instructions, Zikky balled up her fists close to her chest and smiled as she spoke the next part in an obnoxious baby voice, "Then just believe in the power of friendship! Poof! Y'all be there in an instant!"

Wiggling her butt, Zikky kept her eyes closed while grinning from ear to ear. "I'm not hearin' ya believe hard enough."

"Seriously... I hate you," Colin turned toward the mountains and began walking, only to end up swaying when he stepped. "Ugh, this heat."

"Zikky," the scolding came from Lord Valter as he gave her a disapproving look.

"Sorry, couldn't help myself." She chortled before clearing her throat and shouting to Colin, "Get back here ya big doof!"

Even Siroun couldn't help but giggle. If it weren't for Colin bailing her out of a few predicaments, she would have joined in on Zikky's playful teasing. Then again, she was also fighting off the urge to vomit.

Zikky waited for everyone to gather before cracking her knuckles and wiggling her fingers in preparation. As far as one could tell there was nothing within vicinity that showed an entrance point. The Skivat mage stood dead center and pretended to prepare a strange magic trick. Despite the dirt and debris fluttering over the windy peninsula, Zikky scuffed her boot across a small area, to reveal a flat surface underneath. Upon second glance, Siroun saw engravings coming in and out of view. They were standing on a platform, masked by the surrounding environment. No one would guess that this location was a potential entry point except to those who knew about it.

"My selection of this location was for a reason," said Zikky. "One cannot enter The Hive through conventional means. Ya gotta know where the real entrance points are, and those secrets we Skivat take to our graves. So stand back, lads and ladies! Allow me the honor of bein' yer guide this evenin'."

"It's daylight," said Colin.

Zikky pointed at him. "Hush!"

She fished out a tiny marble from her coat pocket and flicked it in the air with her thumb before catching it with a grin. With an object so benign-looking it seemed impossible to guess its true potential as a key to The Hive. Zikky crouched and cleared away the layers of dirt until she revealed an engraved panel, then toiled with the puzzle combination before it clicked and gave way. Siroun and Nikostraz looked on in curiosity while Zikky wove her fingers into an elaborate switch mechanism that let out a burst of hot air upon placing the marble in its receptacle. The gush of pressurized wind swept away the dirt that clung to its surface within a five-foot radius. However, the alter that started sinking was much more extensive. All five of them found themselves caught in a circular platform that started lowering into the depths below.

While the contraption continued to twist and move, Zikky looked up at Siroun and gave the woman a sly grin. "Ya ready to follow me into the wormhole, gel-gel?"

Siroun didn't think she could handle another teleportation trip. "Is it going to make me nauseous again?"

"You're so cute." Zikky chuckled in response before answering with, "Perhaps."

Siroun's cheeks flushed pink from the compliment tossed her way. "Th-there's no standard of etiquette that you live by, is there?"

"What are you talkin' 'bout? I'm bein' very well-behaved right now." Another playful wink and a quick push of the entry mechanism and the door underneath their feet shifted.

With a sigh, Lord Valter replied, "My apologies, Lady Siroun. This behavior is normal for our fire companion."

The earth buckled underneath them, causing everyone to secure their stances to avoid falling. The engravings they stood upon acted as a transportation pad into depths of their destination. The stone plate inched deep into the earth and Siroun glanced up one last time to see the sky. When they became entombed in the darkness only the faint glow of Zikky's animal-print body marks acted as a source of light.

There was a disturbing gleefulness when the Skivat

followed up with, "Oh, I forgot to mention that ya might experience the uncontrollable need to take a nap, followed by a temporary lapse in memory. Best ya not fight it."

Siroun panicked. "What do you mean 'uncontrollable nap'?"

No sooner had she spoken those words when wooziness overcame her, and she dropped to her knees, then to the ground.

PART II

Fi'ro

10

THOUSANDS OF FEET of the pitch-black Di-Metal tubes stretched for endless miles within the underground metropolis that was The Hive. A part remained empty for today's Mak'dor Championship event. Only music blared through the walls from the outside as people waited for the competitors to pass that part of the course. The tube soon hummed to life as something approached in the distance. A green fluorescence emitted from the specialized alloy, and the oncoming sounds of movement increased in strength. Seconds later, a swarm of Skivat flew by. Hoots and cheering echoed through the cut-out partitions of the racetrack as the group of five zoomed through the course at breakneck speed. Twisting and turning, they skated as a unit like a flock of birds while they followed the flow of the Shot Pipes.

"And it's neck-in-neck as the Tumblewheels regain traction on the split course!" The announcer shouted in Vat'tu through a sound amplifying device, relaying what he could from his location. *"This is the closest we've seen the Racerbacks*

come to a potential win as they try to retake the lead from their rivals. It's been a while since I've seen Mikky put this much effort into a Mak'dor Championship. Will the Racerbacks see victory to secure the Pipes turf for themselves? Or will the Tumblewheels shut them out again?"

Fans swarmed the bookies after the two teams bypassed the crowd. In the rafters sat another group of Skivat who examined the match and scribed notes as the action unfolded. Conversations flew back and forth between each of the operators as they captured the progress.

When the track forced the skaters into a harsh turn, they balanced themselves with their palms to keep from falling. Both teams inter-mingled within each other's territory, and the Tumblewheels did their best to throw off their opposition. Each time Mikky or Veska went to take the lead, the Racerbacks blocked them. Mikky's instincts kicked in and he knew the perfect countermeasure his team could enact to reclaim the lead.

"Veska—," Mikky tapped her thrice on the back in a triangular pattern, *"on my mark."*

The team developed plenty of signals over the years. They learned every course and obstacle like second nature. The strategy involved attempting a feint.

He began the countdown. *"One."*

Veska took a jab to the jaw but recovered and pushed the Racerback along so that Mikky had a clear hit. Cheers roared through the tubes like a vibration of thunder that fueled them onward. It wouldn't be long until they saw the finish line.

"Two," Mikky continued.

Once Veska was free of her assailant, she reached over

and grabbed the other Racerback by the shirt. With a firm grip on the skater's vest, she throttled him forward as hard as she could, nearly toppling him, giving both Racerback skaters a substantial lead. Mikky and Veska watched as both opponents exchanged confused looks. The Racerbacks didn't realize the danger they were in before the cuffs on Mikky's wrists emitted a bright glow.

"Three!" Mikky jerked his hands upward before they jumped high into the air.

Chains materialized from the tubes, and the cuffs clamped around the Racerbacks' ankles, yanking them to the floor. Both opponents fell face-first against the Di-Metal floor as the Tumblewheels sailed over them in tandem. When the flats of their skates landed on the airy magnetic cushion of the tunnel, the road to triumph was theirs. With one more obstacle remaining, the Tumblewheels made another left turn into the gentle curve of the pipe. They lowered their stances before the course dipped, then tossed them into one of the most challenging maneuvers in the race. Curling into sideways somersaults, they spun against the resistor plates that floated in mid-air. They bounced side-to-side in a zig-zag motion toward the next tube. They cleared two sets of acrobatic obstacles before twisting their bodies onto the receiving ramp.

Onlookers packed the surrounding space below, roaring with cheers as the two stuck their landings across the finish line and made their way toward the loading rink. Other team members tumbled and flipped through the air in a nod to the fans below, completing the course and securing a solid finish.

"The Tumblewheels claim victory again!" shouted the

announcer over the masses. Both cheers and jeers from those who placed their bets when the results came. *"Bik'aroth's Shackles strike again as their competitors forget that the turf artifact can be in play at any point in the competition. Better luck next time, Racerbacks."*

The rest of the team swarmed Mikky and Veska as celebrations begun. Another year, another win under their belts. Each member exchanged congratulations via pats on the back and ruffling of hair, Mikky most of all. Celebratory music boomed around them, enticing Veska and a few others to join in on a group victory dance. Their skates synchronized to the beat of a sultry little number toward the Racerbacks to further mock their loss. Veska even pinched her right nipple and pointed out the Racerback's leader as a gesture of further insult. Fans loved every minute, mirroring the moves as they razzed those who bet on the other team.

A voice cut through the noise in Vat'tu, *"Are you sure you didn't cheat to win this year?"*

The team halted their joy as they turned to see who dared challenge their honor at the sport. All eyes focused on Zikky who stood before them with her arms folded and wearing a smirk. Confusion soon turned back into delight as the group dog-piled her and exclaimed, *"Zikky!"*

11

SIROUN LEAPED BACK to keep from getting slammed by the onslaught of hugs for Zikky. Overjoyed, the Tumblewheels clamored in their Vat'tu tongue as questions sailed left and right. During this time Siroun noticed something different between Zikky and the rest of the Skivat. Long, thin tails with tufts of fur at the ends flicked and curled in delight, but Zikky was devoid of such a limb.

Mikky ruffled Zikky's hair before the rest of the crew backed away. The two Skivat chatted back and forth, the language too quick to pick up. Even though Siroun heard Zikky speak several fragments here and there in Vat'tu, it was a different experience to hear it in fluent conversation. Zikky then cleared her throat and nodded her head over to Siroun and the others.

"*Let me introduce you,*" she said in her native language. "*These are my colleagues; Colin Lockwood and the fancy guy is Lord Valter Flynn. Then we have Siroun and her tag-a-long partner Nik-ah… uh. Nikoflips? Nicodemus?*"

"Nikostraz," he hissed before shaking his head in disgust.

"Ooo!" Zikky whistled. "Do ya speak Vat'tu as well?"

"No, but I can tell you're butchering my name on purpose."

"Ah yes. Everyone this is Mikky." Zikky turned her attention toward Mikky and added in Vat'tu, *"Fun one that guy is."*

"You don't say," Mikky replied with a smile before changing the language back to something the group could understand. "Welcome to Hive. I hope enjoy here. Much fun!"

Mikky swooped in and took Siroun's hand to shake it in a gesture of greeting.

Overwhelmed by his enthusiasm, she stammered out, "H-h-hello?"

"He ain't exactly bi-lingual," said Zikky.

"I noticed," Siroun said through more rigorous hand-shaking. Soon, the male Skivat glimpsed the opalescent scales that covered her arms. Curiosity took hold, and Mikky pulled her toward him to get a better look.

"Amazing!" He said in his native language before speaking in broken Adami, "Arm like shine! How to get?"

"Um," she murmured and fidgeted with a strand of her hair. As intriguing as it was to meet new people in a foreign land, Siroun was still way out of her comfort zone. She stumbled on how to best answer him. With such a limited vocabulary she couldn't predict what he would understand. She decided on, "Born with?"

Then he locked eyes with her and noticed Siroun's reptilian pupils and gasped again. "Eyes like Dragon People!"

"Yeah, that too." Siroun mumbled, unaccustomed to the Skivat lavishing so much attention upon her.

Mikky processed the words before his eyes grew wide and he switched back to the Vat'tu language, *"Amazing!"*

"That's enough," Nikostraz stepped in and extricated the Skivat off of Siroun's arm. She appreciated having her personal space back. Although Mikky meant no harm, he was too touchy-feely for her liking.

Colin turned to Zikky. "How do you know each other?"

The question caused two members in the Tumblewheels to laugh, namely the Skivat with the pastel green hair that hung near her shoulders now that her headgear was removed. "I see, you not know?"

Her common was also broken, but there was a smoothness of tone to it as she addressed Colin. With a hand touching Mikky's shoulder, she gave a coy smile denoting an intimate familiarity with their leader.

"He is Mikky Halim-Isa of Tumblewheels. In Hive, we call him Boss," she said with pride. Then she gestured to Zikky and added, "But first leader home, she now Boss again. She takes Bik'aroth's Shackles."

Both Siroun and Colin stood there dumbstruck as it took them a minute to realize Zikky's identity within The Hive. Lord Valter reflected no such surprise on his face as he maintained his stoic disposition.

"You mean," Siroun looked to Zikky, "Mikky's your brother? And you're a Boss?"

"Technically, the term is Hive Lord," said Zikky.

Colin turned to Lord Valter in alarm. "You knew this?"

Lord Valter gave a non-committal nod of his head.

"The guild likes individuals of influence in various places, even the Hive Lords."

The chime of Veska's laughter came back to them. "For friends, too many secrets you keep."

"I don't tell them everything, Veska," Zikky replied in Vat'tu.

"What a pity."

"Are we done with this family reunion?" Nikostraz interjected. "I believe we have more pressing matters at hand."

The comment garnered him a hard clap on the shoulder by Zikky, "Mind yer manners, Grumpy Scales. There's no safer place than with family."

Nikostraz's knees buckled, and his eyes widened in surprise.

"The real Boss returns," said Mikky as he approached Zikky and reached out his arms with the shackles upon his wrists. *"Would you like them back now, or later?"*

Zikky stopped him with a slight of her hand. *"Keep them. I won't be here for long."*

The siblings exchanged a warm embrace before she spoke in the common tongue again, "Besides, they're an awful fashion statement! Ha!"

"You have a sense of fashion?" Colin quipped, before regretting it. An arm wrapped around his neck as Zikky brought his head down to her level, rubbing her knuckle deep into his scalp. No amount of yelping for mercy saved him this time.

"I think Colin's tired from traveling, don't y'all agree?" she said with a cheerful tone through gritted teeth. "Veska, be a dear and hook my friends up with a place to stay?"

Lord Valter stepped in and placed a hand upon Zikky's shoulder which halted her tormenting of Colin, "Given our encumbrances, it might be best to see what the Highrise sector has to offer."

"Tigernach's turf?" Mikky eyed Lord Valter before looking back at his sister and shaking his head. His tongue slipped back to Vat'tu, *"We don't have those kinds of strings available to us anymore."*

Raising a hand, Zikky nodded to her brother before looking over to Lord Valter. "The Blood Oath Butterflies gang require payment to stay at the Highrise, and they ain't cheap."

"I realize this," said Lord Valter. "At least allow me to speak with their leader to determine what accommodations are available."

"Makes sense. I'll see what I can do. No guarantees though." Zikky glanced over to Siroun before returning her gaze to Lord Valter and Colin. "I already have a place to crash by the Pipes with the rest of the gang, so that shaves off part of the cost."

"I'll stay with you," Colin added. Before anyone asked he followed up with, "As you said, it cuts costs. Besides, if Felthane is here, then we need more eyes in other places."

"You should stay in the Visitor's Quarter," said Lord Valter. "See if the Hive Lord from that turf has seen him."

"Pixie-Pop is cool with us," Zikky said with confidence. "I'm sure she'll hook us up with some sweet digs. Just try to act pleasant for a change. We might get some good information off of her."

Colin glared in Zikky's direction, but responded with, "Fine, agreed."

With the plans somewhat mapped out, Siroun asked, "What are we doing now?"

Zikky opened her mouth, but before she could answer, a voice echoed over in their direction. *"Zikky Halim-Isa."*

Siroun witnessed an uneasy look on Zikky's face as she winced and turned to face the one speaking to her. Behind two bodyguards with arms folded stood a petite-framed Skivat with an ombré of purple hair cascading through her long pigtails, multiple piercings, and a tattooed spider's web that laced over the left side of her eye, around the ear, then down her cheek and neck. Her looks belied her age, but she carried herself with authority to show that she was the boss and no one else. While she smacked on a piece of gum the punkish-looking woman grinned.

Crowds split a path between Zikky and the other Hive Lord as they faced off for all to watch. Siroun found herself pulled back by both Nikostraz and Lord Valter in tandem. She looked up at the nobleman and a flush of heat radiated across her cheeks as his stern features observed the interactions between the two Skivat. Unfortunately, Siroun had to assess the exchange without translation. Now more than ever, Siroun wanted to find anything that helped her better understand the cryptic tongue that was Vat'tu.

"Spyder," Zikky said with bemusement. *"Long time no see."*

With a wide grin, the other woman blew a small bubble with her gum before digging her molars into it and making a loud snap. *"You should know better than to come back when debts are owed."*

"Debts? Me?" Zikky feigned ignorance as she looked over to her brother and noticed that he averted his gaze

before turning back to her collector. *"I don't recall accruing anything during my tenure here."*

"You are the rightful Hive Lord of the Tumblewheels, are you not? Any debt accrued in your gang's name is still a debt owed."

"Oh, I see." Zikky played coy. *"Well, I don't have any money. Shall we settle things the usual way?"*

"I figured you would say that," Spyder's eyes shifted toward Siroun and Nikostraz before she raised her right hand and gestured with her fingers to the stout bodyguard to step forward. Cheering roared throughout The Hive now that a fight was beginning. A hulking-looking individual stepped forward, and Siroun gripped at Lord Valter's coat for comfort.

"What's going on?" Siroun asked with wide eyes as she visually digested the beastly man. "She's not going to fight him, is she?"

"My apologies that you must witness this, Lady Siroun," said Lord Valter before turning his attention to Colin and asked, "Is this your first time in The Hive?"

Colin nodded. "I vaguely remember Zikky babbling about this place. From the looks of things, I think she's fighting her way out of something she can't repay."

Siroun looked over to the rest of the Tumblewheels and waved down Mikky to get his attention. The Skivat shuffled his way through the crowd with Veska close behind, and leaned in only to have Siroun scold him with, "Aren't you going to stop this?"

Mikky paused and conferred with Veska before they both agreed on what they heard. He then turned to Siroun and responded with, "Zikky fight, I not object."

Siroun growled and slapped a palm over her forehead. She couldn't decide what was worse: Zikky fighting, or that Siroun didn't know the language to facilitate a solution. Tugging on Nikostraz's sleeve she said to him in Drakish, *"As soon as this is over will you help me find a library?"*

"Gladly," Nikostraz replied.

With that established, Siroun made her way over to Zikky. "What are you doing?"

"My brother racked up some debt while I was away," said Zikky as she limbered up for the impending fight. "I need to square it."

"Square it, how? By having your bones crushed in by," she gestured at the beastly man, "...this?"

She likened him to a small mountain. His broad physique paralleled that of the nimble Skivat, but he navigated through the crowded area with ease despite his bulk. The shale plates all along his body complimented the blunted horns atop his head, and the curved tusks protruded from his lower jaw. Small lines of orange hues underneath the stone-like skin radiated the molten blood coursing through his body.

"Rokür," said Zikky.

"Excuse me?"

"He's a Rokür if that's what yer wonderin'. Goes by the name Cable. Rokür are kinda hard to kill since their blood burns through yer skin. To answer any further questions ya have: Yes, I know what I'm doin', and yes, I've fought a few before. I'm surprised ya've never seen a Rokür in those books of yers," Zikky removed her coat and dumped it into Siroun's hands before sliding on a pair of fighter's gloves lined with leather and strange metal plating. With a pat on Siroun's cheek, she replied, "Yer cute when ya worry over me, gel-gel. Don't worry, I got this. There's a reason I'm the offense of the team. Just relax and enjoy the show."

The answer left Siroun dumbfounded as her cheeks turned pink while stammering out, "B-but y-you... Zikky...what?"

With Zikky's mind made up, Nikostraz pulled her away from the impending brawl. Siroun felt powerless to stop the events unfolding in front of her. Zikky's body flexed and tensed as it prepared for battle. Both fighters finished a quick stretch and a warm-up before knocking knuckles with each other as a gesture of good faith. Meanwhile, Spyder gave Zikky a long, hard stare before dragging a thumb across her chest and then pointing at her own eyes before flicking away her hand. The gesture looked like a taunt. One that Zikky shrugged off as she cupped her hands together and murmured a series of equations to begin her spellwork. Fragments of light sparked between her palms. The sparks turned to flames, and with a firm clap of her hands, it dispersed and scattered across her skin. As the fire traveled along her body, the original clothing she wore changed form into leather and segments of plate mail. Zikky crossed her fingers over her chest with her right hand, and the flames continued down her shirt and transformed the clothing into additional armor. Last, she slapped both of her hands upon her knees and her boots fortified with the imbued spell that geared her up for this fight.

When the spell finished, she punched her right fist into her left palm. "Ya ready?"

Zikky distanced herself a few feet from her opponent

and took a fighting stance. Both arms came up parallel to one another to help guard her face while she set her left leg forward, turned at a forty-five-degree angle, while the right leg positioned behind her in a box formation.

"I have to admit, that's incredible," said Siroun in awe, jealous that she couldn't do something similar.

Lord Valter chuckled and leaned into her ear, "This is just a warm-up for her, My Lady."

His voice sent a wave of heat across Siroun's body, and she averted her gaze while swallowing the lump in her throat. Both Colin and Nikostraz saw the exchange, and while one kept silent, the other spoke.

"Something wrong?" said Colin.

"Oh!" Siroun came back to her senses before shaking her head and focusing on Zikky's fight. "Nope, not at all."

Colin's stare hardened, before he turned to Lord Valter and lowered his voice, "Zikky's going easy?"

"There might be a reason for it," said Lord Valter as he, too, scrutinized the fight.

Cable shifted his footing and reached in with a right punch. Despite the Rokür's size, his speed was impressive. He didn't wait for any bell or indicator that the fight was starting and went in for a strike. Zikky pulled up her arms to block the surprise move just in time. The mass of her opponent's fist combined with the velocity of the punch caused Zikky's body to buckle and drop. Cheers deafened the surrounding area, and betting started as it had during the Mak'dor Championship. Siroun couldn't believe how quick the Skivat could turn any event into a profiteering extravaganza.

Though the strike hit true and knocked Zikky down,

she took the fall with finesse and tumbled to the side before returning to her feet. Her eyes locked on Cable before rolling her left shoulder around. "Ya got better."

Cable grunted and lunged in for another strike with a left hook. This time Zikky brought together her right knee up and her elbow down to take the hit and disperse the force. A wave of gleaming orange and gold reflections ran along her body from the impact point as Zikky blocked his next strike once more. She rooted her stance and leaned her weight forward to strike him in the abdomen with her left leg. The audience looked on with anticipation when Cable paused after the kick. Though he didn't appear hurt, Zikky pulled her leg away revealing an imprint cracked into his shale skin. Similar damage reflected on his hands where his punches landed on Zikky's armor. The two of them moved back into their original stances and Cable glanced at his fist, but his features remained unchanged.

"Ya never were the talkative type," Zikky said with a grin. "Now that we've given each other a handshake, shall we fight for real?"

Both of them leapt forward and clashed in a flurry of kicks and punches. Cable struck with power while Zikky's agility allowed her to change up positions and retaliate with several sweeps that knocked him off of his feet. The Rokür's slower reaction time made him an easy target for Zikky to overwhelm him with a few well-placed power strikes to the chest and face. When Cable ambled back up to his feet for the eighth or ninth time, Siroun winced as she watched the man get struck in the abdomen and go flying backwards into the crowd. The group of Skivat caught him and pushed him into the make-shift fighter's ring with nothing but swarms of people surrounding the two as the barrier.

Cable used the momentum of the group push to land a nasty right hook into Zikky's shoulder. Though she softened the blow with a partial block, the strike made her stumble sideways. When he went in for another attack, she lifted both of her arms and blocked the punch. Sparks flew off of her battle armor, and every muscle in her body tensed. Cable snuck in a third punch only to land his fist upon her fire-enhanced battle armor once more. The skin of his knuckles that lacked the shale plating seared against the enchanted armor each time he made contact. Yet, he appeared unhindered by the element she commanded.

Siroun watched as the dance between the two brawlers had her gnawing on her fingernails with each passing second. She wasn't well versed with fighting, so she couldn't tell who had the advantage. When she glanced toward Nikostraz, she saw him engrossed in the match. His reptilian eyes darted and followed the brawl, scrutinizing every move between the two fighters. Across the room, Spyder and her other bodyguard, Jinx, watched as their chosen warrior held his own in the fight. Jinx was a Sylvani with a tall frame that offset the short and stout dimensions of her Rokür colleague. Unlike others of her kind, her skin reflected a honeydew cream color, with dark brown hair and ear lobes that curled like leaves on a vine. The two women chatted back and forth between one another while keeping their eyes on the fight, but it was anyone's guess what they were saying with all the noise in the area.

Zikky changed up her stance so she could move around the fighter's ring with better fluidity. Lord Valter and Colin watched in silence as the minutes progressed. By now any regular fight would have been long over, but both fighters still exchanged blows resulting in further cheering and gambling among the masses. Siroun kept watching as the battlemage hopped from side to side, giving and taking hits. She only saw Zikky in action during their time in Pustelia Crest where she ambled about with little regard of urgency. Now the Skivat looked alert and calculated every move with precise focus, but her breathing became labored. Another massive strike came toward her face and forced her to block. She kept her balance but lost ground when the attack pushed her back.

"Whoops," said Zikky, her tone of voice sounding oddly nonchalant.

Siroun gasped when she saw the next oncoming attack and shouted, "Zikky, watch out!"

The sound of Cable's fist pounding into the Skivat echoed throughout the room and silence befell the crowd. Zikky's body slammed to the ground, face down, immobilized. For a second no one moved or spoke. Then an eruption of cheers and jeers echoed throughout the rock-carved walls of The Hive. Even Mikky and the gang appeared stunned to see their boss receive a beating like that, but they didn't move. With no one to help their fallen colleague, Siroun wrinkled her brows before taking a step toward Zikky. However, an arm crossed out in front of her, and she looked up and saw Lord Valter's stern gaze watch the rest of the scene play out.

"That's your subordinate, isn't it?" Siroun huffed at him. "Why won't any of you help her?"

"My Lady," Lord Valter spoke, making eye contact

with her. "I understand your distress. Please maintain patience, for my sake?"

Caught between wanting to help and not angering Lord Valter, she bit hard on her bottom lip and forced herself to remain still.

"Is that all the Vanis Aer Guild's got?" Spyder boasted as she sauntered over to Zikky's limp body and gave it a little nudge with her foot, "Looks like surface dwelling made you soft."

When Spyder nodded to Cable, the Rokür picked Zikky up and flung her over his shoulder. The Tumble-wheels moved in to intervene, but other members of the crowd halted them. Siroun saw Mikky swipe his hand in Spyder's direction, and the sound of chains clanging filled the air. Several shackles clamped onto Spyder's ankle and wrist. As a third aimed for her throat, she reached out with a spare hand and caught it in mid-air. Her gaze drifted toward Mikky who stood, unflinching.

She smirked. *"Are we upset?"*

"Let her go," he commanded.

"I do not intend to harm her. We have an important matter to discuss between us."

"This was never a debt issue, was it?"

"No," said Spyder. *"But this is a concern outside of The Hive. Release the shackles. I won't harm your beloved little sister."*

For a moment Mikky didn't budge, but in time he gestured his surrender as the ghostly chains released the other Hive Lord and returned to their solid state around each of his wrists. His gaze dropped, and he refused to look anyone in the eyes. When Lord Valter noticed Mikky pulling back, he stepped forward. Spyder's attention shifted to the newcomer and raised a brow before waving her hand at him dismissively.

Not appreciating the gesture, Lord Valter spoke up, "I am afraid we are here on official business. Zikky is my subordinate, and I will not permit you to hijack a member of the Vanis Aer Æther Guild."

Spyder rolled her eyes at him and replied in fluent Adami, "Your rank within your guild's authority does not supersede that of The Hive, outsider. However, I'm not an unreasonable Skivat. I assume you all require accommodations while you are here, yes?"

Lord Valter said nothing. The ever-so-slight softening in his expression made her smirk. "I thought so. Given your particular quality of dress, is it safe to assume you need me to contact the Highrise for you? In exchange for your subordinate's time squaring away old debts that is."

The group looked to Lord Valter to see if he would disregard the offer. Instead, he nodded. "Agreed. With the addendum that Colin accompanies you for assurance of Zikky's safety. He is not versed in your tongue so I assume that is acceptable regarding confidentiality for you?"

She smiled at the Lord's attempt to strike a bargain. "I'll be the judge of that."

Making her way over to Colin she approached the guy with a mischievous grin. With only a few inches of personal space between them, she spoke some casual sentences in Vat'tu while monitoring his reactions. The other Skivat around him snickered, trying to hold back their fits of laughter.

"What is she doing?" Colin asked Lord Valter in frustration. Spyder snapped her fingers at him to recapture his attention. Her next sentence ended with a tonal inflection that suggested she was asking him a question. Colin's temper surfaced, "What you want from me?"

Closing the gap so they were almost nose-to-nose, Spyder had a big grin on her face as she replied, "I told them that you have an undersized package for your kind, and that you wet yourself in your sleep."

"WHAT?" Shards of ice began forming in Colin's hands, but Lord Valter grabbed him by the shoulder and shook him to snap out of it.

Spyder laughed and stuck her tongue out at him. "He passes my test. Let's go!"

The ice mage glared at Lord Valter before ripping his shoulder away with a furious jerk and followed the capricious Hive Lord from behind. He muttered to himself while Jinx covered the back to make sure no one else followed the group into their turf. Everything rested in the hands of Zikky and Colin as far as handling Spyder.

"What now?" said Nikostraz, eyes wide.

"Spyder not bad," Mikky stated in his broken common tongue the best he could. "Words strong, must change over."

Siroun turned to Nikostraz and said in Drakish, *"I have to get my hands on a dictionary, or I may lose my mind here. Especially since our only translator in this crazy place disappeared."*

Meanwhile, a light tap landed on Lord Valter's shoulder, and he turned around to find two women standing behind him, one Sylvani and the other a Skivat. They wore skin-tight uniforms with red denim jackets, and each brandished a red and black butterfly tattooed along their necks.

"You require our assistance?" the taller Sylvani asked, devoid of any emotion in her voice.

Siroun couldn't help but admire her silvery-dark gray skin, and pale hair. She carried herself with a militant posture as tendrils of black smoke rolled off of her body.

"Lord Tigernach, it has been a long time," said Lord Valter, but the Sylvani Hive Lord raised a brow at him, forcing him to bypass the usual pleasantries and get to the point of his conversation. "The three of us wish to find suitable accommodations under your protection."

"Very well," said Tigernach. "Let's discuss the details of your payment after we have situated you and your retinue. Follow us."

The crowd split apart as the two women led them out of the area and toward a metal cage system that moved up and down to the different levels of The Hive. As they walked, Siroun stayed beside Nikostraz. His long cumbersome tail bumped into things when trying to thread through the herds of people in an enclosed space. Hundreds of sets of eyes stared at her, and she scratched at her arms as she walked through the masses.

"Have you ever experienced anything like this before?" Siroun asked Nikostraz in their Drakish language while making their way to the moving cage.

"What, the overwhelming feeling of being stared at by hundreds of people?" he replied with a sarcastic tinge of humor in his tone. *"Yes, I daresay I'm a tad familiar with it. You'll get used to it in due time. Although wasn't Pustelia Crest worse?"*

Siroun contemplated the question, then said, *"I guess the thought hadn't occurred to me."*

Nikostraz gave her a warm smile and patted her on the head with his claw. *"Time desensitizes you to familiar places, doesn't it?"*

The staring was different here. Instead of it feeling like harsh criticism, it was an abundance of overwhelming curiosity. Stares of disgust back home were fleeting and then people went about their business. Here, the interest made her cheeks flush hot as they continued their walk. While Lord Valter remained at the front, and Nikostraz walked along her right side, she felt the presence of another individual on her left. It was none other than Mikky who met her gaze with no sense of shame.

With a broad smile on his face, he spoke to her, "I follow. Good host to sister-guests."

"Uh, thank you?" Siroun said, scooting closer to Nikostraz without trying to be too obvious about it. Switching to her native language again, she whispered, *"This one is so strange, Nik."*

"He likes you," the Dragomyr replied.

Siroun blinked at him before doing a double take at Mikky's amorous expression. She averted her gaze to avoid dealing with the awkward encounter.

"Step on board," said Tigernach. When Mikky attempted to tag along, the escort halted him and switched to the Vat'tu language, *"Guests only."*

Mikky frowned, but complied to the orders. He gave Siroun an enthusiastic wave goodbye before the doors to the cage shut.

As Siroun let out a massive sigh of relief, Lord Valter

noticed her exasperation and couldn't help but chuckle and say, "You have a secret admirer, My Lady."

She groaned as the cage climbed to the top.

12

*I*T ONLY TOOK a few minutes to reach Spyder's abode within the Network turf. Colin waited in a separate room for an hour before Spyder let him step inside. He wondered if he needed to pry Zikky's unconscious body from the Hive Lord. However, when they let him enter he stood there with his mouth agape. There sat the two Hive Lords upon plush cushions, laughing and exchanging light banter as Zikky wrapped a small bandage around her hand. She displayed a few bumps and scrapes, but otherwise, she came out of the fight unscathed. A far cry from the look of being knocked out and unconscious an hour ago. When the door closed behind him and the deadbolt clicked, Colin realized he was alone with the other two women.

"Welcome to my tea room!" Spyder spanned her arms into the air with joyous warmth before setting them back down to grab her cup again. "So you're Colin, eh? You're a cutie. May I add you to my harem?"

If it weren't for the proposition making him recoil in disgust, he would have applauded Spyder for her audacity.

"I'm an elite mage of the most reputable guild in the world, not your pleasure boy. Besides, isn't there a physiological incompatibility between Adami and Skivat?"

Spyder ran her tongue across her lips as she looked him in the eyes. "There are multiple ways to have fun, handsome."

Colin balked, his face turning a deep shade of red as he sputtered through an attempt to fire back an insult but lacked the words.

"She's jokin', Ice-Brains," said Zikky while stifling her laughter. "Sit down already."

"Adami men sure get touchy, don't they?" Spyder quipped in Vat'tu as she took another sip of her tea.

"Just this one," Zikky replied.

Colin sneered, but did as Zikky asked despite Spyder's hungering stare. He scrutinized the tea she poured before giving it a sip, not trusting that Zikky would watch out for his well-being. The tea carried a soft floral body from a plant that must have been native to Fi'ro. Not the worst thing he ever tasted.

"Hmm, interesting," said Colin in response to the beverage before setting down the cup and facing his Skivat colleague. "Tell me, Zikky, why did you throw the fight with that substandard battle armor spell?"

Spyder propped her chin upon her palm and smiled. *"He noticed."*

"He wouldn't be in the guild at his age if he didn't." Zikky mused in return before changing the language back to Adami again. "We're bein' watched. Probably by the very person we came here to track."

Colin thought back on the interactions that transpired

from the fight, before looking at Spyder. "That taunt you did earlier."

"I hope it was subtle enough to keep them from noticing," the Hive Lord smiled. "I'm uncertain if the fight assuaged them, or made them feel cheated."

"That'll be somethin' we'll find out in due time." Zikky shrugged with nary a care before she quirked a brow and said, "I know that artifact of yers reveals more than what yer leadin' on, Spyder. What gives?"

The other woman took her time drinking her tea, forcing the other two to wait for her reply. Then Spyder spoke up, "Allegiances have been changing while you were away. Ponfass is tired of ruling just the Midnight Quarter, and The Twelfth gang wants to go for the Heart."

"It wouldn't be the first time another Hive Lord tried to move in on The Heart before," said Zikky. "Won't be the last, either."

"His motivations are different," said Spyder. "Ponfass wants to dominate the entire Hive."

"He'd have to every artifact to respond to his command. It can't be done."

Spyder quirked a brow at her. "Can't it?"

Colin watched the two Hive Lords exchange suspicious looks with each other, then Spyder elaborated, "As I recall, a certain someone left the chain of command to her brother, yet the artifact still responds to its original master. Tell me, Zikky, how did you get Bik'aroth's Shackles to adjust its terms of ownership? Especially knowing that they bind the presiding master to The Hive and cannot leave it if they are to rule over their turf?"

The silence between the two women made Colin

wonder if another scuffle would break out. His knowledge of Hive politics was marginal. He knew the entire Skivat culture based itself on an oligarchical kleptocracy. Hive Lords ruled over turfs, but he didn't know what determined these hierarchies.

A soft chuckle came from Zikky's lips, but it lacked the humor that everyone expected from the carefree Skivat. "It ain't easy to do, doubt I can do again it."

"But it was done, and now rumors are floating around about how you did it," Spyder's tone sounded like a mother scolding a child. "You've stirred the nest, and I'm not thrilled to be chasing rumors, but here we are. Not to mention your target has me by the tongue."

"Ah, that's unfortunate." Zikky replied, flicking dirt off her sleeve. "Would I at least be able to ask ya who in The Hive does translation work?"

Spyder tucked her arms under her pits and contemplated the question before answering with, "Niskertail, in the Visitor's Quarter. She can translate any of the racial tongues in Clayne for a decent price."

"That won't help us," Colin said to Zikky, only to receive a dismissive gesture.

"I'm afraid what we have on our hands is more divine," said Zikky.

Spyder's eyes narrowed. "You speak of the Immortal Languages?" A nod of affirmation caused the Hive Lord's countenance to tense. "What is your target up to?"

"I dunno the motive, but if he's goin' through all this trouble to prevent you from talkin' to us, then I'm guessin' it's bad. Though I doubt his real target is Fi'ro. Still, that's not to say you shouldn't research those rumors. I just don't have time to stay for damage control."

The Network Hive Lord tilted her head and frowned. "How typical of you."

"Hey, I speak the truth," Zikky said with a shrug. "I can ask the guild to aid ya if that's what ya want."

Spyder gave them a dirty look. "You know full well the Hive Lords take care of our own. We don't need the Vanis Aer poking their noses in places they've got no business investigating."

"Suit yourself."

"Fakil," Spyder spat out afterward. "The one who runs that joke of a junk shop called the Hooker's Eye in the Midnight Quarter."

That name caused Zikky to groan. "By the sands, not that guy. He's double-crossed my crew more times than I can count. The last thing I want is to go to him for help."

"He's the only one I know in The Hive that can translate a god's written word. Not sure which ones he knows." Spyder leaned back with a devious smile upon her lips. "Can't guarantee he won't try to kill you either."

"He can try," she scoffed. "But we both know I'll fold him into a kite if he tries anythin'. Anyhoodle, it's best we get goin'."

Zikky stood and signaled for Colin to follow her to the exit. As they both headed out, she turned toward the other Hive Lord and changed to Vat'tu, *"Appreciate all your help."*

"Don't thank me yet," said Spyder, her humor long gone.

With nothing further to say on the matter, Jinx and Cable returned to escort them out. Colin almost reached the door when Spyder cleared her throat loud enough to catch his attention. Zikky's ears twitched having heard the summon, but she kept walking. Meanwhile, the door shut in front of Colin, forcing him to face the Hive Lord again.

"I wasn't kidding when I said I would like to bring you into my fold," Spyder mused before pulling out a page of parchment and an assortment of enchanted inks. Her fingertips traced over the bottles as her demeanor softened now that they were alone. "Zikky told me you manipulate ice magic, is that correct?"

Colin's upper lip curled. "You don't give up, do you?"

A wry smile reflected on her face as she selected a vial and used the quill to scrawl a message. When she finished, she blew on the paper, folded it in half, and slid it toward Colin. "I'm persistent when I want something. I take excellent care of my consorts, and since you're a capable individual, I believe you're worth what I offer on this paper."

"I'm not int—."

"Please realize that you are in Fi'ro and bound by our customs and jurisdictions. I remind you it is frowned upon to refuse acknowledgment of my goodwill."

If this was her method of intimidating him, he wasn't impressed. "I'm not kowtowing to your advances without fighting back."

"All I am asking," she injected with a calm voice, "is that you take this paper and consider its contents. The offer stands long after you finish your little game of cat and mouse with your colleagues. I've selected an ink that responds to your… skillful touch. Be a dear and humor me just this one time?"

"Tch!"

Colin snatched the paper off the table and stormed out of the room without saying goodbye. He planned on tearing it to shreds once he exited the Network's turf and hasted his steps along the way. But when he hit dead-end after dead-end through the labyrinth of corridors, he relented to asking for directions. He discovered a nearby Skivat who was eyeing him from a distance and realized that Spyder was always watching people. Perhaps destroying the paper wasn't a good idea until they were far removed from the continent. Between Zikky being accused of starting an impending turf war, and Felthane most likely being the one who threatened her to silence, it didn't take a genius to understand that Spyder had the entire Hive sweeping for information that helped her maintain her turf.

For now, he found himself saddled with this offer he never wanted. It took a while to weave his way out of the Network and toward a general commuting area where people walked from region to region within the underground metropolis. When he felt he had made decent strides away from his seductress, Colin found a quiet corner and stared at the folded offer. With only a few moments to himself among the bustling people, his overt disgust at the parchment turned into curiosity. He didn't understand the drive that made Spyder so confident with her offer. After staring at it long enough, his fingers slid between the folds.

Blank. The paper was blank.

Colin flipped it several times to make sure he had missed nothing. His eyes did not deceive him. There was nothing there.

"What kind of sick joke is this?" he muttered to himself. Thinking back on her words, he remembered something about his touch being the key to all of this. "I'm touching it. What's the catch?"

Even when he held it up to the light, he couldn't find anything. Spyder wrote something down. He watched with his own eyes. There had to have been a trick to reading it, otherwise she wouldn't have insisted for him to take it.

Then he realized he was looking at this all wrong. Spyder used an enchanted ink to write the note. He touched the paper with his fingers, and a soft swirl of frost danced across the fibers. It triggered a reaction in the exact spot where Spyder made her mark. When Colin completed his handiwork, he took a moment to read the inscription. His aqua eyes hardened at the contents inside. After taking a moment to reflect on the message, Colin stuffed the paper in his coat pocket and went to visit Lord Valter.

13

PIXIE-POP SLAMMED OPENED the door with gusto. "And this is where you'll sleep!"

Time flew by as Siroun met up with the Hive Lord of the Visitor's Quarter, Pixie-Pop. This turf was more for commoners like her and Nikostraz while the Highrise remained exclusive to influential entities and people of global interest. Though Lord Valter requested an exception to include them both, Tigernach denied him. She and Nikostraz would have to make due in their separate accommodations. A situation that Nikostraz held no qualms accepting.

Their room hosted four single beds with minimalistic decor, and the same magic-infused technology that ran throughout The Hive appeared here too. The color schemes were an array of rustic reds, taupes, and browns to match the mountains. A few desert plants littered the room, and wooden furniture gave the place a warmer touch. Siroun honed in on the small bathroom equipped with blue orbs over the sink, bath, and waste receptacle. A light tap of the orb and the enchanted object came to life, spouting streams of water depending upon the use.

"Careful how much you use," Pixie-Pop said as she watched Siroun explore the technical nuances of each orb's role. "The orbs have limited charges before they gotta go back for refills."

"How are they refilled?" Siroun waved her hand over and under the orb floating above the washing basin.

"That's a trade secret. The hard part is keepin' 'em away from kingdoms that wanna pilfer 'em from us. So, don't get any ideas," she took this moment to glance at Lord Valter, who was still negotiating payment terms with Tigernach.

Siroun shifted her attention to the beds and test out their plushness by bouncing on them with her butt.

Pixie-Pop took this time to approach each of them and latch a thin chain around their wrists with an insignia stamped onto a charm. "Y'all will be right as rain here. Only our guests may enter this turf, but we made sure Zikky can come and go 'round here as needed. For now, I best be off. Got things to do an' all. Later!"

With one Hive Lord shuffling on her way, Tigernach turned to Lord Valter, "This way."

"Stay safe," Lord Valter nodded to the two of them before turning to leave.

The door closed as Siroun finished jumping on the bed. Now that she was just among kin, she felt relieved to speak in her native tongue without Zikky always showing up. *"I wonder if we're able to visit Valter in his quarters while we're here."*

Nikostraz wrinkled his muzzle. *"I assume not, since the Highrise is for people of title or wealth. You heard Tiger-*

nach tell the man we couldn't stay there. I doubt they permit visiting."

"Oh," said Siroun with disappointment reflecting in her frown.

"Even without that restriction, he's still a Lord from Anastas. Nobles don't mix with commoners. Not even his two comrades share the same accommodations as him, so don't get too heartbroken about it." Nikostraz unloaded a few grooming necessities from his satchel, then reached into the air to stretch before eying the dirt on his scales. With a grunt of disgust, he picked at the excess grime.

Siroun used this time to pull up her leg and untie the laces to her boots so that her poor feet could be free of their bonds. "I just thought that wasn't an issue anymore, given how we've all camped out together and whatnot."

"There were no fancy quarters out in the wilderness," said Nikostraz as he made his way to the washroom to grab a damp cloth. "He had to make do with his circumstances. That all changes now that we're back in this strange semblance of civilization again. It would be best if you treated him in the same capacity as a Grand Regent. Be thankful for his kindness, but understand it's limited. Once this mission is over, I doubt he will accommodate you further."

Siroun struggled pulling off her second boot. Her lips twisted to the side hearing his advice. Though Nikostraz conversed with her a thousand times over of what life was like in places such as Finnlock and Anastas, she wasn't good at remembering those conversations by comparison to the written word.

With a heavy sigh, she said. "Forgive me, Nik. I thought this situation made things different. Lord Valter doesn't seem *to be the type that adheres to those social restrictions. I thought I— I mean, we were special."*

The change of wording didn't go unnoticed, but it had been a tiring day.

"There's nothing to apologize for, Siroun," he said. *"I'd make the same mistake. He might be a member of the Vanis Aer guild, but he's a Lord of Anastas above all other things. It is how he carries himself, which leads me to believe that he's of higher rank than he lets on."*

She snapped her gaze in his direction. *"Higher rank? What kind? Are you thinking a prince? Or a king?"*

Nikostraz twitched his snout. *"If he were that high up he'd send someone else to complete this mission. My guess is that he is betrothed too, so you might want to curb that crush of yours."*

Siroun felt her skin grow hot. *"I-I don't have a crush."*

"Uh-huh," he replied, unconvinced. As Siroun opened her mouth to inquire about other noble ranks, Nikostraz chimed in ahead of her, *"You said you wanted to find a library?"*

All thoughts of Lord Valter left as she nodded with enthusiasm. *"If I could just get my hands on something that outlines their language."*

Nikostraz gave her a sympathetic look. *"I admit I'm frustrated too."*

"I might have been the town outcast at home, but I knew where my boundaries were. I had my family, and you as my friend." Siroun met Nikostraz's gaze with warmth. *"It was enough for me. But ever since I left home, I realize just how little I know about the world. If I'm supposed to make a new life out here, I need to arm myself with knowledge. I can't*

keep being this helpless individual who needs to rely on others to protect me."

Giving her a toothy grin, Nikostraz reached out and placed his claw upon her hand. *"I can help with that."*

"You could?"

"If there is a library here, I will find it for you. How about I explore the trader's square and see if I can find something that will help us translate Vat'tu?"

Hope lit up her face as she reached back and clutched at his claw with excitement. *"Yes, let's go!"*

When she tugged on his claw he hesitated, and her smile faded. *"What's wrong, Nik?"*

"I think it would be best if you stayed here for now."

Her lips pressed together. *"But I want to go."*

"I know, Siroun." Nikostraz didn't want to insult her. *"But it will be faster and safer if I went alone since Felthane is targeting you. Here you're under the Hive Lord's protection. I can slip out, find what you need, and bring it back."*

Siroun tried holding back her lower lip from quibbling in front of him but failed.

"Can you at least sit tight until I 'arm' you, as you so put it?" A coy grin forming as a few of his sharp teeth flashed.

She hated when he changed her mind with gentle coercion. Nikostraz wasn't the type to dissuade her in the past, so she made the exception this time with, *"Be quick."*

He saluted her and said, *"Yes, ma'am. By the way, do you still have the reliquary I gave you?"*

Siroun patted her hip, and he replied, *"Good. Keep it close. I'll return in an hour or two."*

"Be safe, Nik," she said as he made his way out of the room.

Silence followed his departure. For the first time since Siroun left home she had privacy. It was crazy to think a little over two weeks ago she was living her usual mundane life, and now she was on a journey to prove her innocence and explore a world unknown. Her thoughts drifted to her father and brother. She hoped they were safe and in good health. With no time for a proper goodbye, her thoughts were always of her family. No letters came her way. Then again, they were always on the move.

"Maybe there's parchment and ink somewhere," she said to herself as she meandered around the room and explored the nooks and crannies, only to be unsuccessful.

Siroun flopped on the bed and looked up at the rustic colored ceiling. She found it strange living underground with no windows to the outside world. The entire metropolis thrived on artificial light. The room was bright as day, but she hadn't a clue as to how to turn the lights on or off. She assumed it had to be similar as the water orbs in the bathroom. She approached the closest sconce and gave the orb inside a soft tap. The magic within ceased to radiate light. With another tap, it brightened again.

Her mind wandered to the reliquary Nikostraz handed her. She fished it from her inner pocket and inspected the strange heirloom. For something so important, she never saw Nikostraz carry it with him before. With the cylindrical shape and long chain, she assumed he hung it around his neck. The cumbersome size made it too large for her to wear as jewelry, so she kept it pocketed instead.

The vial contained a viscous liquid set in silver filigree, tarnished and scratched from either age or lack of care. Any trace of paint rubbed off long ago. Once upon a time this piece looked alluring, with the real mystery residing in the crystalline core. Closer inspection revealed a shimmering black-emerald liquid that produced small bursts of light. What appeared to be a dull, dead trinket came to life the more she stared deep into the recesses of its center.

She tipped the reliquary back and forth until a loud banging came from the door. The sound made her jolt, loosening her grip on the heirloom, and reaching out to reclaim it before it tumbled to the floor. Uncertain of whom to expect, Siroun hid the thing into one of her boots before sliding off the bed to answer the door. Hazel eyes peeked out to find Zikky propping an elbow against the frame. There appeared to be patches of bruising along her face, but she was in good spirits as usual.

She greeted Siroun by flicking two fingers at her in a salute. "Yo!"

"Zi-Zikky!" Both relief and disbelief washed over Siroun as she tried to find words, "I thought that crazy Hive Lord abducted you!"

"Who, Spyder?" Zikky shrugged off the concern. "She was protectin' us from our boogie man."

Raising a brow, Siroun couldn't help but say, "She considers that protection?"

Siroun had no time to reflect further on the matter as the Skivat clutched her by the wrist and tugged. "Let's go!"

"Wait!" Siroun resisted, reclaiming her wrist. "Where are we going?"

"It's a surprise," Zikky said with a wink.

In a split-second, Zikky gripped Siroun's wrist again and pulled her out of the room.

"What about my boots?" said Siroun.

"Yer not gonna need those where I'm takin' ya! C'mon, we're gonna have so much fun!"

With Siroun extracted, the door shut behind them. 'Determined' was an understatement when it came to Zikky's resolve. Without the means to resist, Siroun swept past the Visitor's Quarter and onto the next venture within The Hive. She only hoped the reliquary remained safe in her shoe while she wandered off. Not to mention she didn't want Nikostraz worrying about her when he returned.

Maybe this would be quick.

14

"**Z**IKKY!" SIROUN SHOUTED at her friend, "Please tell me where we're going?"

Siroun's legs moved as fast as they could to keep up with Zikky dragging her from behind. Her bare feet often came into contact with some sharp debris along the floor. The only thing Siroun kept hearing from Zikky's lips was, "C'mon, faster!"

As they ran through the crowds, she observed the Skivat who called The Hive their home. This underground metropolis bustled with activity. Siroun wove through the throngs of people, bouncing off others' shoulders before turning a sharp corner. They traveled through the heart of The Hive where the locals traded, conversed, and commuted from location to location. Whenever she had a moment to breathe, she marveled at the architectural wonder that was The Hive. Firelight and magical orbs illuminated the massive metropolis within the hollowed-out mountain. Levels of neighborhoods and turfs interlocked at each elevation point, with the epicenter resting at the very bottom.

"The Heart is the very soul of our city. Everythin' links to this location," Zikky turned another corner and dashed up the staircase. "This way!"

Siroun's hand hit the rails, but Zikky continued to pull her along. The fire mage radiated unbridled excitement while Siroun hadn't the faintest idea why. If she tried inquiring about where or what they were doing, she fell behind to Zikky's merciless agility. The further down the halls they went, the darker it became. Siroun ran with blind faith before coming to a halt, and collided into Zikky's backside.

Clutching at her face, Siroun grit her teeth in pain and muttered, "Zikky."

The feeling didn't last long as a loud boom of music assailed her ears, and sounds of people whooped with joy. Artificial lights illuminated the room like stars, and Siroun took in her surroundings. The place held a large rink that people floated across with special footwear. Dark tunnels surrounded the rink where people came in and dove out of the area. People raced, chatted, and wasted time before breaking away and traveling into the other tunnels.

"What is this?" said Siroun, admiring the floating footwear.

Upon further observation, the shoes looked similar to what she saw Mikky's team use during the Mak'dor race. Much of the clothing, or lack thereof, only covered the necessities. The glowing birthmark patterns that coated the Skivat acted as natural light against the dark rink. Those who lacked the luminescent birthmarks painted themselves with viscous liquids that glowed in the dark. The visual effect made the skaters look like fireflies over water as they moved around the rink. Those who hung out on the sidelines were warming up or socializing.

Zikky flashed her teeth with a large smile. "Like it?"

"I don't even know what it is," Siroun replied with curiosity.

"It's called Shot-Pipin'. One of our most popular sports in Fi'ro and exclusive to The Hive. My brother and I own this territory. We make the tubes themselves out of Di-Metal from the Fi'ro mines. They run all over The Hive allowin' for some excitin' travelin' about the place. We Tumblewheels consider it home, and yer gonna try it!"

"What?" Siroun lifted her hands and waved them about in refusal. "I'm not sure that would be such a great idea. What if I fall?"

"Everyone falls. Don't worry about it so much. Yer gonna be a natural in no time!" She turned to a group hanging out nearby and used her fingers to whistle for their attention. Smiles showed upon their faces as they turned and saw Zikky approach them.

"Hey, Zikky!" The familiar Skivat with the ombre greens in her hair waved and gave them both a sly smile, *"Come back to claim your mantle as Boss again, yes?"*

Siroun remembered that the Skivat went by the name of Veska and was a racer from the Tumblewheels teams. She tried listening in on the conversation, but the music was loud, and they were speaking in the Vat'tu language that she wanted to learn.

"Nah, my brother Mikky can wear that title until the end of time if he wants," Zikky laughed, and the other two joined in before they noticed Siroun and gave her a nod

of acknowledgment. One even waved at her, to which she responded in kind.

"*At least the turf's still ours for another year,*" said Veska.

"*Yeah, I saw that,*" replied Zikky before glancing in Siroun's direction. "*Looks like the Racerbacks are getting better.*"

"*It's nothing we can't handle. The Racerbacks keep forgetting about the shackles. Every year they implement countermeasures for techniques we used on them the year before. Don't they know we're not going to hit them with the same strategy twice? It's pathetic.*" Veska then gestured toward Siroun. "*That your girlfriend?*"

Zikky gave her a cheeky grin. "*Why, you wanna steal her from me?*"

As the exchange of conversation continued, Siroun frowned at her inability to ascertain the linguistics. Instead of waiting on the sidelines, she took a risk and stepped out on the rink to socialize. When Siroun's bare feet touched the Di-Metal floor, a thrum of energy vibrated through her entire body. An overwhelming, yet pleasant, electrical pulse tingled her nerves. Her knees shook, yet she forced herself toward the group step-by-step until she reached out to Zikky for support.

"Ah! Careful, gel-gel," said Zikky as the group caught her before Siroun's knees gave out. "I forgot to mention the Di-Metal in the Shot-Pipes are hyper-charged with Æther. I have to admit, I've seen no one's legs turn to jelly like this before."

"*Geez!*" One of the other Skivat said with a tone of concern, "*This girl's got no smarts to come waltzing out here in her bare feet. Tch!*"

The clicking of their tongue conveyed a hint of disgust,

to which Veska gave the other a soft slap on the chest with the back of her hand. Siroun's cheeks flushed. It didn't take a linguist to understand tones of disgust.

"Should I turn back?" asked Siroun.

"Ha!" Zikky guffawed before shaking her head. "Nah, I just need to get ya some proper shoes. I had 'em sent over this way. Should be here any moment."

They all looked over to see that outside of the rink there was an area set up to send and receive items. A clerk monitored the process, and giant hollow Di-Metal containers shaped like eggs surfed through the mailing tubes. When the clerk opened the most recent inbound package, Zikky smiled and recognized the contents. She spoke a few words to the other Skivat, waving them farewell before guiding Siroun off the rink. The magical energy left Siroun's body, allowing her to gather her wits while Zikky retrieved the Shot-Pipe gear.

When she found a place to sit, Zikky returned and brought an armload of equipment. The pile comprised boots, a helmet, pads, and a small cylindrical tin with foreign writing on it.

Zikky placed the tin in Siroun's hands. "Put this on yer face and arms."

Following instructions, Siroun removed the lid to find the contents glowing a brilliant purple hue. It was the same paint she saw other skaters wear who were not Skivat themselves. She dipped her fingertips into the gelatinous substance and held it up to her nose to give it a sniff. The paint smelled musty but not unappealing. She experimented with it by gliding across each of her cheeks, and noticed the paint glowing within her peripheral vision.

"Give it a couple minutes to dry," said Zikky. "Just make sure it covers ya well enough that people can see all yer limbs from any angle."

Siroun tried her hand at painting a few designs on her body. Meanwhile, Zikky took one boot along with Siroun's foot and mashed their bottoms together for measuring.

"Yep! I guessed right!" She grinned before handing it over. "Put these on."

Siroun's fingers trembled in excitement as she set aside the paint and slipped into the first shoe. At first glance, the footwear didn't look too out of the ordinary. They were ankle-high, black boots with lacing up the front and a buckling strap for further security.

As Siroun fumbled with the laces, she asked, "So when did you first learn that you could manipulate fire?"

A brow arched in response, but Zikky wasn't surprised by any of it. "Me? Not sure how much ya know about Skivat from those dusty ol' books ya read. Like Sylvani, we have a high affinity with Æther, spirit callin', and tappin' into other life forces."

"Really?"

"Mm," Zikky nodded. "Sylvani are considered the children of the Mother of the Wilds, Drya."

"Drya?" Siroun tilted her head in confusion. "Is that another one of your so-called gods?"

"She ain't my patron god," said Zikky, pressing a palm to her chest as she spoke, "but the Sylvani think highly of her. If ya ever meet one, don't go dissin' their favorite goddess. Got it?"

Siroun nodded, but couldn't help but stifle a giggle. "Sure."

"Anyway, lots of nature-based casters hail from that kingdom because of it bein' bio-diverse. That's where we get the body paint. Sylvani can connect to supernatural skills even if it's minimal. Skivat have a lower connection percentage per capita. There are still more Skivat at my skill level by comparison to the Adami or even the Dragomyr. But Adami who have the talent... well, ya saw how it works with Colin. That kid has more control than me and Lord Sparkles put together. Kinda makes me sick that he's burnin' his life away on this mission."

"Is it because of that Hemo-Hemo——."

"The Hemophæther State, yeah. The kid keeps pushin' himself beyond his limits and triggerin' it every chance he gets. If only I could do what he does with such abandon. I got things to live for, y'know?"

Despite the twinge of jealousy at the end, Zikky still smiled. Siroun enjoyed learning about the differences in talent. Though the Skivat had an advantage in producing more mages, it didn't guarantee they were better. Still, Siroun frowned at the mentioning of the dreaded Hemophæther State.

Other questions popped into her mind as the conversation continued, "What about Valter?"

Zikky chuckled. "That man's a powerful caster. It's why he takes the passive route or lets me and Colin take the lead."

"Is he that strong?"

"It's a different kinda power," said Zikky. "When he's serious, his spells level the playin' field. Problem is, lightnin' is hard to control. There's no guarantee that the spell makes its mark. Ya follow?"

Pulling up the sleeve of her guild coat, Zikky flashed her right arm to show off the scars that marked her animal-patterned skin. It didn't take a genius to understand the implication.

"Is this Valter's doing?" asked Siroun.

"Yeah, I call them my combat experiments."

Siroun's curiosity piqued. "What do you mean by that?"

Until Siroun could read about the Vanis Aer Æther Guild and the individuals it employed, conversation was the only way to expand her knowledge of them. There was only a slight problem with learning through discussion. A lesson her friend would soon learn during this little bonding experience.

Zikky finished putting on the rest of Siroun's protective gear and pulled the woman to her feet. "I'll answer that question after ya get on the rink and skate!"

The fire mage secured Siroun's boots, activating the skates as she explained, "The first rule of Shot-Pipin' is simple: Maintain balance. It's gonna be like walkin' on air. Leanin' forward cause them to speed up, and leanin' back is the brake. Side to side allows ya to hug the curves as ya turn, but be careful. If yer leanin' forward or backward it translates to movin' faster into the curve or slower. Gives yer knees and back a workout 'cause crouchin' at different levels keeps the speed in yer control. Got it so far?"

Siroun returned a blank stare back at her, and Zikky decided it was better to show than explain. With Siroun's wrist in possession, the two made their way onto the rink. The moment her skates hit the Di-Metal; it became a whole new world. Siroun sensed the Æther within the floor surge into her shoes as Zikky let her loose to test out the weight-less sensation. The Skivat wasn't kidding when she said the key was balance. Her ankles trembled at putting her body weight on air. Nothing felt firm, and the buoyancy would take time to adjust.

Meanwhile, Zikky drifted around the rink as though she had never left this arena.

"Try movin'!" she instructed as she skated another lap around the rink.

"Moving," Siroun murmured to herself. "Moving... moving... moving..."

Zikky stopped and watched in confused awe as Siroun shoved a foot forward while clutching the rails, tilting the shoe back by accident. When the heel stuck into place in mid-air, Siroun grit her teeth at the lack of cooperation in her equipment. "No, stop doing that."

"Oh boy," Zikky sighed in Vat'tu before catching up to the hapless cohort, and pulled Siroun along as she skated backwards. "We need to work on yer memorization skills, gel-gel. Okay, let's try this again. Forward is 'go'. Back is 'stop'."

Siroun held on for dear life, entrusting Zikky to keep her upright. She repeated the instructions a few times aloud while executing the actions. Once her body started aligning with the motions, her grip loosened. Learning the new activity took time to work through the balance issues, but she refused to quit. They continued practicing for the next hour. Siroun stumbled and fell multiple times, but soon got the hang of the basics to where she could turn on a dime without tripping.

In their second hour of practice Zikky replied, "I'm Fancy Pants' conduit."

"Huh?" The answer caught Siroun off-guard since the conversation they started a while ago picked up where they had left off.

"Ya wanted to know more 'bout Mister Prim-and-Proper's abilities, yeah?" said Zikky. "I got the scars bein' his conduit."

"A conduit to what?"

"The bracers on my wrists ain't for decoration, gel-gel. They're enchanted so I can empower myself with other Æther magic. Fancy Fingers harnesses lightenin', but strikin' with his full powers can cause a wide area of damage. It's more efficient for him to hit me, and I get a power-up that most opponents can't touch. We've found it reduces the collateral damage."

"Makes sense." Siroun deliberated before adding, "Still, striking you with lightning? Isn't that dangerous?"

"Only when he misses," she grinned. "The rest of the time it's called empowerin'."

"You could get killed."

"That's the job, gel-gel. Besides, what's a fight without risk?" Siroun couldn't believe Zikky was so laissez-faire over these dangerous situations. "Aren't you worried in the slightest?"

Zikky paid little concern to Siroun's alarm over the subject. Instead, she pulled the newbie by the wrists and, as they passed by a tunnel, threw her to the tubes. "Level up! Time for the next stage!"

"Whaaaaaaa! I'm gonna diiiiiiieee!" Siroun's shrieking

echoed throughout the tunnel as the whooshing of bodies flew past her, heightening her anxiety.

Wave after wave of sound and lights sped by Siroun as she flailed her arms. When a soft bump came up behind her, Siroun freaked out, but they shushed at her and said, "Gel-gel, stop it. Yer overreactin'."

"Zikky!" Siroun clung to her friend, her entire body trembling. "Get me out of here!"

"That might be awhile, but this tube ain't so hard. Look," Zikky pointed to all the strips of luminescent lights that guided directions from within. "Just follow the path and it leads ya along. Follow me!"

They transitioned to holding hands, and as the Skivat began speeding up, it forced Siroun to lean forward to match pace. The tube itself was spacious enough to host several skaters side-by-side.

"Ya can't stay in one spot once yer in the tubes," Zikky instructed before crouching down and making a soft turn which Siroun mimicked. "The rinks are a restin' point, but it's the tubes where ya find most of the thrills. There's bends, tight curves, ramps, and launch pads. This tube has a little bit of everythin'. Yer gonna love it!"

"Launch pads?" Siroun gulped. "You're putting me on launch pads?"

They rounded into another turn, and Siroun understood the amount of muscle control needed to move. It explained Zikky's athletic physique. Years of being a Hive Lord in the most aerobic sector did wonders for her body. Even Siroun was a touch jealous.

"So, you run this place?" she asked.

"More or less," replied Zikky. "My brother is the

standin' Hive Lord for the Tumblewheels while I'm out on missions. When I'm discharged, I come back to visit everyone. They keep offerin' for me to retake command, but I'm recalled too much to make it worth the hassle. Besides, Mikky has everythin' under control."

"Do you ever plan to return home permanently?"

"Prepare to jump."

Confused, Siroun crouched to mirror Zikky as the two reached an upcoming wall with an enormous bio-luminescent green square painted with odd text. The moment the two of them crossed onto the panel, a wave of energy surge into Siroun's legs turning them buoyant and springy. They both jumped and rocketed into the air.

Siroun clutched to Zikky again, squealing in both fear and exhilaration as they ascended to the upper level of the tube. The skates landed, hovering inches above the Di-Metal floor, and the mage shook the novice off of her arm.

"As much I'd love to cuddle with ya, gel-gel, the Shot-Pipes ain't the place," said Zikky.

Siroun released her friend with flushed cheeks and replied in a panic, "I'm sorry!"

There was no response from the other woman, only a giant grin plastered the Skivat's face. With another smooth turn, the anxiety of the leap had left, and Siroun felt more confident with the Shot-Pipes. Skaters flew past them while others maintained a leisurely pace, waving to Zikky as they passed. Siroun noticed that slower traffic stayed to the left side while the racing types occupied the right. Siroun wondered what happened if someone were to wipe out on such a dangerous sport.

Before long she noticed that their speed picked up, and now they began to pass others from the middle lane. The next turn was easy to recognize, and Siroun leaned into the curve with less hesitance. The music continued to echo throughout the tubes, while she bopped to the rhythm and followed the fluidity of the tunnel. Siroun was nothing but smiles from here on out.

"Jump!" said Zikky.

The familiar panel of lights appeared ahead, and Siroun tucked her legs to replicate the position from earlier. When her skates crossed the threshold, buoyant magic surged into her legs, and she jumped up as hard as she could. Instead of fear, the joy of weightlessness took hold. Her legs wobbled when she landed, but mastering the sport came with practice.

"Yer gettin' the hang of things," Zikky shouted back to her. "How is it?"

Siroun was careful not to nod with too much enthusiasm as she said, "This is fantastic!"

"See? Glad I brought ya!"

When the tunnel ended, they popped out into another rink that looked identical to the first. This one stationed itself over the Trader's Square, and the two glided toward the guard rails to see the bustling on the main floor. In the distance, a different song boomed and lights flashed.

"That's the Entertainer's Quarter," Zikky pointed to a stage far off in the distance. "I believe the turf is still in the hands of the Birds of Paradise gang. They host live music every night. I will take ya there before we go. They're not selective with whom shows up to party with them. Y'all will have a blast, I promise."

Siroun grinned. Despite the turbulent first few hours into The Hive, she enjoyed the boisterous party-going spirit of the Skivat. She turned to Zikky and said, "Is it always this lively?"

"It ain't without its issues. Not everyone is allowed in each other's turf. But we tend to live in the moment and enjoy life to the fullest. Ya won't find this kinda atmosphere in Ysile Marden. When royal butts rule the roost, it's always 'bout bowin' and scrapin' to the whims of puffed up nobles. It has its good points too. Guess ya gotta find out."

"I suppose," Siroun said with trepidation. "The more of the world I experience, the more I wish I had traveled beyond Niravad's borders sooner."

"Ha! Didn't I tell ya to treat this like an adventure?"

"Yes, I suppose you did," she smiled, then shook her head. "Am I to assume you'll never let me live this down?"

"Nope!" Zikky tilted her head. "Shall we get in a few more rounds before we head back to the room?"

It wasn't even a question that needed asking. This time Siroun took Zikky by the wrist and led her toward another tunnel. Even if their visit to Fi'ro was fleeting, she wanted to experience everything.

15

*T*ELLING TIME IN a city that operated underground felt impossible. With no indicator by the sun or moon, it was easy to get caught up in the endless thrills of the Shot Pipes. Both Zikky and Siroun were sweating from head to toe as they made their way down the hall within the Visitor's Quarter. Zikky could tell that this was the most exercise Siroun had gotten in a single excursion based on how easy it was to tire her out.

"Ya gonna be okay, gel-gel?" said Zikky. "Yer not gonna die on me, are ya?"

Siroun grinned through heavy breaths and said, "I'll try not to."

They giggled through the halls until they reached Siroun's room and noticed that Pixie-Pop and a few of her underlings were chatting with Nikostraz. Concerned looks reflected on everyone's faces. As both women approached, they all turned their heads toward her and Siroun.

"Siroun!" Nikostraz ran over and scrutinized her sweaty appearance. He snorted before saying, "Where were you?"

"I was with Zikky. She taught me how to ride the Shot Pipes. Why?" Confusion turned to realization as Siroun winced and replied, "I'm so sorry, Nik. I should have written a note before I headed out."

"Yes, you should have," he scolded. "But that's not the main problem at hand."

Zikky didn't wait for acknowledgment by the Dragomyr. He didn't trust her, so she snuck past him and greeted the other Hive Lord with a nod before looking into the room. The destruction wasn't anything she hadn't seen before, but that didn't make it any less astounding.

Nikostraz wasted no time in explaining to Siroun, "The room is demolished, and I thought Felthane attacked or kidnapped you!"

"Demolished?" said Siroun as she glanced into the room to confirm what Nikostraz was referencing.

When Siroun went to take a step forward, Zikky swung out an arm and stopped her. "I'll investigate."

She made her way inside and scanned the room, her eyes analyzing every detail inside. The room received a thrashing, but there was a purpose for its current state. She looked past the damage to read the process. Each step she took was slow and methodical. Zikky searched for any clues that identified who could have done this. Her fingers graced across a gash in the desk, noticing its size and style. The animal-like claw marks tore through the plush beds and gouged the walls. Traces of necrotic magic lingered in patches throughout the place. She conjured a detection spell that triggered parts of the room to emit small flashes of light due to the magical traces left behind. All the while she imagined the sequence in which they unleashed their rage. The damage originated from inside before the individual left in a hurry, as there was less wreckage near the entryway. Zikky felt she had enough information to name the culprit. Luckily, she faced away from the others so they couldn't see her frown.

It gave her enough time to put on a smile as she turned to the others. "Well, I think it's our usual suspect."

Zikky glanced toward the doorway and waved to Pixie-Pop to grab the other Skivat's attention. To make sure her colleagues weren't eavesdropping, she spoke to the other Hive Lord in Vat'tu and said, *"I thought you said no one visits this area without your weird jewelry? Wasn't anyone on guard?"*

Pixie-Pop blinked at the accusation. *"I post teams on every floor. Our barriers alert us to unauthorized intruders. No system's perfect, mind you. But my crew's pretty diligent over something of this magnitude. This must have been an inside connection."*

"You are the inside connection," said Zikky with emphasis.

"You know not everyone's loyalties are genuine, Zikky. Even my gang has its moles and traitors."

There was truth to those words, causing Zikky to draw additional conclusions that, for now, she would keep to herself.

She tromped over to Nikostraz with confidence in her strides. "Good thing she was with me, eh? Who knows what would have happened to our gel-gel if that beast got hold of her." She then clapped Siroun hard on the shoulder. "Yer such a pain to be a bodyguard for. Seriously, how do ya think Lord Fancy Pants is gonna feel knowin' he's gotta front the bill for this whole ordeal?"

Siroun turned red again. "Oh no, we can't have him pay for this. That wouldn't be right. Perhaps I can find another way to come up with the money."

Pixie-Pop cleared her throat and said with a grin. "You can always work fer me, Luv. I need a new handmaid."

Siroun pressed her lips to the side before turning to Zikky. "Does Lord Valter need an assistant back home where he's from?"

"Only if ya wear a uniform and call him Master," Zikky chirped back with a devious glint in her eye. Nikostraz's head swerved in the mage's direction and snorted into her hair. She waved away the blow of annoyance before turning to Pixie-Pop and switched back to Vat'tu, *"So how are we going to handle this little mishap?"*

"You call this a little mishap?" Pixie-Pop replied, *"No wonder you're always on Spyder's shit list."*

"Eh," Zikky shrugged, *"it can't be helped."*

During that time, Zikky noticed Siroun and Nikostraz step into the demolished room. She picked up a fragment of the conversation between them but had to keep her attention on the Hive Lord in front of her if they were to get some place new to stay. The pair slipped into their Drakish tongue, making it impossible for Zikky to understand them.

Turning back to Pixie-Pop, Zikky said, *"Think you can pull some strings for us? Trust me when I say this could have gone worse."*

The younger Skivat placed a finger on her chin as she thought it over. *"I don't know, Zikky. You've kinda burned through your remaining favors these days, and you haven't been around to pay any of them back. It will not be cheap repairing these damages either."*

"This wasn't our fault. It's not our job to keep tabs on security, that's what we paid you to do for us."

"True," said Pixie-Pop. *"But you knowingly endangered The Hive with whoever's following you. So you need to handle some financial accountability. You know my rules, Zikky."*

That caused Zikky to chew on the inside of her cheek. The Hive Lords operated their individual turfs with complete autonomy. If Pixie-Pop wanted to charge them for the damages, it was within her jurisdiction. Zikky had been absent far too long because of her missions with the Vanis Aer Æther Guild. Soon she would face the hard decision of either leaving the Ysile Marden and the guild to rebuild her reputation with the Hive Lords, or not return to The Hive at all.

For now, Zikky chose the path of least resistance. *"How much would this favor cost me money-wise?"*

Pixie-Pop raised a brow. *"Aren't you broke?"*

"I'm traveling with a set of deep pockets."

"Oh, that's right. The nobleman from Anastas."

Zikky leaned in and waggled her eyebrows while replying in a sing-song voice, *"And he's a friend of the King."*

The look of pleasure on Pixie-Pop's face signaled Zikky to reach out a hand toward the Hive Lord. Though there was a moment of hesitation from the other woman, she grabbed Zikky's hand and shook.

"Deal," she said.

Zikky savored the victory before making her way back to Siroun and her cantankerous companion, smiling at them brightly. "Good news everyone! We're gonna be chargin' ol' Fancy Britches' tab on this endeavor."

No sooner had she spoken those words, one of Pixie-Pop's cohorts showed up and tossed a pair of keys in Zikky's direction. With a quick catch, she nodded her thanks to the crew before jingling the pieces of metal to Siroun, "Next floor up is now yours, gel-gel. It can accommodate our whole group, assuming our frozen colleague intends to join us. Haven't seen him since I woke up from my little scuffle. Wonder if Spyder forced his hand with that proposition of hers."

Both Siroun and Nikostraz asked in tandem, "Proposition?"

A wide grin shot across her face. "I'll tell ya all about it on our way to the other room. C'mon!"

With a 'come hither' gesture of her hands, Zikky led the way to the new room, regaling them with the tale of Spyder's offer of a permanent place of sexual employment to Colin. Siroun looked worried halfway into the story, as her brows furrowed while exchanging glances with Zikky. The Skivat interjected with, "Stop that pouty face of yers, gel-gel. Ice Bucket always shows up sooner or later in his usual grumpy state. Trust me."

"I suppose," said Siroun. The uneasiness in her tone made her sound unconvinced.

16

PROTECTION IN NUMBERS was the name of the game for this area. The Midnight Quarter was part of the seedier areas of The Hive. Every corner was riddled with trash and vagabonds lurking in the darkness. People slunk about as though they had something to hide by looking over their shoulders every few seconds while interacting with others of their ilk. Unlike the central regions full of music and laughter, the Midnight Quarter was quieter with the occasional sound of a quick scuffle or scream echoing down the alleyway.

They all stood out like sore thumbs with their lighter-colored clothing. Even Siroun's earthy-toned garments seemed bright in an area that lived in the shadows. As a result, she kept to the middle of the pack, protected on all sides as Zikky took the front, Colin and Lord Valter to the sides, and Nikostraz behind them all. Insisting that he could hold his own, the Dragomyr's eyes darted at any movement and kept alert.

"Hm, which one is it again?" Zikky pondered as she analyzed several buildings while they walked.

"You can't remember?" said Colin with no surprise. "Lovely."

"Hey, it's been a while. Don't worry. I got this," Zikky said as she inspected every doorway and building. Signs weren't commonplace for this turf.

A good hour had passed before she made a final decision on which door led to Fakil's shop. The building was shabby, with its dilapidated roof, dirty windows, and faded paint. Then again, most of them looked like identical to one another to appear as unassuming as possible. The group approached, and Zikky knocked twice with the side of her fist before entering the establishment. Siroun followed behind her and leaned forward while shuffling in to take a gander at everything inside. Books, scrolls, ancient relics, and maps took up every square inch of the space, leaving almost no room for them to walk around. The shop was a treasure trove of goods to any adventurer looking for something out of the ordinary to aid them on almost any off-the-wall journey.

Once they squeezed their way through the narrow entrance, loud raspy wheezing belted out from the other side of the room. Siroun squeaked in fear as she backed up into Colin. The teen predicted her reaction and already had his palms out to halt her progress.

"Watch it," he muttered before breaking away from the group, his eyes scanning the store's merchandise.

Feeling a twinge of embarrassment, Siroun shuffled along and watched as Zikky and Lord Valter headed over to a burly old Skivat looking less than happy to see them.

His facial expression looked almost as dour as Colin's. He took a heavy drag from a long, thin pipe and remained silent as the mages approached him. His gaze fixated on their clothes before meeting them eye-to-eye. A few seconds later he glanced over to Siroun. Feelings of unease came over her, and she took a step back.

He turned to Nikostraz, ignoring the two in front of him, and said, "Hatmir wants you to return the book, reptile."

The Dragomyr raised a scaly brow. "I beg your pardon?"

"You heard me," Fakil grunted. "Your loan time is up on that book you nabbed yesterday. Best do it quickly before he sends folks to acquisition it by force."

The entire group turned to Nikostraz, and the Dragomyr sighed in frustration before giving a response, "Very well. Siroun, if I may?"

It took a moment before she realized what he was requesting.

"Oh, um… yes." Siroun opened up the satchel that hung against her hip and removed the tome from its protection to hand it over. "Here you go."

Nikostraz ignored the suspicious glares he received from the three mages, and retrieved the book from Siroun.

He switched to Drakish and said to her, *"It's nothing to concern yourself with, I assure you."*

"I understand, Nik. Do what you must. Just be careful." A smile crossed Siroun's lips to let him know that she trusted him.

Laying a claw upon her shoulder, the two gave each other a nod of reassurance before the Dragomyr made his way out of the store and shut the door behind him. Siroun noticed the scrutinizing looks of her other traveling companions. Specifically, Colin, whose eyes narrowed on her to where he was burning her skull with his gaze. She drew in a deep breath and said, "Is something wrong?"

"When did he loan you a book?" said Colin as he raised a brow.

Siroun's fingers fidgeted as she looked at Zikky and Lord Valter and realized that they, too, appeared eager to receive an answer. With a quick clearing of her throat, she replied, "Nikostraz left just before Zikky took me Shot-Piping to find me something to read."

She thought she would have to explain further, but Lord Valter appeared satisfied and waved a hand in Colin's direction. The ice mage shook his head and returned his attention to the shopkeeper, all the while crossing his arms in a huff. With that interlude out of the way, Lord Valter cleared his throat and said, "We are looking for an individual who came to your establishment to have some translation work completed."

The shopkeeper snorted in amusement while he set aside his pipe. "You don't say. What makes you think I'm the one in question? Plenty of individuals in The Hive are multi-lingual."

"Yes, but you translate the written word of gods, which makes you special."

"Lucky me," said Fakil, yet his tone spoke otherwise.

The silence that followed felt suffocating. Siroun held her breath while Lord Valter and Fakil maintained their stares, and Colin glowered from the sidelines. Zikky leaned against the high-top shop counter and admired all the old trinkets hanging on display hooks, and poked at them. The silence was a waiting game, and Siroun could see Fakil was trying to think his way through this impending altercation.

"Hmpf," the man grumbled. "Vanis Aer have no business here. If ya aren't buying anything, you need to leave."

"You realize we could lay waste to this place and disappear before anyone would notice," Colin replied as he took a step forward and the room began to drop in temperature.

A flashback came to Siroun as she remembered this exact experience before Colin saved her from the undead. Zikky wasn't kidding when she said that, out of the three of them, Colin had the most control over his powers. Siroun wrapped her arms around herself and hoped this interrogation ended soon.

Even Zikky shivered before turning to Colin and said, "Really, Frosty? Ya tryin' to freeze us too?"

The younger mage smirked. "Small sacrifices."

"Ah yes," Fakil's mustache twitched. "This is why I don't make deals with Vanis Aer mages."

Lord Valter took over the conversation again, "What resulted from the translation you performed for Felthane? I will ask this only once."

Fakil's facial muscles kept twitching as his eyes darted to each of them before lingering on Siroun again. He pulled together whatever amount of composure he could as his hands fidgeted underneath the counter and returned his attention to Lord Valter. "Felthane? Is that some kind of alias? I've translated several works for people in the past few weeks. All of them claiming they found things belonging to gods. Some were right, and others were not. If this Felthane was among them, he didn't go by that name."

"Then allow me to revive your memory. The item in

question is a map that is missing a corner," Lord Valter pulled the portion he had kept under guard and flashed it in front of the man whose mustache bristled in reaction. "This corner, to be exact."

The shopkeeper grunted in response to the interrogation, and the more they cornered him, the more Siroun watched him sweat. Lord Valter exuded an aura of calm despite the stern tone in his voice. With Colin on the right taking an aggressive stance, and Zikky standing next to Fakil looking carefree as ever, he had nowhere to run. All the while the sound of a steam clock ticked away the seconds in the distance.

They kept their eyes on the shopkeeper while they could see the wheels of thought grinding to a slow halt. Fakil's jaw tightened in frustration, and he slammed his fist on the count. "I told that man to keep his business out of my territory! Now I'm stuck with the lot of you."

"Well," Zikky mused, "that's the price ya pay for havin' bad guys for customers."

Fakil's eyes jerked in her direction. "You're no better, you Tumblewheels wretch."

"Ya want a piece of me, grandpa?" she turned and rested her chin upon her palm.

"Enough!" Lord Valter placed his hand upon the counter, and small tendrils of electricity danced across as a warning to all. Siroun looked onward with curiosity since this was the first time she saw the Lord use his Æther to threaten someone. Regardless the reason, she wanted to see how he wielded the wild lightning magic. Lord Valter tucked the map piece back into his jacket, and said with a little less patience, "Where is the map?"

"I don't have it anymore," Fakil replied with a higher pitch in his voice. "I-I couldn't translate it, so he took it back."

Colin closed in and slammed a fist on the counter. "What do you mean you couldn't translate it? That's what you do!"

Fakil leaned back and grimaced. "Yes, w-well... I can translate several of the gods' languages. Out of all of them, Arcandus is the most common. The man who asked me to translate the map told me it was likely Arcandus' work. After I inspected it, however, I found the writing didn't match that damn deity."

"Whose is it then?" Zikky asked out of genuine curiosity.

To this question, Fakil shrugged. "Don't know. Never seen the writing before in my li—!"

Colin reached over and grabbed him by the collar, shaking the shopkeeper and yelling, "You're lying!"

"I am not. Now, get off me!" Fakil tried shoving Colin away, but the mage's grip was like a vice.

"Why should I believe someone like you, huh? Someone who lives and breathes in the lowest of places. Now tell me where he is!"

The room plummeted in temperature and frost etched around the edges of the windows in seconds. Siroun looked at her fingertips to find they were already hurting from the cold. Her brows wrinkled in Colin's direction as she worried they would all become a casualty of his rage.

"Colin," Lord Valter's voice was calm but deadly. The glare he shot the younger mage spoke volumes, and Colin sneered back at the higher-ranking guild member before releasing the shopkeeper in an abrupt thrust and walking away. Colin wasn't just retreating from the counter, he was walking out of the establishment. Felthane's actions flared up an unspeakable hatred within the teenager that made her wonder the cause. Though she wanted to listen in on the conversation between Lord Valter, Zikky, and Fakil, she felt something tug at her chest. Colin's state of mind was important too.

As the door slammed shut, she looked back at the other two mages. "I'll go check on him."

"Stay close," said Lord Valter.

"Wait!" Fakil's tone laced with urgency, but he quickly composed himself when Zikky and Lord Valter moved in to block him.

As Zikky kept a watchful eye on their target, Lord Valter gave Siroun a reassuring nod. "Go ahead, My Lady. We will handle things here."

Siroun didn't want to guess what those ominous words meant. She concluded it was best not to witness the scene play to fruition. Escorting herself out, she didn't have to venture far to find Colin standing only a few paces away. He stared out into the street, watching people slink into the shadows the moment they laid eyes on him. She watched him wipe his nose once or twice with a kerchief before pocketing it discreetly.

"Are you okay?" she tried to get a read on him, and glanced in his direction only to find his expression still incensed from what transpired inside the Hooker's Eye.

"I don't need your sympathy," he hissed.

Her mouth twisted to the side before she responded with equal sharpness, "It's called concern. Also, what's with the constant attitude toward me? Am I beneath you or something?"

Colin stayed silent, so she glared at him. A few seconds later when he realized she was still staring, he sighed, "You look creepy right now."

"At least it's temporary. You have this look all of the time. There's still hope for me."

That little jab elicited a look of surprise from him. Instead of a dour response, he quirked his brow. Both of them paused when they heard a crash inside the shop and a faint cry for mercy from Fakil. For a while the two of them listened to the mayhem going on inside before Colin shook his head and continued the conversation, "You've been hanging out with Zikky way too much."

"I hate to break it to you, but we all have." Siroun took a moment to smile. "That's part of her charm."

"She's never thrown up on you," Colin grumbled.

"No, she — wait, what?" Siroun blinked a few times, and her jaw dropped in disgust. That was enough to put Colin in a better mood.

"So is your guardian always this secretive?" he asked, changing the subject.

It took her a second to figure out whom he was talking about, then replied, "Who, Nik?"

When Colin nodded, the muscles tightened in Siroun's jaw. "I know you're all suspicious of him, but he's been the one person who's never judged me back home. The elders thought I was a cursed child. Most don't think I'm worth treating with any modicum of dignity. However, Nikostraz, my father, and brother have always stood up for me."

Colin smirked. "That explains why you're so meek."

"H-hey! Where do you get off saying those kinds of things?" she said.

"It's true. You put up with a lot of crap, especially from that village."

"Thank you for that riveting observation," she gave him a light smack on the arm before the two of them stared back out into the streets. All went quiet inside the Hooker's Eye, and they both glanced back at the shop wondering if Fakil decided to cooperate.

Colin distracted her by asking, "What do you plan to do after this is all over?"

"That's a good question," her finger reached up and twirled a lock of hair while thinking about what kind of answer to provide. The Hive seemed to be a viable location, but so far it was the only one she had seen since leaving Niravad. As much as she wanted to return to her home country and try a new life in a different region, it wasn't possible. At least not right now. The Dragomyr were adamant about keeping the continent free of outsiders. That made her think about her father and brother, and whether she would ever see them again. Given her father's age and overall health, it wasn't likely that he could travel outside of the continent and brave the violent seas to pay a visit to wherever she stayed. It also reminded her she needed to write a letter letting him know that she was well.

"I asked you a question," said Colin as he tapped his fingers upon his folded arms.

She shook her head to snap out of her thoughts. "Hmm? I'm sorry. I don't know. I've never been outside of my village. I am still trying to absorb all of…this."

Gesturing the whole of The Hive with her arms, she looked to Colin and asked, "Do you have any ideas of where I might fit in?"

"You? Fit in?" He scoffed, leaving pause for Siroun to regret ever asking. To that, he waved his hand to signal that he was joking. "You might find work in Anastas, not sure what type. Just keep your eyes open. I'm sure there's something they'll find useful about you."

"Oh," she nodded, but in sooth, she didn't find his advice helpful in the slightest. She had no idea how she was to make a life-changing decision of this nature with so little knowledge of the world.

"Listen," he said, "we won't just dump you on the street after this whole thing is over. I'm sure Lord Valter has some connections in mind. Plus, Zikky's too attached to you to leave you in the lurch. You'll be fine."

That sentiment brought a little comfort to her, and she smiled at Colin knowing that he was saying that to act nice. "What about you?"

"I don't consider you a friend. I barely know you," he didn't have to glance at Siroun to feel she was radiating a level of sadness at hearing those words. He added, "But I don't consider anyone a friend, so don't take it personally."

"May I ask why?" Not expecting to receive an answer. Perhaps a snarky remark, and a subsequent dig at her lack of intelligence. Instead, she received an alarming surprise.

"That's simple," Colin replied. "I don't plan to live through this mission."

A lump formed in Siroun's throat as she chuckled to his candid response. When her awkward reaction subsided, she said, "You were joking, right?"

"Hardly," his face resolute, not reacting to the uncomfortable laughter. "My colleagues believe I'm impetuous, but I intend to kill Felthane. That's the only reason I'm here. Lord Valter has orders from the guild to capture him alive if possible, but that necromancer shall never have the luxury of mercy by me."

Now Siroun realized why Colin had aged so much faster than the other two. He sacrificed his youth for the chance to go after Felthane. The reason why remained unanswered. Something terrible must have elicited these kinds of feelings from him.

"What about your parents?" she asked. "Won't they be angry if you died and could never see you again?"

Those questions caused the aged teenager to grit his teeth and shout back at her, "Don't you ever stop?"

He stormed off, forcing Siroun to wonder what just happened, and debate whether she should go after him. Given that she knew nothing about navigating The Hive, she stayed put while Colin disappeared from sight. Tears pooled around her eyes and she wiped at them with the back of her hand. All she wanted to do was befriend him, but everything she tried always seemed to be the wrong approach. She couldn't imagine that Felthane's downfall was the only thing that motivated him. But here she was, standing alone on a corner with Colin long gone. Not a second later the sound of a door opened behind her, and she turned to see Zikky bouncing out with Lord Valter two steps behind her. With their business concluded, Siroun patted at her face to hide her tears.

Zikky noticed Colin's disappearance first and said, "Where'd Ice Fingers go?"

Siroun hung her head in shame while pointing toward the street. "I made him angry, and he walked off in that direction."

A hand touched her on the shoulder, and she looked up to find Lord Valter nodding at her reassuringly. "Do not dwell on it too much, Lady Siroun. Our colleague is not himself when unpleasant topics are broached. Give him a chance to collect himself. I am certain he will return."

No words of solace lifted her feelings of guilt, so she deviated to another topic. "Did you find out anything more about the map?"

"Eh, Fakil is a pain in the ass as always," Zikky mused. "It was nice gettin' to rough him up a tad, though."

Siroun should have known that Fakil's muffled screams were Zikky's doing. Shaking her head, she said, "Ah, there's the reason you look so pleased. Don't let Colin overhear you say that."

"I only pinned him down and kissed his face with my fist once or twice," she cracked her knuckles with pride. "Colin would kill him; that's the difference."

There were no words for that response, and Siroun turned her attention to Lord Valter as they started walking back to the Visitor's Quarter. "Did you find out anything more after we left?"

"Very little, My Lady," Lord Valter stifled a sigh, but everyone saw the look of disappointment on his face.

"What about when he tried to stop me from leaving the shop? That seemed strange. Don't you think?"

"It is best we converse on the matter elsewhere," the expression on Lord Valter's face looked grim as he scrutinized the ally dwellers that were now showing up from the shadows with eyes transfixed on the group. "We may have drawn some negative attention."

"I gotcha covered, Sparkle Buns. Watch me work my magic," said Zikky as she cracked her knuckles then wiggled her fingers in mid-air. Within seconds, she reached over and tickled Siroun along the ribcage. "Raaaawr!"

The surprise ambush made Siroun shriek as the feathery touch caused her to leap forward. "Ahh! Zikky!"

"I'm the great tickle beast!" the Skivat bellowed before diving in again to deliver another round of tickles. "I feast on the laughter of others!"

"Gah!" Siroun giggled through Zikky's onslaught before breaking free and retaliating in kind. "Take that!"

Zikky's laughter echoed through the streets as she hopped back a few times. "No, I am weak against my own punishments! What a sad turn of events."

The two ran around Lord Valter like children while they used him as a barrier to sneak in tickle attacks. Lord Valter pinched the bridge of his nose with his fingers and sighed. Their boisterous antics started driving off the street folk within the Midnight Quarter, and it wasn't long until a familiar face showed up to find them. Siroun practically jumped out of her skin when Tigernach appeared from nowhere, and even Zikky halted their game once the other woman arrived. The Sylvani approached the group but kept her focus on Lord Valter.

"My Lord," Tigernach greeted the nobleman with her deep, velvety voice, "have you concluded your business here?"

With reluctance he replied, "Yes, I believe we have garnered as much we could."

Tigernach took a moment to count the group before adding, "You are missing two."

"The Dragomyr went to return a book, and my other colleague headed back early." When Lord Valter saw her eying him, he said, "I assure you they will not cause trouble."

A nod came from the Hive Lord before she turned her gaze to Zikky and acknowledged the Tumblewheels's former master. Zikky gave her a two-fingered salute before the three of them followed the Sylvani's lead back to the Highrise and Visitor's Quarter.

17

THE ENTERTAINER'S QUARTER surged with activity by the time Zikky and crew strolled onto the scene. With Siroun in hand, the two women navigated their way to the designated bar and claimed several seats as the earlier patrons left.

Zikky planted her butt on a chair and raised her hands into the air. "I win!"

The others took their time arriving. Nikostraz, found it harder to maneuver since his body was so long. His tail made it challenging when he tried fitting into the small seats. He endured the discomfort for Siroun's sake, who was watching the pop idol on stage with wide eyes and a smile to match.

"That's Sonestrelle," Zikky shouted loud enough for Siroun to hear her over the music. "She's a very famous singer out here in The Hive!"

Siroun tilted her head and blinked. "Sonestrelle?"

"It's a stage name. No one knows her real identity, though."

While Siroun nodded in acknowledgment, Lord Valter leaned in so he didn't have to scream in her ear. "People speculate she is of the Foxsong royal family in Seda. If she is, she keeps her identity well disguised."

Even though the proximity was out of respect for Siroun's poor ears, her cheeks flushed and turned red. Nikostraz picked up on the intimate interaction and sneered at the nobleman, a hiss escaping his lips. Siroun might have been oblivious to the Dragomyr's response, but Lord Valter noticed the reaction and pulled away.

"My apologies," he said, but Nikostraz snorted and looked elsewhere.

Already the noise was getting to Colin. "I'm going to investigate. Find out if anyone has encountered our target."

"Don't scare 'em off, Ice Brains," Zikky shouted back as he departed the group. Even with Colin's retreat, that didn't stop the fire mage from turning to the bartender and making a circular gesture. "One for all my friends here."

Nikostraz could only grunt. "We are friends now?"

"Hush!" The fire mage scolded him playfully. "We drink, then we bond more! Time to crack that dour look on yer face."

"Because it worked so well on Colin?"

Zikky's intentions were genuine, but Nikostraz didn't appear convinced. It took Siroun's pleading expression to get him to relent while the bartender served them. Once everyone had a drink in hand, they clinked their glasses in a wordless toast. The liquor combination looked exciting to Siroun as she examined the drink. Swirls of purple, pink and gold enchanted her. While Zikky downed hers, Siroun took the cautious approach and dipped her finger into the concoction before dabbing it on her tongue. The medley of flavors was indescribable. There was a sharp sting on her palate from the alcohol, but the sweetness subdued it. The flavors swirled upon her tongue layer-by-layer like a trip through a garden. Notes of elderflower and cherries dazzled her tongue while the honey harmonized them together. A hint of nectarine concluded the journey, and Siroun was in heaven.

"What is this stuff?" she asked, this time Siroun took a sip. The taste continued mixing on her tongue, adding a greater punch of flavor than before. Her reservations of the drink falling to the wayside the more she consumed.

"It's called a Seda Sonata," Zikky answered. "Always the house specialty whenever Sonestrelle performs."

"It's lovely!"

"It is deceiving with its potency, Lady Siroun." Lord Valter added in as he sipped at his drink. "I recommend taking your time."

Siroun tried emulating the nobleman's approach while noticing that Nikostraz had only taken a small sip before setting the drink aside. Curious, she scooted beside him and tilted her head. "You don't like it?"

The Dragomyr glanced and saw that, despite trying to be dainty, Siroun was on the last few drops of her drink. Nikostraz shook his head and slid the drink toward her. "I'm not into things like this. Here, have mine since you've reached the bottom on yours."

Siroun's eyes widened as she looked down to find nothing left in her glass. With a sheepish grin, she set it aside and took the one he offered.

Nikostraz chuckled and said, "Careful. As much as I

hate to admit it, the Lord is right. You've not consumed alcohol before. It muddles the senses if you're not paying attention. I would prefer not to be picking you up off the floor before the night is over."

Siroun nodded as a soft hiccup escaped her lips, "I understand."

She didn't live under a rock. Back home, the locals visited taverns every night. Dragomyr often flopped around the village afterward with slurred speech and silly grins on their faces. Once or twice she tried the local brews, but they had a vile taste that made Siroun lack the desire to try anything alcoholic again until now.

When she finished the second drink, the music switched tempos, and new dancers came on stage. In a manner of seconds, the room transitioned from wild cheering to quiet awe as the next song began. Siroun wondered what the fervor was all about and got up on the seat to look over the crowd. Sonestrelle's outfit started transforming in front of their eyes. Golden plates darted off in all directions as a mist swarmed her body to form a new change of clothing. The audience cooed at the magical transition. The gold dress morphed into an uneven skirt and a coat made of pastel suedes with semi-puffed shoulders and long sleeves. Her hair changed color into a dusty silver with an array of desaturated blue-green tones. Each motion within the transformation paired with the beats of the song. After transformation finished, Sonestrelle started singing the next song. Music washed over the audience, hypnotizing them with her alluring notes. Siroun watched with admiration and imagined being up on that stage with Sonestrelle.

Zikky locked arms with Siroun's and tugged her toward the dance floor. "Let's get this party started, shall we?"

Siroun hastened to set the emptied glass aside before relinquishing all control of her location to the will of her friend. Already the liquor made her feel light as a feather as they navigated through the throngs of people. The music started into a slow crescendo before Sonestrelle began her lyrics, and the dancers burst into movement. People made their way onto the floor and lined themselves out in a checkerboard pattern. Their moves all synchronized as they swung their right arms side-to-side and clapped their hands before transitioning into a half turn. The next set of moves involved another series of claps before shimmying into a turn and starting the first half of the sequence over again. Their feet skipped to the beats, and more joined in on the dance once they understood the sequence. Lights powered by more glowing orbs flickered and strobed all over the room, giving it a wild and colorful effect. Upon further observation, Siroun realized that the Skivat dancers summoned the elements of fire and water to bring forth a dazzling visual spectacle.

The two women found a spot on the dance floor and Zikky melded into the dance sequence mid-step. Looking around, Siroun noticed the ubiquitous motions within the crowd, and attempted to copy the moves.

Zikky blew a raspberry at her, "No, no, no gel-gel! Ya gotta give it yer all!"

She closed the gap between them and took Siroun's hips to guide her into the twists before performing the claps that marked the end of the segment. With Zikky as her guide, Siroun relaxed and surrendered herself to the music, both adding their own styles to the sequence. Zikky performed more shuffling into her footwork and Siroun undulated her shoulders with the turns. Whenever Sonestrelle went into the chorus, lights flashed and changed direction while the dancers moved to their choreographed numbers.

Siroun noticed several stage performers slowed their dancing just as she was getting into the groove. A glowing, aquatic bubble pulsing with Æther floated in their hands. They pulled back their arm and pitched the bubbles high into the air. At the pinnacle of their ascent, the magic-laden spheres exploded in a torrent of icy foam that sparkled and cooled the entire room. The audience cheered, and Siroun found herself bathed in refreshing bubbles that fluttered everywhere. Applause deafened the room as the performer ended her song and bowed.

"I love you all, good night!" Sonestrelle's joyful voice said in her Sylvan language before she departed the stage with the rest of the band.

The guitarist took their pick and looked Siroun square in the eyes before flicking it into the air. The small item glinted as it sailed right into her hands. Nearby on-lookers gave her the side-eye but kept their tongues in check while waiting for the next performer to arrive on stage.

Zikky elbowed Siroun in the arm and waggled her eyebrows. "Yer popular with the women, I see."

A wave of heat washed over Siroun as she elicited an awkward chuckle. If it weren't for her friend pointing out the guitarist was a woman, Siroun wouldn't have realized it. Skivat physiques were androgynous. Then again, Dragomyr anatomy was nowhere near the same to the rest of the kingdoms. Being popular with other women never crossed Siroun's mind until now.

Next, local Skivat performers took the stage, and several regions of the room cheered as the three situated themselves with their instruments. The lead singer remained hands free while the other two donned a guitar and a portable-sized instrument that appeared to be a piano.

"*Allo!*" he greeted the audience in Vat'tu in his tenor voice. Fans screamed throughout the entire Entertainer's Quarter in response.

Siroun understood why so many reacted to him the way they did. His features were slim with a boyish charm to his face. Heart-shaped cat marks traipsed down his collarbone over the darker skin compared to the rest of his band-mates. Even the way he carried himself spoke volumes toward charisma, and the drawl in his dialect had everyone swooning.

"*We've got a new little number for ya, Luvs. Find yourself someone special and take them out for a slow hop or two, eh?*"

Siroun caught herself sighing while her gaze drifted toward Lord Valter chatting up a local diplomat. It surprised her to see a Skivat dressed in formal attire.

As usual, Zikky pressed her palm against the small of Siroun's back. "Why not get ol' Fancy Britches to dance with ya. It'll be the only chance ya get."

The suggestion made Siroun blink and look back to her friend. "Who me? I couldn't ask him. No—. Wait, what do you mean it'll be the only chance?"

"Well," Zikky hesitated as she dragged her voice, searching for the best response. "Given that he's an aristocrat and everythin', this might be the only opportunity ya have at enjoyin' some private time with him and all. Y'know them fancy folk and their marital obligations an everythin'."

Before Siroun absorbed that last comment, Zikky gave her a playful smack on the rear, causing her to squeak in surprise and leap forward. She stared at him, with her eyes wider than usual, and every inch of her body trembled with fear. Thoughts of running away whizzed through her mind, but Zikky's bizarre words of encouragement echoed behind her, "If ya don't ask him, I will do it for ya. I'll make sure it'll be way more embarassin'!"

Siroun blushed for the umpteenth time tonight, and the thought of dancing with Lord Valter made her nauseous from the butterflies flapping in her stomach. Despite all of this, she braved approaching him and his diplomatic acquaintance.

To her chagrin, Lord Valter noticed her arrival, and halted his conversation to shift his attention toward her. "Yes, Lady Siroun? Do you require something of me?"

The other individual now stared at her, and Siroun's heartbeat pounded so hard she felt she would vomit and faint at the same time. Her lips parted as if to say something, but no words came. Siroun closed her eyes and took a deep breath to calm her nerves.

"Are you ill?" the Skivat diplomat asked in their feminine voice.

Siroun snapped her eyes open and looked shocked to see that the decorated Skivat sounded female. The height and build deceived her, yet again, but Siroun admired the Skivat's attractive features. Had she not harbored such a crush on Lord Valter, perhaps there would have been room in her heart for this lovely stranger. Even now, she found her thoughts wandering to devious places before she had to snap herself back to reality and address the question before too much time had passed.

"Uh—no, I am well. T-thank you!" she said, all the while wanting to crawl under a table and die of shame.

Lord Valter raised his brow at the odd behavior. "Is this something of grave concern, My Lady?"

As questions kept funneling in from both people, Siroun inched backward while saying, "N-no, it was n-nothing. I'm sorry. P-please continue!"

She almost retreated, even turned away, when she paused and acknowledged her cowardice. Perhaps it was the booze with Zikky's idle threat only moments ago, but she turned to face Lord Valter and held her chin up. "No. No, that's not what I meant. Lord Valter, I'd like to dance with you."

After the words slipped off her tongue, she wanted to vomit right there in front of him. Every muscle in Siroun's body trembled while the thoughts in her head turned to panic. All she could think was that she had gone mad. Alcohol was the nectar of shame. However, she stood her ground despite the fear and nausea, waiting for him to respond. She hoped for the best while expecting the worst.

Seconds passed before he understood the situation and excused himself from his guest. The diplomat obliged, allowing Lord Valter to break away from the conversation and approach Siroun. "I must admit, it has been a while since I was asked to dance."

Her heart leaped into her throat, and Siroun cleared it

several times before she looked him in the eyes and faced her fears.

He listened to the tune, and counted the beats before asking, "Have you ever danced a Pavana before?"

Her brows furrowed as though he had spoken a foreign language. "A Par-what?"

"My apologies, I meant to say a Shyvtan," Lord Valter frowned. "I keep mixing up my regions for certain dances."

"Too many to remember?"

"Quite," he chuckled.

"To answer your question, yes," said Siroun. "I am familiar with the Shyvtan. It's a popular dance for Dragomyr during the summer, though I'm not sure if it goes very well with this song. The dance is quick in its steps by comparison."

"Shall we improvise?"

Siroun felt herself beaming as she opted to nod in affirmation rather than trip over her words. From here Lord Valter offered his hand and took the lead. Instead of hopping into the first few steps, they both took long strides to slow the tempo and match the music. Siroun's head felt fuzzy from the alcohol she consumed earlier and found a rhythm that they were both able to follow.

"I'm curious, Lord Valter," she began, "what region in Anastas are you from again?"

The question caused him to raise a brow. "I was born and raised in Firenz, located southwest of Ysile Marden."

"That's nice," Siroun smiled. "Do you have a family?"

He hesitated before responding, "I have family in Firenz, but I prefer to keep those details private while in foreign territory, My Lady."

"So, you are married?" she emphasized to extract a direct answer from him this time, and Lord Valter nodded his head. Though Siroun had her suspicions confirmed, the knowledge didn't hurt any less. A lump formed in her throat she forced herself to swallow. She endured disappointment many times in the past, and she would do it again. "Why aren't you wearing your wedding band if that's the case?"

"It is not typical for someone like myself to be traveling beyond the shores of Anastas without more assistance than that with which I came. It is a matter of personal security that I keep certain information private. I hope you can understand."

She didn't understand the logic behind the reason, but she kept the veneer of nonchalance plastered upon her face while they continued the dance.

"Have you written to your father yet?" Lord Valter inquired as they moved together.

Shame reflected in her eyes as she shook her head. "It's been difficult. We move around so much. Not to mention, I've lacked access to supplies."

He looked concerned by that answer. "Strange. I thought I had requested a stationary set brought to your room."

"I think it got destroyed if you had it delivered to the first room."

"Oh yes, you are correct." A sigh of disappointment escaped his lips, and he continued through the steps. "Our business here will conclude soon, and we shall sail to Ysile Marden. Perhaps during the boat ride you can draft a letter for your family and have it sent out once we make port.

I imagine both your father and brother want to know if you made it out safely. I apologize for not providing the opportunity to write sooner."

"It's all right," she said, hearing Colin's words in the back of her head again declaring her a pushover.

Despite having an unending love for words, she lacked the ability to conjure them in Lord Valter's presence. Small talk wasn't a quality she possessed. Seconds later, Lord Valter changed up the steps and twirled her to break up the flow of the dance. Siroun stumbled through the movements, only to trip on her own feet and bump into him. The fumble took him by surprise as he grunted from the collision.

He caught her with his hands and smiled with amusement. "My apologies, My Lady. I figured I would change things up."

"T-that's fine," she stammered. "I haven't danced like this before. The village barred me from joining social events. The only reason why I know how to do a Shyvtan is because I watched others."

There was a hint of concern in the Lord's tone of voice, "I must say, my limited observation determined that the villagers treat you like a lesser individual despite being of similar status among your people. Is your physique that abrasive to them?"

"It's—," she shook her head. "It's complicated. I wish it weren't, believe me. It's unfortunate that they can't see me as a helpful member of society, but what can I do? I've read the history books. Their treatment of me stems from wars and political upheavals way before my time. Is it right? Of course not. But I can't just erase decades of fear and mistrust."

"I see your point."

"Every day of my life I've regretted who I am and how I look. I thought, maybe if I tried hard to exemplify a model citizen they would accept me for who I was. It has the opposite effect. They always think I have an ulterior motive. I soon came to terms with the fact that I have to accept them for who they are and learn to live by myself, for myself. Don't cause trouble. Don't stand out or give them a reason to hate me more than they already do. Do I like it? No. Do I have a choice? No."

Lord Valter stopped the dance and reached out to Siroun. His fingers touched the bottom of her chin to tilt it up and meet her gaze. "You have a choice now."

Siroun felt comfort in that statement. Talking about home made her feel like she had returned there. However, Lord Valter's words brought her back to The Hive where she could break free of the shackles of mistrust of those surrounding her.

He changed the subject by taking Siroun's hand again and continuing their dance. "Perhaps I could interest you in a few dancing lessons when we arrive in Anastas? Many of the royal courts enjoy such activities and might ask you to join them."

Siroun laughed before giving it consideration and replied, "I appreciate your offer, My Lord."

In the back of her mind, the dance lessons allowed her to look less foolish. Then she realized Lord Valter mentioned other people would ask her to dance, and the excitement transitioned to anxiety. She chewed at the bottom of her lip while ruminating on how best to learn the techniques in a short time span.

When the song ended, Siroun gasped, "I just realized that I interrupted something important between you and that other person."

Lord Valter reassured her with his smile. "That is all right. The conversation was a light exchange of information."

"Oh," she blinked, "on what?"

"Felthane, and whether The Hive has anyone else besides Fakil who is a master at reading divine languages."

Siroun recalled the shopkeeper's unnerving stare. "Were you able to find out anything? You know, before I rudely interrupted you."

The applause in the room increased, forcing Lord Valter to raise the volume of his voice as he leaned in to further explain, "Unfortunately, no. Translators of divine languages are becoming rarer as the years pass. Too many centuries of chasing ghosts with nothing to show for it reduces faith… and funding."

Siroun adjusted her volume to match his. "There are too many other things to support that take financial priority?"

"Exactly."

As the next song continued, Lord Valter placed his palm upon the small of her back and led her to the bar as they continued their conversation.

"If I may ask," said Siroun, "who thought this artifact belonged to Arcandus in the first place?"

"Alas, I may not disclose that information. Even if

I could, His Majesty did not provide us the clearest of details. It only leads to further questions."

"Questions that you didn't ask before accepting this mission?"

"Questions I may not ask when assigned to me. Propriety is a tricky beast sometimes."

She took a few seconds to mull over that response. Despite her personal beliefs on which gods were real, she acknowledged there were things beyond her understanding. For now, she humored the fact that Arcandus was a powerful deity and that there might be others just like him creating powerful artifacts, like the Sinefine Bible.

"Based on what you know, is there anyone else you think might have created this dangerous artifact we're chasing?" said Siroun.

"That is the troubling part. Our understanding of the gods that influence Clayne is incomplete. No one knows how many deities are out there. We discover them by accident when we stumble upon things kept secret to us, or when other gods leave behind clues to the past in their texts, temples and relics. We pay the price for playing with things we do not comprehend."

"You're saying this artifact might be more dangerous than surmised?"

Lord Valter went to speak when a loud boom resounded through the room. The thundering noise forced the musicians to stop their performance. The ground only shook once, like the snapping of a towel when trying to shake off the debris into the open air. It was enough to topple people, including Siroun, to the floor. Panic ensued from the audience, sending them fleeing in waves of screams.

Lord Valter pulled Siroun to her feet. "Are you all right?"

Though her legs trembled, Siroun nodded in response.

"Stay here, I need to find the others," said Lord Valter before disappearing into the crowd.

She wanted to go with him, but with everyone fleeing and screaming past her, it was better that she stayed in one spot so the others could congregate. Through the cacophony of noise, something else swooped into the Entertainer's Quarter. A warbling shrill echoed, followed by a large bird gliding onto the main floor. A waterfall of miasma poured from the balcony above, and tendrils of the energy darted out to grab people. They wove around furniture and snaked up peoples' legs as they ran, causing them to trip and fall. Bystanders scattered everywhere, trying to avoid contact with the ominous energy.

Siroun's thoughts wandered to Nikostraz as she searched through the chaos to see if she could spot him. During the insanity, a fleeing patron tripped and hit the ground next to her as a tendril loomed in to capture them. Instinctively, Siroun reached over and helped the young Skivat to their feet.

"Run!" Siroun commanded in Vat'tu.

They didn't hesitate and continued fleeing. Meanwhile, the wandering tendril jumped out and latched around Siroun's wrist. She tried yanking herself free, but it only tightened its grasp. The bird that had made its landing moments ago closed in, soaking part of the tendril-shaped energy into its body and transitioning to the familiar form Siroun saw in the library that fateful night. Eyes widening, she halted her struggle as he stepped ever closer.

"Ah, there's my lovely little survivor," the voice as smooth as she remembered it, and the layers of robes and dark garments continued to hide his face. After spending all of this time chasing threats and shadows, Felthane showed himself. "Come, we have a date with destiny."

Siroun couldn't believe how fast the warlock appeared and tipped things in his favor. When he closed in, she tried again to wrench herself free from the mysterious power to no avail. He stretched out his hand, and Siroun pulled back her fist, preparing to fight him. A wall of ice shot up between them and locked Felthane's hand in place, severing the tendril's grasp on her. Before the warlock turned to see who cast the spell, a bolt of ice whizzed past his face and clipped the tip of his nose. Now he knew the trajectory of the spell and turned to his left to see Colin running toward them with a handful of icy Æther at the ready.

Felthane growled, and his right hand transformed into a demonic claw that shattered the glacial blockade. He met the ice mage face-to-face with a wide swipe, forcing Colin to summon another ice barrier that covered the palm of his hands, but it fell apart upon impact. As Felthane struck again, Colin took both hands and made quick twisting gestures that coated the ground below them in a sheet of ice. The momentum of the warlock's attack slid him off balance. While Felthane strove to regain his footing, Colin went over to Siroun.

"Thank The Great Three, you're safe," she said.

Colin ignored her, grabbed her hand, and guided her over to the bar. "Off the floor, off the floor!"

Frightened, Siroun did as he commanded. Once both of them finished climbing atop the bar table, a wave of electricity shot across the floor, enveloping Felthane. The warlock's cries echoed throughout The Hive. When the spell subsided, Felthane couldn't help but chuckle as he turned to find Lord Valter's hand pulling away from the ground.

"Ah, the Duke of Firenz graces me with his presence." A cough escaped Felthane's lips. "That took me by surprise. But it lacks punch, don't you think?"

The title didn't go unnoticed by Siroun, "Duke?"

This reaction brought a curl at the corner of the warlock's mouth. "I find it rather amusing that he hasn't required you to address him as Your Grace yet, given the fact that he's such a stickler for titles."

Colin jumped off of the bar and slammed his heel into the ground, shattering the ice spell, "Shut up, prick."

When he began muttering another spell, Siroun grabbed him by the jacket and pulled him back "No, don't!"

A look of pure contempt reflected in Colin's eyes as he shouted, "Let me go!"

"He's too strong for you," Siroun protested. "You'll get hurt!"

"That's my business," he ripped his arm from her grasp and shoved her away, causing her to tumble behind the bar table.

"Lady Siroun!" Lord Valter tried to step in her direction, but Felthane closed in and backhanded the man.

The force behind the strike knocked the nobleman to the ground as the warlock raised his palm and part of the miasma-like shadows that still floated around the room took the shape of a small demonic creature on four legs with multiple rows of teeth in its maw. It looked like a charred canine, but lacked eyes and used its sense of smell to find Lord Valter. When the demon found its target, the creature lunged on top of the nobleman, pinning him to the ground with its taloned paws.

With Lord Valter preoccupied, Felthane prepared to execute a killing blow when Colin closed in from behind. The warlock reacted by grabbing Colin's casting hand and turning it back on the mage. When the ice spell released, Colin found himself paralyzed by his own doing. Felthane used this opportunity with his claw to swipe a mighty gash across Colin's back, eliciting a cry of pain, and then shoved the younger mage face-first into the floor. Frigid and injured, Colin stirred once then passed out.

"I grow tired of this," Felthane grumbled, turning his attention to the nobleman.

Lord Valter fended off the bloodthirsty demon by pulling a dagger from his boot and lancing it through the throat. It made a high-pitched shriek as its life force bled away before going limp on the floor. Black blood oozed from the wound before its physical form turned to ash. Wiping the demonic remnants from his cheek, Lord Valter stood with a lightning spell at the ready only to find Felthane stealing his sword from his hip. The warlock lunged forward, and Lord Valter blocked it with his casting hand, releasing the electrical spell. For several seconds the voltage coursed through the weapon, while the edge of the blade sliced into Lord Valter's hand. It wasn't until the flash of a kunai zipped across Felthane's left cheek and struck the ground that the two men broke away, and the sword clattered to the floor.

Blood trickled in tiny beads down Felthane's face as he dabbed at the injury and looked above to find a series of Skivat dressed in skin-tight leather jump in and surround both he and Lord Valter. The arriving Blood Oath Butterflies acted as a distraction, allowing Siroun to sneak past the bar, wrap an arm around Colin, and pull him to safety. Meanwhile, Tigernach jumped into the center of the dispute with Zikky trailing right behind her.

"Outsider," Tigernach said with no emotion behind her tone. "You have broken the rules of conduct within The Hive and are subject to the laws admin—."

Siroun watched as miasma flooded the room, clouding everyone's vision. She felt her lungs constricting against the noxious energy that sought to suffocate them all. She heard scuffling and wondered if the Blood Oath Butterflies got him. When the smoke cleared, Felthane vanished. Tigernach scrutinized the disappearing act, then noticed a bird's wings flapping above them.

Her eyes honed in on a black hawk flying toward the upper levels of The Hive and gave the command in Vat'tu, *"After him."*

As the women bounded toward their prey, the Hive Lord looked to Lord Valter and said, "Your presence is a danger to The Hive, Your Grace."

"My apologies," Lord Valter replied, wincing through the pain of his hand still bleeding while he retrieved his discarded sword. "He has always been discreet with his ambushes. I did not think he would expose himself out in the open like this."

"He's gettin' bolder by the day," Zikky spat at the charred demonic remains.

"Mistaken indeed," Tigernach replied before nodding to Zikky. "Settle your business. Out of respect to Hive Lord Halim-Isa of the Pipes, I will not remove you today. Instead, you are to leave within the next two moons lest we deem sooner. Are we clear?"

"Sure," said Zikky, her lips scrunching to the side.

Once her business concluded, Tigernach followed the rest of the squadron by leaping up to the second floor in one jump and following her team's trail. Siroun gaped at the acrobatic prowess the Sylvani woman had and could see why they would accept her as a leader despite not being a Skivat.

When Zikky approached her, so many thoughts raced through Siroun's head as she said, "She's incredible."

Zikky chuckled as she crouched down and checked on Siroun first before looking at the wounds sustained by Colin. She spoke the equation of a warming spell in her palm to press against his chest to thaw the ice and said, "She's incredible all right. Incredibly strict. Unfortunately, we're on her bad side now, so we gotta do as she says and shove off in the next day or two."

"But we don't have the map," said Siroun. "Where will we go?"

Lord Valter coughed behind a kerchief as the nobleman meandered his way over. "We return to Ysile Marden and inform the Division Magistrate of our findings."

"He ain't gonna like the fact that we're comin' back empty-handed," said Zikky.

"Yes, well," he cleared his throat, "sometimes to move forward, one must take a step back. We now know Fakil could not do it, therefore we must return home to find out who in the world can. We can only hope our efforts come to fruition first."

"That's a hefty bet yer placin'," said Zikky as she wrapped Colin over her shoulders and hoisted his body up to carry him. Meanwhile, Siroun looked around for any sign of Nikostraz. People started returning to assess the damages, forcing Siroun to hop chairs to search for the Dragomyr from higher ground.

She cupped her hands around her mouth and shouted at the top of her lungs, "Nik? Niiiiik!"

Lord Valter and Zikky kept watch for Nikostraz while Siroun continued calling his name.

"Niiikostraaaaaz!" Siroun shouted again through the clusters of people. After several minutes of searching, a familiar face showed up among the crowd appearing somewhat banged up. Her heart soared as she ran over and hugged Nikostraz. "By The Great Three, you're safe!"

He returned the gesture with less enthusiasm. Afterward, he backed away and shook off the debris that coated his clothing.

"Yes, I am in satisfactory condition, all things considered," he said before coughing a few times.

Siroun saw the injuries along his cheek and reached up to wipe some of it away. "You're bleeding."

"It's just a scratch."

"Come, I'll patch you up. We have to leave this place per Tigernach's orders. Lord Valter says we're going to Ysile Marden next since we couldn't get the map."

Those words caused Nikostraz to shake off Siroun's insistent prodding at his face to reach back and produce a folded-up mess of parchment that he handed to her. "You mean this map?"

At first, Siroun couldn't believe it. The map went through extensive wear and tear since the last time she laid eyes on it. The missing corner looked identical in shape to the part Lord Valter had in his possession. Speechless, Siroun stammered through her reactions, "This is—! How did—? Where—?"

"I saw him drop it on the second floor as he made his getaway. I figured I would grab it before all those Blood Oath whatever-they-call-themselves confiscated it."

"I can't believe this!" She cried in elation, and then stiffened up. "I seriously can't believe this."

Nikostraz shrugged and walked toward the Vanis Aer mages, "I don't care to understand the enemy, I'm just here for your sake. I apologize for not being here sooner. Once the chaos started, it was impossible to get here any faster with everyone running away."

Siroun ambushed him with another hug before darting off to Lord Valter and Zikky shouting, "He found it! Nikostraz found it, can you believe this?"

It occurred to her from Felthane's earlier words that Lord Valter was a Duke, and she slowed her strides. While knowing this detail didn't change the aim of the mission, it bothered her he hid his true identity until now. When Siroun handed the map to Lord Valter, he didn't act any different now that she knew. Instead, she watched as he and Zikky's eyes widened at the document, unable to believe their luck.

When he unfolded the Map of Selvarethon shock overcame him as he asked, "How did you come to find this, Siroun?"

"Nikostraz said he found it on the second floor after Felthane dropped it." Siroun tapped her fingertips together as she said with excitement. "Having the map changes everything, doesn't it?"

"Yes," Lord Valter sounded reticent in his enthusiasm. "That changes things in our favor."

He folded the map and tucked it away in his coat, doing his best not to bleed all over it. "I commend you, Nikostraz. Well done."

Something in the way Lord Valter gave the compliment conveyed suspicion to Siroun, but Nikostraz ignored it with, "Yes, well... I'm just trying to help the team so that Siroun can be free of this entire affair. The sooner, the better."

"Agreed," said Lord Valter. "Let us return to our quarters so we can bandage Colin up and get him conscious again. Thank you for taking him, Zikky."

"Meh, I kinda owe him for all those times he dragged my drunken butt around." With that, Zikky took one of Colin's limp hands and slapped his face with it. As everyone sighed at her antics, she could only giggle. "Not that I won't have fun with it."

With a gesture for Siroun and Nikostraz to lead the way, Lord Valter and Zikky stayed a few paces behind to converse about the sudden twist of fate that had dropped into their laps.

Meanwhile, Siroun turned to Nikostraz and smiled as she spoke in their Drakish tongue, *"I'm so glad you're safe. You had me worried when I couldn't find you during the scuffle.*"

The Dragomyr smirked. "*It'll take more than a scuffle to get rid of me.*"

"*I hope so,*" she said, as they started the trek back to their guest quarters.

18

*C*OLIN SENSED SOMEONE touching his exposed back, and his eyes snapped open while scrambling into a sitting position. Along the way, he smashed into someone head-first who yelped in pain before he looked over to realize that it was Siroun holding her jaw as she shot a glare at him.

"Hey! Be careful," Colin snarled before looking around to find himself in the medical room within the Visitor's Quarter. "Why are you touching me?"

She shot him an incredulous look before clearing her throat and changing her vocal inflection to replicate his. "Gee Siroun, thank you for pulling me out of that fight when I was unconscious. Oh, and thank you for nursing my wounds so they wouldn't get infected. I appreciate it."

Mortified, he replied, "I don't sound like that."

Siroun's eyes narrowed, and she reached out and punched Colin in the arm, causing him to yelp and suck in his breath.

"Would it kill you to say something nice for a change?" she said.

Before Colin replied, she got up and stormed toward the exit, tossing another wet cloth toward a pile that stacked up on the floor. The door slammed, and he winced in reaction before looking over to the discarded towel pile. Every one of them stained red with his blood. As much as he wanted to shout at her through the door, he couldn't help but linger on the sight of the blood-soaked cloths. Colin navigated his hand with precision toward his back and felt the bandages covering him. A knock came to the door, and the younger mage reached for his shirt while Lord Valter entered.

"How are you feeling?" Lord Valter asked.

Putting his shirt on was an exercise in extreme care, but Colin endured it while grimacing every step of the way.

Slipping into his uniform one piece at a time, Colin noticed the haphazard stitching where Felthane cleaved through his clothing, "I've been better, but I'll heal."

"It appears we require new uniforms once we return home," Lord Valter said as he leaned down to appraise the pile of bloody towels. He shifted his attention to the younger mage. "She did not leave your side, you know."

With a sharp flap of his collar, Colin finished easing himself into his pants. "I didn't ask her to do that."

"No, but she insisted."

Colin scoffed. "Women are stupid."

At that moment, the mage found himself face-to-face with his leader who looked less than happy after those words slipped from his mouth.

Lord Valter replied, "Do you wish to correct that statement?"

Colin clenched his jaw and tried to wait it out, but when Lord Valter didn't budge nor release his penetrating stare, he huffed in frustration. "Fine, I'll be more appreciative next time. You happy?"

"No," said Lord Valter with a disappointed tone, "but that is a start."

The ice mage huffed in annoyance before his eyes traveled to the bandage around Lord Valter's hand. Despite the nobleman always condemning him for his own recklessness, Colin never understood why Lord Valter took similar risks.

He reached out and said, "Let me see your hand."

Lord Valter complied, allowing Colin to remove the bandage and assess the wound. It was a decent cut, but nothing out of the spectrum of his ability. The verbal components of the spell rolled off of his tongue, and numerical symbols glowed around him before transitioning to swirls of soft snow. With a swivel of his hand, the spell gathered into Lord Valter's palm before Colin pressed it down into the wound. When the ice mage released Lord Valter's hand, he revealed a mended wound with little more than an insignificant mark that would go away on its own in time.

The nobleman flexed his hand a few times before saying, "You should have saved that spell for yourself."

"I can handle myself," said Colin. "Besides, you're too important to go around with unsightly scars."

Lord Valter gave a hearty laugh as he touched the lightening marks along the side of his face, "It is too late for that."

Seconds later, Zikky bounded her way into the room. "Oh hey, the Grumpy Butt is up! How's it feel to be back among the livin' again?"

Being in no mood to tolerate his pluckier comrade, Colin groaned, "Lovely."

Lord Valter turned to her. "I think it is time we put our prize to use. Would you mind fetching the Lady Siroun for me, please? I believe she stormed back to her room after Colin overwhelmed her with his charming personality."

"Sure, not a problem!" A hint of mirth glinted in Zikky's eyes as she reached over and gave Colin a big slap on the back. "Glad to see you up and runnin' again!"

"Ow!" Colin howled as Zikky bounded away to find Siroun before he could do anything in retribution.

He looked to Lord Valter to see if their leader would admonish the action, only to find the nobleman pulling up a chair and settling in to await the fire mage's return. Since it was moot to argue further, Colin returned to the small couch and conjured another healing spell through spiteful hisses.

19

WITH THE FIVE of them now on a deadline with how long they were permitted to stay, every minute counted in getting closer to the artifact. Zikky went to knock on the door when she heard Siroun and Nikostraz's muffled conversation. Deciding to be nosy, she pressed her ear against it to listen until she determined when it would be a good time to interrupt. Meanwhile, her fingers worked on casting an unlocking spell.

"What do you expect from a brat like him?" said Nikostraz's muffled voice.

This surprised Zikky since they often spoke in the Drakish tongue when the two were alone together.

Siroun sighed as she washed her hands. "I know I'm naïve, but sometimes I wish Colin would open up to me… or respect me at the very least."

"I don't think he respects anyone. Now that they have the map, most our work is done, and I can take you to visit my friends in Finnlock. I'll figure out how to get you back to Pustelia Crest."

Zikky stuck out her tongue in disgust at the idea. Yet, it sounded like she wasn't alone in questioning the suggestion.

Nikostraz sighed and spoke again, "Do you not like that idea?"

"Of course not, Lizard Lips," Zikky whispered to herself in Vat'tu. *"It's a terrible plan."*

"Huh? Oh yes, that will be very nice," the tone in Siroun's voice gave off the opposite impression.

He sighed. "What's wrong?"

"You're a clingy annoyance that keeps holding gel-gel back," Zikky muttered as her fingers continued toiling with the unlock spell.

"N-nothing's wrong," said Siroun with hesitation. "It's a great plan!"

Zikky couldn't help smirking at Siroun's inability to lie.

Nikostraz must have thought the same thing, because Siroun follow up with, "Listen, Nik. It's not that I don't like the plan, I do. I appreciate everything you're doing for me. But despite everything that's gone wrong, I'm liking it here."

The Skivat pumped her fist. *"Atta girl!"*

"Who's saying you won't like it in Finnlock?" said Nikostraz.

"I know. I'll give it a shot. I promise I will. Just—," the conversation paused before Siroun said, "—maybe I could consider settling here too."

Before either of them spoke further, Zikky burst into the room, shouting, "TA-DAH!"

Both Siroun and Nikostraz screamed and clung to each

other in fear. When they realized it was Zikky, they saw the position they were in, released their embraces, and tried looking normal.

Nikostraz composed himself first before he hissed in Zikky's direction, "Why must you be so brazen with your intrusions?"

Siroun interrupted with a different concern. "Never mind that, how did you get in here? I distinctly recall locking it."

"A question I'd love to answer... another time," Zikky grinned before advancing on Siroun and clutching her by the wrist. "C'mon! We have a date with destiny!"

When she pulled Siroun to drag her along, the other woman tugged back, halting the Skivat's advances.

"Wait a minute, Zikky," said Siroun. "Where are you taking me now?"

"Takin' ya?" she blinked, then grinned. "To read the map, silly! Lord Fancy Pants needs yer help since yer the only one who can read it. Ya ready?"

Zikky pulled on her wrist again, but Siroun continued resisting. "What about Nik?"

"Unless he can read that crazy language, we don't need him," Zikky glanced over to the Dragomyr and gave him a shrug. "No offense, Scaly."

"You're not taking her anywhere without me," said Nikostraz.

"He's right," Siroun replied. "Every time I separate from him, bad things always happen."

"Pfft, nonsense!" Zikky waved her hand at the two of them. "She's takin' ten steps to the other room. Nothin' will happen."

"Then why can I not join you?" By now Nikostraz stood to his full height to intimidate the mage, but Zikky didn't fall for the scare tactic knowing that she could take him in a fight if required.

"Sorry Nickle-Fart," Zikky playfully stuck out her tongue at him. "Vanis Aer personnel only, Sparkles' orders. Can't be helped."

Zikky noticed Siroun knitting her brows before locking eyes with her.

"Promise me," said Siroun.

"Eh?" she tilted her head.

"Promise me that after I translate the map, Nikostraz comes with us to recover the artifact."

The Skivat flicked her gaze between Siroun and Nikostraz. They were serious. She didn't understand why Siroun was so paranoid in leaving the disgruntled Dragomyr behind.

"Ya know we wouldn't do that, gel-gel. Now let's go!" said Zikky. This time she pushed Siroun toward the door.

As they exited, Siroun glanced back at Nikostraz, who looked perturbed. "I'll be right back, Nik. I promise."

When the door closed behind them, Zikky heard Nikostraz slamming his claw down on a piece of furniture inside the room.

Siroun balked, but Zikky kept nudging her forward. "Sheesh! He's as bad as the Angst Bucket when he's grumpy."

"Zikky, I can't keep doing this to him."

"I understand, gel-gel, but we have bigger issues that take priority over his hurt feelin's. The sooner we end this, the sooner ya get to go to Finnlock or wherever else he has planned."

Siroun's body language relaxed, but something must have occurred to her because Zikky felt the tension in her muscles return as she said, "Wait, how did you learn about Finnlock?"

"Not important!" Zikky replied before nudging her harder. "Let's go!"

20

S IROUN SAW THE whole Map of Selvarethon up close
for the first time and took a deep breath. Though
she had encountered it once before at the library, it didn't
compare to seeing it unfurled in its entirety. When she
compared the corner piece to the rest of the map, she realized how much abuse it weathered until now. The paper
should have disintegrated eons ago. As the three mages
gave it a cursory scan with their magic, they discovered
much more.

Colin was the first to chime in on his findings as he
pulled back his hands. "Every fiber is woven with some
potent form of Æther I've never seen before. Maybe that's
why it survived this long."

Siroun glared at the younger mage, who ignored her
by staying focused on the task at hand. His behavior from
earlier weighed on her mind, and she still harbored an
unspoken animosity toward him.

"Then ink is enchanted too," said Lord Valter as he

finished his analysis of the piece. "I concur with Fakil, I have never seen this style of writing."

While the two mages conversed, Siroun looked upon the Map of Selvarethon reflecting a sheen of copper-colored light. As much as she tried to pay attention to the others, she couldn't help but reach out and place two fingertips along the edge of the paper. Meanwhile, Lord Valter and Colin kept their focus on each other while Zikky stood silent and watched Siroun interact with the ancient document.

"Think the guild leaders might have an inkling of who made this?" asked Colin. "Or even our Councilor of Artifacts?"

"It is possible," Lord Valter replied. "However, time is not on our—."

The light flashing off of the Map of Selvarethon caused Lord Valter to stop his train of thought and look over in Siroun's direction. Something about the enchanted parchment put Siroun in a trance. Voices whispered and buzzed in her mind as her eyes glazed over. The three mages stepped away, watching her place her palms upon the paper. The muddled voices in her head were hard to discern at first, but the words became clearer over time.

"*We need to destroy it,*" said the first voice in an ancient language Siroun did not recognize but understood.

"*Oh psh!*" said the second. It's tone higher in pitch with a gravelly response of, "*You know we can't do that.*"

"*Then what do you suggest?*"

"*Give it a mortal form and see if it can adapt to this world instead.*"

The first voice did not sound pleased. *"Have you lost your mind? Revanine did not instruct us to do that."*

"It's impossible to satisfy Revanine. Regardless of how we handle this, we lack the resources. Besides," the second voice cackled, *"aren't you the even the slightest bit curious to test this little experiment?"*

"Not when we're bound to this world," retorted the first.

"Existence ends for everyone at some point, old man. Even immortals like us."

"Old man?" the indignant voice quipped.

"Tell you what. We build it like a lock and key, and then we seal both pieces in separate locations. We make sure one cannot function without the other."

"No."

Frustration grunted from the second voice, *"Oh, come on, what's the worst that can happen?"*

"Besides world destruction?"

"Not if we do our jobs right."

"You just said we didn't have the resources to do it right."

"No, I said we didn't have the resources to do it to Revanine's satisfaction. There's a difference."

The first voice paused for a few seconds before saying, *"Fine."*

Other whispers surfaced, voices blended, and everything became muddled. Meanwhile, the Map of Selvarethon radiated a bright light and started mending itself. Letters and lines lifted off of the parchment, transforming the room into a holographic replica of the entire world of Clayne. It outlined the lands of a desert continent in mid-air and reassembled various markers and broken lines.

"It can't be a coincidence that Felthane ran to Fi'ro after he stole the map," Colin commented as he took in the landscape.

The nobleman shook his head. "Fi'ro is home to thousands of old ruins that once belonged to another era of time. I am not surprised that the artifact resides here."

Zikky could only murmur words of amazement in her native tongue as the other two continued gawking. With careful analysis they attempted to make sense of the layout, but the fire mage was the first to understand the locations and pointed to a cylindrical set of lines that appeared to be marking the spot.

"There!" said Zikky as she pointed to a marker. "That must be the location. It's somewhere near the Bat'filin-ear Ruins."

Before they analyzed any further, the map radiated an intense glow. All three shielded their eyes against the brilliant light. The enchanted lines zoomed toward Siroun and absorbed into her body. By the time the three of them realized what had happened, it was too late to perform a counter-spell to stop it.

The voices within Siroun's mind came to an abrupt halt, and she realized that something trapped her within the confines of her subconsciousness. Though she recalled reading a book on astral projection in the past, the thought of practicing it seemed folly. Now she relied on that book's insight as it appeared in her mind and realized that her first order of business was to ground her form. She imagined standing on soft grass, and her feet touched a dewy patch of land to help bring her to a focal point. With that feat accomplished, a voice spoke up in billowing echoes.

"If you can hear this, that means you have found the key to your reawakening," the voice sounded gravelly, just as she heard earlier. *"It also means that time is short. There is no other choice but to lift the seals and see what happens. Seek the black pillar in the sands, and you shall soon come to know your truth. Find me after you reunite with your other self. I will answer your questions."*

Siroun twisted her lips at the presented riddles. "My other self? And what truth?"

There was no reply. Instead, Siroun felt herself slipping back into darkness, and when she opened her eyes, she found Zikky patting her on the cheek.

A few snaps of the fingers, and the fire mage smiled in approval. "Yep! She's awake!"

Siroun didn't realize that she stood throughout her entire trance. Blinking, she wiped at her eyes to remove the excess tears that formed since they were so dry a few seconds ago. "What did I miss?"

Taking a moment to regroup, they looked at the parchment paper that was now blank and dull.

"It is not a map in the normal sense of the word. It was a scroll. As soon as Siroun completed casting its spell," Lord Valter picked up the paper and the fibers turned to dust, "the map lost its power."

That explanation didn't make sense to Siroun. "What about the other times when I activated the corner?"

"You were invoking its desire to make itself whole again," he said.

"The creators designed this map to be a muddled mess until someone knew the language to induce its activation," said Colin, somewhat impressed. "Siroun, what did the spell do to you?"

With all eyes upon her, Siroun bit at her bottom lip as she tried recalling the voices along with the instructions. She rubbed her forehead and replied, "Something about a black pillar in the sand, and they made the map for me. There was some added stuff, but I'm having trouble remembering."

Colin frowned. "You're not great at remembering verbal instructions, are you?"

"At least I try," she glared back at Colin. "Which is more than I can say for some people in this room."

To break up the tension, Lord Valter said, "Do you remember any details of what the map looked like?"

"Huh?" Siroun blinked before realizing the question. "Oh, yes. I should be able to redraw the map without issue. Assuming that is what you wanted?"

All three reacted in tandem, "What?"

"I might be terrible at remembering large quantities of verbal commands," she shot another sideways glance at Colin and continued, "but I have a perfect memory with the written word or line work. I thought I explained this before."

Zikky grinned. "I knew ya were a bookworm that read fast, but not to the extent of eidetic memory, gel-gel."

"Oh," Siroun's expression shifted as she bit at her lip, but then folded her arms and straightened her posture. "Then yes, I suppose speed reading isn't an unusual talent. The only reason I found work at the library is that I can memorize and recall anything I have ever read word for word. It was useful for duplicating books that went missing or destroyed."

"Do you know of the poet, Finneas Dallfirth?" said Lord Valter.

Siroun shook her head. "Pustelia Crest isn't the central hub of literary knowledge."

"Interesting," he said as he brought a finger to his chin and rubbed at his beard before saying, "Sislstrad's poem of Path to Knowing if you would, My Lady?"

Taking in a deep breath, Siroun recited the poem word for word without stumbling in the Drakish tongue. Once Siroun completed the poem, she paused and recited it again. This time in the Adami's tongue:

"Path to Knowing by Sislstrad

Here I take my lasting steps,
I see the dawn anew.

Knowing those behind me
Have yet to see the truth.

Shadows bar my way no more,
Deceptions revealed through smiles.

Friends were enemies, and enemies, friends.
On this path traversed through miles.

Yet this path is mine alone,
The journey left me broken.

'Ere I saw the end of all,
This was the path to knowing.

The Collective Works of Sislstrad, page
one-hundred and twelve, second poem."

When she finished her recitation, Siroun looked at the three of them and waited for a response. It wasn't the best test of her skills since anyone could recite poetry. Perhaps it was the only thing that Lord Valter knew within Drakish literature to test her.

Zikky, meanwhile, murmured in her native tongue, *"That was awesome!"*

Siroun recognized the words and with a humble smile, replied to her in broken Vat'tu, *"Is not speak poetry exciting."*

Despite the butchered sentence, Zikky's eyes widened to saucers, and she squealed with joy. *"No way! Did you learn the language? When? Tell me! Tell me everything!"*

"Slow down! Learn still. Structure sentence different," Siroun pleaded, but Zikky leaped upon her in a flurry of hugging and bouncing.

"That book Nikostraz borrowed," Colin interjected, his eyes narrowed in both disbelief and with some level of disturbance. "What was it?"

After Siroun pried Zikky off of her body, she said, "A dictionary of the Vat'tu language. It only provided rudimentary grammar information though. If you understood what I said you would have noticed that I butchered those sentences."

"Is it something you learn the longer you listen to others speak?" Lord Valter inquired.

"That's the problem. As Colin noted, it's a challenge remembering full conversations. The content only sticks by reading. Without a grammar book, I'm afraid I'll just be stringing together words and hoping a Skivat understands me long enough to realize what I'm conveying."

Lord Valter furrowed his brows in silence for a minute before saying, "This changes everything."

"Lord Valter?" Siroun looked at him with concern. She wasn't ready to call him Your Grace just yet since he didn't require it of her for the time being.

Lord Valter forced a smile. "That is quite a skill you have, Lady Siroun. You mentioned someone made the Map of Selvarethon for you?"

"I'm not sure what it means, but it explains the strange connection I have toward it."

"When we locate the black pillar of sand, I am certain we shall discover the reason." Lord Valter looked to Zikky and said, "Do you think you can find us a way to get there?"

"No sweat, I'll get right on it!" The Skivat looped her arm into Siroun's once more yanked the other girl along with a grin. "Yer comin' with me!"

"Gah!" Caught off-guard again, Zikky tugged her around before Siroun stopped and said to the Skivat, "Don't forget we need to get Nikostraz."

"Yeah, yeah, I'm on it," Zikky said and dragged Siroun along, leaving Lord Valter and Colin with the pile of dust.

21

*C*OLIN DIPPED HIS fingers in the dusty remnants and rubbed at the debris. Despite every attempt to seek any sign of residual magic, there was nothing.

His expression reflected displeasure. "You realize we're heading into a trap, right?"

The information brought to light regarding the map and Siroun's part in this puzzle illuminated the reason of why Felthane's obsession honed in on her and no one else. Zikky also wasn't in the dark anymore about the cryptic message from Spyder to Colin. However, Lord Valter worried how long the Skivat could hold her tongue given all that had transpired. He wasn't the only one thinking this.

"We should tell Siroun," said Colin, interrupting the nobleman's thoughts.

"Not now," replied Lord Valter with regret lingering in his voice.

The response created an edge to younger mage's tone. "Why? We're not protecting her any more or less if we do."

"Felthane still has the upper hand. If we are wrong

in this assumption, she will not look upon us favorably, and I can tell her heart and mind are strained with other concerns."

To that reply, Colin sneered, "It makes you wonder what kind of sinister quality this artifact possesses. What's more disturbing is that this map was made for her. Which means—."

"The artifact was made for her too. Yes, I am aware. It also brings up how much the Regents of Niravad knew about her, along with the map and the artifact it leads toward. They locked it away in a restricted vault within the same village Siroun lived. That is not a coincidence. She was meant to inherit it, and it scared them. The real question we should ask ourselves is: Why?"

Colin scoffed and said, "It explains her isolation and later exile after Felthane recovered the map."

"True, and I doubt they intend to offer us their explanation. For now, we need to do better in keeping Siroun under our watch."

22

"**G**OING TOP-SIDE ARE you?" Spyder snapped her gum with a grin as she clomped her way toward the lower regions of The Hive. Everyone followed from behind as the Hive Lord had her usual bodyguards take the rear. Siroun snuck a glance over to Nikostraz who was silent and inattentive as he lingered near the back.

"It's not the best idea to go during daylight," she said.

"Ever see a black pillar near the Bat'filinear Ruins?" said Zikky, now dressed up in her desert rider clothing native to the Skivat.

Even Siroun and Colin had matching outfits to suit the desert landscape while Nikostraz had nothing that fit his shape. Lord Valter remained in his usual attire but welcomed the goggles and added safety gear that prevented the sand from blasting his skin.

With a pop of the gum and a shake of her head, Spyder made her way through a metal-linked gate and turned toward a darker part of the underground metropolis.

"Nope! Besides, I'm not allowed to leave The Hive. Even if I had, you couldn't afford the answer."

"Figures," Colin grumbled.

To which Spyder halted and faced the ice mage. With a wink and a wag her finger, she said, "Was I not the magnanimous hostess when I helped you earlier despite preferring to accept you as currency? By the way, my offer still stands."

When Spyder reached toward him, Zikky clutched her by the wrist and said in Vat'tu, *"Hey, knock it off. He's already had a rough enough day."*

The Hive Lord raised a brow at the other Skivat. *"Since when did you become the paragon of piety?"*

"I'm learning as I go," she said, giving the other woman a warning glare. Leaning forward, Zikky murmured, *"Come on, Spyder. Not now. We'll be out of your hair soon enough."*

Everyone stopped walking to see if another fight would escalate between them. While Zikky kept her gaze on Spyder, the Network Hive Lord glanced around to make eye contact with everyone else. The time that lapsed felt uncomfortable, but Spyder soon clicked her tongue and yanked her wrist free.

"You're no fun anymore," she said and continued onward.

After a few more twists, turns, and pulleys, the group made it to a sector that opened up into a huge underground hangar. The Skivat in this territory worked on an assortment of mechanical vehicles. Mixtures of obnoxious whirling and buzzing pervaded the senses as the grease monkeys toiled on building and repairing the intricate monstrosities. Siroun covered her ears as she continued to follow the rest of the group down a staircase that led them to the ground level.

"If you want to go top-side, then you will need transport," said Spyder. "The Garage turf is home to the Dune Thrashers, their leader is Rocky Samara."

The introduction was for the outsiders rather than Zikky. As the group cleared the last step, several nearby mechanics halted their work and looked up to see who approached. The name 'Rocky' began echoing throughout the hangar from the workers to relay a summons. Meanwhile, a mechanic meandered over to Spyder and performed a special series of handshakes in greeting before following up with a brief hug.

"*Spyder!*" they said in a chipper tone. "*What brings you to this corner of the rock?*"

"*Some visitors need a favor from your leader. How's the Dune Thrasher life?*"

They grinned. "*I like it. Not that I didn't enjoy my time with The Network.*"

"*Yeah, you always had a penchant for Rocky's toys. No hard feelings. I see your skin's a few shades darker. Looks good on you.*"

"*Thanks!*" They rubbed the back of their neck. "*It's nice spending more time top-side.*"

"*If only I could do the same. The curse of being a Hive Lord.*"

"*Not every Hive Lord,*" the mechanic flicked a glance in Zikky's direction until Spyder redirected the conversation.

"*Have you seen your boss around?*"

They nodded and pointed a few feet away. The individual approaching was one of the tallest Skivat that Siroun had ever seen. Even though the Skivat physique was short, lean, and lithe, Rocky looked like a taller, beefed up version of Zikky by comparison. Every muscle on their body rippled, while a hardened expression reflected on their chiseled face. Once Rocky closed the distance between them all, Siroun stepped over to hide behind Lord Valter. The Skivat saw this and scoffed at her before meeting gazes with Spyder.

"Lookin' to take your minion back from me?" said Rocky with a feminine tone. Once again, Siroun found herself fooled between male and female. No one else around her looked shocked by this revelation.

Laughing, Spyder shook her head. *"No, you won him fair and square. Besides, he's happier here. This visit is unofficial business. I have visitors here that need to go treasure hunting up top."*

Rocky grinned before nodding to the guests and noticing the emblem on Lord Valter's lapel. "Ah, I see. Vanis Aer?"

"That is correct," said Lord Valter.

"Which division?"

"Ysile Marden."

She appeared satisfied with that answer. "Good division. They pay well, and on time."

"It helps when your employer is a monarch."

"Not all of them do," Rocky retorted before turning away with a gesture for them to follow. "Come, I'll get you accommodated."

Lord Valter nodded his head in appreciation. "We are much obliged."

The group followed while Spyder and her retinue

lagged. Siroun and Colin noticed this and wondered if they would follow.

The Gothic-looking Hive Lord waved with a grin. "This is where I leave you. Good luck. Don't die."

Wandering further into the hangar, the sounds of machinery intensified. Metal clanged, bouncing off different surfaces to create a symphony of noise. This was music to a Dune Thrasher's ears. The Hive thrived on a plethora of interests and technology. Each turf held a purpose to the collective, and the gangs acted as its foundation with their specific functions to the rest of society. To Siroun, the whole Hive Lord concept seemed like nothing more than a competition of resources that improved the overall statuses of those living within its walls. She looked on in fascination while Rocky gave them the formal spiel. Lord Valter was the primary negotiator since it was by his link to the Anastas treasury that gave him the clout to decide on prices. Both parties shouted at each other given the level of the surrounding noise.

"I don't need to get into too many details on the dangers of the Fi'ro desert," said Rocky. "Don't travel during the day if you want to avoid death by heat exhaustion. At night you'll be dealin' with various scavenger animals, but as long as you stay alert and keep driving, it shouldn't be too much trouble. The only real monsters you have to worry about are the Tyth'var. They eat anythin' that breathes or bleeds, so make sure you're well-armed."

Siroun leaned into Zikky's ear and asked, "What are Tyth'var?"

"Massive, carnivorous sandworms," she replied.

"Oh," pulling back, Siroun swallowed hard.

Rocky glanced over her shoulder. "How many goin' top-side?"

"Five," said Lord Valter.

Rocky double-checked the headcount. "Since one of you is a Dragomyr, you'll need some stretching room. I can offer you either the Claydozer that seats eight or two Sand Skirters that seat three apiece."

"Any difference in speed?"

"A little. The bigger difference is in maneuverability. The Claydozer has a ton of power, but the Sand Skirters have better responses in their turning and agility on rougher terrain. Both use Di-Metal, which attests to their durability. The standard power cores last three days, give or take how much you travel. I can use the spare seats to load up extra if you think you'll be needin' them."

"Please," Lord Valter answered. "I believe the two Sand Skirters are our best options."

"Smart choice," she said. Rocky curled her bottom lip over her teeth and emitted a high-pitched whistle. The nearby mechanics looked up to find their boss making several hand gestures before waving in a circular motion over her head. The groups dropped their current projects and headed over to two specific vehicles to administrate the order. With things underway, Rocky turned back to the group and folded her arms. "Will you be payin' upfront, or do I bill your superior?"

"You may send notice to His Majesty, King Nathaniel," said Lord Valter. "When will we be able to depart?"

"Soon, but I recommend waiting a few more hours before you leave. It's still blazing hot outside."

"I must emphasize that time is of the essence."

To this remark, Zikky tapped Lord Valter on the arm. "Rocky's right. Better wait until dark, then go."

"I recommend trusting the Skivat's expertise on this one," Nikostraz further impressed as he scanned the nearby tools that were being used to work on a vehicle in their immediate vicinity.

Lord Valter put a finger to his chin, and scratched at his beard before saying, "What about the black pillar? How will we be able to see it in the middle of the night?"

"If we have Siroun re-draw us the map," said Colin, "we can determine distance and the time it will take so we'll have the light of dawn on our side."

They looked at Siroun before Lord Valter replied, "That solution appears reasonable."

Turning to Rocky, Zikky asked in Vat'tu, *"Have a place for us to hang for a few hours while we wait out the day?"*

"Sure," said Rocky. *"Through the right corridor, there's another set of stairs that lead to a padded room. Should help with the noise. I'll put the stay on your tab."*

"Deal!" Zikky turned to Lord Valter and said in Adami, "Rocky's gotta nice place to crash for a bit while we wait."

"Oh," the tone in his voice perked up. "How generous."

"Yep, she's a gem like that. Follow me!"

As they headed toward the designated room, Siroun waited until they were going up the stairs before tugging on Zikky's arm and saying in Vat'tu, *"Bill you charged room?"*

She gave a cheerful wave of her hand. *"Ah, don't worry about it. The King's pockets are deep with this stuff. Besides, Fancy Pants would have done the same thing."*

When they reached the designated room, the group settled in and searched for whatever writing materials they could find for Siroun to recreate the map. Those items included a light rag, some oil, and a screwdriver. Disappointed but not discouraged, Siroun worked on reconstructing the map's layout. She noticed Zikky watching her as she struggled to use the alternative tools to create a copy. By the time she finished the map, the Skivat could see her hand muscles tightening up. While Siroun nursed her fingers back to sensation, Zikky and the other two huddled around it to study.

"Memorize it well," instructed Lord Valter. "As soon as we go outside, Zikky will burn it."

"Burn it?" said Siroun. "Why?"

"We don't want anyone else accessing the ruins. Also, if we fail, it's best that no one finds it," said Colin as he analyzed the drawing before curling his lip a little. "It's all goopy. There are blobs everywhere."

Siroun balled up her fists and shot a glare toward him. "You try drawing in oil. See how masterful you can be with it on a first attempt."

She felt a gentle tap on the shoulder by Lord Valter who diverted her attention away from the teenage mage.

"Someone went to great lengths to ensure that only you could read the directions, Lady Siroun," he said. "It would be irresponsible of us to not maintain that level of secrecy in respect to its creator."

Though it made sense, she couldn't help but lament having to destroy all of her hard work. While Lord Valter and Colin calculated the distance and travel speeds that would determine their departure time, Zikky glanced over and nudged shoulders with her. "What's wrong, gel-gel?"

A small sigh left Siroun's nose. Too many things bothered her. "I'm just frustrated."

"About what?"

"Nothing? Everything? I don't even know," Siroun rested her chin on her palm. "I still can't figure out if this whole escapade is a blessing or a curse. When I fled Pustelia Crest, I was certain my life was over. Now I'm not sure it was a bad thing, but dealing with this Felthane guy is scary, and I have no idea if anything I'm doing is right."

"If it's one thing I've learned bein' a field agent, gel-gel, is that nothin' we do is gonna be one-hundred percent correct all the time. Even Lord Sparkles over there gets it wrong. Though I doubt he'd ever admit that," she smirked before giving Siroun another nudge. "For a first timer with no trainin', yer doin' great."

"That's the point. I want combat training so I'm not helpless all the time."

To that statement Zikky placed a finger to her chin and contemplated the request. "It would be useful to have ya pick up a few things when the time permits. Only problem is that we've been on the move a lot. Then again, we're due back to Ysile Marden after our business here is done, and I know that it'll be a long boat ride for us. Plenty of time to teach ya some basics! Sound good?"

The fire mage offered a hand, and Siroun gave it a shake before smiling back. "Deal."

By now the men finished memorizing the map and moved their conversation to a different topic. Zikky and Siroun soon noticed Colin narrowing his eyes at Nikostraz. "I'm going with you."

"What's going on?" said Siroun.

Lord Valter sighed at the two, but forced a smile when he went to answer her, "I figure we could grab some additional supplies while we wait for our transports. Nikostraz volunteered to assist."

"I told you, I am perfectly capable of navigating The Hive on my own," Nikostraz snarled at the ice mage.

"There is something I need to pick up too," Colin grumbled. "I'm coming with you."

Siroun couldn't determine if what Colin was saying held any truth behind it.

Eventually, the Dragomyr snorted, "Fine. Let's go."

After the two of them exited, Siroun stared at the door before saying, "Why don't I believe Colin?"

"He is unconventional with his communication methods, Lady Siroun," said Lord Valter with exasperation in his voice. "But he means well."

"I know, Lo — I mean, Your Grace. However, I wish he wouldn't be such a complete jerk to Nik. I can deal with him being rude to me, but my best friend is a different matter."

Zikky patted Siroun on the shoulder. "Trust me, gel-gel, yer bestie doesn't hold back his tongue when Colin gets sassy with him. He only acts pleasant when yer around."

Lord Valter followed up with, "On another note, Lady Siroun, I do not require you to use that title until we are in Ysile Marden. To which point I must call you Miss Fatima as per protocol."

Zikky then snapped her fingers. "I just had an epiphany! Sparkles, keep an eye on gel-gel for a bit. I have to go fetch somethin' for her."

Siroun fidgeted with her hair before saying, "I want to come with you."

"Nope. Where I'm goin' is restricted to outsiders. I won't take long, promise," she gave Siroun a wink before skipping her way out of the room and leaving the two alone together.

For a while, all was quiet except for the distant sounds of all the grease monkeys working on machinery and vehicles that littered the hangar in varying degrees of completion. Siroun tried to think of something to say to Lord Valter so it wouldn't feel so awkward.

"So," Siroun cleared her throat, "any idea what that was about?"

She didn't notice that Lord Valter's attention returned to the oil-blotted map. When she asked again, he shook his head and said, "Zikky has always been the spontaneous type. It takes a while to become accustomed to her capricious endeavors. Truth be told, I still find myself caught off-guard from time to time."

"Oh, okay," Siroun wanted to smack herself in the face in embarrassment. Instead, she got up and headed toward the door. "I'm going to watch the Skivat work on these weird machines. It looks interesting."

"They have quite the knack for technology. It is unfortunate that the Skivat are not compelled to share much of it with us."

"They keep it on lock-down?" she said with confusion in her voice. "Why?"

"Di-Metal is a rare substance found only in The Hive. This whole metropolis used to be a mine that the Sylvani and Dragomyr fought wars over several millennia ago.

They enslaved the natives into unearthing it for them, but there was a revolution. Once the Skivat won their freedom, they made it their business to ensure every piece of Di-Metal returned to its source location. However, it was not the only thing they confiscated along the way."

This information stunned Siroun. "They stole their former masters' artifacts and relics as well?"

"Indeed. When the Skivat recovered every piece of Di-Metal scrap from the other kingdoms, they became a powerhouse of illicit goods and trade. For the Skivat, it was not just about recovering what others stole from them. They wanted retribution for their suffering. Each kingdom reacted different to the shift in power. Some negotiated peace treaties. Others secured alliances, and one in particular—."

"—closed its borders to the rest of the world," Siroun finished as she realized the real reason behind the Dragomyr's xenophobic mentality.

"Correct," he replied. "The Skivat go to great lengths to protect their technology from the outside world. It is the reason we cannot remember how we get in and out of The Hive. It is also the reason this continent is a graveyard for artifacts and relics. Every kingdom keeps secrets, My Lady. Including Niravad."

The information Lord Valter provided brought additional insight regarding the cause and effect of why things were the way they were within Niravad's borders. It was a lot to digest, and as she reached over to open the door to the hangar, Lord Valter spoke up once more, "Do not wander far, My Lady. The hangar is dangerous, even for me."

Nodding, Siroun headed out to a loud blasting of noise but sat at the top of the stairs, plugged her ears, and watched everyone toil away. A twinge of jealousy reflected in her eyes as she watched the mechanics work together in small teams. Siroun hoped that after this mission finished, she might find a place in this world.

23

No MATTER THE time of the day or night, The Hive always bustled with activity. The Entertainer's Quarter didn't waste a moment getting the place up and running again after Felthane's attack. Both Colin and Nikostraz wove their way through the turfs and into the Trader's Square where the merchants haggled endlessly in selling their wares.

Nikostraz finished purchasing a satchel of dried meat and fruit while Colin followed up close behind with a rucksack of water slung over his shoulders. When their shopping exploits ended, Nikostraz couldn't help but notice that the ice mage never left his side.

With an arc of his brow, Nikostraz felt compelled to comment, "I thought you said you had something to do."

"I do," said Colin, plucking a small pouch of chewing candy and paying the vendor. "I'm keeping my eye on you."

Nikostraz paused momentarily but played off his discomfort by pretending something caught his attention elsewhere. He reached out to a random trinket dangling on a string, and replied, "Me? For what? Do you think I will interrupt your little game of chase with this necromancer you've been hunting? Please. I have more important concerns than the affairs of Ysile Marden's elite."

"Do you, really?" Colin raised a brow at the Dragomyr as he followed Nikostraz out of the marketplace.

"Yes, really," Nikostraz stopped and turned to the mage, hoping to size up the teen. "I don't know what you're playing at, child, but I suggest you keep that unpleasant tongue in your mouth before I force your silence."

"Is that a threat, old man?" Colin took a further step forward, and a chill crept into the surrounding air. Now Nikostraz took the defensive as the younger mage continued with, "You might have Siroun wrapped around your claws, but I don't trust you."

"Good," said Nikostraz with indignation. "I've trusted none of you this entire time. I'm glad we're able to come to terms with this out in the open for once. Now put your spells away before you hurt someone, little boy. After all, you don't want your superior sending you home early before you've had your chance to show off, would you?"

That remark forced Colin to scowl and relax his hand which had been holding onto a small spell in secret.

Colin brushed past the Dragomyr and continued on their pathway back. "Let's go."

24

*L*OUD CREAKING ECHOED throughout the hangar as the two Sand Skirters fired up their power cores. By now the group had returned from their excursions, save one.

Lord Valter frowned and turned to the others, "Where is Zikky?"

The question became drowned out from the deluge of mechanical noises, forcing the Duke to exaggerate his annunciation so that everybody could read his lips.

Halfway through articulating the query a second time, Zikky shouted out with, "Here I am!"

The fire mage ran at maximum gallop to rendezvous with them. A massive shoulder bag flopped side-to-side as Zikky sprinted to the vehicles and climbed into the one occupied by Siroun. When the Sand Skirter jostled from Zikky's unceremonious leap, Siroun clutched at a nearby railing to keep her balance.

"Didja miss me, gel-gel? These are for you," said Zikky as she swung the bag over her shoulder, and plopped the spoils into the empty seat next to Siroun. The men stared at the luggage, curious about its contents.

Siroun's nimble fingers set to work loosening the bag. She withdrew the first of many works and marveled at its size. "By The Great Three, how many books did you pillage?"

"*Surprise!*" The mage cackled with joy as she switched to the Vat'tu tongue, "*I could only grab so much. I got you several books you will love. I found one on ancient gods, historical heroes, a spell book to mix things up, and a textbook on Raven Knights!*"

"*Raven Knights?*" Siroun responded in her rudimentary grasp of the dialect, "*What they are?*"

"*Something about a goddess of death who chooses mortals to be her champions and grants them powers, yada yada. They're like demigods that existed in history. Trying to find texts on them is nearly impossible, but the Treasure Vikings gang must know a trick to hunting them.*" Zikky then beamed. "*Jak'rileh owed me a favor that I cashed in to secure these for you. So, how'd I do?*"

Siroun felt so overwhelmed with elation that she reached out and embraced Zikky in a tight hug, returning to the Adami language with a resounding, "Thank you!"

Zikky grinned as she peeked over to see Nikostraz curling his lip at them and before turning away.

Rocky's voice chimed in a few seconds later, interrupting them. "You're in luck. The moons are full tonight. You should have an excellent view of the terrain. Also, I had the crew put a few pulse beacons in the back in case you come across any Tyth'var that don't want to leave you alone. They hate high-pitched sound waves. Just flip this side switch, and they should change course real quick."

"Thank you for everything you have done for us," Lord Valter said with sincere appreciation.

"Don't mention it. Once you leave through the hangar, you'll drive through a few miles of tunnel before it leads you to the desert. From there you'll head northwest to follow the correct route of the Bat'filinear Ruins. After that, it's up to you. Oh, and another thing," Rocky plucked out a small vial with two tablets inside and tossed them to Lord Valter. "These are for your other operator so they don't fall asleep while leaving the garage. There's only enough for one person to leave and return. Make sure if you don't return, it's because you're dead. Good luck finding your black pillar that we've never heard of before."

Everyone equipped their goggles and began loading into the Sand Skirters. Colin acted as the chauffeur for the first vehicle, thus being the recipient of the pills. Meanwhile, Zikky operated the second that Siroun occupied, who was already halfway done with the compendium she started reading. Nikostraz looked in Zikky's direction before turning away to load up into the vehicle with Colin, while Lord Valter joined the women. Siroun, however, was nose-deep in the Raven Knights book to where she didn't notice anyone select their transports. Readied, they took off through the tunnel and into the desert expanse of Fi'ro.

25

*E*NGINES CAME TO a halt as Siroun finished up the Raven Knight book. One deity by the name of Revanine turned the hands of fate by empowering a worthy mortal seeking to overcome a significant obstacle. The rest of the details involved explanations of various heroes and their mighty deeds, but the one thing that didn't match their stories and hers was the fact that this deity of death riding a giant equine had never visited her.

By now Zikky leaped out of the vehicle and chatted up the others, "We've been drivin' around forever. What gives?"

"I thought you were the expert in these regions?" said Colin with a snerk.

Zikky opened her mouth to retort when Lord Valter interjected, "It is dawn, and our time is running out. Ideas?"

No one said a thing.

Lord Valter glanced over at Siroun, and watched her put aside her book, stretch, and rub her eyes before looking out into the vast stretches of desert. Not a moment later she performed a double-take, "Oh, we're here."

The Duke tried to find the pillar, but saw nothing for miles that indicated their arrival. Siroun disembarked from the vehicle and walked along the sandy terrain. Reaching out into open air, she wiggled her fingers to find that the illusion she could see was a pillar of energy. It resembled black sand floating toward the heavens with a sensation of cold steam on the skin. From the others' points of view, she was groping air.

Nikostraz stepped up behind her. "You see it?"

Nodding, Siroun continued to explore the phenomenon on her fingertips. The power it radiated brought a sense of calm that she couldn't describe as she let the particles dance across her palm and along her wrist. After a minute of playing, the black pillar swirled and words materialized from its energy.

Speak your true self to enter.

The others joined her in mulling over the meaning as she repeated the sentence aloud. Zikky spoke first on the matter, "Somethin' ya desire?"

"Perhaps it is asking for your origin of birth?" said Lord Valter.

"A name," said Colin, and the others quirked their brows in his direction. He clarified again, "I bet it's your name."

"Sure, we can give that a shot," Siroun replied and took a slow breath before saying, "Siroun Fatima."

They waited for a few seconds, then a few minutes.

Nothing changed. The sun rose higher into the sky, and the surrounding air heated.

"Try again," said Nikostraz. "Maybe a little louder?"

She took a deeper breath and shouted, "Siroun Fatima!"

Still nothing.

All eyes waited on her as Siroun toiled over the answer behind the riddle. Of the five of them, Zikky's body adapted the fasted to the harsh desert climate, while the others began dabbing at beads of sweat along their necks.

"We're gonna have a serious problem if we don't figure this mystery out soon," said Zikky as she raised a brow in concern at the rest of them.

"No," Siroun replied with determination in her voice. "I need more time."

"A luxury we do not have to give you," Colin quipped.

"If you do not intend on being of any further help, then remain silent," Nikostraz hissed back at him.

Colin stepped forward and approached the Dragomyr. "You haven't contributed to this escapade since we started, so why don't you just back off."

"Didn't I warn you, boy? Do not start something you can't finish."

When the bickering didn't show any signs of stopping, Lord Valter muttered a series of equations and flicked his hand in their direction. A small blast of lightning hurled between them, and caused sand to launch everywhere, halting their tongues long enough to garner their attention.

"Enough!" Lord Valter's tone full of impatience.

Even with the Duke's efforts, it didn't ease the pressure put upon Siroun to figure out a way to activate the black pillar. While she nibbled on her bottom lip, she studied the riddle and sifted through multiple books within her mind to see if anything provided an answer.

Meanwhile, Zikky's left ear shifted and caught a sound in the distance. "We've got company."

Though slight, Zikky wasn't wrong about what she heard. Sand shifted around their feet in an S-shaped pattern as the five of them realized they weren't alone. Colin spotted the subtle movement to the left of them and reacted with a snap of his right wrist to conjure a spell. What was supposed to be a lance of ice looked more like a giant blob of slush as it splattered into the ground where the unknown creature slithered. All movement stopped for a second, only to have the muddied ground burst open revealing a massive worm with a giant maw lined with teeth. Colin dodged, barely missing being a meal by less than an inch.

As he tumbled out of the way, Lord Valter followed up with an incantation while Zikky made a beeline for the vehicles. Siroun remembered Rocky saying she equipped the Sand Skirters with tools to deter them. Siroun didn't believe it until she found herself face-to-mouth with the sightless Tyth'var. Only muscle and teeth embodied this carnivorous desert dweller. When it redirected its path after Zikky, Siroun ran up along its side and kicked the beast as best she could. Its flesh was as hard as a blacksmith's anvil, and her efforts went unnoticed as it raced after the fire mage who almost the reached vehicle.

"Siroun, get out of the way!" Nikostraz shouted as he dodged the Tyth'var's tail.

Meanwhile, Siroun got walloped from the side, the

sheer force knocking her to the ground. As she recovered, she heard Lord Valter speak another series of equations, readying a spell. She kept low to the ground to avoid receiving an electric death as the crackle of lightning arced from the mage's hands and struck the worm. Upon impact, the bolt spread across the creature like a net before exploding everywhere. A deafening thunderclap followed. When Siroun pulled her hands away from her ears, she noticed the worm was shaking off the effects just as Zikky emerged from the vehicle with a glowing spike in her hand. It was the pulse beacon that Rocky provided them for emergencies such as this. Though Siroun wanted to watch the fight unfold, she felt a hand grab her by the wrist and pull her to her feet.

"Do your job, and we'll do ours," Colin scolded as he pushed her toward the general area of the black pillar. Then he took a defensive stance and conjured forth an ice barrier that turned to slush and plopped into the sand.

While a stream of cursing flowed from Colin's mouth, Siroun returned her focus to the entrance point. She puzzled over how to decipher the code when it hit her: She had another name.

As the fighting continued around her, she shouted it into the sky, "Beskonerynth!"

A burst of wind flared up from the center of the pillar, blowing away the sand and revealing a plate that sunk into a staircase toward the depths below. The stench of stale air bellowed out, striking Siroun in the face and causing a coughing fit.

When the movement ceased, she stared at the entrance,

muttering, "And now I feel dumb for not figuring that out sooner."

Nikostraz came up from behind and pushed her forward in haste. "It happens to the best of us."

The Tyth'var barreled through the sands before leaping to the surface with the intent on swallowing the Skivat whole. In a fluid motion, Zikky slammed the beacon against her leg to activate the hypersonic sound and waved it at the oncoming Tyth'var. The sandworm tensed up and bellowed in agony. Zikky did her best to plug her ears with a shoulder and spare hand, as the vibrations picked up just enough to be annoying. The worm's massive body writhed from the sound, blasting Zikky backward as it dove into the ground to escape. Before the last of its tail could vanish under the sands, she summoned an amplification spell on her right arm and stabbed the beacon into the beast's hide to ensure it would keep fleeing long after it was out of range. With a victorious flick of her hand, Zikky dusted off her body before scrambling to join the rest of the group.

By now, Colin and Lord Valter made their way inside and were leading by several paces. Siroun poked her head out to see if the fire mage caught up only to find the Skivat giving a gesture of victory with her hands.

Zikky shouted out to Siroun, "See? Nothin' to it, gel-gel!"

"Yeah," Siroun forced a hesitant chuckle. "Nothing to it."

One-by-one they filed through the narrow corridor with nothing but darkness up ahead to guide them. As they progressed further into the tunnel, Colin conjured a sphere of light in the palm of his hand and held it out to get a better picture of their surroundings.

"By the way, how'd ya know the answer to the entrance, Salt Lord?" said Zikky.

Colin balled up the fist that wasn't holding the light and punched Zikky in the arm. Though it caught her by surprise, she did very little in reaction other than wiggle her tongue at him.

"I played a lot of word games with Sebastian when I was younger," he replied.

"I didn't realize yer so smart."

"You don't notice much, do you?"

"Sebastian?" Siroun chimed in, "Who's Sebastian?"

"He's no one," muttered Colin.

"Ha!" scoffed Zikky. "Yer such a liar. Ol' Seb is a childhood friend of his. Super smart guy too. Always gettin' himself into trouble with his experiments though. Reminds me of another individual always pushin' himself too hard."

The Skivat folded her arms and stared at Colin who ignored her in favor of moving forward. Siroun couldn't help but smile at their banter as they made their way further into the underground ruins. A desolate tunnel directed them into a barren, circular room with nothing further to notice other than the stone walls and thin streams of sand creeping into the place. Colin tossed the light spell into the air where it illuminated things enough for them to assess the limited space of the room.

After several minutes of investigation, Zikky stuck out her tongue. "Bleh, just a dead end. I never thought I'd describe an ancient ruin as borin'."

Nikostraz stepped slower than the others, running his

claw along the walls and pausing whenever he thought he noticed something, only to follow up with snorts of frustration. Siroun found his snorting a common occurrence as of late.

Zikky's comment about the ruins made Nikostraz grumble, "It feels strange to agree with you."

"Whoever made this place was in a hurry," said Colin, wiping away some debris that clung to the walls revealing faded ink. "But there's more of that bizarre writing style again. Siroun, look."

All four of them closed in around Colin as Siroun removed more of the dirt and scanning the faded lettering. Again, the language used to convey the next riddle was as familiar to her as breathing.

Knowledge is the key to expansion.

Zikky snickered. "Ha! That's somethin' Arcandus would say."

"Yet, it is too vague to understand the context." Lord Valter plucked at the nearby debris and rubbed it between his fingers before adding, "Hold that thought."

He walked over to the other side of the cylindrical room, and Zikky followed him while the others continued to puzzle over the current findings.

No matter how many times Siroun re-read the text, she seemed perplexed on how to approach the ancient statement, "I don't get it. Am I supposed to learn something and repeat it back?"

"Maybe it has something to do with the artifact itself,"

Nikostraz swept his claw along the rest of the wall. "Perhaps there's more."

Colin and Nikostraz continued their search, while Lord Valter found an irregularity in the wall and dug his fingers against the caked-on dirt to pick it away. When a small part of faded writing appeared beyond the remains, it motivated both mages to clear away the debris.

Eventually, they uncovered the message in full, and Zikky called out to the others, "Over here!"

Everyone moved to the other side of the circular room to find another passage on the wall. This time the words were written in the Drakish tongue:

To touch is to empower.

After Siroun read the statement aloud, a set of hands started rubbing her shoulders. She blinked in confusion before glancing behind to see Zikky doling out a massage.

"It says to touch is to empower," said Zikky with a wide grin. "I figure a little massage should do the trick. I'm just followin' instructions."

Siroun couldn't help but roll her eyes despite her amusement. "I don't think that's what it meant."

"Well, they need to be more specific. Why do these places have such silly riddles anyway?"

"So idiots like you don't have immediate access to dangerous things they shouldn't be touching in the first place," remarked Colin.

Now Zikky landed a sucker punch on Colin's arm, but the difference in strength was clear as the ice mage grunted and almost fell over. Her voice dripped with sarcasm, "Oops, my bad."

Their bickering remained ignored as Lord Valter analyzed the two pieces of wall scripture and tried to piece together their meaning.

"Is this still your beloved Arcandus at work?" said Nikostraz to the Duke.

Lord Valter shook his head in response. "Not to speak poor of the Archmage, but he is far too prideful to write in a mortal's language. These two messages pose a different question: Why is Drakish text showing up in the Fi'ro ruins?"

"Did The Great Three built this place?" said Nikostraz through wild assumption. He ran his claw along the walls one more time to poke at the stones holding the place together.

Zikky burst out laughing. "Oh please! Are ya really that forgetful, Nickle Drops? Dragomyr used to rule these lands with the Sylvani ages ago, remember? The whole reason y'all are so uptight about foreigners in yer lands now is because we ransacked the kingdom after we threw y'all out of The Hive."

Every muscle in Nikostraz's body froze as he struggled to find an appropriate response. He settled with, "I was born and raised outside of Niravad. Forgive me if I lack the standard xenophobia you've come to expect from others."

"Hm." She contemplated before saying, "Fair enough."

Meanwhile, Siroun vacillated back and forth between the two statements before inspecting the more recent scripture. Although the instructions were vague, it didn't appear as though they were written to be cryptic. She mulled over the black pillar, and that all she had to do was speak her real name. An idea came to her as she stepped in closer and placed her fingertips against the text. The reaction was immediate as the writing lit up, and the sound of stones shifting echoed within the chamber. Everyone heightened their caution as more sand snaked its way through the cracks. They could feel the entire chamber shifting in a circular direction ever-so-slowly. After a few minutes, another doorway along the wall opened up on the opposite side of the entrance. Once the new opening was free of obstruction, the chamber stilled. Zikky's ears shifted toward the entrance as she fanned out her hand to gesture no one to move.

"Somethin's comin'," she whispered.

Indeed, the others listened as something came from the entrance hall. An unnatural wind flared up from where they had entered. Sand whipped and scratched at them, forcing everyone to hunker down and cover their faces to wait it out. The howling deafened the senses, and they wondered if there was a sandstorm trying to make its way in from the outside. When the gale stopped, it allowed the group to stand and dust off their clothes. As silence settled in, they heard a voice crying from the unexplored tunnel. The words muddled together, but they recognized it as pleading. Listening closer, Siroun recognized to whom the voice belonged. When she looked around, she saw one of their party members went missing. She wasn't the only one to notice either.

Zikky scratched her head, dumbfounded. "How'd he disappear like that?"

Siroun looked at the floor to see something else.

Dread washed over her as she saw fresh splatters of red trailing toward the mysterious doorway. Every muscle in her body tensed as she assumed the worst. Without words her feet took flight, and she raced through the hallway to pursue Nikostraz.

"Gel-gel, no!" Zikky's voice shouted behind her before a gate slammed shut, separating Siroun from the rest of them, and leaving her to face her fears alone.

26

Though Siroun heard Zikky calling her name from a distance, she kept pressing forward. Darkness pervading her sight. It was by touch in which she now navigated the hall. Nothing but her footsteps and the muffled sounds ahead led the way forward. Adrenaline rushed through every inch of her body. She understood that her decision put them all in danger. Even now, as she crept blindly through the hall, she recognized that Felthane could lurk next to her without knowing. Those doubts washed away when she saw the soft glow of light up ahead. Instinctively her pace quickened as she progressed from a careful trudge to a brisk walk, then into a sprint. She eventually saw the chamber up ahead with her best friend lying upon the ground. When she entered the room, she slid to her knees next to him. There was bruising along his face and gashes along his sides, but they were shallow upon closer inspection. He would heal.

Her eyes softened to tears as she said in Drakish, *"Oh, Nik."*

"Siroun?" he rasped.

"What happened? How did he do this to you?"

"He grabbed me with some kind of claw and dragged me down here."

Siroun's eyes widened in disbelief. *"How is that possible? We never saw him following us."*

"I don't understand it either, but we don't have time to figure that out right now. He tried taking the Sinefine Bible, but I warded him off for now." He raised a claw to point to something past her shoulder.

"This doesn't make sense," Siroun shook her head and looked up to find floating only a few paces away, a small tome encased within a beacon of magical light: The Sinefine Bible. The source of their heartache and strife. But the victory was cut short as she heard more clanging of gates and the echoing of spells down the hall.

Something didn't feel right, but Siroun couldn't place why. *"How did Felthane find us this fast?"*

Nikostraz coughed. *"You need to take it."*

"I need to wait for the others to get here."

"If you don't take it, he will find a way to get it himself. We can't risk that. Go on!"

Her fingers trembled, and she hesitated. Gathering what little courage she had, Siroun approached the foreboding object. Every step felt heavy as she made her way to the artifact and placed a hand upon the wall of light. A pressurized force field prevented her from being able to touch it. There were no clues to reveal how she was to obtain the Sinefine Bible. But she thought back on the previous riddles within the ruins and knew that there was a connection.

Siroun gathered her courage and whispered, *"Beskonerynth."*

Her palm passed through the barrier, allowing her to access the Sinefine Bible with ease. When she took possession, the beacon dispersed into multiple small lights that floated around the ceiling to illuminate the room. The Sinefine Bible sagged in her arms when she held it. When she secured the artifact, Siroun returned to Nikostraz's side.

"We need to find the others," she said.

"I need a minute," he replied, struggling to stand. When he got to his feet, he said, *"May I look at the object that got you exiled with the elders?"*

Siroun furrowed her brows. *"Don't you think you have more pressing problems?"*

Nikostraz's lips curled a little, only to relent with, *"I know, silly me."*

Siroun juggled pulling his arm over her shoulder while holding onto the Sinefine Bible. She heard her name echoing from a distance. The second Siroun lowered her guard she slammed to the ground with the book ripped from her arms. Her palms and knees stung as the rough terrain tore through her clothes and dug into her skin and scales. With clenched teeth, she sucked in some air before looking up to see Nikostraz holding the Sinefine Bible in his claws and taking several steps back. A sneer appeared on his face as a familiar black smoke surfaced around him.

"My sweet little Siroun. How far we have come together throughout these years."

She shook her head, thinking her sight deceived her. "Nik?"

The sound of footsteps became louder as the Vanis Aer

mages filed their way into the chamber. Oddly enough, they looked unsurprised that Nikostraz held the Sinefine Bible and took a defensive stance. Zikky rushed to Siroun's aid by stepping in front as a shield. Not perceiving the gravity of the situation, Siroun watched as Nikostraz's visage changed to that of the one person they didn't want touching the artifact: Felthane.

This had to be a trick of the eyes. "What did you do to Nikostraz?"

The pale figure chuckled, taking a small step toward her, but the three mages took equal steps to halt his advance. "For someone so well-read, you lack wisdom, my dear girl."

Too distraught to process the insult, Siroun asked again, "Where's Nik?"

"He's dead," said Felthane. "I killed him long before you ever knew a soul by that name."

Through gritted teeth Colin said, "The Nikostraz is an illusion, Siroun. He's a Reaper Warlock. He siphons the souls of others and takes on both their skills and image."

No one saw Felthane move as he appeared behind Colin and struck him so hard that the mage flew against the wall and dropped to the floor.

"Colin!" Siroun screamed in horror.

A long, content sigh escaped Felthane's lips. "You do not understand how much I enjoyed that. Honestly, I'm impressed by the level of restraint you all have around that brat."

When Zikky attempted to strike him with a fireball, the warlock turned to shadow and moved around the chamber. Though Lord Valter and Zikky tried to follow his movements, they found themselves tossed with equal force against the wall, and the wind knocked out of them. With everyone but Siroun unconscious, Felthane reformed into his Adami shape and dusted himself off. His features were too calm for her comfort. Despite wanting to run away, her legs froze in place, trembling at everything that just transpired in a matter of seconds. Satisfied at his handiwork, Felthane leaned in and swept a lock of hair away from Siroun's face, making her flinch in reaction.

"Do not tremble, little lamb. I should thank you. Without you, none of this is possible. At the very least, you should witness the power this book possesses."

Steeling her gaze, Siroun gathered up her courage to speak, "Why are you doing this?"

Felthane gave her a look of mocking pity. "One as naïve as you could never understand the aspirations of those born to power. Fate placed a tremendous burden upon you, my dear. A responsibility that I am happy to lift from your shoulders."

Felthane stepped back and analyzed the Bible's construction. His fingers explored its uneven texture and enclosed around its small shape. Though the Sinefine Bible gave him a shock to the hand in retribution, he shook it off and continued onward. He pored through the pages before his smirk twisted into a frown.

"You have it now, so what happens next?" Siroun said, still baffled as to how he pulled off the entire ruse.

His voice lacked patience, but he humored her while further pawing at the Sinefine Bible. "Have you ever aspired to become more than what you are? I suspect not, given the fact that you resigned yourself to living in abject isolation without the slightest bit of motivation to go beyond the walls of that little hovel of a place you call home. I am not the same. My bloodline detests such a mundane existence. With the Sinefine Bible I will force the hand of fate back in my favor."

It was hard to understand what he was talking about. Without knowing his origins, there was little more to go on other than the sheer need for power. She watched as Felthane flipped faster through pages, eyes darting from side to side, the lines in his face becoming harsher as he kept going. His jagged fingernails scratched across the ancient text as his movements became sharper and erratic. Sometimes he lifted his hand and muttered in an incoherent language, but then paused half-way when the Sinefine Bible remained inert.

Eventually, he slammed it shut. "By the Liar's Tongue!" When he made eye contact with her again, Siroun sucked in her breath and her heart pounded. "There must be a catch," he muttered, more to himself than her.

Siroun noticed his hesitation in deciding what to do next. Based on what she observed, Felthane intended to use the Sinefine Bible moments ago but stopped. It took a second to fit the pieces together, but given what she learned while entering the ruins, something occurred to her.

"You can't read this, can you?" Siroun slunk back after she asked the question.

Felthane's eyes narrowed. His hand reached out to yank a fistful of her hair while hissing, "What I can or cannot do with the artifact is irrelevant to you."

Siroun shrieked in pain and clutched at her head. He didn't cling to it for very long, and the moment he shoved her aside, she rubbed at her throbbing scalp and bit back the urge to cry. With his temper already being short, Siroun needed to come up with a plan to stall for time and regain possession of the artifact. It was hard to stop her body from trembling, but she suppressed her fear and lunged at him with the palms of her hands, aiming for his chin.

Felthane reacted by clutching one of her wrists and shouting, "Get off of me!"

However, the force behind her ambush threw him off balance, and he dropped the Sinefine Bible with a hearty thud. Siroun felt like she now had the upper hand. She used her hands to push him. When the warlock lacked his demonic spells, he made for a feeble opponent. With a final shove, Felthane toppled to the ground, and Siroun made a dive for the Sinefine Bible. The warlock's groans of pain echoed in the chamber as he stood. This time his hands transformed into the demonic claws she encountered before. With nimble fingers she opened the book to find any spell she could while he descended upon her. However, Lord Valter placed himself in front of Siroun and summoned a minor shock spell with the palm of his hand. The spark hit Felthane in the chest and the man recoiled in discomfort.

Lord Valter looked over his shoulder. "Are you all right, Lady Siroun?"

She nodded, still too shaken to say anything in response.

"Good, keep that thing safe. We have some business to wrap up with our treacherous stowaway."

A clap resonated within the room, and the light

of flames emanated from Zikky's hands as she finished her transformation spell to reveal a new version of her enchanted battle armor. The outfit had elements of chain and plate mail that covered the entirety of her lower body and most of her upper torso. The style appeared sharper too, as parts of the armor glinted in orange and yellow. Meanwhile, the room's temperature dropped to a chilling level. Despite the freezing discomfort, Siroun felt relieved as she witnessed Colin staring down Felthane with a blood-lust never seen until now.

Felthane could only chuckle at them. "Four against one? That doesn't seem like a fair fight. Then again, I'm not limited by the abilities of just one person."

Zikky brought up her fists and widened her stance. "Besides Nikostraz and a druid, what other soul have ya got tucked away in there?"

"I'm surprised you haven't figured it out already," the warlock remarked with a cheeky grin.

The three mages muttered incantations, and Zikky took the lead since her maneuverability was on par with the warlock's shadow-stepping skills. Colin barraged the nec-romancer with ice spells designed to slow or stun Felthane, however the desert climate weakened their effects, making them slower to cast and lacked their usual vigor. Lord Valter's spells took longer to recite the incantations, and they were small or short-lived at best. It was not the display that Siroun had once seen back in Pustelia Crest, but she remembered that their enclosure was the reason behind Lord Valter's restraint.

"What's the matter, Fancy Pants?" Zikky razzed the Duke as she exchanged a punch with Felthane only for him to disappear and strike her upside the back. "Yer gettin' timid at a time like this?"

"You know I do not take extreme risks in tight spaces," he replied as he went to pull out his sword only to have Felthane descend upon him.

"Then allow me, Your Grace," said the warlock as he backhanded the man with a demonic claw, sending the nobleman to the ground. Felthane went in for another strike, and a wall of slush barreled at him, forcing his attention toward Colin. When the warlock moved in to attack, Zikky popped up in front of him.

"Nu-uh!" She surprised Felthane with a roundhouse kick to the face that sent him flying against the wall. The fire mage propped her hands upon her hips and laughed. "Ha! Thought ya could get past me?"

However, Felthane sprang back up, and the fighting continued. While the titans clashed, Siroun opened the Sinefine Bible in her arms and flip through pages. With so many topics to search through, she chewed on her lip as each page displayed a fragment of a different, yet familiar, book. She eventually found a spell that would do the trick. Meanwhile, a small bolt of lightning struck a few feet away, causing her to scream in surprise. Siroun scooted to a safer location before taking one last look at the spell. She read the foreign words aloud only to find the Sinefine Bible unresponsive. Over and over she recited the words only to have nothing happen. Then she remembered: To touch is to empower.

Her breathing quickened as she placed her palm upon the pages, and the Sinefine Bible lit up in response. Black ink crept up her hand along the skin. Her jaw tightened against the pain, allowing it to work its madness hoping to save her friends. She watched the Sinefine Bible's power seep out from underneath her, stretching across every inch of the floor. It took on the shapes of intricate circles that spun like gears in a machine. Some moved faster than others, allowing her to see additional words and symbols within the rings whose meanings were vague to her. When the circles of power locked into place, and the spell manifested, it caught everyone's attention. Despite never having studied magic in her life, Siroun lifted her free hand and pointed in Felthane's direction. Runes radiated underneath him, and chains launched from the symbolic letters that glowed near his feet. They surrounded the warlock creating a net that confined his movement. When he tried to twist through an opening, several more doubled over and locked him in place.

Felthane seethed at Siroun, "You think I don't know how to break free from a binding spell?"

It might not have been the strongest of choices, but it was enough to give the others time to recover. The room dropped in temperature as Zikky slammed into the warlock to disorient him. Fragments of ice crept up Felthane's lower body and encased him. He wasn't the only one suffering from the cold. Colin gritted his teeth through the spell as the tips of his fingers suffered from frostbite. Felthane struggled and resisted, taking every ounce of mental fortitude Colin had to keep the frigid binding in place. The struggle didn't last forever. Felthane twisted against the icy bonds, cracking and shattering the ice into pieces. The chains that held him exploding along with it.

Desperate to find another solution, Siroun searched

the pages again, only to have the Sinefine Bible snatched from her hands by Felthane. When the mages attempted to retaliate, the warlock evaded both fist and fire, changing forms whenever necessary to evade capture. In a wave of insanity, Siroun ran at Felthane and swung at him only to have a stunning spell strike her in the chest. Her knees gave out and almost hit the floor when Zikky came to the rescue, catching her by the upper body so she wouldn't crack her head on the ground.

"Nice try, but I grow tired of playing," said Felthane. "Enjoy presenting yourself to your false King empty-handed."

The warlock transitioned to his avian form with the Sinefine Bible hooked in his talons and escaped through the tunnel. While the tingling sensation in Siroun's body subsided, Lord Valter caught Colin by the scruff of the neck to prevent the teen from chasing after ghosts that had long vanished.

Colin tried yanking himself free while shouting, "Let me go!"

The older man adjusted his grip, but remained firm in waiting for the younger mage to calm himself. "We need to regroup."

"We need to go after him!"

"Colin, you have triggered the Hemophæther State," Lord Valter ran his forefinger down the ice mage's jawline and flashed the blood in front of him. "You need to stop."

Red painted both of his ears and nose, and he gained another streak of white in his hair.

"He's not the only one, Glitter." Zikky pointed to Lord Valter, and the nobleman dabbed at his face in several places until he realized it was trickling along the corner of his mouth. He swished the blood off of his tongue, then turned away to spit it out before pulling out his kerchief to wipe off the excess.

"No," he said. "Felthane struck me in the face."

Turning to Siroun, Lord Valter followed up with, "Lady Siroun, are you all right?"

It took a moment to calm herself. By now Siroun felt the effects of the paralysis spell wear off. She lifted a hand and wiggled her fingers before looking up at Lord Valter and said, "I'm fine. Thank you for asking."

"Good, let us retreat for now," Lord Valter's tone sounded grim. "We head for Ysile Marden as soon as possible."

"Felthane is gonna be houndin' us every step of the way, Fancy Britches," said Zikky.

"I'm sorry," Siroun interjected.

"Sorry?" Zikky blinked. "For what?"

Siroun's gaze lowered. "For letting him get away with the Sinefine Bible. First, it was the map, now the artifact. This is my fault. I should have stayed with you."

Colin started yelling with, "Damn right it's—."

Lord Valter silenced the ice mage by clapping a hand over the teen's mouth. "This is not your fault, My Lady. At least we do not have to pretend to play the fools anymore. Let us retreat and mend our injuries." Turning to Colin, Lord Valter's eyes narrowed at the young mage. "Understood?"

Colin pried the Duke's hands off of him and shot back a surly look before walking out.

"Tigernach's not gonna want us stickin' around to heal

up, Glitter Fingers," said Zikky. "We should leave Fi'ro as soon as we give Rocky back her toys."

The nobleman nodded in agreement. A slight pause followed before turning to his Skivat colleague and asking, "Do you have a way to get us to Ysile Marden?"

"Pfft!" She waved her hand at him with a carefree expression. "I can get ya on a ship outta here, no problem."

Siroun furrowed her brows. As far as she knew, The Hive lived deep within a vast mountain range at the epicenter of a vast desert continent. How they got into the place remained a mystery since she couldn't recall entering. With that in mind, Siroun said, "Does it involve forgetting how to get there?"

"Yes," said Zikky. "Hive rules, remember? But don't worry, gel-gel. I'll get y'all there safe and sound. Haven't broken my promise yet, right?"

A few seconds later the three of them heard Colin shout, "Are we leaving?"

With a roll of her eyes, Siroun marched on up ahead, leaving Zikky and Lord Valter to follow her from behind.

27

While living miles within an underground metropolis was something Siroun never experienced before, traveling on a ship was also new. Zikky made good on her word to find transport from Fi'ro to Anastas. However, the details on how she secured such a trip remained a mystery. They sailed upon the Hymn of Sailune, a brigantine vessel carrying both passengers and cargo to Ysile Marden. With days turning into weeks, it was hard not going stir-crazy as Siroun spent her days training with Zikky on the top deck.

By now, Siroun had lost count of how many days they had been out at sea as she searched for an opening and struck out her right fist only to have it captured and twisted behind her. Her feet then kicked out from underneath, and she slammed face-first onto the wooden deck. A deep grunt elicited from her lips, wincing from the pain only to pound the floor several times to tap out.

Zikky smirked and released Siroun, offering a hand to help her up. "Ya got better that time around!"

"Thanks," Siroun replied, although it didn't feel like it to her. She accepted Zikky's hand up and rolled her shoulder a few times. "Between Lord Valter's dance lessons, and our sparring matches, I don't think my body can take anymore."

"Yer a lot tougher than ya think, gel-gel. It's helpful that we can draw up the stances and yer able to memorize 'em so fast. It's just a matter of muscle memory now."

"True," Siroun didn't have the heart to tell Zikky that she was a terrible artist.

"Why are you so interested in learning how to fight?" Colin asked. The ice mage's body rested leisurely along some shipping crates near the rail to get a better view of the ocean horizon. His aqua eyes diverted from the waters over to Siroun and Zikky to watch their sparring antics.

Siroun straightened her posture before answering, "Because I'm sick and tired of being a damsel in distress. I want to help."

"You'll just get in the way."

Normally the response bothered her, but she grew accustomed to his hurtful quips and came back with, "Big words from someone who always pushes himself into the Hemophæther State for the silliest of reasons and doesn't get anywhere with it."

That retort sent a wave of shock to both of the mages as Colin's mouth dropped and Zikky burst into a fit of laughter. Speechless, he slid off the boxes and stormed toward the cabin.

"Was it something I said?" Siroun rolled her eyes before hearing a sailor cry out from the crow's nest that land was in sight.

"He's not very good at takin' a dose of his own medicine," said Zikky.

"I wish he wasn't so abrasive," she said as she grabbed a hand-cloth and wiped the sweat from her face. "Can't he at least give me credit for trying?"

"Eh, Colin has a weird way of showin' he cares. Luckily for us, he's willin' to tolerate anythin' as long as he gets revenge for Felthane. He'll get over it," Zikky grinned then snapped her fingers. "That reminds me, if Colin starts actin' grumpier than usual, pay it no mind. He's upset Felthane escaped."

Siroun got back into her stance and waited for an opening. She advanced with her right elbow, and Zikky blocked the strike with a left palm before grabbing her, sweeping her leg, and planting her back on the deck.

Sighing, Siroun relented to defeat as she said, "He's angry with me that Felthane escaped."

"Eh." Zikky tried to play it off as untrue, but her facade dropped as she said, "Yeah, sorta."

"I didn't intend for us to lose both the Sinefine Bible and Felthane."

"I know, gel-gel. It ain't anyone's fault. The kid's got anger issues, but that's not because of anythin' ya did."

That comment was an understatement. Perhaps it was best if Zikky continued sugar-coating things. Siroun took a deep breath and returned to her feet, dusting herself off. "May I ask what Felthane did to Colin?"

After several seconds of silence, Zikky nodded and ended the training session so she could fetch two chairs for them. While the ship swayed back and forth, Siroun listened in to hear what the Skivat had to say.

Zikky opened her mouth to begin, she stopped herself. "Oh, that's right."

Siroun blinked, but Zikky darted to her feet and descended to the orlop deck. Several minutes passed before she returned with parchment, ink, and a writing utensil.

"Aha!" she exclaimed, holding up the materials high in the sky with a victorious grin. "I knew I'd find somethin' to write with!"

Now that Zikky had everything in place, she sat next to Siroun and tested the quill. When everything proved to work, she waggled her eyebrows. "I'll jot down the main points as I explain. Hopefully, my hand doesn't cramp up again."

Siroun reached up and twirled a lock of hair from embarrassment as Zikky began with, "Colin's parents worked for the guild as historians. The Lockwoods were kinda like Fakil, translators of deity-based languages. Best in the business too!

"One day King Nathaniel comes and hands 'em a pile of old texts and other things. Said they found 'em in one of the abandoned wings of the castle and wanted 'em to look into it. Could've been important stuff, could've been junk. Either way, the King requested to have it analyzed to see if there was anythin' of importance for the archives. Everythin' was junk, except one thing: A diary."

Zikky flipped to the back of the page and scrawled a diagram to go with more notes. "It belonged to King Evander Hanmel, one of Anastas' greatest rulers of the ancient age. In the diary, he mentioned somethin' 'bout a great power that conquers kingdoms with ease. No one's sure how he found it, but his searchin' soon led to his permanent disappearance. In later years, the Explorer's Guild excavated the diary only to go missin' again.

"Anyway, findin' King Evander's notes was both important and dangerous. To protect the interests of the kingdom, King Nathaniel had it locked in his private vault. By now the Lockwoods had delved into the tome and examined its contents. If anythin' King Evander had written was true, the discovery would be monumental. All they had to do was crack the cipher that King Evander had written."

"What was the cipher about?" said Siroun.

"The very quest we're on, gel-gel. The information King Evander gave toward the Sinefine Bible appeared reminiscent to Æther spellwork. Folks just assumed this might've been Arcandus's collar or somethin'."

"Collar," Siroun brought a finger to her chin and tapped at it. "Haven't I heard you mention that before? What is it?"

Zikky shrugged. "Not sure how the details work, but every deity wields an artifact crafted for 'em that they call a collar. When they wield it, it amplifies their powers, but there's a catch. What that catch might be, I haven't the faintest idea. No one does, to be honest."

"Wouldn't Arcandus tell you?"

"Eh—," Zikky scratched at the back of her head, "he only teaches us what he wants us to know."

"By The Great Three," said Siroun, swallowing hard afterward.

Zikky flipped another page and cracked her knuckles a few times before continuing, "King Nathaniel ordered to destroy the diary. He determined that whatever his ancestor was chasin' couldn't have been good. The Lockwoods preserved the diary by destroyin' a fake. Somehow Felthane found out, so he waited, then cornered 'em.

"Through torture he extracted every known thing about the diary, the cipher, and the Sinefine Bible. When he got what he needed, he siphoned their souls from their bodies and moved on."

Siroun cupped her hands over her mouth, while tears welled in her eyes. Words could not come to her lips to express her sorrow for Colin.

Zikky finished with, "Colin was five years old. His parents hid him in a research closet when it happened. I can't even guess what's re-livin' in that head of his every day. I might give him a lot of flak, but it's just done as a diversion to keep him from goin' over the edge. Ya saw how many times Sparkles has had to reel him in after reachin' the Hemophæther State."

Siroun's voice trembled. "He's so young."

"Yeah. I still can't figure out why the guild put some-one this young on our team knowin' his mental state with our target. Seems cruel to me. They even promoted him to field agent just before assignin' him to me and Fancy Pants. No one up top cares."

Zikky set aside the pen and cracked her knuckles again. "Sorry to hit ya with this depressin' stuff, but now ya know."

Thinking back on her interactions with Colin, it made sense. "I always knew there was something off with him."

"It's not in his nature to be chatty 'bout his personal life," said Zikky. "Don't take it too hard."

Siroun bit on her lower lip while taking a moment

to digest the information. She tried thinking back on any clues she missed during this mission, other than Nikostraz's betrayal. "The other thing I've meant to ask: Who is Felthane? I mean, is that really his name?"

Zikky shook her head. "It's an alias. I dunno his real name, and neither does Lightnin' Rod. The King handed this mission to us himself, which means there must be a history between this warlock and the royal family. He's only notorious 'cause of the Lockwood incident. Before that, no one's ever heard of him."

"Strange," said Siroun, knitting her brows together.

"Yeah, makes no sense. I only get paid to capture or kill Felthane, not to sweat the details. They couldn't have picked a better gal, 'cause I'm awesome at bringin' down the baddies!"

The two shared a moment of laughter. Even with the sobering information, at least there was light-hearted banter to have with Zikky along the way. To that, Siroun was thankful.

The conversation shifted as Zikky plopped next to her and bounced in her seat with excitement. "Okay, enough tales of woe. C'mon, gel-gel. I've got a lot more to teach ya, and not much time before we get to port."

"Ah, okay," said Siroun.

As they retook their stances, Lord Valter arrived on deck. "My apologies for interrupting."

"No worries, Sparkle Buns," replied Zikky, who received an unpleasant glare from the nobleman as she followed up with, "What can we do ya for?"

"Please do not call me that." There was an edge in his voice before he cleared his throat and turned his attention to Siroun. "My Lady, there is one more topic I wish to review with you before we reach Ysile Marden."

His words caused both women to blink, but it was Siroun who asked, "Oh? What topic is that, My Lord?"

"Does Niravad have courtiers in your culture?"

Siroun shook her head. "I don't think so. We have Regents of different ranks that govern our lands. Is a court-ier something like that?"

Lord Valter ruminated on the question before reply-ing, "Yes, and no. Either way, I need to prepare you for the royal court and the requirement regarding social decorum."

"O-okay," she said, glancing in Zikky's direction. When no one moved, she blinked and pointed at herself. "O-oh! You mean now."

Lord Valter raised a brow. "Is that a problem?"

Sheepishly, she laughed. "O-of course not! I was just surprised."

"I figure now is a good time to cover more material before the ship makes port."

"Oh boy," Zikky smirked before sauntering over to collect the remaining parchment and writing materials, then walked over to Lord Valter and dumped the supplies into his arms.

Caught off-guard, he struggled to handle everything at once, but stabilized his grip on the supplies. "What is all of this?"

"Gel-gel has trouble keepin' large quantities of verbal material, remember?"

"Aha, I remember that being the issue," said Lord Valter. "My apologies for the lapse in memory. I recall the challenges mentioned earlier."

Siroun waved her hand at him. "Don't worry."

"Yer hand is gonna cramp up faster than goin' swimmin' after ya eat," the Skivat continued.

While Lord Valter didn't look displeased by Zikky's remarks, he wasn't smiling either. Instead, Lord Valter kept his expression neutral while turning to Siroun. "I trained with the most prestigious professors in Firenz. They taught me to take copious notes with the utmost alacrity. We shall tackle this challenge together."

His confidence brought Siroun comfort. "I look forward to the lessons, My Lord."

When Siroun glanced in Zikky's direction, the Skivat waved her hands and shook her head. "Nu-uh, don't look at me. I'm not studyin' a bunch of Adami etiquette nonsense. That ain't my thing, gel-gel."

"You, of all people, would benefit the most," said Lord Valter under his breath.

Zikky's ears twitched, and she gave him a mischievous smirk. "Would I?"

Siroun had to agree with Zikky. Even if the fire mage bothered to take the time to learn any social decorum, there was zero chance of her implementing it. To that, Siroun waved Zikky farewell and strode alongside Lord Valter. "I believe that is a mission best left for another day, My Lord."

"Yes," he said as he led the way back to the cabins. "I am afraid you are correct."

PART III

Anastas

28

THE AIR SMELLED of salt and city. Workers bustled about the docks as passengers disembarked and crewmen restocked the ships. Despite what Siroun heard about the majesty of Ysile Marden, nothing prepared her to see it in person. Her mouth gaped as she took in the scenery, all while trying to follow her companions off of the ship.

Tapping Siroun on the shoulder, Lord Valter leaned in and whispered to her, "This is where I must ask you to act with formality."

Her cheeks turned pink as she nodded in agreement. "Y-yes, Your Grace."

A satisfied smile crossed his lips before leading the group to disembark. Siroun chided herself for still reacting to Lord Valter whenever he came in close. The feelings would fade in time, but they acted as a nuisance. Her disappointment only compounded when she noticed a bright glint off of Lord Valter's hand and saw both his signet ring and his wedding band on display.

Zikky snatched Siroun's hand and wove their fingers

together. "Don't worry, gel-gel, I'll hang in the back with ya. I prefer yer company anyway."

A tug came to the corner of Siroun's lips as she said, "Same."

Servants and guardsmen greeted them from the royal palace. Two carriages came to retrieve the group, and Lord Valter rode in the first one while the others huddled into the second. As the horses pulled the vehicles through the city of Ysile Marden, Siroun gaped at the enormity of the realm before looking over at both of her companions.

"This is amazing! I can't believe you live here," said Siroun.

"That's the only thing it has going for it," Colin remarked in a blasé tone. "Wait until you get inside the palace. The place is a social death trap."

"What do you mean by that?"

Zikky tried dismissing the exaggeration. "Eh, he's just sayin' that the Hanmel royal family are big on image."

Colin glanced over to Zikky and raised a brow. "The whole family?"

"Okay, just one in particular. Prince Anthony doesn't say much 'cause he ain't the brightest. He smiles and nods a lot, but you can tell he ain't got a clue what's goin' on around him."

Colin shook his head and rested his chin upon his hand as he stared back out toward the streets. "Proper King that one will make."

This information alarmed Siroun. In Niravad the Grand Regents that ruled over the regions had to be both swift of mind and physique to take on such a mantle of high prestige. She wondered how Ysile Marden survived on a system that favored birth rite over capability. "Can the King not pass his legacy onto a more qualified descendant?"

"That's the problem, gel-gel," said Zikky. "The most qualified of the bunch is a woman."

Siroun raised a brow. "Is that a problem?"

"Try convincin' the entire patriarchy that it's totally okay if a woman rules over 'em when their wives and daughters ain't allowed that same privilege."

"Oh, I see your point."

"Princess Antoinette, King Nathaniel's eldest daughter, pulls the strings behind the curtain," said Colin. "Try not to cross paths with her if you can avoid it."

Siroun tilted her head at him. "Is she that bad?"

"She's one of the sexiest creatures I've ever laid eyes on, but she bites with venom, gel-gel. Even I know not to mess with that one," Zikky's haphazard smile hinted at the seriousness of the remark.

"Noted," Siroun nodded as she turned her attention toward the window to watch as they got closer to their destination.

Hjarta Castle was enormous and easy to spot from far away. Its shadow blanketed most of the city, but its pristine brick and mortar acted as a beacon glinting in the sun. Siroun swore the palace emanated a soft light. It gave off a twinge of hope, even when they passed by areas known to be seedier by comparison to the main roadways. Some people came up to the carriage to beg for alms, while others stared at them as they passed. A few times Siroun wanted to pull down the window flap to block out the attention given to them by strangers. But her curiosity to take in the city made her sneak multiple peeks along the way. Though inhabited by Adami, Ysile Marden was home to smaller groups of people from other continents of Clayne. They came together to chat and trade within the protective walls of the Hanmel Kingdom.

An expansive courtyard opened wide to the approaching carriages as fountains danced along the front of the palace doors. Servants and guards escorted them into the palace toward the Throne Room. Opulence radiated off of every wall, door, and decoration. White Marble floors contrasted with the plush red carpets running through the halls. Crystal chandeliers of every shape and size lit up the rooms. Every rail, step, corner, and baseboard were born from the talent of artisans who hand-crafted every detail in its architectural design.

Through the bustle of servants and courtiers, the group approached the royal throne room. Massive double doors remained open for people to leave once their business with the King had concluded. Siroun followed along as they shuffled toward the side where a smaller entrance allowed newcomers to filter into the throne room. Siroun felt confused by the covert practices she had to follow, but intrigued at how fluid the system operated.

As they made their way out from behind the curtain and into the grand courtroom, Siroun listened to the disjointed sentences spoken by a towering woman standing before the King. The center area remained reserved for those addressing the monarch, while further back there were a series of stairs that elevated up to reveal the thrones of the royal family members. No matter where you stood within the grand room, the royal family remained visible, and they saw you in return.

Several individuals dressed in red-orange and gold uniforms approached Lord Valter and gave their formal gestures of salutation. "Your Grace, the days have been dreary without your presence. So glad you have returned to us safe."

"I appreciate your kind words," said Lord Valter in return.

Zikky pulled on Siroun's hand, indicating for her to fall back so that the guardsmen could surround the Duke and lead him before the King. The three of them remained on the sidelines. However, their disheveled state made them stick out like sore thumbs in a realm of pristine cleanliness. Colin redirected the group behind a row of courtiers, leaned in and whispered, "We should stay out of sight for this. Don't want the King's diva to see us under-dressed."

Zikky stifled a scoff while listening in on the remaining conversation.

King Nathaniel stood and extended his arms to the court. "Then it is settled. Ysile Marden will provide aid to the Titanian chieftains in exchange for an alliance. As a symbol of good faith, our beloved Captain to the Royal Order of the Sanguine Sword, Desmond Gilchrist, shall take the Titanian Priestess, Lyonesse Foulkes, as his wife."

A round of applause filled the room, and the trio mimicked the crowd in clapping along. However, Zikky and Siroun picked up on commentary scattered around the room:

"She looks awful small for a Titanian."
"Must be the runt of the litter."

"She is still beastly to look at."

Gossip flooded the room, and Siroun tried to catch a glimpse of the woman they were so harshly critiquing. The constant shuffling made it difficult to pinpoint the priestess in question. One person she found was the stern-looking Captain of the Royal Guard standing to the side of the room, towering over everyone and wearing a displeased look upon his face. Topics of conversation moved forward, and now the trio overheard Lord Valter's introduction to the King by one of the court chancellors.

"His Grace, Lord Valter Flynn Alexander Rosario VIII, Duke of Firenz."

"That's a lot of names," said Siroun, in her hushed voice.

Zikky shrugged, unimpressed. "Part of bein' important, gel-gel."

"Guess I didn't realize how important he was."

"Titles sometimes impede missions. Lord Fancy Pants uses his title out in the field only when required."

"I've noticed." Siroun remembered his words from the night they danced in The Hive.

"—Siroun Fatima of Pustelia Crest," Lord Valter declared before gesturing in the area where the three of them stood.

The courtiers that first blocked them from view stepped aside to allow everyone to focus on Siroun. Caught by surprise, she swallowed hard and noticed that Lord Valter waited for her to approach. Colin gave her a soft jab in the back to force her forward.

Hazel eyes flitted in all directions as Siroun made her way to Lord Valter's side and kept her gaze to the floor as the King towered over her. At the monarch's sides sat a young woman and a man who were the King's eldest daughter, Princess Antoinette, and Prince Anthony. Princess Antoinette looked dressed to the nines over everyone else in the room. The elaborate train of her embroidered dress cascaded over the stairs like a waterfall of white gold. Every glittering gem was stitched with such care that the stars in the heavens looked upon the Princess with envy. When she stole a glance at the royals, Siroun realized how under-dressed she was by comparison. Her fingers fidgeted on the cuff of her weathered garments with the only solace being Lord Valter appeared no less traveled than she. Though he had cleaned up the best he could on the ship, his guild uniform was weathered from extensive travel. He tapped Siroun upon the arm to convey that she needed to enact the rules of etiquette with the King.

Her trembling knees lowered her into a curtsy, humbling herself before the royal family and following up with a shaky, "Y-y-your Majesty."

Whispers flared up around her. If the things she overheard prior were any sign, she assumed they were not fantastic.

"Well now, this is rather peculiar, Your Grace," said the King as he leaned in to get a better look. Siroun kept her eyes to the floor as he investigated her figure before saying, "I did not know they allowed Adami to live with them."

"Your Majesty, Siroun was a special exception since half of her bloodline is Dragomyr."

King Nathaniel's brow lifted. "Was, Your Grace?"

"Circumstances in direct correlation to my recent travels have now changed that status among her people."

The whispers turned into loud murmurs of conversation. Even the young woman next to the King let out a soft titter in reaction but hid her lips behind a fan as she leaned toward another young woman beside her dressed in a simpler blue gown that appeared to be her sister. As the volume in the room increased, the King projected his voice over everyone, "I will have silence in my court!"

Siroun shut her eyes tight and kept her head down in obedient reverence as to not appear improper.

"Always with the whispers." The King shook his head with displeasure before returning his attention to the Duke. "Your Grace, I hope you don't expect me to believe this tale at face value. Half-breeds of that origin never live beyond their infancy, much less come into the world bereft of physical deformities."

"I assure Your Majesty that I, too, was skeptical of her origins at first. However, I speak the truth. Miss Fatima has risked everything to aid my team with our mission at the expense of banishment from the only life she has ever known. Her sacrifice is a testament to her character and eligibility for a place within Anastas. I request that we treat her as an important guest under my protection. I take full responsibility for her actions while she is here."

"That is quite a high regard for a low-born of foreign origins, Your Grace," said King Nathaniel as he stroked his graying beard. "Are you sure?"

"She is most vital to recent events, and I regard her as a friend to the Vanis Aer Æther Guild. Perhaps, even, a future pupil. For now, let us leave that conversation for a different day."

"Most certainly," said the King as he eyed Siroun one

last time before looking to his councilors who didn't object. He shifted in his seat before making a flick of his wrist. "Very well, Your Grace, I agree to your request. We shall speak in private regarding other matters later this evening."

"Your Majesty is most gracious," said Lord Valter with one last bow, then directed Siroun back toward Zikky and Colin.

They called the next issue to order now that Lord Valter's business concluded. Every muscle in Siroun's body trembled, and she forced herself to remember how to walk straight. Her eyes glanced sideways long enough to realize that she was still receiving stares from multiple individuals. One, in particular, caught her attention. A rogue-ish looking man dressed in a manner that reflected a nobleman of high station. He wore his clothing in an unconventional style with his collar buttons and cuff-links opened. Every part and piece was there, but they lacked in presentation. His scruffy appearance added charm and personality to his devilish features. As soon as she locked gazes with him, a sultry smile crept across his lips. He then followed up with a wink before diverting his attention back to the main floor. Siroun could only suck in her breath as Lord Valter steered her through the crowd and the other two joined them. The group took their leave, with Lord Valter's guards aiding a path out the door.

When they exited the room, a noblewoman stood before them with a young boy in her arms. She had to have been of the same high station as Lord Valter, for her dress was made of the finest fabrics, and swallowed her frail frame whole. That led to another observation. Her lithe physique bore similar electrical scars to Lord Valter's that marred her body in jagged patterns on almost every part of her visible skin. Despite this, she radiated an aura of warmth. Guardsmen surrounded her, and her face lit up when Lord Valter arrived.

The boy struggled for release, and barreled toward Lord Valter with a gleeful shout of, "Daddy!"

Lord Valter's features lit up as he scooped the boy into his arms and greeted the lad with a hug. Soon after, the noblewoman leaned in and kissed Lord Valter on the cheek. "It is good to see you safe, husband."

"It is good to be back in one piece."

Siroun knew she would meet Lord Valter's family sooner or later. That didn't stop the pang of jealousy she felt in her heart toward the Duchess. For now, she swallowed the lump in her throat and put on a smile.

When the couple closed in on each other, the Duchess Ammeline brought a hand to her nose and tittered, "Dear me, it appears you need a bath."

"I am certain we all could use one," he chuckled before nodding toward Siroun. "My Lady, this is Miss Siroun Fatima. Miss Fatima, this is my wife the Duchess Ammeline DeFleur Rosario, and my son, Lord Donato Valter Flynn Rosario IX."

"It is a pleasure to meet you, Siroun," the Duchess gave a nod of respect before looking to Colin and Zikky with a smile. "I give you my sincerest thanks in ensuring my husband's safe return. It must have been awful out there in the wilderness."

"Eh, I'm not too bothered by it. Can't say the same for the others," Zikky replied as she nudged the other two.

Colin remained silent but responded with a nod.

Siroun, however, became fascinated by the palace decor. When the Duke cleared his throat to recapture her attention, she snapped back to reality and gave a series of non-committal gestures. "Oh—yes. Yes, it was quite dusty."

The Duchess Ammeline furrowed her brows in concern. "Are you all right, darling? You look pale. Should I fetch a cleric?"

"Hmm?" Siroun didn't plan to admit the real reason behind her sudden change in behavior. "No, no, I'm fine. I'm just overwhelmed by these new surroundings. Not to mention the trip here was the first time I've ever sailed, so I'm still a little uneasy getting back on solid ground again."

"Yes, I see where this might be intense for you," the Duchess's voice jingled like a bell in the crisp winter morning. Every bit happy and light-hearted. "Do not fret for you are most welcome. Having the Duke vouch for you ensures your stay is pleasant."

Siroun gave a silent nod.

Zikky raised a brow in suspicion before turning to Lord Valter while pinching Siroun's cheek and wiggling it side-to-side. "Duke Fancy Pants, mind if I take our dear gel-gel to the guild and get her situated? We might be here a while."

The discomfort sent a shock through Siroun's face as they awaited Lord Valter's response.

"Certainly," the Duke replied. "That gives me some time to catch up with my family and converse with His Majesty and the guild. We shall reconvene when I have concluded my business."

"Excellent, let's go, gel-gel," turning, Zikky gave Colin a nudge of her elbow. "I'm gonna go introduce her to Seb."

There was a roll of his eyes, but Colin waved the women away. "Don't get blown up in the process."

"Blown up?" murmured Siroun to herself.

29

$\mathcal{G}$ ETTING TO THE Vanis Aer Æther Guild was a long walk. The areas that housed the guild integrated into the palace, but navigating the routes were complex and riddled with fake entrances. One of Zikky's favorite paths brought them through the kitchen where she pilfered a snack and moved along. They pressed onward through a secret wall within one of the storage closets. Once she found the door, Zikky tapped in three specific areas followed by reciting an incantation that emblazoned the spot she selected with a rune. The stones gave off a few flickers of light before pulling them both through the portal. When they came out from the other side, Siroun stared in fascination as other mages bustled through the halls. Though everyone had the Vanis Aer emblem upon their lapels, the uniforms varied.

"What's with the different uniforms?" said Siroun.

"It signifies their rank and occupation in the guild," Zikky replied. "There's always gonna be yer fancy magistrates and council that oversee the different locations and hierarchies. Then ya got yer students and professors, but the field agents come in several classes. Besides the apprentices there's the Standard, Red, Bronze, and Silver guards. Then there's the Arcandus Elite which Frosty and I are a part of, while Fancy Pants is part of the Council Elite since he's a councilman of the King."

Siroun knew she already forgot half of what Zikky said almost immediately. "Wow, that's a lot."

"Speakin' of which, looks like classes are just wrappin' up," Zikky said before pointing west. "C'mon. I think he's this way."

Even though Siroun followed without hesitation to keep up with her fleet-footed friend, she wondered, "He?"

However, Zikky didn't pay attention to the question. Her sole focus involved navigating through the throngs of students and making sure Siroun wasn't too far behind. As they wove through people, they made their way to a hall that wasn't as populated.

"They've got him sectioned off from the rest of the guild."

"Are you referring to this Seb person you've mentioned before?"

An explosion echoed through the hall several feet in front of them, stopping the women in their tracks. Stone and debris billowed everywhere, choking them from the dust clouds. Siroun heard another person coughing, but they needed to wait for the dust to settle before she saw the mysterious person. They sat slumped on the floor, their back smashed against the wall opposite from where the explosion had originated.

"Yep, that's gotta be him," said Zikky with a smirk.

"How can you be so calm?" Siroun waved away the dust and studied the individual who looked like a pile of robes covered in debris.

"This is commonplace for him," she replied as she offered a helping hand. "Always good to see ya haven't died or dismembered yerself, Seb. How's it goin'?"

Groaning, Sebastian pulled himself upright with Zikky's help and dusted his hair off to smooth out his short brunette locks. Sebastian looked average in both height and build and appeared to be in his mid-twenties if she had to guess. One could tell he hadn't gone outside or taken a bath in a while given his scruffy facial hair and disheveled clothes. He donned a robe with his uniform peeking out underneath, and both looked as worn out as he did.

"Thanks," he replied, coughing one more time before shaking his head to clear the buzzing from his ears. When he gathered his wits, he looked over to Siroun with an expression of intrigue. "Oh, who's this?"

"Seb, meet Siroun Fatima," Zikky gestured to the other woman, then gestured back to Sebastian and said, "Siroun, this is Sebastian Di Mercurio."

Sebastian reached out his hand and gingerly shook Siroun's. "Pleasure to meet you, Siroun."

"Likewise." When Siroun pulled away, she felt the dirt on her palm and refrained from grimacing. Instead, she tucked it behind her back and wiped it on her clothes.

"Sorry about the explosion," said Sebastian. "My research gets a little volatile."

His apathy toward blowing up a room stunned Siroun. Still, his pleasant demeanor made her comfortable in dismissing any negative first impressions from the unfortunate event.

"That's okay." Zikky pointed to her unkempt clothes. "We just got back into the city today, and I figured I'd introduce ya to one of our new teammates."

Sebastian's eyes widened. "You're done with the mission?"

"Nah, but we're makin' progress."

"I see." He turned his attention toward Siroun. "Try not to let Zikky rope you into doing anything crazy. She loves living recklessly."

Siroun smirked and replied, "Says the person who almost blew himself up."

"Ah yes, that," Sebastian chuckled before clearing his throat.

A knock came to the broken wall, and everyone turned to see Colin gesturing at Zikky to follow him, "Valter and the others want to see us."

She whistled before saying, "Man, that's fast, I was hopin' to have Siroun hang here for a while."

"She's not invited to the meeting," said Colin, "so she can stay as long as Sebastian doesn't mind."

"Well, damn." She turned to Sebastian and said, "Think ya could keep gel-gel company while I deal with the big-wigs, Seb?" Zikky didn't even give him time to respond before turning around and heading out with Colin. "Awesome, thank you!"

Both Siroun and Sebastian stood there in amazement.

"That was… swift," said Siroun.

"Yeah, it's like that around here," he replied as a loose piece of stone clattered to the floor breaking the silence.

He gestured for her to follow him. "Come on in, I'll show you around."

They navigated their way through the loose rubble of the opened wall with calculated steps. Broken remnants of equipment were strewn everywhere. But there was no charring or heat when Siroun touched an affected spot.

She touched the broken wall several more times before asking, "What exploded?"

Sebastian used the sleeve of his robe to sweep off a pile of debris from the table as he answered, "I was tapping into an arcane leyline from a remote device that I constructed to bend the energy to a different location. But I over-calibrated the reactor and caused the event you just witnessed. This is only a small model, but now I have to trek back out to the main source to make sure the explosion didn't cause a backlash."

Though Siroun understood the underlying issue behind his explanation, she couldn't make sense of the details and feigned wisdom over the matter. "That sounds frustrating."

"Sorry, I get caught up in my work," he replied in a sheepish tone while using his forefinger to draw a rune upon the table before walking away. The symbol pulsed a blue light before disappearing, leaving the table pristine with his tools back in order.

"There's no need to apologize for something you're passionate about," she said, staring in awe. Siroun watched as he traveled the room and made various gestures and taps against the different surfaces with similar reactions. Within minutes the exploded mess vanished, then everything returned to normal. Only a few things didn't make it through the cleaning process, to which he discarded and walked over to the blown-out wall to analyze the structure. The one thing she knew was using Æther had a price, the cost of their life essence. Sebastian wielded his magic with as much finesse as Colin, if not better. The difference in the aging process seemed different, and she felt compelled to ask, "How is it you can cast without words and not age?"

Sebastian scrutinized the damage before marking several spots along the destroyed rim, then spread his palm to channel the arcane power upon the stones. The rubble sprang to life, and the pieces regrouped themselves before the final pulse of energy fused them back together. When the spell finished, the wall was back in order, give or take a few cracks and minor corners.

Picking up a chunk of melted metal that appeared to be part of his reactor, he tucked it under his arm to dust his hands off, and turned back to Siroun. "I guess they didn't tell you everything about me before you got here."

She shook her head. "No one elaborated on who you were, only that they insisted I meet you."

There was an uncomfortable chuckle in reaction to that comment. "Yes, in any normal circumstance, I shouldn't be able to do this without paying the physical price for it. I am supposed to appear older than Colin or the Duke of Firenz with as often as I cast my spells. However, I'm an exception to that rule."

"Why's that?"

"Because my father is Arcandus, god of the arcane."

Before Siroun replied, they both heard someone knock on an actual door from the opposite side of the lab. When it opened, a head popped through and called out to them, "Hello, may I come in?"

"Niamh!" The surprise caused Sebastian to drop the metal chunk upon his foot, and he grimaced in pain as it clattered along the ground. The young woman winced in reaction, and Siroun took a moment to observe the two of them. Niamh had a limber physique, with straight brown hair and matching eyes. Her ears had the same tips as an Adami, but there were a few flourishes of vines weaving along the edges through her ears. Soft hues of green shimmered off of her skin along the sides of her face and down her neck. She took cautious steps through the lab and toward Sebastian. Concern reflected on her face as she looked him over and furrowed her brows.

"I heard an explosion," said Niamh. "Are you hurt?"

A strange pause cropped up after Niamh asked the question. When Siroun glanced over to Sebastian, he stood dumbfounded, mouthing random words with no sound coming from them. The intelligent and articulate individual was struck mute, struggling to craft any sound into words.

"I... I... ah, I uh..." he mumbled.

Siroun cleared her throat. "I think his head hit the wall pretty hard."

Niamh squeaked in surprise before turning to Siroun and blushing. "I'm so sorry, who are you?"

"I'm Siroun, nice to meet you Niamh." Siroun put out a hand to shake, and the other girl hesitated before reciprocating the greeting.

"Likewise," Niamh replied before making her way over to Sebastian who was still battling speech demons. She picked at a patch of hair at the back of his head to look. Her lips twisted sideways as she continued to inspect other spots before sighing. While Niamh dug into her satchel to fish something out, Siroun noticed the emblem on the woman's uniform resembling that of a tree leaf. After a minute or two of rummaging through her bag, Niamh pulled out a salve and placed it in his hands.

"You're lucky that you didn't get a concussion this time," she said with an admonishing tone toward Sebastian. "I recommend conjuring something cold for the back of your head. This salve should help with any scrapes or bruises. I made it as part of my senior project, but I made extra. I know you're always hurting yourself." Her words trailed off as she fidgeted with the buttons on her uniform. "Anyway, I need to get to my next class. It was nice meeting you, Siroun."

"Same," Siroun nodded, and Niamh flitted out the room as fast as she arrived. A soft smile appeared on her face as she glanced over to Sebastian. "She was nice."

The researcher remained silent. His face flushed red, holding the salve stationary in the same position when Niamh gave it to him. Siroun waved her hand in front of his glazed expression with no reaction. She tried snapping her fingers instead. "Sebastian?"

With a final clap of her hands, she shouted, "Seb!"

He jolted and blinked before meeting Siroun's gaze. "What? Oh, s-sorry!"

Siroun giggled. "She's cute. Have you asked her out yet?"

"What?" His face turned a darker shade of pink. "O-oh, oh no. There's no way."

"Why not? From where I was standing, the affections appeared mutual. Here, let me see that," Siroun plucked the salve from his hands, and pointed over to a nearby chair. "Sit. I'll fix you up while you do the ice part that she recommended."

Sebastian obeyed with a sigh as he opened his right hand and a wave of ice swirled around before infusing into his palm, turning it a light blue. He then reached back and placed it flush against his head, "You just arrived in Ysile Marden today, right?"

She nodded. "Although Lord Valter mentioned something to the King of me becoming a future pupil here. So, it's possible that this might be my new home. I guess I shall see in due time."

Opening the salve, Siroun administrated the medicine over the scratches and bruises that littered his face, hands, and arms. The olive-green mush had an earthy scent that wasn't unpleasant but was still strong on the nose. As she worked through his injuries, she broached the question again, "You never explained why you hadn't asked Niamh out yet."

"Huh? Oh, yes, well—." Clearing his throat, he opened his mouth a few times before answering with, "I'm not permitted. The guild told me that my father would not be pleased if I were to engage in any amorous relationships."

"But he's okay with you blowing yourself up?" she shook her head, not expecting the response that followed afterward.

"Actually, yes." Sebastian winced at Siroun's next application of the salve before soldiering onward. "Arcandus has a direct investment in my research over the leylines that envelope this world."

"And he doesn't want you getting involved with anyone because—?"

"Because he's afraid that fraternizing might impede my research."

She smiled at that response. "Well, he's not wrong. The instant Niamh came into the room your brain turned to putty."

Sebastian's jaw dropped while Siroun smiled and said, "But that's because you've not admitted your feelings to her yet. Believe me when I say I was in a similar situation not too long ago."

She finished covering the last of his wounds with the salve, wiped off the excess, then closed the container. Setting it aside, she sighed and stared at the ground. Meanwhile, Sebastian concluded his ice spell and covered his arms back up with his sleeves before looking over to her. "What's wrong?"

Siroun kept forcing her smile. "I'm a hypocrite."

Sebastian tilted his head with a brow raised, but Siroun hesitated to say anything further.

"I should find a place for this," he stood and went to store the salve in a safe location in one of his smaller cabinets.

By the time Sebastian returned, Siroun sucked in her breath and blurted, "I have… feelings… for Lord Valter. Well, not have. Had. In the past tense."

Sebastian paused with widened eyes before he walked over and sat beside her. "The Duke of Firenz? He's been married for a long time."

Siroun's tone went sharp. "Yeah, I realize that. It doesn't stop a person from liking them. It just… it takes time to get over it."

He gave her a sympathetic smile. As much as she hated to admit it, Nikostraz, or Felthane, had warned her not to get too attached to the noble. Zikky dropped similar clues at The Hive.

"I wish I had known sooner about those personal details."

"The Duke of Firenz is a private individual. Too many people try to take advantage of him, so he only illuminates information as it becomes necessary. I've always known him to be protective of the Duchess Ammeline since she gave him a son. No one thought it would be possible."

Siroun blinked. "Why is that?"

"Being a lightning mage is a double-edged sword. It's powerful, but erratic at the same time. If you don't have proper control over the element, it has ways of afflicting not just you but others. With the Lady Ammeline, she miscarried several times before Lord Donato was born. Childbirth almost killed her every time they attempted. The Rosario family stems from an ancient bloodline of the first lightning mages. Any child of Lord Valter's has the highest probability of inheriting the power and its repercussions."

"You mean those lightning scars on the Duchess are from—."

He nodded. "Every child she's tried giving birth to has left their mark on her. As you can see, if she ever tries to give him another child she will perish. That is why they stopped once Lord Donato was born. Truth be told, I'm surprised she's survived this long. It's a testament to the Duchess' constitution." This brought an awkward silence between them before he asked one more thing, "Not that it accomplishes anything, but do you ever plan to tell him how you feel?"

"Oh no… no, no, no. That's a terrible idea," Siroun plucked a piece of debris from the floor and rolled it between her fingers. "Please don't tell anyone. I'm not even sure why I told you. I'm sure Zikky already knows. It's scary how she reads my mind sometimes."

"Zikky's an intuitive individual. But don't worry, I won't tell a soul," he replied, and the two sighed simultaneously over their current plights. Sebastian then changed the subject. "So, you might be a future student with the guild?"

Siroun welcomed the new topic. "That's the plan. I'm not allowed to go back to my homeland anymore. It appears Lord Valter is trying to find me a new place to live."

"You were exiled? From where?"

"I used to live in a small village within Libstravad with my father and brother called Pustelia Crest. Then something happened, and the council banished me. Right now, it's convenient for Lord Valter and the others to keep me around due to this mission they're on. Once it's over, I have nowhere to go."

"Libstravad?" he said while scanning her physique and tapping a forefinger against his facial hair in thought. "You don't look like a Dragomyr."

"I'm a half-blood."

He gaped in silence, and she knew he was processing the answer. By now the reactions became comical, if not predictable. Sebastian cleared his throat and added, "You mentioned you're vital to the mission, so you have spell-crafting capabilities, right?"

She thought upon the Sinefine Bible and frowned. "It's a long story, but I don't know what abilities I have other than speed reading and mass retention."

"Oh, a fellow bookworm!" Sebastian said with perked interest. "I have a couple to loan you if you're bored."

Her mood lifted at the offer as she responded with, "That would be great!"

Ysile Marden was anything but boring, but she was not going to refuse new reading material. The researcher made his way over to an enchanted cabinet that he opened by tapping on the cabinet doors. The shelves revealed a vast collection of tomes on magical topics.

He scanned through a few items before asking, "Do you prefer books on practical applications or theoretical history?"

She pondered that question before answering with, "How about both?"

He looked pleased by that answer and plucked two from the collection before shutting the cabinet. The magical locks glittered along the doors, signaling their reactivation before he made his way back and set them on the table next to her. One was thicker than the other, with leather bindings that appeared well-read by the weathered state of the cover and yellowed pages.

"These two are my favorite," he said. "The bigger one here is an encyclopedia of spells and practical uses for arcane and elemental Æther. This other one is a personal selection of mine on the theory of leylines and how Æther relates to an individual's connection to specific types of magical energies. If you plan to be a student here, they will hit you with an aptitude test inspired by this textbook. It might take you a while to get through the material, but if Lord Valter is vouching for you in some capacity, then that counts for something."

"It does?"

"From what I know, Vanis Aer field agents often vouch for their direct replacements. Lord Valter is influential since his missions come only from the King. If he's backing you, that means there's something special that he believes the guild needs within their ranks. Even if you don't know what you're capable of, he does. In a place like this, speed reading and mass retention will place you ahead of the curve."

A blush came to Siroun's cheeks as she placed her fingers upon the books to touch their textures.

"Perhaps there might be a home for me here," said Siroun with her spirits lifted.

She wrapped her arms around the tomes, and she pressed them to her chest, causing her sleeves to scrunch and reveal the shimmering scales that replaced her skin above the wrists. Sebastian caught a glimpse and reached out in awe, but she pulled back and frowned.

"I'm sorry," he said, offering out his hands. "I didn't believe it at first. May I take a closer look, please? I swear I mean you no harm, I just want to see."

She hesitated at first, but relaxed when he took her hand into his. Sebastian's touch was calloused, and scars marred his fingers from all the research gone awry. Yet, there was a gentleness in how he handled her, and he turned her wrist from side to side so he could analyze by sight. Nothing more.

"If it weren't for seeing it with my own eyes, I would never believe it to be true."

Siroun reclaimed her hand and fixed her sleeves while juggling the books so she wouldn't make a further spectacle of herself. "I know, people tell me that a lot. I can't explain the reason I became the exception to the rule. All I can assume is that my existence is by a stroke of luck."

"What if it wasn't?" said Sebastian. The question caused Siroun to tilt her head in confusion, but he continued, "What if you're created for a purpose, like me? If I could analyze your biological make-up, I might unlock the reason you defied the odds over others. Perhaps I coul—."

"Hey, gel-gel!" Zikky burst through the door, and Siroun felt her heart leap into her throat from the sudden intrusion.

"Zikky?" she blinked as the Skivat bounded over to them. "How are you back so soon? It's not even been an hour."

"Oh man, that meetin' is so borin'! Luckily, I escaped." Zikky flexed with pride before adding, "I see ya kept Seb entertained, but now we gotta go."

"Go? Go where?"

"I wanna show ya around the castle more!" Zikky flicked her gaze over to Sebastian. "Ya don't mind if I steal her back, right Seb?"

"Um…" he started.

Before Sebastian responded, Zikky dragged Siroun out of the room while shouting, "Thanks for keepin' her company, Seb! We'll chat soon!"

"Wait, Zikky," Siroun looked back at Sebastian, who stood there wide-eyed and dumbfounded at how the Skivat could swoop in and change the energy of the room in an instant.

"No time for hesitation, gel-gel. We gotta move before a mob of angry higher-ups finds me. Let's go!"

30

THE NEXT MORNING Siroun opted to stay in her guest chambers as she nibbled on some breakfast and watched the farmers tend to the fields in the distance from her window. Zikky spent most of yesterday dragging her around the castle to avoid her duties of the paperwork sort.

When a knock came to the door, she finished up the last bite of fruit and meandered over to see who came to call. No sooner had she turned the knob, a swarm of people infiltrated the chamber and placed scores of boxes across the floor and furniture.

It took Siroun a minute or two to summon words before stammering, "Wh-who—?"

A lanky Sylvani man dressed in an upscale tailor's uniform made of scarlet hues and silver embellishes fit for high nobility entered and replied in a snarky tone, "Oh good, you're awake."

His complexion was a pale gray with small, knotted crimps of skin outlining his facial silhouette around the bridge of his nose and sides of his neck. Everything from his snow-white hair to his manicured fingernails maintained the utmost care. Not a single part of him appeared out of place.

Bolts of fabric, boxes of shoes, and embellishments from lace to rhinestones invaded the room. Siroun gawked at the tidal wave of luxurious items and couldn't speak, much less move. The Sylvani tailor wasted no time as he clapped his hands and summoned his assistants upon her. They shoved Siroun onto the one-step platform, while others flitted about in a torrent of swatches and accessories to bring to the man in charge. They waited for him to say something as he took slow strides around Siroun. His eyes scrutinized every imperfection before reaching out and lifting a piece of her skirt as though it were a dead rodent. Perhaps he thought he was being polite, but she could tell he was not used to serving commoners as part of his clientele.

He turned up his nose, then addressed the main assistant next to him, "At least she bathed the night before."

Siroun balled up a fist as she repressed her urge to snap back at him.

Clearing his throat, he looked at her. "Miss Fatima, I am Tavris Silverthread, Master Tailor among the royal kingdoms of Seda and Anastas. The Duchess of Firenz commissioned me to ensure you are arriving in style tonight. Ladies, if you would."

When he stepped away, the assistants descended upon Siroun, stripping her to the undergarments. A wave of gasps and whispers fired up the moment they saw what they weren't expecting. Siroun covered herself as best as possible with only her hands for of concealment. The clamoring grabbed Master Tavris's attention as he clapped with rigor to enforce some semblance of order.

"What is this?" he snapped. Making his way back to Siroun, his lithe hand snatched her by the wrist and yanked her towards him. With careful inspection, he glowered at her iridescent scales and even moved her arm side to side as they reflected soft, rainbow hues against the light of day. His brow raised as he said, "Interesting."

He analyzed the scales that covered her arms, shoulders, and legs with the elegant merging into the parts that were flesh. Her skin displayed intricate black tattoos that flowed like wings and bore scripture of an unknown language down her back. He eyed the small protrusion from her backside and clicked his tongue in disapproval before turning her around to see the center of her chest displaying another tattoo.

Whispers rose among the gaggle of seamstresses, and Master Tavris flicked a hand at them and snapped, "Oh, do be quiet!" Then stepped back and rested a finger to his chin. He puzzled over Siroun's physique before concluding with, "Your bust is lacking and your thighs are on the thicker side, but you are an amalgam of beauty and taboo with your physical... eccentricities. I guess that explains the gossip with the aristocracy as of late. Between that ridiculous marriage arrangement and your arrival, it's no wonder the gentry of court are all atwitter." He rubbed at his temple before sighing in defeat. "Very well, I suppose this gives us the chance to be creative. Ladies, the silks if you please. Stick to the bolder colors, we can't have her looking washed out."

In unison they replied, "Yes, Master Tavris."

Before long, Siroun had swaths of fabrics placed against her body to determine the base color of the impending dress. Then Master Tavris took her measurements while barking orders on what shapes to cut and in what sizes for the bodice, skirts, and sleeves. The flurry of activity displaced Siroun's sense of time. One moment there was a bolt of fabric, the next they were already pinning it together into the shape that would soon sweep across the ballroom floor. Siroun noticed that Master Tavris designed the gown to accommodate her unique features while hiding the unsightly tattoos.

As the stitching continued with the first group, another team started giving her a make-over. They maneuvered in tandem with the dressmakers, scrubbing at her fingernails, applying a mud mask, and polishing her scales so they glistened. Never in her life had Siroun endured so much poking and prodding. If this was considered normal for a courtier, then it was not the lifestyle for her. Time continued to tick away, and Master Tavris moved on to the next phase which involved stitching the accent pieces to the garment. The assistants toiled with alacrity, hand-stitching the hemline at a furious pace and making sure the seams were well in order. A glint of light caught Siroun's eyes as they stitched away at the dress. Despite the movement going on around her, she recognized the thread they were working with and her lip twitched into a grin.

"Nexus Floss?" she whispered to herself, and Master Tavris's keen ears were quick to pick up on it.

"I'm surprised a woman of your lower breeding recognizes such a thing," he said with a smirk. "Yes, for this design it's imperative we use Nexus Floss since the shape needs to be exact. You'll see what I mean when we finish."

His words left her curious as she blinked at the dress one more time before an assistant turned her away to finish her manicure. As the dress came together through the passing hours, it was time to select shoes and accessories. By now they dolled Siroun up in a short clean shift, her old ones discarded and likely sent to get burned with the rest of the rubbish. The stockings and garters were foreign accouterments that required aid putting on, while another assistant fitted Siroun with a proper corset. This left Master Tavris to narrow the choices between three different pairs of shoes. All of them accented the indigo-blue dress still in process of completion. Setting them in a line with the heels facing her, the artisan tailor stepped back and waited.

"Try them on and let me know which ones you prefer," he commanded.

The shoes were too tall for her liking, and Siroun nibbled on her lip as she tried to figure out which one to attempt first.

"Come on, come on!" Master Tavris said, snapping his fingers at her. "We don't have all day."

She flinched at his impatience. In a fervent response to appease him, Siroun picked the pair to the far left and slipped one foot in after the other. The moment they were on her feet, her ankles started trembling, and she lost her balance. With arms flailing, Siroun toppled sideways upon an assistant who squeaked in surprise.

The clattering mess caused Master Tavris to roll his eyes and say, "How are you this clumsy?"

Siroun extricated herself off of the assistant and huffed

a stray hair out of her face. "Don't you have anything with a flat heel? I've never worn these before."

She lifted her foot and wiggled it in front of him. She was a pile of underskirts and leggings while she awaited the finished dress.

"No." His tone was curt. "This is the style."

"Come, come now, Master Tavris," a female voice interjected, and everyone halted as a sweeping of skirts floated into the room. Blond curls dangled from the elegant hairstyle that emphasized the woman's natural beauty in a somewhat tomboy-ish fashion.

The entire room bowed to the young woman while saying in unison, "Princess Claudette."

A retinue of Ladies in Waiting followed behind, stopping a few strides from their leader. Many whispered amongst each other as they caught a glance at Siroun. When Princess Claudette gestured for everyone to be at ease, she made her way over to help the girl to her feet. The Princess lifted her with one arm with surprising ease. The bulky dress did a fantastic job of disguising Princess Claudette's true physique under the pomp and circumstance of formal fashion.

"Master Tavris won't admit it," she said, "but I was just as bad in these things growing up. I don't know why we make such a fuss over footwear designed for riding stirrups, but here we are." The Princess continued holding Siroun's hand as she waited for the signs of trembling to cease. When things appeared settled, she led Siroun over to the podium and helped her sit. "There we go, right as rain."

"Thank you, Princess," Siroun mumbled, still star-struck.

Waving her hand, Princess Claudette smiled. "Claudette is fine while it is just us in this room. Once I leave it is back to formalities again, understood?"

"Yes… Claudette." The casual response felt unnatural upon her tongue.

"Excellent! Now, Master Tavris, show me what you have been up to with our honorary guest. I hope you have not traumatized her too much. We need her to be in good spirits when she arrives for the party." Snapping her fingers, her eyes lit up. "Oh, that reminds me. Lady Jeanne, bring me the gift from You Know Who."

One of the Ladies in Waiting came forward holding a mahogany box the size of a large book between her arms. While the assistants and other seamstresses twittered around her, Master Tavris saw the emblem on the container and rolled his eyes. "Drya's withering roots, not that philanderer again."

Princess Claudette frowned. "You would do well to hold your tongue, Master Tavris. Lady Jeanne, if you will."

Everyone's eyes were upon the Lady Jeanne as she unlocked the clasp and opened the hand-crafted box to reveal a gift of extraordinary expense. Within the velveteen interior, forged in platinum filigree, and beset with an array of gemstones as iridescent as the scales on Siroun's skin, rested an exquisite necklace with earrings to match. The room gasped, except for Master Tavris. Already overwhelmed by the events of having a personal tailor hand-craft a dress from scratch, this final gift of lavish expense made Siroun pale.

She slipped out of the heels and stepped back. "I-I can't wear such a thing."

"Do not be alarmed, darling, it is only a gift from a secret admirer. Quite the catch too," Princess Claudette gave a mirthful wink, but Siroun was not having any of it.

"What type of person gives a complete stranger a gift this expensive?" said Siroun. "It's not normal."

"Shocking," Master Tavris replied. "For once I agree with a lowborn."

Princess Claudette waved it off. "It is not a big deal. Besides, every girl needs jewelry to go with her gown. Did the Duke of Firenz give you a budget for that, Master Tavris?"

"No, because he's married and maintains his propriety, not to mention common sense."

Reaching into the box and plucking the necklace from its container, Princess Claudette made her way over to Siroun and fastened it around her neck. "You would let this poor young woman commit one of the biggest fashion faux pas in front of my sister? I know you're not fond of commoners, but I never thought you to be cruel."

When Princess Claudette clicked her tongue at Master Tavris, people could see he was getting testy. The color on his cheeks wasn't from benign embarrassment as much as checked rage. He took a deep breath and calmed himself long enough for a tight smile to creep across his lips. "Forgive me, Princess. I sometimes forget my place when I judge others."

"All is forgiven," said Princess Claudette as she finished up the clasps and took a step back to admire the piece from afar. "It looks ravishing on you. Once we put the pieces together, you will become a walking piece of art. How much longer until we finish the dress, Master Tavris?"

Everyone looked over to the assistants who were putting the finishing touches on the gown. One of them answered, "Not much longer, Princess."

"Excellent." Princess Claudette turned to the retinues behind her and said with a wave of her hand. "My ladies and I shall take it from here."

Siroun watched as Master Tavris clapped his hands to have the unused materials whisked away. With half of the crowd gone, Siroun breathed easier, placing a hand on her chest to where her fingertips touched the gem necklace. Now it was the Princess Claudette with her Ladies in Waiting, along with the remaining seamstresses that were sewing the rest of the garment with alacrity.

"You must forgive him. He isn't the easiest individual to get along with. Those who were born and raised within the region of High Seda are a touch… arrogant." A devious smile crept across her face. "Still, they mean well."

"I realize that I shouldn't judge a group based on the actions of one individual," said Siroun, with thoughts of both Colin and the villagers back home coming to mind as she spoke those words.

"My sentiments exactly." Princess Claudette smiled before gesturing to the swarm of skirts that followed her. "Let me introduce you to my ladies."

The five women lined up so that each could be introduced. There was no way Siroun could remember their names or ranks as Princess Claudette went down the roster from right to left, but every young woman came from other noble families within the Anastas kingdom.

Siroun's hand trembled as she waved. "Pleasure to meet you."

"With that out of the way," said Princess Claudette, "I believe we have an appointment to keep in ensuring your transformation. Ladies, it is time."

Excitement filled the air as they pulled Siroun into a chair and tended to her hair and make-up. Princess Claudette sat on the sidelines to guide the seamstresses on any last second additions or adjustments. Siroun remained silent throughout the process. She let the others gossip about the recent betrothal between the Captain of the Royal Guard and the Titanian Priestess. The intrigues behind the marriage alliance went over Siroun's head as the Ladies in Waiting discussed the implications of the match.

"Prin—, I mean Claudette," said Siroun. "This isn't normal for a person such as myself. It's not that I'm not grateful, I just don't understand the deviation from protocol."

The Ladies in Waiting stopped their grooming exploits to exchange glances before going back to work. Princess Claudette finished sipping on her glass of wine and set it down.

"You are correct, Siroun. However, circumstances are unusual for you. The Duke of Firenz is involved in a mission for my father which includes the Vanis Aer Æther Guild. Your other companions traveling with him are not titled either. Yet, because they serve my father, the King, that grants them limited privileges within the palace.

"Your involvement in our beloved Duke's mission is vital to protecting the royal family and requires your attendance at specific events. Of course, you cannot arrive at a party unless you are properly dressed. Hence, the Duchess Ammeline has made these arrangements on your behalf so you can attend in style per your current condition. We cannot have someone show up looking like a vagabond within the royal courts. Does that make sense?"

Siroun pondered it for a second, reflecting on Zikky's comments in the past regarding the connection between the mission and the King and answered with, "Thank you for clarifying."

"You are most welcome."

As they completed the finishing touches on Siroun's hair and make-up, the gown was ready to try out. With a resounding sweep of the fabrics, the ladies enveloped her in the dress and began to fasten the clasps while Princess Claudette watched in anticipation. At first, the dress sagged off her shoulders and hips. For something that Master Tavris claimed to require exact fitting, this appeared to be a complete failure.

She tugged on the straps, and hiked up the skirt before she heard the Princess say, "Wait, darling. Give it a minute."

Siroun did as she was told and stared at herself in the mirror. The fabric looked glamorous with its rich, blue hue and silken texture. Yet, she felt anything but regal in this messy bunched up heap of cloth. However, that changed when the dress twitched to life and shrunk itself around Siroun's body, hugging every curve. Nexus Floss had way more uses than stitching badges to jackets.

"Whoa," she breathed ever-so-delicately.

When Siroun turned around, Princess Claudette smiled and said, "You're ready."

The gasps of awe made her skin flush red. "I don't think this is a great idea."

"Nonsense," the Princess Claudette placed her hands upon her hips and held her chin high while eying the other woman. "Allow me to impart some advice: Never let them smell your fear. If I have learned anything from my sister, self-confidence is the number one thing you must always have. Swallow your fear and hold your head high. Cowering in a corner is not what the people should see from those who are on a mission of great importance to the King."

It was easier said than done. But when the Princess placed a palm upon Siroun's cheek and looked her in the eyes, she sucked in her breath.

"Can you do this for me?" said Princess Claudette.

The request was honest and earnest. Now Siroun was compelled to prove to both Princess Claudette and the rest of the royal court that she could do this. "I will, Princess."

"Excellent," she smiled. "Now go out there and make me proud."

31

"OH, HEY ZIKKY," said Sebastian before taking a step back and permitting her to enter his room. "Thanks, Seb!" She shut the door behind her and noticed that he had gone back to scrubbing at his hands with a damp cloth. "Whatcha doin'?"

"Getting ready for the ball tonight," he replied and glanced in her direction. "You?"

A burst of laughter slipped from her mouth before she clapped a hand over it and forced herself to stop. She could tell by the look in Sebastian's eyes that her little outburst hurt his feelings. Clearing her throat, she said, "I'm sorry, Seb, that wasn't very nice of me. I thought ya swore off goin' to these kinds of hoity-toity parties. That's the reason I came over here. Figured I might borrow a cummerbund or somethin' since ya wouldn't be usin' any."

Now it was Sebastian's turn to chuckle. "Shouldn't the same be said for you? The last time you went to a soiree like this, I distinctly recall you telling me you've sworn off the fancy folk."

"Oh yeah," Zikky mused. "I did say that."

He shook his head at her before gesturing over to his closet. "Take what you need, just remember to give it back."

"Right-o!"

Within seconds she descended upon the closet, sifting through endless amounts of formal-wear pieces before she found a cummerbund, cuff links, and a tie that matched her chosen attire. It entertained her to watch Sebastian have a vast selection of clothing, yet, wore none of it unless forced. He favored his guild uniform and robes marred with burn marks and patches. Having found what she needed, Zikky shut the closet, pocketed the cuff links, and draped the other items around her neck before glimpsing a suit laid out upon his bed. The tawdry color caught her eye, and she meandered over to get a closer peek at its odd shade of green.

Zikky looked over her shoulder. "Is this what yer wearin'?"

Sebastian swallowed hard from across the room. "Y-yes. W-w-why do you ask?"

She couldn't help but shake her head at the outfit. "Out of everythin' in yer closet, yer pickin' this? Ain't ya afraid Her Royal Diva-ness will make yer evenin' a pain in the patoot?"

"No, and I'm not changing my mind either." Sebastian then added, "I wanted to match."

"Match? Match what?"

Even Zikky noticed terrible fashion choices when she saw them. Then it dawned on her, and a wolfish smile crept upon her face. When she turned to face him, she saw the expression of panic in his eyes.

"Or should I be askin'…match whom?"

Sebastian broke eye contact and returned to scouring the oil and arcane burn marks off of his fingers.

While he pretended to appear too busy to notice her, Zikky scooted beside him and bumped her shoulder into his. "C'mon, smarty pants. Dish. Who's the girl?"

Sebastian scrubbed his hands faster. "I have no idea what you're insinuating."

The man could play coy all he wanted, but Zikky had a strong inkling over who it was a long time ago. "It's that Sylvani-esque herbalist girl, ain't it?"

When the soap slipped out of his hands and dropped into the washing basin, Zikky knew she was right. She saw his cheeks flush, and now he rubbed at his eye with his upper wrist when the soapy water splashed up and hit him.

As he bemoaned the stinging, Zikky grabbed a nearby towel and handed it to him. "Here ya go, silly."

"Thanks," he said, and cleaned up his face. "How long have you known?"

"Long enough to see she's a good fit. Yer clumsier than usual around her, but that's what makes it fun to watch."

Zikky heard him sighing while she pulled up the small armchair in his room and leaned back. "So can I assume yer her date this evenin'?"

The rest of his face now matched the reddish color of his cheeks. "Who, me? No! I could never get away with that?"

She tilted her head. "Why not?"

"The Headmistress said my father does not want me fraternizing with mortals."

Zikky raised a brow in disbelief. "And ya believe her?"

"Yes," he said before hesitating. "I mean, no. Well… maybe."

The feet of the chair made a soft thump when Zikky leaned forward and said, "Listen, I may not be a master scholar regardin' deities, but if it were me, I wouldn't buy a word of it unless I heard it from the big man himself. Y'know?"

She could see the wheels turning in his head as he stared at the water basin in silence. Continuing the conversation, she asked, "Yer how old, twenty-four? Twenty-seven?"

"Twenty-six," Sebastian answered before stepping over to his bed to look at suit he chose for the party.

"And how often have ya seen yer father since he left ya to the guild?"

Sebastian's voice cracked as he replied, "Never."

"Don't ya think the Headmistress is pullin' yer chain a little? Even if she was tellin' the truth, how long are ya gonna let yer old man keep ya cooped up in this castle?"

Sebastian didn't respond at first. Instead, he continued to stare at his suit before taking a deep breath and exhaling. "I have always wanted to leave this place and see the world. I will admit I fear the ramifications of my actions if I disobey my father's will."

Zikky understood what he was saying, but she shrugged. "There's always gonna be that risk, but I've found it worth the cost. Ya should be as adamant with yer life choices as ya are with that suit ya insist on wearin'."

That last sentiment garnered a chuckle from Sebastian,

who turned around and shook his head with amusement. "You've never been one to mince words, have you?"

She grinned. "Ya travel the world as much as me, ya pick up a nugget or two of wisdom."

"Why do I feel you copied that sentiment from the Duke of Firenz?"

Now it was Zikky's turn to have her mind read. With a half-hearted grin, she said, "Fancy Britches always has lots of nuggets to spare."

The two shared a moment of laughter before Zikky tapped the articles of clothing she borrowed. "Thanks for lettin' me use these tonight. Yer not the only one hopin' to impress a lady."

Sebastian blinked and tilted his head before saying, "This is a first for you. Should I be concerned?"

Zikky waved his question away. "Nah. She's oblivious, but that's one of her endearin' qualities."

"Do you plan on telling her?"

"It's complicated," Zikky replied as she got out of the chair and began heading toward the door. "She's got a lot goin' on in her life. I'm not gonna add more stress. I wanna help her have fun tonight, y'know?"

His concern shifted to a smile. "I know what you mean."

With their conversation concluded, Zikky opened the door to leave when she paused and looked in his direction. A devious smirk crept along her lips as she wiggled her eyebrows and asked, "Seb, answer me this: How many times have ya pictured Niamh naked?"

It took a second for Sebastian to register the words.

When he did, his eyes widened, and he clapped a hand over his nose.

Zikky cackled, before waving goodbye and saying, "Thanks again for the clothes!"

When she shut the door, she kept laughing all the while wiping tears of mirth from her eyes.

32

"Colin!"

Weaving his way through the crowd, Sebastian dodged around throngs of courtiers to reach his destination. Colin looked him up and down then raised a brow. Though Sebastian's attire was technically formal, all of that eclipsed the outdated style of the garment. The color choices were garish, with dark brown breeches and a long olive-green waistcoat trimmed with discolored ivory lace, and a faded gold-colored vest, making him look drab and out of place.

Clearing his throat, Colin remarked, "Not that I'm a fashion expert, but what are you wearing?"

"What, this?" Plucking the edges of the overcoat, Sebastian gave his friend a bashful expression. "I wanted to look nice."

"You should have stuck to your guild uniform with the rest of us. You will have a target on your back for the rest of your life if Princess Antoinette sees you. Even I know that."

Sebastian furrowed his brows. "Did Zikky tell you to say that?"

"No, but it's reassuring that we both agree your tastes in fashion are questionable."

Colin wasn't wrong, Princess Antoinette ruled the bourgeoisie with an iron fist. Those within the royal court understood that while the King was the authority, his daughter held the keys of access to him. Sebastian cared not for those trivialities, but he checked anyway to see if Princess Antoinette was looking in his direction. When her eyes panned in their direction, Sebastian shuffled behind his friend. Colin shook his head and continued watching the events play out around him.

Everyone in Anastas attended this evening. Lords and Ladies filled the grand ballroom with boisterous laughter as the King and his family greeted guests while keeping watch on the party. Music echoed everywhere, giving off a joyous tone as the décor of the palace held an extra gleam tonight. Sebastian kept an ear out for the guest names as they arrived. So far he hadn't heard Niamh's name called, nor had he bumped into her. Then again, there was little guarantee of her attendance given her position and rank within the guild.

He fidgeted with his cuff-links while envying how composed Colin remained in this social environment. Since the teenage mage was of common blood, he remained unknown to most of the guests in attendance and had no issue standing around and watching people. Sebastian felt awkward just standing next to him in silence. Despite his anxieties toward these events, he felt at odds with himself on whether to emulate the younger mage.

Eventually, the silence broke him. "How is the mission coming along? I see you've added another addition to the team. I enjoyed conversing with Siroun when she visited me yesterday. Is she enrolling in the Vanis Aer Æther Guild when the mission finishes?"

At first, Colin appeared to ignore him, but when Sebastian kept staring at the side of his face and fidgeted with his clothing, the ice mage sighed in defeat. "Don't you tire of asking a million questions at once?"

"I wouldn't be in my position if that were the case. I take it things aren't going as well as you hoped?"

Colin's jaw tightened, "Siroun's future after the mission is not a concern of mi—."

"Heeeeeyooooooo!" Zikky came in and draped an arm around each of them. Booze wafted in the air, and a hiccup slid out. "I see ol' grumpy butt here is being miserable as usual, eh? Eh? Eh?"

Her endless prodding elicited a groan as Colin pulled himself out of the bear hug. Sebastian buckled under the sudden weight placed upon him, giving her the chance to look him up and down in glee. A barrage of hiccups and giggles now prevalent.

"Ya went with that suit of yers."

Before Sebastian could respond, her face lit up, and she dug a pointer finger into his chest. "Have ya seduced that lil' herbalist gal yet?"

"What?" Sebastian's face turned so red that it eclipsed the drunken blush on Zikky's cheeks by comparison. "I-I… it's just… well… she… no wait… what are we talking about?"

Zikky leaned back in laughter, and Sebastian to tilted

with her. It took every ounce of strength for him to not topple to the floor. The surrounding courtiers glanced at the Skivat's antics and disassociated themselves by walking away.

Colin grabbed Zikky by the shoulder and pulled her upright so that the Skivat at least stood straight.

"We can't take you anywhere, can we?" he growled.

Zikky stared at Colin for a few seconds before her head arched toward Sebastian. "He's such a spoilsport."

To Sebastian's relief, the fire mage removed herself from his neck and toddled away from the two of them. "Maybe the crowd over yonder is more interestin'."

The two men turned their attention to where she was pointing and saw the Earl of Baldurholt, with his expansive family, swigging pints of wine and ale alongside the Viscounts of his region.

Colin shook his head in disgust. "At least she picked a group of her ilk, socially speaking."

"Lord Wolfram is an agreeable individual. I don't see her stirring up that much trouble within that family when they drink," said Sebastian before he saw someone approaching them at the corner of his eye, and straightened his posture out of respect to the couple. "Y-Your Graces, it's an honor to see you again."

Lord Valter and his wife smiled before gesturing him to relax. Colin made no such reaction of subordination, but he nodded to the both of them in respect.

Lady Ammeline's voice was full of kindness when she spoke, "Councilman Di Mercurio, I've heard much about you and your research of Æther-based leylines and how best to harness them."

That news caused Sebastian to swell with both pride and surprise. "You've read my thesis, Duchess?"

"I hope you don't mind. My husband and I take great interest in your work. Naturally, the guild allows us to be privy to your progress given our financial involvement."

"Wait, you're sponsors? How come I was not told?"

"It is not something I wave as a badge of honor, Councilman," Lord Valter said as he flagged a servant and passed around flutes of a bubbled liquor to raise their glasses in a toast. "To the pursuit of knowledge."

The other three raised their glasses with him and repeated the sentiments before clinking them together and taking sips.

At that moment, the party's herald announced, "Miss Siroun Fatima of Pustelia Crest."

The group looked over toward the top of the staircase in the distance to marvel at her attire. Sebastian caught, at the corner of his eye, Colin's jaw drop.

33

*T*HERE SIROUN STOOD, her silver hair pulled up into a sweeping bun laced in braids. Ribbons of silver woven in flower shapes, and small crystal drops added in for extra flair decorated her tresses. From the top of the staircase, she saw the entire ballroom and the people within. Anxiety welled up in her chest, but she closed her eyes and took a deep breath. Her presence drew so much attention that even Princess Antoinette took time to eye the newcomer when Siroun inched her way down the stairs. As her hand gripped the railing, she tried her best to exude confidence per Princess Claudette's advice.

The deep blue hue with the mermaid silhouette stood out in the sea of whites, beiges, and pastels. Some gasped as they caught glimpses of her iridescent scales shimmering through one slit on the side of her upper skirts. The top bodice covered up the back and around the neckline in silk and lace, ensuring that the tattoos marring her body remained hidden. Her dress also featured open bell-sleeves with sheer fabric and blue hemming exposing the scales along her arms while still giving the illusion of being covered. The pièce de résistance that completed the ensemble included the raindrop earrings set in platinum filigree with onyx stones in a Briolette-shaped cut gifted to her by the unnamed admirer.

From across the room, Siroun saw the royal sisters exchange smiles and converse after taking time to look her way. She struggled to not reach up and twirl her hair out of nervousness. At the corner of her eye, she caught Colin and Sebastian gaping at her from afar. Two seconds later, the ice mage averted his gaze.

When the song changed, people cleared the dance floor so that a couple could perform a special number. Siroun used this time to blend into the crowd, skirting behind on-lookers while her eyes fixated on the ground. She wove through the throngs of people before she saw a set of shoes block her path. Looking up, Siroun found Lord Valter and his wife there to greet her.

"Good evening, Your Graces." Her curtsy lacking finesse as she tried not to topple over in the heels.

"You look most lovely tonight, Miss Siroun," said Lady Ammeline. "As usual, Master Tavris has a discerning eye for beauty. I am most pleased with the results given the lack of time."

"Thank you, Duchess. I'm flattered," said Siroun as she rubbed at her left arm before adding, "a-and grateful."

While Lady Ammeline was smiling, Lord Valter reflected the opposite expression. "Agreed. Though I must inquire, who provided you the earrings?"

Siroun's hand reached up to finger the sizable gemstone and replied, "I'm not sure. Princess Claudette said they were from a secret admirer."

The answer caused Lord Valter's jaw to tighten, making Siroun happy that she didn't mention the matching necklace. Even with Lady Ammeline's delicate touch upon his arm, he knew something Siroun didn't.

"Is that a problem, Your Grace?" Siroun's confidence somewhat shaken seeing Lord Valter in a disapproving state. However, she wasn't going to shy away from him when she had done nothing wrong. The awkward silence that befell Lord Valter enticed Siroun to continue with, "Princess Claudette said it's shameful to arrive with no jewelry, and I didn't want to embarrass you, so I accepted the gift if only to appear suitable to an event such as this."

When there was no reply, Lady Ammeline nudged him. "Your Grace?"

Coming back to his senses, Lord Valter blinked and shook his head. "Oh, yes. Well, Princess Claudette is insightful with those things."

His gaze redirected toward the dance floor where the same roguish man with the unbuttoned collar and tousled hair performed a number with another woman. The music's fast-paced tempo energized the crowd, while the pair moved through the sequences with quick steps. Everyone watched in awe, but Siroun's eyes returned to Lord Valter who appeared unimpressed by the center display. When the song came to a close, rounds of applause filled the air, and the dance pair took their leave off the floor.

Lord Valter watched the gentleman like a hawk. The Duchess tugged on his arm twice and said, "Come, Your Grace. Let us engage in pleasantries."

Siroun couldn't help her curiosity as she asked the Duchess, "Pardon me, but who is that person?"

The question caught the Lady Ammeline by surprise. With a slight stutter, she attempted to explain, but Lord Valter answered the question instead, "That is the Duke of Vasile, Marcus Rovani." His words lacked the usual tone of respect whenever he addressed people by name. "He is a philanderer and unscrupulous with his business practices. Do well to avoid him while you are a guest within this castle, Miss Fatima."

Siroun blinked in shock at his blatant command. Lord Valter's unnatural behavior, along with Lady Ammeline's reaction, showed a tense history between the two Dukes. She flicked her gaze at the Duke of Vasile before looking Lord Valter in the eyes and replying, "I promise to take your words to heart, Your Grace."

Lady Ammeline smiled in relief as she nudged Lord Valter toward another group of guests. With a thankful nod, she gave Siroun a gentle squeeze on the arm. "My husband and I need to pay our respects to his cousin. Please, enjoy the party in the meantime."

They shuffled off, and Siroun did her best to maintain a happy facade. Once they were out of sight, her posture relaxed, and she took this time to watch the room. The people on the dance floor twirled to the song, Colin and Sebastian disappeared from sight, and she could hear Zikky in the far distance roiling in laughter with another Lord and his family.

At the opposite side of the room, she noticed the betrothed Titanian Priestess who dwarfed everyone around her. While the woman looked stunning, her face reflected nothing but disappointment. Every few seconds she scanned the room to search for someone, only to frown while her jaw tightened. Upon further realization, Siroun looked around and noticed that the Captain of the Royal Guard was not present. Figuring the two could keep each other company, Siroun took a step in Lyonesse's direction when the Titanian wiped away a tear and stormed off looking incensed.

During this time of observation, Siroun didn't notice the song finish. However, she sensed folks nearby shift away from her, and looked up to find an outstretched hand and the charming smile of Lord Marcus Rovani greet her, "Care to dance, M'lady?"

Everyone's eyes were upon her. While she contemplated his offer, she searched around for her guardians. With neither Lord Valter nor his wife present, she returned her gaze to the outstretched hand.

Lord Marcus noticed her reluctance and said in a low tone, "I will be most hurt if you left me hanging here, Luv."

"I…" she wanted to say no to this stranger out of fear of what Lord Valter told her earlier.

Lord Marcus raised a brow. "You?"

She searched again for Lord Valter, with no avail. "I-I'm afraid I'm a personal guest of the Duke of Firenz, Your Grace."

"Yes, I know of that." His smile radiated confidence as he took a step forward and murmured, "You need not worry of my intentions, as I'm sure you've heard plenty from your guardian. I am just a man asking for a dance, nothing more."

Siroun reflected on his words and weighed her options.

Lord Valter warned that he was a womanizer, but considering she held no romantic interest in the man, she didn't see the harm in accepting the offer. She slipped her hand into his, and a rush of warmth filled her body. She felt a familiar bond with him, as though she had met him before a long time ago but couldn't place where.

With her hand secured, he pressed his lips upon her knuckles. "I appreciate you saving me from embarrassment, M'lady. My heart would have been most distraught had you left me behind."

Those words made her laugh, and he mirrored her good humor. Lord Marcus led her to the one side of the dance floor, then made his way to the opposite side. Murmurs filled the air as the plucking of strings began the song. Siroun saw the Duke take a bow, and she curtsied. With formalities out of the way, they approached each other.

Confidence radiated off of him as he leaned in and said, "Ignore everyone and relax. We'll start slow so you can follow my lead."

She nodded, while he placed his hands upon her hips and whispered, "Dance."

A warmth spread throughout her body, and the quivering in her ankles from the heeled shoes vanished. The song transitioned into a sultry tune, and Lord Marcus guided her through the beginning steps. Though she had never danced this way before, her body moved on instinct. It was a different experience compared to dancing with Lord Valter back in Fi'ro. With each step to the rhythm of quick-quick-slow, Siroun gained confidence in her ability to nail the moves. Lord Marcus steered her into an outward twirl before pulling her in and dipping her low. Suddenly a pulse of energy rippled through her back. The sensation shook her to the core, and she stumbled, mis-stepping on Lord Marcus' shoe.

Even though his eye twinged from the discomfort, he asked, "Are you all right, M'lady?"

The pain subsided as soon as it came, and Siroun calmed her nerves while stammering out, "I-I'm fine. You?"

"A little shoe-stomp never deterred me," he said before looking concerned. "Are you sure you're well?"

"Hm? Oh, yes," she lied. "I'm still not used to walking in heels, much less dancing in them."

The shoe-stomp was the least of her worries. Siroun wanted to find out why her body shook to the core like that. However, the increasing tempo of the song along with the sweeping steps made it so she had no time to dwell on a sensation that now passed. Courtiers had a field day watching the two of them, but Lord Marcus pulled her attention back to him as the song intensified its pace.

Siroun focused on the moment and listened to the foreign lyrics sung by the performer. The words were a mix of the Adami dialect with Drakish pronunciation techniques. There was more rolling of the letters on the tip of the tongue rather than the back of the throat.

She quirked her brow. "I've never heard this language before."

"Really?" he replied with bemusement. "It's Stzovylic."

"Stzovylic?" she repeated, stumbling through the pronunciation.

"The native language of my homeland in Vasile."

"Oh my, it's lovely. I didn't realize the Adami had more dialects."

Lord Marcus looked at her with a curious smirk. "Is that so?"

When Siroun nodded in affirmation, he replied, "Most interesting. I would have thought one born from Niravad recognized the linguistics given its history."

She blinked while performing another twirl. "History?"

"It is said that Stzovylic is the foundation of the Drakish language when they came into being by their creators."

"That... that can't be right," she replied. "The Great Three created the Dragomyr in their image."

"Perhaps," Lord Marcus mused, "but did The Great Three create them first?"

"I beg your pardon?"

"The Adami were the first mortals created during the ancient era. Were you not aware of that?"

Siroun puffed out her cheeks in both frustration and embarrassment. While she wanted to tell the Duke he was wrong, she didn't want to debate a nobleman in the middle of a dance. He must have realized her displeasure, because he smiled and said, "My apologies if I have offended you, M'lady. Consider this my blunder in trying to impress you with an abundance of arrogance."

To that, she admonished him by shaking her head, but forgave him with a smile while the Duke swept her across the room. The intricate footwork consumed Siroun's focus but transformed into enjoyment as she progressed. She felt lighter on her feet after the weird bout of discomfort from earlier. When the song changed into verse two of the scintillating lyrics, the same steps applied, but at greater speed and flourish. Instead of one twirl, there were three fast-paced ones. Every move more exaggerated than the last. The crowds transitioned from whispering to clapping in unison, while the men in the audience whistled. Siroun picked up her steps as though she had breathed the art of dance her entire life. Even when she made a mistake, Lord Marcus adapted and carried on as though it were part of the sequence.

During the dance, Siroun inspected the room to see who else was watching and caught Lord Valter's stony gaze before dropping his drink. Siroun somewhat regretted the decision to dance with the Duke of Vasile knowing it might disappoint Lord Valter, but she was having too much fun to care.

The song ended, and the two posed on the final note. A round of applause resounded as Siroun regained her breath, and Lord Marcus bowed to their audience. One had to admire the level of confidence the Duke had with this grand display.

When it was on to the next song, the Duke leaned in close making Siroun's face flush and whispered, "You are welcome to my chamber any time, M'lady."

He placed a delicate kiss upon her hand, then bowed in respect before rejoining his retinue. Meanwhile, Siroun drifted off of the dance floor, her fingers tucking the same lock of hair behind her ear as she smiled.

The calm Siroun experienced was shattered when a nimble figure bounded in front of her, shouting, "Surprise!"

"Gah!" Siroun clutched at her chest, then performed a double-take when she realized who it was. "Zikky! You nearly gave me a heart attack."

Even though Zikky was her usual mischievous self, Siroun couldn't help but look the other woman up and down to admire the attire. She wore the formal men's version of the Vanis Aer Æther Guild's elite uniform. Her wild locks of hair now slicked back and groomed. Though she appeared inebriated, she carried herself well. Siroun's heart went from pounding out of surprise, to that of admiration for the other woman. Just like the Skivat diplomat, Zikky looked handsome when dressed up to the nines.

However, Zikky killed the mood by giggling before being cut short by a loud hiccup. "Ya were awesome, gel-gel! I didn't know ya could dance."

"Are you drunk?" Siroun knew the answer to that question, but she hoped that highlighting the bad habit got the other woman to recognize her outlandish behavior.

Zikky grinned. "Maaaybe."

Sighing, Siroun shook her head. "Don't you think it's excessive?"

"Nonsense! It's a party. It's what we're supposed to do. But seriously," Zikky's tone shifted to something calmer, "Ya were amazin', gel-gel."

"Oh." A blush came to her cheeks as she twirled a ringlet of hair around her finger. "Thanks."

Zikky offered a hand. "Wanna dance?"

Siroun let go of her hair long enough to wave the suggestion off. "Zikky, I don't think they appreciate Hive dances—whoa!"

In a heartbeat, Zikky took Siroun's hand and pulled her into a closed dance position. Her left hand snuck around to the small of Siroun's lower back. They were only inches from each other's noses, and Siroun swallowed the lump in her throat. Her heart raced in a way she hadn't experienced before.

"Duke Super-Suave might have a trick or two up his sleeve, but I'm not unarmed in that department," Zikky said with a smirk.

Siroun's mouth opened then shut several times, unable to find the words to speak. All the while finding herself transfixed to the twinkle in Zikky's mirthful eyes. A romantic tune played in the background, the Skivat's athletic physique pressed through the uniform against her body. As they swayed to the music, Siroun rested her head on Zikky's shoulder and sighed while the world around her slipped away. For this one moment, she didn't have to think about Felthane, the mission, or anyone else. Even if they received a glance or two by nearby guests, Siroun didn't care. While violins played, and the piano's keys danced, she enjoyed the safe embrace of Zikky's arms around her and knew everything would turn out fine.

Her bliss ended when a man cleared his throat beside them. They both pulled away and found Lord Valter fidgeting with his cuff links, looking irate.

"Miss Fatima, may I speak with you?" he said. The tone in his voice sounded both amiable and perturbed, like an angry parent summoning their child in public without making a scene.

Zikky started hiccuping again before sliding over to poke him in the cheek. "What's wrong *hic* with ya, Fancy Britches?"

He swatted Zikky's hand away and looked back at Siroun. "Now, please."

"Yes, Your Grace," said Siroun. Her fingers gripped at a small piece of fabric in her skirt and twisted it as she followed Lord Valter out of the ballroom and around the corner. Zikky tagged along, despite the silent glare from the Duke.

"Is it prudent for you to grace us with your presence?" The edge in Lord Valter's voice was becoming palpable with each second as he eyed Zikky.

"Since yer gonna give her a tongue lashin', yeah. I'd say it's prudent," she said, giving Siroun a confident thumbs up through more hiccups. "I got yer back, gel-gel."

Though Siroun's curiosity focused more on how Zikky managed to re-summon her hiccups from thin air, she forced herself to face Lord Valter and said, "Yes?"

She kept the discussion simple given the obvious impending topic.

"Help me understand," said Lord Valter, "how you ended up dancing with Lord Marcus?"

The tone in which he asked his question jarred her. Siroun knew there were hostilities, and she had every intention of avoiding Lord Marcus as much as possible on Lord Valter's behalf. However, she would not be rude to an individual of whom she had no qualms. With this in mind, Siroun straightened her stance and didn't shirk from facing him, saying, "Because he asked me."

Zikky's eyes widened at the response, and her ears twitched in delight. Lord Valter stood there stunned. It took him a moment to find his verbal footing before he said, "Miss Fatima, I realize this environment is new and overwhelming. I thought I considered my protection adequate for you to trust me when I urge you to stay away from specific individuals."

"To be honest, Your Grace, I'm not sure whom to trust these days," said Siroun as she held up her hand to count off reasons on her fingers. "My best friend betrays me and is the very person we've been chasing for the past month or more."

Zikky hiccuped before adding, "That was a surprise."

"Then I find out you're a Duke."

"Yeah, that's our fault," another hiccup followed.

"Last, you interrupted my dance with Zikky so you could lecture me about not socializing with a Lord you have a vendetta against?"

Zikky turned her gaze to Lord Valter and said, "I'm *hic* pinnin' that one on you."

Lord Valter lost patience with the incessant hiccuping and shot Zikky a glare before returning his attention to Siroun, "I do not understand why it is so difficult to obey one simple request, Miss Fatima."

"People were staring at me!" Siroun said with exasperation. "Everyone was watching me. Do you think I was going to be rude and decline him?"

"You are my protected guest, Miss Fatima. They were expecting you to decline."

Siroun felt her skin getting hot with rage. "How am I supposed to understand every stupid social nuance when I just got here?"

"I thought we covered this ahead of time. I gave you one simple command to follow and you disregarded it. That is why I am upset."

"Well, I'm sorry I'm such a disappointment!"

Tears began to pool in Siroun's eyes, and Zikky patted her on the back while shooting a look at Lord Valter, muttering, "Nice one, Sparkles."

He tilted his head, frustration cracking through the

pristine exterior as his eyes narrowed at Zikky. "What do you mean by that?"

"You're so infuriating!" Siroun blurted out. "I can't believe I have feelings for someone as nit-picky as you."

The moment those words slipped from her mouth, she clapped a hand over it and stared at Zikky with wide eyes. She never intended to admit such a thing to him, but anger and frustration overrode her judgment, and now she regretted it.

Lord Valter opened his mouth to respond only to be at a loss for words. When the moment of speechlessness passed, he looked at Zikky and asked, "Were you aware of this?"

With her arms crossed over her chest, Zikky returned to him a sardonic smile. "Obliviousness is a curse plagued by many."

Lord Valter roll his eyes. "How poetic."

"Yer not the only one who can be *hic* eloquent."

Silence overcame the three of them as music from the party echoed into the halls. Lord Valter shook his head. "I apologize, Miss Siroun. I was unaware of your affections. You understand that I do not have those feelings for you. My involvement in your life is in direction relation to the mission at hand. Afterward, I intend to fulfill my contractual obligations and make sure you obtain a stable lifestyle as was my promise to your father and brother."

Zikky winced before shaking her head at the Duke. To that, Lord Valter said, "I am explaining that—."

Siroun gestured for him to stop as she balled other hand into a fist. "I get it. I'm a tool for the mission."

Lord Valter's jaw went slack for a moment before he

composed himself. "Well, that is a boorish way of stating it."

"Keep diggin' that hole, buddy," said Zikky.

Not appreciating the interruptions and being mocked, Lord Valter turned to Zikky. "Do I need to file a report to the guild on your recent infractions?"

"Meh," she waved away his threat, "put it on my tab."

"You know what? I'm fine. It's better this way," said Siroun while standing straighter. "Now there are no more secrets and false assumptions between us. Nik was right, even if he was just Felthane in someone else's skin. I can't expect to garner friendship from someone who only brought me along out of obligation."

"Miss Fatima," said Lord Valter, his voice lacking its usual calm. "You are taking things way out of context, please cease."

"No, Your Grace, I understand that you're bound to your duties. Now, if you'll excuse me, I intend to enjoy the rest of the party on my own."

Without giving the Duke a chance to object, Siroun brushed past him.

"Miss Fatima!" Lord Valter called out to her, but Siroun kept walking.

"Can't hear you!" she said, stomping her way down the marble hall, heels clicking along before her ankle buckled causing her to stumble. But she was quick to recover and continued her march with resolve.

Zikky had already bounded after Siroun when the Skivat reached out and caught her. "Whoa, gel-gel! Slow down."

Siroun clenched her teeth as she crouched over,

grabbed the left shoe, and threw it on the floor before doing the same to the other. In her fit of frustration, she muttered, "Stupid party. Stupid rules. Stupid nobles!"

Zikky stepped in and placed her hand on Siroun's shoulders. "Hey, it's okay, gel-gel. Breathe."

Hearing the Skivat's words didn't lessen her anger. A few seconds later, Siroun hoisted her fore and middle fingers in the air like a V in the direction at the party and said, "This is what I think of your party!"

Zikky burst out laughing at the obscene gesture. Siroun knew this was unlike her in typical circumstances, but she needed to release her frustrations.

"I went through the same thing when I first got here," Zikky said through bouts of chortling. "Nothin' but hoity-toity nobles and snobby royals. Ya gotta suck it up and ignore them sometimes, otherwise they'll drive ya mad. Fancy Pants meant well, but even he gets caught up in his issues. Don't take it too hard."

"By the way," Siroun tilted her head and quirked her brow, "what's with the on-command hiccups?"

"Oh, that?" Zikky waved a hand. "Pfft, I sometimes hiccup whenever I have certain alcohol. That makes people think I'm drunker than I am. In places like this, I use it to annoy nobles. Take Fancy Pants for instance. Did ya see his eye twitchin' after a while? That was great! No one gets to mouth off to my gel-gel and get away with it. Colin bein' the only exception since he's always an ass."

Siroun laughed and wiped at her eyes to remove any excess tears from earlier only to smear her make-up. When she looked at her fingers and realized her mistake, she sighed, "Can we please leave?"

"Absolutely," said Zikky and took Siroun by the hands, looking her in the eyes. "C'mon, I've got somethin' that'll cheer ya right up!"

With a somber nod, Siroun entrusted her friend and took off down the hall. The designer shoes abandoned for the servants to find later.

34

AFTER ENDLESS SEARCHING, Sebastian trudged over to Colin looking abject and defeated.

"I take it you haven't crossed paths with that girl yet?" said Colin.

"I should have never come. Royal parties make me uncomfortable, not to mention people keep asking me about my clothes. I don't know what I was thinking," Sebastian ferreted an hors d'oeuvres from a passing server and gnashed it between his teeth.

"That's what I've been telling you all of this time."

"What's your excuse for coming, then?"

"Because my commander gave me a direct order," said Colin, pointing to Lord Valter from across the ballroom.

"The mission is that high profile?"

The lack of response was all that Sebastian needed to realize the level of importance. Having finished the snack, he fidgeted with his cuff links and stared at the doorways to see when Niamh arrived. Hope rose and sank like the tide with each announced guest until the repeat disappointment pummeled his enthusiasm to the ground.

He turned his attention back to Colin. "Do you ever ponder the future?"

The inquiry caused Colin to glare at him. "Is that a trick question?"

"No, I'm serious."

"You're not going to sucker me into a touchy-feely conversation, are you?"

Sebastian twisted his lips to the side before replying, "I'm just concerned about you. Any good friend would be."

"I thought I told you we're not friends."

"That's just a story you sell to yourself more than the rest of us."

The ice mage sipped at his drink again, trying to ignore the sentiment. "Remind me to push you down the stairs as validation of our non-friendship."

An awkward silence fell between them before Colin smirked, then chuckled. Not long after, Sebastian followed suit. However, with their laughter came uncertainty on the demigod's part of whether Colin was kidding.

"To answer your asinine question: No, I don't think about it," said Colin. "I want closure for my parents' deaths, even if it requires my own."

A chill crept down Sebastian's spine, and his tone softened. "Colin, I'm imploring you not to use the Kingman's Curse. I shouldn't have shown you that spell book."

"Don't flatter yourself," he derided. "I planned to learn that spell, with or without your help."

"Colin." Sebastian took a step closer and lowered

his voice, "That spell does not know the meaning of true death."

Colin's eyes narrowed, and the surrounding air chilled. But the conversation stymied when a young woman approached Sebastian with a smile on her face. "There you are!"

Sebastian recognized the voice and turned. "N-Niamh! You are... y-you-."

Within seconds Sebastian's face went cherry red, and Colin used this opportunity to carry out a silent retreat.

Meanwhile, Sebastian's pulse banged against his eardrums, nearly rendering him deaf to his surroundings. "Y-you look. Uh. Wow! A-a-and I am, this drink, er... I rode a horse here. No, wait — no, I didn't. What am I talking about?"

She couldn't help but smile at Sebastian's fragmented sentences. Niamh's olive-green dress complimented her medium skin tone and brought out the vibrancy in her brown eyes. Tendrils of ivy wove into the braids of her hair as a symbol of the topic she studied within the guild. She looked so radiant that he kept stumbling over his words.

"You look handsome," she said while reaching out to straighten his lapel. "Although I'm confused about the clothing choice. I thought you would be in the guild's formal uniform instead. Imagine my surprise when I found you changed out of your tried-and-true attire to come to a party."

"Ah, oh? Ah... yes, I—well, I thought you—," Sebastian cleared his throat while Niamh remained patient, and waited for him to find his words. Sebastian continued attempting speech through whatever noises he could muster from his mouth. Slipping her hand into his, Niamh pulled him toward the dance floor.

"B-but I can't dance," he said, finally able to string together a cohesive sentence.

Sebastian hesitated and tugged backward. He already faced the throngs of scorns and snide glances because of his fashion choices. He wasn't ready for another round of critiques from the social elite with his footwork.

"That's okay, we'll learn together," she replied, and he melted to her whims.

The jaunty tune playing had people hopping and clapping as they bounced around the allocated dancing space. Both Niamh and Sebastian felt out of place as they watched the others and mimicked the steps at a lagging pace. On a positive note, the steps repeated themselves. With a few haphazard attempts they synced up with the other dancers for the remaining song. Even through their missteps they laughed as the audience cheered on the participants.

After one final round of the melody, the dance came to a close. The men took their partners by the hands and planted kisses upon their ladies' knuckles. Sebastian thought his knees would buckle. With a damp palm, he reached for Niamh's hand and swallowed hard. Even Niamh turned a bright shade of pink as she saw him lower his lips only to pause halfway toward the destination. Every muscle in his body trembled, and at the last second he placed his other hand over hers and gave it an appreciative pat. Too many people were staring, and he wiped his palms against his tunic as they retreated from the dance floor side-by-side.

Neither one had the idea nor courage on what to suggest next at the party. It was by uncanny timing that the Vanis Aer's Headmistress approached them. Niamh noticed her first and pulled away into a formal posture, causing Sebastian to turn and see what had spooked her. Once he understood who stood in front of them, he adjusted his facial expression to match the formality of the Headmistress' disposition.

"Headmistress Von Brandt," they both greeted her with reverence.

"Councilman Di Mercurio. Lady Niamh." Her eyes scrutinized each of them as she spoke their names before keeping her focus on Sebastian. "Councilman, I'm afraid I must recall you from the party this evening."

"What? Why is that?" His glance darted toward Niamh.

The Headmistress' eyes flicked back in Niamh's direction. "You have an important visitor who is demanding your audience."

Confused, Sebastian tilted his head. "Who?"

"Your father."

35

SCONCES ALONG THE walls of the massive room lit up one-by-one, revealing a cornucopia of books from floor to ceiling for what felt like an eternity. When the fire spell completed, Zikky brushed her hands together. "Ta-dah! Welcome to the royal library, courtesy of Yers Truly."

Siroun's mouth gaped with wonder, then stammered through bursts of laughter. "T-this is wonderful!"

"Yeah, well," Zikky put her hands on her hips and waggled her eyebrows. "I know how important this stuff is to ya. Figured this would be the best place to take yer mind off things and whatnot."

Bare feet padded along the stone flooring as Siroun looked through the myriad of texts that came from around the world. She recognized a few titles from Niravad that were books of poems and philosophy, which explained Lord Valter's familiarity with Siseltrad's material. Still, it was fascinating to see literature from different continents congregating in one area. Her fingers brushed across the spines so she could touch the leather bindings.

When the vibration of books dropping in piles echoed in the distance, Siroun postponed her perusal and made her way closer to the sound. More fell, followed by the sanding sound of them shifting around on the floor. Siroun chewed on her lower lip as she investigated the source of the noise. "Zikky?"

"Over here, gel-gel!"

She followed the voice and wove through several bookshelves before witnessing the mess and gasped. Zikky dropped one more pile of books on the floor and adjusted them to construct, what Siroun could only assume, was furniture she couldn't yet identify. Siroun tried her best to hold back the urge to yell at the Skivat as she tempered her tone and said, "Zikky, what are you doing?"

The Skivat grinned, setting the last book down and replied, "Hold that thought."

Zikky disappeared behind the bookshelves, causing more suspicious sounds along the way. This time, the fire mage returned with a giant tapestry in tow. Siroun swallowed with trepidation while Zikky draped it over the mound of books. Nothing appeared special at first. But upon further inspection she could now see it was a backrest. However, that dwarfed the fact that the tapestry was that of the royal family and Siroun panicked. "We're going to get into so much trouble for this! What if King Nathaniel finds out?"

The Skivat giggled. "Gel-gel, ya worry too much. The King ain't got time to grill us over silly stuff. Besides, I'll put it back before they even realize it's missin'."

"That doesn't comfort me," she muttered, still chewing on her lower lip as she watched Zikky settle into her handiwork and make gratuitous comfort noises.

As Siroun continued to watch, Zikky patted the space next to her. "Ya comin', gel-gel? Yer missin' the view."

"View?"

The fire mage gestured upward, and Siroun removed her focus on the travesty of the book pile to understand where they were. The architects constructed this sector of the library with large panels of glass windows, supported and shaped by metal-based craftsmanship and designed as a partial atrium. It overlooked not just the city and sea in front of them, but the stars above as well. Her eyes transfixed on the heavens as she padded her way next to Zikky.

Zikky chuckled. "See? Figured ya'd get a kick out of this place."

The fabric of Siroun's skirt billowed as she plunked to the ground and continued staring at the stars. Then the boning of the corset stabbed her in the ribcage, forcing her to wiggle around hoping to find a comfortable angle in which to situate herself.

Zikky saw this, and reached behind Siroun while saying, "Here, lemme help ya with that."

Her nimble fingers went to work loosening the ties and hooks that kept Siroun cinched into a dress that was too rich for her taste. When the squeezing around her lungs lifted, she took a deep appreciative breath. But Zikky kept working on the ribbons for a few minutes more until she pulled back and smiled in satisfaction.

"There, that should do it. I loosened it for ya, but the dress won't fall off once ya get back up and head to yer room later."

With a sigh of relief, Siroun said, "Thanks, Zikky."

"Anytime."

Pointing to her dress, Siroun smirked and asked, "Is this why you wore your guild uniform instead?"

"Eh," she shrugged. "Those clothes ain't practical for my line of work. I have no interest in wearin' things that don't serve a purpose. Maybe if I needed to dazzle folks with frilly things, it'd be a different story. But Felthane ain't gonna wait for me to chase 'em in a dress."

To that explanation, Siroun burst out laughing. "By The Great Three, could you imagine that?"

Zikky started laughing too. "Yes, and it doesn't end well for me!"

The laughter continued to echo throughout the library before Siroun wiped away tears of mirth from her eyes, and Zikky followed up with, "So, other than that last little interlude with Lord Butt-Hurt, did ya have fun?"

Siroun still resented Lord Valter for instigating that spat, however, looking back on the evening she nodded. "Lord Marcus was entertaining, but I enjoyed dancing with you the most."

"Good," Zikky smiled. "That's how I'd hoped it'd be for ya tonight."

It comforted Siroun that Zikky was looking out for her well-being. Even though Lord Valter was diligent in ensuring her safety, her happiness was not something that concerned him by comparison to the fire mage. She settled in further against the piles of books, and kept her eyes on the stars while asking, "What's up with the feud between Lord Valter and Lord Marcus anyway? Not that I know much about the Duke of Firenz, but he always struck me as an ever-composed person. This is the first time I've seen him angry."

"Yeah, ya'd think Felthane pisses him off more, eh?" Zikky snickered. "He's not attached to the warlock on any personal level. Makes him more objective. Lord Super Suave, on the other hand, has always been the devious little scamp. From stealin' trade routes under Prissy Pants's nose, to deflowerin' his sister, the man has done his fair share of irreparable damage. Supposedly, Lord Lightnin' was the one to get him booted from the Vanis Aer council 'cause he was pissed when he found out his sister bedded him without a weddin' band."

"I never knew Valter had a sister." Siroun didn't even pretend to sound surprised. She wasn't going to comment on the bedroom antics of Lord Marcus either.

"Still," Zikky continued, "what happened tonight ain't yer fault. Lord Super Suave is a kindred spirit because he likes pushin' buttons with those who take themselves too serious. That makes Lord Sparkles an easy target since the Duke of Vasile is a powerful mage in his own right, and not easy to trifle with."

Siroun sat up. "So, he's a mage?"

"Yeah, though I'm not sure what kind," Zikky raised a brow in her direction then smirked. "Why? Ya got the hots for him? Ya both were dancin' real close durin' that sexy little number from his homeland."

Every inch of Siroun's skin flushed with head. "N-no! It wasn't like that."

"Are ya sure?" the Skivat eyed her with faux suspicion. "Yer tellin' me ya didn't try and grope him?"

"Zikky!" An edge reflected in Siroun's voice as she scolded her, "If you're trying to tease me, it's not funny."

Zikky gave her a wink and said, "Sorry, gel-gel. I was just pryin'. Seems like after the whole crush on Fancy Pants ended ya might have moved onto someone else."

"Even if I had, which I haven't, what does it matter?"

Zikky cleared her throat. "I'm just curious 'bout the other types of partners yer into besides the rich ones who look pretty."

Dead silence followed afterward as Zikky stared at her with a curious intensity that was far beyond her normal teasing. Siroun mulled the question over and found there was truth in the Skivat's comments.

"You know what, I never thought of it that way. Perhaps I'm dazzled by people with manners."

"Ya sure it's manners?"

"Okay, okay, I admit that they're attractive, and I'm roped in by the refined ones, but I can't help it. There weren't a ton of options for me in Pustelia Crest with mates. Save for, maybe, Nikostraz." Siroun paused, bringing a finger to her chin to ponder more on the self-revelation.

Zikky tilted her head and raised a brow. "So, there's a chance yer attracted to other types of people too?"

Siroun thought back on the diplomat that Lord Valter chatted with back in The Hive during the Sonestrelle performance, and nodded, "I think so. Why do you ask?"

With Zikky acting uncharacteristically mild mannered, Siroun felt concerned about what was going on inside the Skivat's head. She didn't understand the purpose behind the question. When Zikky sat up and looked Siroun dead in the eyes, a lump formed in her throat.

With a deep breath, Zikky said, "I'm curious because I find ya attractive."

The pitch in Siroun's voice went two octaves higher as every inch of her skin flushed pink. "W-what?"

Zikky soldiered on, "And I wanna be more than just yer friend."

"More than just…" she trailed off.

"A girlfriend," Zikky said with confidence. "I want ya to be my girlfriend."

Despite understanding the words, Siroun sat there slack-jawed, and unable to respond to such a loaded subject. Seeing the look of anticipation in Zikky's eyes added further guilt and anxiety. She questioned if she could return the feelings or not. The more she sat there in silence, the more Zikky's excitement turned to impatience. When Siroun tried to comment, the Skivat leaned in and placed a soft kiss on her lips.

Everything became a blur of warmth and exhilaration as Siroun hesitated at first but then loosened up as she felt Zikky's thin but soft lips press against hers. After a few moments of lingering, Zikky pulled away and winked at Siroun, "Been wantin' to do that for a while."

Siroun blinked a few times, bringing her fingers to her lips. When her brain had, figuratively, returned to her body, she smiled. "How long have you been holding back?"

"I dunno what kinda self-confidence issues ya have, gel-gel, but yer a smart woman with a rockin' body. Ya even had Ice-for-Brains gawkin' at ya earlier. Might be the first time I'd seen anyone make him look that surprised."

"Colin?" That made Siroun belt out with laughter, and Zikky followed. She recalled seeing both him and

Sebastian looking stunned, but thought nothing of it. "If that's the case, it didn't last long."

The two continued to stifle bursts of giggles as they leaned back in the make-shift furniture and stared up at the stars. All the while, Siroun nibbled on her lower lip.

Zikky saw this and raised her brow. "What's wrong, gel-gel?"

Siroun struggled with trying to figure out how to answer that question while analyzing her own emotions.

"About that kiss," she mumbled.

The Skivat flipped to her side and grinned. "Why? Ya want another?"

Another wave of heat washed over Siroun's face. She considered Zikky's feelings and wondered for how long the Skivat felt that way about her. In hindsight, it should have been easy to notice. However, so much had gone on around them it was next to impossible for Siroun to recall the clues. From there, she admonished herself for being so dense at reading social cues.

Soon the cycle of thoughts repeated themselves until Zikky's voice cut through the self-deprecation with, "Take yer time."

Siroun's mind quieted long enough for her to say, "What?"

"I said take yer time." Zikky tapped Siroun on the forehead with her finger. "Ya always overthink things, and from the looks of it, this might have been a little sudden."

"I just," Siroun paused as she reached out and took Zikky's hand in her own. "I don't know how I feel right now, and I don't want to disappoint you."

"Disappoint me?" She chuckled, before squeezing Siroun's hand. "Ya can't disappoint me, gel-gel. I want ya to be happy. My hope is that it's with me. If not, I'm a big girl. I understand."

Despite the words of comfort, Siroun wanted to reconcile a decision now rather than later. Again, Zikky poked her on the forehead. "Hey, do ya at least like me, friend or otherwise?"

"Of course," Siroun said without hesitation.

"Then that's all I need to know," she smiled. "The rest we take one day at a time. Sound good?"

No pressure, no expectations. Siroun took a deep breath and exhaled, while Zikky reached over and gave her a stroke of the cheek with a thumb. It felt good knowing that someone was by her side through this entire endeavor.

"C'mon, these stars ain't gonna watch themselves." Zikky leaned back and offered an arm to Siroun, who nestled in and looked up at the skies above.

Girlfriend.

The word excited Siroun just thinking about it.

36

SIROUN DIDN'T PLAN to sleep in the library. One minute she was lying next to Zikky in a pile of books chatting, the next minute it was morning. When she arrived back to her room, she noticed the castle servants had tidied it up and breakfast served. Her satchel of belongings looked undisturbed, but she double-checked to make sure that nothing was out of place. The reliquary from Nikostraz, the guitar pick she gained from The Hive, and Sebastian's books that he loaned her were all accounted. She found letters stacked neatly upon the table which perked her curiosity. Upon closer inspection, two envelopes had her name written on them. Of the two, she recognized her father's Drakish handwriting and opened it to read the contents within:

My Dearest Beskonerynth,

I hope this letter finds you doing well and in good health. Lord Valter was kind enough to send word that you would be in Ysile Marden. He speaks highly of your perseverance through the current trials and tribulations, and I am so proud to call you my daughter.

No matter where the journey takes you, know that I am always praying to The Great Three for your safety. Someday we will reunite, and I know you have blossomed into a strong and proud young woman ready to take on the rest of the world.

Hold your head high, dear daughter, for you are never alone.

All my love,

Your Father

A tear hit the ink at the end, blurring some of it off of the parchment as Siroun wiped her cheek and reread the letter once more for posterity. When she overcame the wave of homesickness, she tucked it into her satchel and moved onto the next one. She didn't recognize the ragged scrawling. Curious, she opened the envelope and read the letter written in Adami:

To the Master of the Bible,

Allow me to start by saying that you looked ravishing in that gown last night. Master Tavris certainly has a way with fashion when he wants to impress a crowd.

However, I am writing to make you aware that I realized something in our little adventure together. That epiphany made me understand how integral you are to my endeavors, and it means your place is at my side. So, you can understand why I am disappointed when you did not retire to your room when I came to collect you.

Whether you come by choice or by force means little to me. If I must take out your guardians, so be it. Meet me in the abandoned guild tower tonight when the sun kisses the earth.

-F-

The tears that she shed over her father's letter dried as panic and anger took hold of her emotions. Her fingers dug into the paper that held the threatening words. Siroun wanted to crumple the letter and burn it. Instead, she hastened through breakfast and changed into new traveling garments that the servants laid out on the bed. Stuffing the accursed note into her coat pocket, Siroun grabbed her satchel and went to find the Skivat. The stomping of her boots echoed throughout the halls as she stopped guards and servants alike to aid her in finding Zikky. Most of them knew nothing, and she ran the corridors, garnering disapproving looks of the courtiers. With her first attempts going nowhere, she changed tactics and asked for directions on where to find an entrance point to the Vanis Aer guild. That request warranted her better directions, and it wasn't long until she found someone nearby that she recognized.

The problem for Siroun now consisted in remembering her name. She took a wild guess and called out, "Ah, Nicole! Nym!"

Siroun huffed in frustration at not being able to remember the name. By luck, the other woman realized that Siroun was trying to flag her attention.

"It's Niamh," she said with a twinge of annoyance in her voice.

"I'm so sorry, Niamh. Do you think you could help me find someone?" Siroun asked through gulps of breath.

The senior student gave a non-committal nod of the head. "I will try my best."

"Do you know where Zikky might be?"

The original look of hesitation by Niamh changed to confidence as she lifted the magical charms off of the nearby entrance portal and pointed the way. "Down the hall, take a left, she should be somewhere in sector E-12 since she's a member of the Vanis Aer Elite."

"By The Great Three, thank you!" Siroun's initial enthusiasm then transformed to embarrassment. "Would you be able to write that down for me, please?"

Niamh smiled and said, "Sure."

A few minutes later Siroun bolted onward, with Niamh's notes scratched upon a small piece of parchment. When she reached the correct zone, she started by asking people which room Zikky occupied. When that resulted in little success, she banged on each door hoping someone could lead her to the fire mage. By the time she reached the eighth door, it opened, and a hand pulled her inside.

When Siroun came face-to-face with the resident within, she relaxed.

"Have ya gone mad, gel-gel?" said Zikky through a yawn. "What's with all the racket?"

Trying to catch her breath again, Siroun pulled out the letter from Felthane and stuffed it into her hands. "He knows I'm here. He knows!"

"Calm down. Let me see that." With furrowed brows, Zikky read the contents in full before looking up at Siroun, "What does he mean by ya bein' integral to his plans?"

Siroun scratched at her arm, the anxiety creeping up on her. "I have no idea."

However, she retraced her memories to the Bat'filinear Ruins, and she remembered the epiphany she had with him.

"The Sinefine Bible!" Siroun blurted out, "He doesn't know how to use it. I'm sure he needs me to read it for him."

Zikky reread the letter while rubbing at her chin in thought. "That's worrisome. He's been one step ahead of our every move for a while. He's gotta have somethin' on us that's tellin' him where we are."

Siroun watched as Zikky thought through this dilemma. The Skivat's ears twitched, and her foot tapped as she pondered the connections to Felthane's fortuitous endeavors.

A few minutes later she said, "I need to ask if ya have anythin' that belonged to Felthane."

"What? Why would I have anything of his?"

"He came to collect ya last night on the assumption ya would be there, gel-gel."

Siroun wrinkled her nose at the response, "So? Anyone can assume that."

"Yes, but Felthane has found ya multiple times."

"Because he was with our group in disguise the entire time!"

"Only until we rode the boat."

"He knew that we were coming this way—," every muscle in Siroun's body tensed.

Even now, it was hard acclimating to the fact that Nikostraz was an illusion. She pulled her bag forward and rummaged through it until she found the glowing reliquary tucked deep at the bottom. The one thing that Nikostraz gave to her for protection and told her to keep it secreted. To guard it with her life, as it protected her in return.

As she pulled the reliquary out and presented it to Zikky, the two of them saw the contents from within stir and swirl.

This was it.

When she offered it to the fire mage, Zikky pulled back and shook her head. "Nu-uh, I ain't touchin' that. Ya shouldn't be either."

The thing radiated a strange sensation that made Siroun's head buzz, but otherwise, it hadn't harmed her in any capacity. All she felt was a sense of calm.

She stared at it for a few seconds before shifting her gaze to Zikky. "What now?"

"We need to call a meetin' with Lord Fancy Pants and the guild leaders to help us hash out a plan before the evenin'."

"How do we find them?"

"Leave that part to me." said Zikky, giving Siroun a pat on the shoulder along the way. "Meanwhile, ya go find Seb, and he'll find Frost Fingers for us."

The command gave Siroun pause. "Why would Sebastian know Colin's whereabouts?"

"Seb is Colin's only best friend."

Siroun raised a brow. "I thought Colin claimed not to have any friends?"

As Zikky grabbed her guild coat she smirked at Siroun. "Haven't ya learned by now that what Colin says and what he does don't match? The two are brilliant mages who grew up without parents. They've been besties since childhood. The only difference is in their parentage."

Siroun followed Zikky out of the room and said, "One of these days you must run me through this pantheon of deities."

"Are you kiddin' me?" Zikky scoffed. "My hand would cramp up just havin' to write that info. Yer on yer own with that little research adventure."

37

ONVERSATION ECHOED THROUGHOUT the meeting hall as council members, the Division Magistrate, and King Nathaniel with his retinue arrived. Everyone bowed to the sovereign before finding their seats. As Zikky passed with Siroun in tow, she honed in on one specific woman walking by the King with only a nod. Her tall, toned body rivaled that of the fire mage's physique with garments made of soft beige leathers as it hugged her legs and cropped along the upper half of her body. Shimmering tattoos graced the exposed abdomen of her dark, sun-kissed skin. The belts that hugged her waistline holstered two pistols and a series of small storage pockets.

What seemed strange to Zikky was that King Nathaniel didn't bat an eye at her lack of subservience to him. Instead, he nodded in return. Zikky tucked that interaction away in her head and searched for a place to sit. Siroun held fast to her hand, something the Skivat enjoyed as they side-stepped one of the council members blocking their path. King Nathaniel took a spot next to Lord Valter, and the two conversed while sharing mutual looks of concern. On the opposite side of the room, she saw Colin watching others in silence, but didn't spare a glance at his teammates.

A series of gavel bangs resonated around the room, and people quieted themselves as the Division Magistrate adjusted his glasses and began with, "I call this meeting to order."

He swept his gaze across the room to make sure everyone was paying attention. "Thank you. I remind everyone that we have guests with us today. Please be discreet in your conversations you consider classified to those not privy to your endeavors. With that in mind, I shall begin by confirming that the warlock known as Felthane is active within the city walls."

The information was met with silence. Many looked to Lord Valter expecting an explanation on why the mission was not progressing as planned.

"Magistrate," said an elderly female council member whose gray-speckled hair was pulled into such a tight bun that her leathery skin stretched her face up toward her ears. "Given Lord Valter's travels after yesterday's debriefing, how did Felthane make his way here so soon?"

"There are several theories, Councilwoman Brisbois," said the Magistrate. "However, I shall allow our Councilman of Artifacts to illuminate our most plausible reason. Assuming he can arrive on time."

Everyone's eyes shifted over to a man who tripped on the edge of a rug as he made his way into the room. Meanwhile, Siroun's eyes widened. "Sebastian?"

Zikky smirked and murmured in Vat'tu, *"The curse*

to being the son of a god that founded the Vanis Aer Æther Guild."

"Meeting yesterday, not with you. Why?" said Siroun in her broken grasp of the language. Afterward, she paused and counted the words on her fingers.

Zikky enjoyed listening to Siroun work through the Vat'tu language, and responded with, "He's not invited to every party, gel-gel."

"Why?"

"They can't have him meddling in mortal affairs every time."

Zikky expected to see Sebastian speak about the reliquary. But when he locked gazes with the mysterious markswoman, something nagged at the back of her mind.

"Strange," Zikky murmured.

"What?"

Zikky wiggled her pinky finger in the dark-skinned stranger's direction. "See her?"

It took a while for Siroun to notice, but when she did, she nodded.

"She's not part of the Vanis Aer or the King's council," said Zikky.

"How know?"

"Technically, I don't. This is the first time I've seen that woman before, and this isn't an open meeting. She's got her eye on Seb too, and she must know the King... intimately."

She watched Siroun blush before turning her attention back to Sebastian. The councilman made his way to his seat and set the notes upon the table. With a flick of his hand, an enlarged ethereal image of the reliquary that Siroun surrendered earlier that day appeared mid-air in the center of the room for everyone to see. The magical depiction gave off an emerald green glow as people analyzed its design.

Whispers stirred around the room as Sebastian cleared his voice before beginning. "I-I'm sure a handful of you recognize this item, but for those who don't, I will explain. The item is a Soul Chamber Talisman. Every warlock carries at least one of these on them, and it is a physical manifestation of their pact with a demon or dark god. It works as a two-way conduit between the warlock and its master. The reliquary grants them power for a repayment that depends upon the pact made between them and their patron."

The room kept quiet, and everyone's expressions reflected concern. Zikky glanced at the markswoman again to find her sky-blue eyes focusing on Siroun.

Sebastian continued, "I've only been able to perform a cursory analysis before this meeting, but I am confident the nature of the bond a warlock shares with a reliquary is why Felthane knew where to follow. In this case, he gifted the item to Siro—I mean, Miss Fatima in their travels."

He stumbled over his words throughout the rest of the presentation, but maintained his train of thought long enough to relay the details to the rest of the group. It wasn't until another councilman piped in that Sebastian took a seat and tried making himself look small.

"This is absurd! How was he able to gift something of this nature without her knowing what it was? You don't expect us to believe such naiveté," the other councilman said while shooting an incredulous look at Siroun.

Zikky saw the anger in Siroun's eyes and squeezed her hand, then stood from her chair. Despite being smaller in stature, Zikky's physique and general demeanor made up for any shortcomings in height when she shot back, "Ya watch yer tongue."

"You're out of order, field agent," the Division Magistrate banged his gavel to calm them down. "And you're inciting disorder, Councilman Harcourt. Both of you be silent unless you have something productive to add to the conversation."

"We can whittle away the day debating how this came to pass," said the King as he placed his palm upon the table. "My greatest concern is that he intends to appear again tonight. How do we use this information to our advantage?"

"Set a trap," said Councilman Harcourt. When all eyes shifted to him, he continued with, "If the reliquary is a tracking device, as Councilman Di Mercurio theorizes, then let us use it to spring a trap. This plan puts the cards back in our favor."

Sebastian shook his head but said nothing, averting his gaze toward the markswoman instead. Zikky's ears twitched as she listened in on the different members discussing the options.

Siroun squeezed her hand and nodded in Colin's direction. *"Where going?"*

At the corner of her eye, Zikky caught Colin sauntering toward Sebastian to whisper back and forth. She tried to focus in on what they were saying, but the nearby murmurs between the council members next to her drowned them out.

"Nope, no good. I can't understand what they're saying," said Zikky, clicking her tongue in disappointment.

Eventually, Colin stood up and stared at the Magistrate. The rest of the room noticed, and the conversation quieted. The Division Magistrate looked to the ice mage. "You wanted to say something, field agent Lockwood?"

"Thank you, Magistrate," said Colin.

It shocked Siroun to witness the sudden politeness from the aged teenager, as Zikky noticed her tilt back in her seat, eyes wide. She could only surmise that this was the first time Siroun saw Colin act cordial to anyone.

The ice mage looked upon the room before speaking. "Felthane shows no sense of fair play. I'm certain his note is a trap despite our attempt at a preemptive attack, but his abilities put us at a disadvantage. I propose we meet him head-on with only a select few waiting to engage."

Councilors whispered amongst themselves before Councilman Harcourt spoke up once again, "He wants the woman, field agent."

Councilman Harcourt seemed pleased, yet agitated for some unknown reason. Both men glared at each other before Colin spoke further on the proposed plan, "If Felthane wants to take Siroun then he is welcome to try, but he needs to get through me first. I will act as the decoy."

Lord Valter frowned but said nothing as the King and the other council members discussed the validity of the option. Zikky tapped the table with her fist and glared at Colin. She shook her head at him and made several gestures to convey not to go through with this suggestion, but he averted her gaze.

She wrinkled her nose and muttered in Vat'tu, *"That idiot will get himself killed."*

Zikky expected Siroun to agree with her. Instead, she turned to find Siroun standing up to interject with, "No, I will be the bait."

A round of whispers flared up, and the Magistrate banged his gavel to call the room to order.

"Gel-gel," Zikky tugged on Siroun's sleeve in hopes she would sit, only to be ignored. Frustrated, she tugged on Siroun's sleeve again. "What are you doing?"

"I appreciate the amount of courage it takes to volunteer for such a task. I cannot, in good conscience, allow others to take this kind of risk on my behalf," Siroun turned to Colin only to find his aqua eyes glowering back at her. She tilted her chin up and added, "After all, Colin is just a boy, no matter how much his abuse of magic has aged him."

Siroun must have known that hit a nerve because the room temperature cooled while everyone else surged into a crescendo of conversation. Only the King and the markswoman sat silent in their chairs as they watched the others.

The Magistrate banged his gavel again to put everyone in check, saying, "Order!" He then pointed to Colin. "Field agent Lockwood, if you use Æther in this room again while a meeting is in procession, I will strip you of your rank and privilege within the guild. Is that understood?"

It took every ounce of self-control in Colin to keep his face neutral while the chill in the air went away. Though Zikky saw that it pained him to say it, the ice mage responded with, "Yes, Magistrate."

"Miss, er...," the Magistrate peered down at his paperwork before looking up at Siroun, "Fatima, I understand your feelings of responsibility in this matter. However, given that you're a civilian, a protected guest, and a liability should Felthane succeed in your apprehension, I cannot condone such a risk at the expense of the kingdom's safety. Also, I warn you not to insult members of the Vanis Aer Æther Guild regardless of their age. With that said, I approve of field agent Lockwood's proposition. Let us take a vote. All in favor, raise your hands."

Siroun clutched at her chest and skulked into her chair as the vote commenced. A majority were in favor of the idea by a count of six to three, with Lord Valter begrudgingly backing the King's decision to move forward with Colin as the decoy. Zikky, Sebastian, and Siroun glared at Colin when they raised their hands against the plan.

"Field agent Lockwood has two hours to prepare himself. In the meantime, have the Council see that we use appropriate resources to secure the palace and the city should things go awry. This meeting is adjourned."

When the gavel banged, the monarch's retinue left with King Nathaniel giving orders to call forth the royal guard and ensure they were ready for the worst. The guild council also occupied themselves with figuring out the logistics of the trap. No one seemed concerned that a junior elite field agent volunteered to sacrifice himself for the greater good. Sebastian attempted to stop Colin from leaving, but Zikky saw the markswoman stand up and flick her palm upward, making the demigod halt in his tracks.

As if things weren't complicated enough, Siroun stood up to go after Colin. Zikky knew the ice mage well enough to know this wasn't a good idea, and reached for Siroun's wrist. "Yer only gonna anger him, gel-gel."

"So what? Angry is better than dead," Siroun yanked

her wrist from Zikky's grip, and wove her way out of sight. Things were spiraling out of control. People were so eager to come up with a plan that no one stopped to consider if it was the right plan.

"Zikky," she heard Lord Valter call for her.

Turning around, it appeared everyone cleared out except for him, the markswoman, and Sebastian. She blinked and said, "Wow, that was fast. I guess people are in a rush to send our Lockwood lamb to the slaughter."

The nobleman's brows creased. "You know that is not the sentiment behind the votes."

"Coulda fooled me," she stuck out her tongue. "So, who's the observer?"

Lord Valter gestured for Zikky to follow him. As she approached the strange woman, she noticed that the reason Sebastian couldn't move was because his feet were stuck to the floor with ice. The Skivat whistled. "I didn't know a little frost kept ya down, Seb."

Usually, the man took her teasing in strides, but this time she noticed he wasn't acting bashful, nor responding with a sheepish tone in his voice. Sebastian tapped a finger against his folded arms while staring at the markswoman. "It doesn't, Zikky."

It took a second to understand the implications behind his quip. Taking one more look at the frost spell, she realized that if Sebastian could have gotten out, he would have. He was a grand master of the arcane arts. An ice spell, even the best of them, rarely stopped someone like him, unless the individual was a higher deity by comparison. The pieces came together as Lord Valter said, "This is the Archmage, Arcandus."

Zikky paused and assessed the woman's physique. "No way, the Arcandus?" It took her a minute to visually digest everything. Not only was the deity's appearance a rare treat, but the form Arcandus took was not his typical silhouette. "Why'd ya choose breasts this time around? Not that I'm disappointed or anythin'," she asked before leaning in and poking at the Archmage's derriere in appreciation.

Lord Valter smacked his face with a palm, groaning, "Must you accost our patron god?"

Arcandus slapped Zikky's hand away. "My appearance is not a concern of yours. I'm here to ensure that you have a plan to handle the warlock. It is imperative the necromancer does not acquire the girl while the Sinefine Bible is in his possession."

"With all due respect, Archmage," said Lord Valter, "are there any details you can provide for us regarding what the Sinefine Bible does?"

Arcandus raised a brow at the Duke. "You need not know what it does, only that the girl is not to use it. Moreover, if your Skivat subordinate doesn't stop poking me in the rear, I will flay her in half, and sear her skin where she stands."

Zikky saw Lord Valter widen his eyes at her, to which she pulled her hand away and replied, "Haha, I like him a ton! C'mon Lord Tight Sphincter, let's figure out how we're gonna help Frosty Fingers beat that warlock into the dirt."

After Zikky's enthusiastic response, Sebastian broke free of the spell and said, "I'm helping Colin too."

"No," Arcandus flicked her fingers once more and conjured a chair to pull up behind Sebastian, forcing him into a sitting position. "You have a different purpose to fulfill."

Sebastian tried freeing himself with a counter-spell only for it to fail. The difference in power was apparent, and he remained still as Arcandus turned his attention back to Zikky and Lord Valter. "I recommend you end this little game with the warlock sooner rather than later."

"Yes, Archmage," Lord Valter bowed, and Arcandus sauntered out of the room while Zikky glimpsed the god's backside one last time.

"Hot damn, he picked a good form," Zikky grinned, only to find herself get zapped in the cheek by Lord Valter's electrified finger. "Yeow!"

"Do not embarrass yourself like that again."

38

$\mathcal{A}$LL REMAINED QUIET as Colin sat in front of a mirror and worked on securing the wig into place. There were plenty of resources provided to him that emulated the clothes Siroun wore when she landed in Ysile Marden. The worst part was trying to fit into them. The tailors departed after they cinched him into a corset and padded his chest to give him Siroun's modest physique.

Fitting into the clothes wasn't the hardest part of the disguise. Instead, he felt overwhelmed at the droves of containers that held a myriad of make-up essentials which boggled his mind. Never had he attempted a ruse to this degree. It made him regret dismissing the princesses' dressing servants after they helped him with the corset. As he poked and sniffed at the various jars, a knock came to the door. He hoped it was a servant coming back to check on him.

"Colin?"

When he heard Siroun's voice, he scowled, "Go away."

A moment of silence followed, and he returned to the

plethora of containers full of powdered pigments. But his concentration broke with another knock, and his grip on a blush container tightened as he shouted, "I said go away!"

"Colin, open up!"

"No!"

Another pause.

Then the silence broke again. This time by the repetitive pounding of Siroun's fist. Through the heavy wooden door, her muffled voice seeped into the room, "You can tell me to go away all you want, but I'm not going to stop!"

The banging continued, and Colin opted to sit and wait it out. Perhaps if he made her do it long enough, she would tire and give up. So, he sat there, resolute, and waited.

And waited.

And waited a bit more.

By the time several minutes passed, Colin's patience wore out. His brow twitched at every pulse of the knocks that Siroun made him endure. A brief respite came, only to hear her talking to the guards. The conversation got muffled from the barrier between them, but the intent was clear. She was to keep knocking until he permitted her entrance.

One guard answered Siroun with hesitance in his voice, "Very well, carry on."

That answer caused Colin's anger to hit a peak, and he banged his fists on the vanity table. Containers tumbled to the floor, and the room turned cold as swirls of frost laced the mirrors and windows from the inside.

"Fine, do whatever you want!" he said. "Just stop doing that!"

The subsequent silence soothed his weary ears until the door clicked open, and Siroun's head popped inside. While meandering her way toward him, he watched her gawk at the accommodations provided. The beige silk bedding, the elaborate fireplace, the hand-woven rugs. No matter where the woman went, she was always in awe. Now Colin realized that living in an isolated village for one's entire life skewed their perception of normalcy. Despite being of common origins, Colin's privileged life within the Vanis Aer Æther Guild cultivated apathy toward opulent environments that were not an everyday sight for common people.

When Siroun reached him, she crunched her lips to the side. "Really? You think I look like that?"

Colin jerked his head back. "I'm not finished yet. Why are you here?"

Her reptilian eyes glowered at him as she said, "I came to convince you not to do this."

Without hesitation he replied, "You're wasting your time, now get out."

"No!" Blurting that out so suddenly caused her to turn red before she said, "I mean, no. I'm not going anywhere. Besides, Sebastian told me you would be stubborn. So at least let me help. If I cannot deter you, then the least I can do is support you."

He scowled. "You realize that you just said two opposing decisions, right?"

"I realize you have this whole aloof teenager thing going for you. That doesn't mean the rest of us are on board with you sacrificing yourself for the greater good."

"You don't get it. I'm not doing this for you or the

guild, I'm doing this for myself." Colin grabbed a random container full of purple eyeshadow and mashed it on his lips. "And when did you grow a backbone?"

Siroun snatched the make-up from his hands and set it aside. "Since someone told me I was an obligatory doormat. Now sit still. You look like a grape with a wig."

As Colin tried making sense of how he lost that argument, Siroun tidied up the make-up that he scattered everywhere. She checked each one by dabbing a finger into the product and running it across the top of her hand. It was entertaining to watch her smudge a few more colors onto the scant areas of flesh, then blink at them in confusion.

Colin rested his chin upon his hand and muttered, "Are you going planning to color yourself with them all day?"

"Oh hush," Siroun grumbled as she attempted to organize the jars in a manner beyond Colin's understanding. "I'm trying to remember how Princess Claudette and her Ladies in Waiting used these when they did my make-up. We're both lucky I don't wear much of this stuff."

"Can we please just move on?" Colin scoffed, triggering Siroun to clutch his chin and analyze his facial features.

Once she took in every curve and pore on his face, she grabbed a cloth and wetted it with some soap and water from the nearby wash basin, then scrubbed his lips clean of the purple eyeshadow. She then stared at the smeared color on the cloth and clicked her tongue in dismay. "Leave it to someone like you to waste make-up made for royalty."

He rolled his eyes, but didn't make any comments since she could take her frustration out on his face with the vibrant color palette at her disposal. His eyes followed her every move as she rubbed a dollop of oil into his skin before covering him with a light-toned powder. Any time he tried to turn his head toward the mirror, Siroun redirected his gaze back to her. Then she moved onto using the eye pigments, and Colin remained a statue. He didn't speak nor move while she selected the different colors through a barrage of options.

"Ugh," muttered Siroun as she opened up the lids to the colors and puzzled over two hues that appeared identical to Colin. Her lips wiggled side-to-side as she continued staring at them before saying, "There are so many. How do these noblewomen do it every day?"

"Are you kidding?" Colin smirked. "They live for this nonsense."

"I'd be exhausted," said Siroun, finally selecting a soft taupe and dabbing some of it on her finger before blending it over his eyelids.

She moved onto his mouth by blending a drop of oil with a pink flower petal and mashed it into a poultice. With her pinkie finger, she rubbed the hue onto his lips. Last, she grabbed a brush and took a few moments to center the wig upon Colin's head before securing it with some pins.

When one of them stabbed him behind the ear, he growled, "Ow! Watch it."

"Sorry," said Siroun, but he noticed it lacked her usual submissive demeanor. Before he had the chance to ask, she followed up with, "Zikky told me about your parents."

She knew.

It was bad enough that he endured Lord Valter's

endless platitudes about finding another way to punish Felthane. Now the whiniest one in the bunch knew his history, and his jaw tightened.

Siroun continued talking, "I understand why you feel you need to do this. If that happened to my father and brother, I would want to take justice into my own hands too."

"If this is your way of convincing me to end this plan, you're doing a piss-poor job." He felt the soft whap of the brush against his head and winced. It didn't hurt as much as it caught him off-guard.

"Just because you're moody doesn't mean you get to be rude," she scolded. Colin gave an indignant grunt in response but otherwise remained quiet. She grabbed a hair tie and some clips then began twisting the bulk of the wig up. "As I was saying, I know Felthane did horrible things to your parents. Do you think they would want you to do this?" The strokes of her brushing getting rigorous as she spoke. "We will capture him. I know we will. But let's capture Felthane on our terms, as a team, so that no one has to die. No one has to—."

Siroun gasped as Colin's hand reached around and clutched her by the wrist. Frost magic crept across her skin as she attempted to wriggle free. Meanwhile, it took everything in his power to keep his emotions in check. He hated when she spouted her opinions so flippantly at him. The horrors of that night came back every time she spoke that name, as though it were happening all over again. Flashes of his parent's fear-stricken faces and tortured screams appeared, muddling his sense of reality. As he felt Siroun tugging to break free, tears pooled at his eyes and rolled down his cheeks.

Through gritted teeth, he said, "I saw my parents tortured, and their souls fed to a dark god to forge that reliquary he gave to you. I relive that night every day of my life. There is nothing I want more than to see him dead. No matter the cost."

Her eyes widened, and Colin realized that he almost went over the edge, releasing his grip. Siroun tucked her wrist under an arm and shivered but said nothing. He turned toward the mirror and saw Siroun's image instead of his own. As Colin blinked away the tears, Siroun's began to fall instead.

He quirked his brow at her. "Are you cr—?"

His question was cut short as she wrapped her arms around him. He grit his teeth in reaction and was at a loss on how to respond.

"I'm sorry, Colin," she sniffled through the tears. "I realize you've been through some horrible things, and I want to help you make it right again. But not like this. Please, don't die like this."

Speechless, it took him several attempts to pry her off while trying to compose himself for the sake of the situation. They were so close to putting this whole ordeal behind them. He couldn't let anything deter him, not even Siroun in her tear-filled glory. With remarkable resolve, he calmed himself and said, "Your nose is running."

That got her to stop crying while her brows knitted in confusion. "What?"

"You have boogers dribbling from your nose," he said.

"That's gross. I can't be friends with people who let their boogers run rampant down their faces."

Frantically, she wiped at her face with a sleeve before stopping to see his dead-pan expression. She couldn't help but laugh through her subsiding tears and runny nose. Her disheveled appearance made him smirk. Slight as it was, he felt a sense of genuine hope that this plan would work. He then shooed her with his hand. "Go fix your goober face. It's hard to look at you."

Nodding to the jest, Siroun made her way toward the door. Colin used this moment to lift the frost magic from her wrist. When she realized the frostbite subsided, she turned to look at him as Colin smiled back and said, "I won't fail you. I promise."

She returned the smile while sniffling and wiping at her nose again. As she headed for the door, he noticed her pause before exiting, leaving the door open. Colin clicked his tongue in frustration at her forgetfulness only to see Lord Valter step into the room. The Duke analyzed the disguise while Colin gave him the usual monotone greeting, "Your Grace."

"Is she all right?" Lord Valter pointed behind him from where Siroun exited.

Colin shrugged it off. "I told her to go clean up her face. I can't deal with her crying."

Lord Valter stared at Colin's semi-red eyes. "It appears you were joining her in that activity."

"Shut up, I was not!" Colin turned toward the mirror to clean up the streaks down his face. "Dammit, I just had this make-up done!"

The Duke took pause at the rude comment, but shook

his head and didn't press the matter. Colin knew Lord Valter came for a similar reason, but they were past the point of talking him out of things now.

"Are you ready?" Lord Valter kept a stern face through the question.

"As long as you don't start blubbering like a fool too," he muttered

"Colin, should the worst happen—."

"Don't order me to retreat, because you know I won't. I've waited too long for this chance." Colin would not let the Duke take this moment of closure away from him. Even if they took Felthane alive, it was likely that there would be no trial.

Pain reflected in Lord Valter's aging eyes as he took a deep breath. The two reached out and shook hands only to have the Duke pull Colin into a firm embrace. The younger mage didn't speak nor move, allowing the moment to settle in before the Duke said, "Don't miss."

With a pat on the back, Lord Valter released the teenager, and gave him a firm nod. Everything in this plan was at stake, and neither he nor Lord Valter wanted to think about the consequences of failure.

39

OUT OF ALL the places Felthane picked to have a showdown, the abandoned watchtower within the Castle Hjarta of Ysile Marden was fitting. Had it not been for his colleagues waiting for the warlock's arrival on the floor below, Colin would have died to deaf ears just like his parents. He finished setting up the remaining components that supported the last spell he would ever cast in this world. Small quartz stones bathed in leyline energies along the rim of the room helped amplify his connection to the amount of Æther magic he intended to conjure. With each stone's placement his hands trembled in both fear and anticipation. When finished, he reached into his guild coat and gripped the reliquary with disgust. The faint glow of its hypnotizing light mocked him, knowing that his parents' sacrifices crafted this accursed thing. Eventually, he ripped his gaze away and looked out toward the horizon where the sun was setting.

With a deep breath, he closed his eyes and spoke the incantation of the spell he saved for this moment. Flecks of blue ice danced off of his fingers, absorbing into the floor and walls around him. Once the first phase of the incantation was complete, a large blue glyph radiated off of his left wrist, then vanished. With everything in place, the countdown started. As long as the rest of the Vanis Aer guild performed their correct functions, all would go as planned.

When the sun touched the horizon, a large bird of prey swooped through the window before transitioning into the man that everyone dreaded. A bead of sweat rolled along Colin's cheek in front of his right ear as the wig added a layer of heat to his frazzled nerves. Felthane smiled and stretched out his arms.

"My dear," said Felthane with a silky tone. "I am most pleased with your compliance. Allow me to apologize for having to be so demanding. I am so close to seizing my rightful place on the throne that delays become most... discouraging."

Colin remained silent. To speak would give away the ruse, and he wanted to ensure that the slippery warlock wouldn't get away again. As much as he wanted to pounce the murderer and freeze every vein in his body, he remembered Lord Valter's lessons of restraint and waited for an opportunity instead.

"My, my, my. It appears we've gone through a little growth spurt since I last saw you," said Felthane.

The warlock placed a hand upon Colin's shoulder and the ice mage jerked himself free.

A chuckle followed with the words, "I know my real appearance is disheartening. However, I'm afraid I had to release Nikostraz in favor of a different skin this time around."

Though Colin couldn't have cared less about the fate of the real Nikostraz, he swallowed the forming a lump in his throat knowing Siroun likely overheard the comment. Not to mention the fact that Felthane admitted to taking another life as a new disguise. He turned to face Felthane with a hardened gaze but continued to bite his tongue.

"You're quiet, considering you had no trouble telling me off in the library all those months ago," Felthane gave a little sneer. "Has fear caught your tongue? Or perhaps you cannot speak because your true identity might reveal itself?"

Colin felt his stomach tighten with those last words.

As Felthane descended upon the decoy, his grasp only snatched the wig, revealing Colin's short brunette locks. Disgust flashed in the warlock's eyes as he tossed the fake hair aside and slunk toward the window that granted him an escape route. Colin stomped his foot, causing a thick wall of ice to gloss over the windows and nearby stairwell along the floor, forcing Felthane to halt and face him.

"Ah, the little boy wants to fight? Very well, I'll indulge you for a moment." The tone, however, conveyed anything but the desire to entertain Colin.

A hum of power resonated within the stone walls of the abandoned tower, but it came not from Felthane. The entire room gave off a hue of pink, causing Colin to exhale in relief now that the magical barrier erected.

It didn't deter the warlock as he looked at Colin with a cheeky grin. "You realize, boy, that this won't hold me forever?"

With no retort, Colin shifted his body with giant sweeps of his arms and the floor became coated in a layer of frost. A wave of ice rampaged in the warlock's direction before a jagged spike punched into the air. Felthane transfigured into a bird and escaped, but Colin throttled a handful of ice shards that numbed Felthane's wings upon contact, forcing him to the ground. A barrage of ice arrows followed suit, and the bird struggled to avoid them as one punctured his wing. Felthane shook off the injury by changing his shape into a canine-like creature and lunged at Colin. With another sweeping arm gesture, a barrier of ice curled to protect the mage against the impending attack. But Felthane's enchanted fist swooped in and smashed through the spell before taking a step back and waiting for the mage's next move. With belabored breathing, some locks in Colin's hair began to transition from brown to white. The gemstone on his ring finger shattered and fell to the ground. Felthane raised a brow at the change and began to circle Colin while looking him up and down.

"Isn't this a curious outcome? I know the cost for such skill is great, and your lack of affinity toward the offensive spells is wanting compared to your colleagues. But I doubt these paltry attacks are triggering your transformation with this level of alacrity. What are you hiding?"

A droplet of blood hit the floor, and Colin could feel the warm liquid seeping from his nose. Without keeping his eyes off of his opponent, the mage wiped at his face with a sleeve, while searching for an open shot. Neither one of them let their guard down as they both made cautious sideways steps and waited for the other to strike first.

"You can't keep wasting time, little Lockwood," said

Felthane. "Your parents couldn't stop me. What makes you think you're any different?"

The words made Colin's jaw tighten as he prepared to lunge at the warlock when he heard a thumping noise behind him. Siroun's muffled cries got his attention, and he despised her uncanny timing. Never would he admit his thankfulness to her, Zikky, and Lord Valter for letting him get this far.

With a deep breath, he dropped his guard and turned to make eye contact with Siroun. He watched the panic strike her face as he left himself open to attack. Felthane returned to his Adami form and leaped in with his demonic claw at the ready. Despite Siroun's inaudible screaming at him to turn around, Colin raised his left hand at her. The blue hue of the glyph gave off a noticeable glow from his wrist as he nodded to her.

"No! No! What are you doing?" Siroun's hands slapped against the ice. Tears poured down her cheeks as she pleaded, "Please don't do this!"

The pain reflected in her eyes made him wonder if, in another life, the outcome could have been different. Felthane moved in, and Colin closed his eyes, succumbing to the ambush to draw the warlock into his trap. The moment the two made contact, and a blinding light exploded from the watchtower causing the mages to all fall to their knees as the barrier ice walls shattered and the magic soaked the rest of the damages.

40

THE STAIRS SHOOK beneath Siroun's feet and Zikky swooped in to catch her before she toppled over. The guild mages scrambled to their feet and continue their incantations to keep the magical barrier going. When Siroun regained her footing, she noticed something else enveloped the room above her: Frost. The same surreal calm stirred her memory from when Colin first made his magical presence known in Pustelia Crest.

She rushed up the stairs with Zikky and Lord Valter following behind. The effects of the spells exploding shattered the ice barrier that pervaded her from entering before. Siroun jammed her shoulder into the blockade, the ice crumbled apart, and she climbed up to the top floor. A shiver ran through Siroun's body as she wrapped her arms around herself and searched for Colin. Only snow and ice saturated the place. The source of the snowy weather came from an ethereal orb of magic with a pile of clothing laying underneath. Behind the orb of magic rested an

Adami-sized ice block. Black shadows danced within the crystalline sculpture of Felthane's form.

As Siroun approached the source of the frozen storm, she put her hand out to touch it, only to phase through the energy. Her knees gave out, and she collapsed next to the clothes, sobbing. Nothing of Colin remained except the radiating power of the icy storm that chilled her to the bone. As her fingers delved through the garments, she felt a piece of parchment in one pocket. She plucked it out and unfolded the wrinkled note. The chilling cold that swirled around the room caressed the fibers of the paper and revealed the enchanted ink written upon it: The friend is the enemy.

At first Siroun wasn't able to connect the dots, and she didn't recognize the handwriting. But Zikky knelt next to her and wrapped an arm around in comfort before looking at the scrap of paper and saying, "Oh, I didn't realize Frosty Fingers was still holdin' onto that note from Spyder."

Siroun's eyes widened. "Wait, you knew Nikostraz was Felthane?"

Zikky scratched at the back of her head. "Ah, well... sorta? I mean, I didn't see the note, just heard the theory."

"Still." Siroun's gaze hardened. "You knew my best friend was the person we've been trying to hunt?"

With Zikky at a loss for words, Lord Valter replied with, "We did, but only after Spyder took Zikky and Colin with her."

Siroun furrowed her brows and shifted her attention to him. "And you didn't tell me?"

"Would you have believed us?"

She paused and stared at the note, her fingers thumbed

at the ink as she mulled over the question before answering with, "No, I suppose not."

As she set the note aside, something else caught her attention: The Sinefine Bible. Even though it was a mere arm's stretch away, she hadn't noticed it until now. Siroun snatched the artifact from the ground and ran her hand over the intricate cover. Memories of the Bat'filinear Ruins came rushing back as she thumbed through the ominous tome and recalled Felthane's frustration when trying to use it. Curiosity overcame her as she searched through the pages to reaffirm every spell was written in the same language as the Map of Selvarethon. Not only that, but as she turned each page, the Sinefine Bible displayed text from other books she remembered reading in the past. The more she flipped through it, the more the pages reflected verses from old Dragomyr fables and other stories. Out of sheer panic, Siroun snapped the Sinefine Bible shut, catching Zikky's attention.

"Is that what we think it is?" the Skivat asked.

"Uh." Siroun tucked a lock of hair behind her ear. "Yes?"

"Oh-ho! Way to go, gel-gel!" Zikky bumped Siroun in the arm with her fist before turning to Lord Valter and saying, "Hey, Fancy Pants! Gel-gel found the artifact!"

Meanwhile, Lord Valter focused on Felthane's frozen prison. Stepping behind the encased criminal, the Duke unsheathed his sword, and positioned the tip of the blade close to the neck region. Zikky held Siroun's hand and nodded to their leader to proceed with the execution.

The sword sang as it moved through Felthane's encased body, swift and unrelenting. Ice shattered and fell to the ground. The Duke's features changed from solemn to disturbed when he cut through a hollow shell with nothing but black smoke inside. Upon realizing Felthane's body was missing, Lord Valter transitioned into a defensive position.

Zikky picked up on the nobleman's caution and pulled Siroun toward the stairwell. An ominous pressure befell the room, and soon Siroun could not move. Both women searched the floor to discover a demonic claw gripping Siroun by the ankle. It reached out from the heap of Colin's clothing. Cackling echoed around the room, and shadows expelled from the pile before forming into Felthane's body once more. This time the hood revealed the full shape of his face. He was a regal-looking man with striking eyes and platinum blond hair. Everything from his facial features to his presentation reminded Siroun much of the Ysile Marden's royal family. But this individual in front of her had sharper features, with a sickly countenance by comparison. The decades of dabbling in necromancy dulled his skin, showing off veins and corrosion of his flesh around the hairline. Despite Siroun's struggling, he pulled her foot into the air, yanking her off-balance, making her stumble to the ground. His other hand held the reliquary he gifted Siroun.

Felthane's laughter subsided as he said, "I knew the boy had a vendetta against me, but I did not know he learned the Kingman's Curse. I'd commend him, but he's not part of this plane anymore."

He yanked Siroun back, ripping her out of Zikky's arms and throwing her against a wall behind him.

"How did you—?" Zikky began, but the warlock expected her question.

The warlock's upper lip curled into a sneer. "Where's the joy in the chase if I tell you all of my secrets? But if you insist." Once again, his visage changed to the features of Councilman Harcourt. With the councilman's voice, he said, "Obviously I knew of this little counterattack. In fact, you could say that I was the one to lay the groundwork. The one thing I love about organized groups is that they're so easy to predi—!"

A fist cracked Felthane across the jaw as Lord Valter closed in without warning. The strike knocked the warlock back while the Duke shook off the discomfort.

"By the mountain's fury, that hurt," Lord Valter cursed under his breath as he shook his hand then wiggled his fingers to make sure he still felt them.

Zikky placed her hands on her hips and belted an appreciative laugh. "That was amazin'! Can ya do it again?"

"I try not to debase my reputation by engaging in common brawling," he muttered before eyeing Felthane with disgust. "This is an exception. Though I must admit, I did not expect it to smart this much."

"Seriously?" Zikky chuckled, wiping a tear of mirth from her eye. "Ya never decked anyone before?"

Felthane used this time to recover from the surprise attack as he glanced over to Siroun still writhing on the floor, and said, "I can see you held back in Fi'ro. I thought Spyder was smarter than that."

This comment brought a smirk to Zikky's face. "Ya don't expect us Hive Lords to kowtow to threats, do ya? We might bicker, but we always look out for their own. Guess ya shoulda known that before pissin' the lot of us off."

The Skivat's remark was met with Felthane taking a

swipe at her only to catch the Duke's blade in his hand. Blood trickled down the edge as the warlock released his grip and backed away, allowing Lord Valter to move in and guard his comrade. Lightning crackled through the saber as runic equations glowed off of the steel.

Meanwhile, the mages below called out to him, "Shall we assist?"

"Your priority is to keep the shield up," Lord Valter commanded.

That split-second conversation gave Felthane the opportunity to shift his body into that of a large feline-looking creature with which to begin his next assault. Demonic energies dripped from its sharp canines, and rolled along its coarse fur, giving the illusion it melded into shadows as it lunged toward its target. While the sounds of punching and swordplay rang in the air, Siroun pushed herself into a sitting position. Her head throbbed and ears rang, but she shook off the discomfort and regained her bearings just in time to see Felthane's sharp teeth bite through Zikky's battle armor and into flesh.

"Zikky!" Siroun gasped, but remained unheard by the fire mage.

"I think it's 'bout time to bring the big spells out," Zikky said through gritted teeth as Felthane chomped into her right shoulder.

Siroun saw Lord Valter cast his empowering spell only to have Felthane change targets. Before the Duke completed half of the vocal components, the warlock slammed into him. Dual-wielding both spell and sword became a clumsy affair. Lord Valter sheathed the weapon and rolled away from another pounce by the bestial creature to avoid losing a limb.

When he fired up the incantation once more, he heard Zikky shout, "Duck!"

As Lord Valter crouched, Zikky came up with her right arm out and clotheslined the warlock mid-air. Both mages tumbled away as Felthane landed on the flat of his back and gasped for air.

"Gettin' tired here, Fancy Pants." Zikky panted and wiped a few beads of sweat from her cheek. "We're gonna be joinin' Colin if we don't do somethin' quick!"

"I know that," said Lord Valter as he gawked at how fast Felthane sprang to his feet. Frustration creased into his face as he worked on his next spell, and a few seconds later he said to Zikky, "I'm going high, catch!"

While not the smartest of decisions to give away strategies, there was no choice. Electricity crackled around the Duke's arms as he cast the spell without words. As the lightning coalesced, he caught the creature lunging toward him at the corner of his eye. The Duke pulled away in time but clicked his tongue with disappointment for having another spell interrupted. Even when attempting to surprise the warlock, it seemed too little too late. When Felthane leaped at him again, Lord Valter braced for impact. But Siroun rushed over and slammed her body into the beast, toppling him to the floor with her. While Felthane laid dumbstruck, Siroun scrambled to her feet with the Sinefine Bible still in tow.

Lord Valter used this opportunity to re-summon the spell, and called out to Zikky, "Take it!"

The fire mage used Felthane's body as a springboard to launch herself into the air. A bolt of lightning flew from Lord Valter's hands, and Zikky moved her gauntlet into its path, causing the gemstone to clip enough of the energy to trigger the instant transformation. Blinding rays of light burst forth from her figure, and the armor glittered with fiery gold as it changed form. Small metal plates layered together like the scales of a dragon, with sharper edges and dramatic etching to give it a reptilian look. Siroun watched as Zikky lunged and slammed her elbow into Felthane's upper body. The force caused bursts of snow to billow throughout the room. The three of them covered their faces as it became impossible to see anything.

Despite the sudden calm, Siroun took several steps back until the stones of the tower wall pushed against her back. At least Felthane couldn't sneak up from an unseen direction. A small comfort as her lungs tightened from the cold air. As the seconds ticked by, she saw movement in the center of the room as powdery snow cleared. When visibility returned, the three of them blinked at each other.

"Where'd he go?" asked Zikky, only to have her question answered in the form of blood-curdling screams and sounds of gore below.

Siroun watched the battlemage dash down the stairwell with lightning speed, followed by the sound of brawling and scuffling. With one more scream, and the sound of guttural splattering, Siroun noticed the magical barrier fading away, leaving the windows open for escape.

"Oh no." Siroun slid over to the stairwell and shouted, "What happened?"

When she saw the gory scene below, a wave of nausea overcame her. The mere glimpse of the spattered blood and dismembered bodies caused her to shut her eyes and move away. Luckily, the fire mage used her lightning-enforced speed to zip back up to the top floor to rejoin them. Clutching at her abdomen, Zikky spat some of blood from her mouth, "He got 'em. The whole team."

Lord Valter limped behind Siroun. "Did you see where he went?"

"No," said Zikky. "He's vanished again. Stay alert."

The Skivat's eyes glanced to Lord Valter and her brows furrowed. She pointed at his face before tapping her fingers to her own upper lip. Siroun recognized this gesture and went to see what Zikky was addressing. It was here that Lord Valter dabbed at his face and realized that blood was running from his nose.

"I had no choice," Lord Valter's somber voice replied.

Siroun's eyes widened as she tore off a loose piece of cloth from her outfit, but he turned away in refusal. "I am fine, Miss Fatima. The fight is not over yet. Like Zikky said, stay alert."

Already she sensed Felthane's foreboding presence surrounding them. A dark miasma crept up the stairwell, causing the three to back away. The tar-like substance bubbled and coalesced into Felthane's Adami shape. This time his skin was black as the void of space.

Zikky cleared her throat. "Oh, that's not good." An ear flicked in Lord Valter's direction. "Got any bright ideas, Sparkles?"

As Lord Valter struggled to prepare himself, he replied, "Hit him with a rock?"

The Skivat chuckled at the ill-timed joke. "How about a fist?"

"Sure."

When Zikky dashed in to strike, Felthane caught her

fist and throttled her against the wall. Neither Siroun nor Lord Valter saw either individual move when the exchange happened. When the Duke tried retaliating with a spell, something crumpled him to the ground. Felthane stood upon the nobleman and dug his heel into the mage's hand, making Lord Valter grunt in pain. The warlock then gripped the nobleman's shoulder and uttered words of a spell Siroun had never heard before, eliciting cries of agony from the Duke.

Through his shrieking Siroun shouted, "Stop! Just stop, please!"

But the plea fell on deaf ears as Felthane relished in the torment he wrought upon the Duke. As much as she wanted to avoid testing the power of the Sinefine Bible, Siroun's frantic fingers opened the tome and searched for anything that could help save her friends. She didn't know what the ramifications of using the Sinefine Bible would be, but she had to try. Her palm pressed upon the pages and the spell came to life. Inky black lines crept along her skin, while feelings of vengeance coursed through her. The dark marks traveled down her body and into the floor, creating an elaborate sephirot of moving gears and runic marks that etched their way over to Zikky. The summoned energy dug into the fire mage's skin just as she was rebuffed again from Felthane's demonic abilities.

Through gritted teeth, Zikky murmured, "Ya gotta be kiddin' me."

Felthane came at the Skivat again, but the empowering spell deflected him, forcing a pause in awe at the trans-formation spectacle. Siroun saw the pain she inflicted on Zikky and regretted the decision. Instead of helping, the spell appeared to be torturing her companion. Though she tried to pull her hand away, the book stuck to her palm.

"No, no, no! This is not what I wanted!" Tears formed in Siroun's eyes.

"Gel-gel, I got it," said Zikky through belabored breathing, then diverted her attention to the power that attempted to consume her. "How 'bout a compromise?"

When Zikky stopped struggling, the black energy engulfed the rest of her form.

"Zikky!" Siroun screamed while a surge of power merged with both the fire and lightning that coalesced within Zikky's armor.

The energies twisted and turned as the plate armor melted into the Skivat's skin, enhancing her musculature. Her hands turned to blackened claws. Spikes grew from her shoulders and back with a mixture of curled shapes. Boots turned to black steel while the rest of the armor became part of the Skivat's body. When the merge of powers finished, a burst of energy exploded off of her, knocking everyone back. Zikky's battle armor radiated with tendrils of black and gold lightning cascaded off of her in crackling waves. She squeezed her knuckles with each hand, the popping audible as she grinned. The moment Felthane moved to find an opening, he took a blow to the face and slammed against the wall.

"Oh man, this is amazin'!" Zikky hopped around, twitching with anticipation. "Ya okay, Fancy Britches?"

Lord Valter grunted as he spat out a mouthful of blood and clutched at his arm. "I shall live."

"Good!"

As Felthane recovered from the surprise attack, Zikky

tried landing another punch, and the warlock dodged. When her fist struck the wall, the ferocity of the impact made the stones crack. Even the Skivat seemed amazed at her newfound strength, and said, "I feel lighter than air."

The two forces danced around the room in a flurry of attacks, making it hard to determine who was winning. Soon, Zikky found the upper hand. With a swing of her right leg, she kicked Felthane across the chest, and the intensity throttled him to the opposite side of the room. Bricks crumbled at the point of impact, causing a small hole to open up through the tower wall.

For a moment, everything was still.

The Skivat leaned forward with her hands on her knees as she panted and waited for the warlock to make his next move. Instead, a roar of frustration assailed their ears before Felthane's visage transformed into an avian shape and made his escape out through the wall opening. Zikky chased after him, but stopped herself in time before she would have plummeted out the window. Her fist pounded at the stone wall as she watched the warlock fly away into the twilight sky, "Get back here, ya bastard!"

With the fight over, Siroun removed her palm from the pages. The black ink slithered off of Zikky's skin and around Siroun, forming into a series of symbols along the floor. When Siroun tried to stand, her body froze to the ground. Panic reflected in her eyes as Zikky tried reaching out only to be rebuffed by the aura Siroun emitted.

"Gel-gel?" Zikky said as she shook her hands and stepped back. "What's going on?"

"I don't know," said Siroun. The Sinefine Bible floated up into the air, and before she could determine what it would do next, it rocketed toward her chest. The pressure upon impact felt like her ribcage was being squeezed. She endured the throbbing pain until the Sinefine Bible disappeared into her body. When the pain subsided, she shuffled to her feet.

"Are ya okay?" said Zikky as she poked Siroun a few times. "How'd ya do that?"

She nodded in response to the first question, then furrowed her brows at the second question. "Surprisingly, I feel okay. Better than okay. But I haven't a clue as to what just happened."

Siroun couldn't explain why Sinefine Bible's presence comforted her. However, their priorities shifted the moment they both heard Lord Valter's belabored breaths, and they rushed to his side. Zikky helped move him into Siroun's lap so she could clean away the blood with a spare kerchief from her jacket. Tears ran down Siroun's cheeks as she toiled to get Lord Valter cleaned up.

"What happened?" his voice somewhat raspy.

"Felthane got away again," said Siroun, and his gaze reflected disappointment. She couldn't blame him. Every time they gained a victory, it always came with a caveat.

Lord Valter followed up with, "… and the bible?"

"It's safe."

That response elicited a sigh of relief from the Duke.

"I'll get help," said Zikky as she stood and descended the stairwell.

Siroun didn't want to think about the floor below where Felthane left behind a gruesome scene. Then there was Colin. The heartache caused Siroun to go from tearful to crying. Lord Valter's palm pressed against her cheek, and she clutched at it only to cry even harder. The ethereal frost continued to billow waves of powdery snow that dusted the floors and settled into the cracks of the stone walls. It was all that remained of Colin.

41

*A*S THE MESSENGER hawks settled in for the evening, the Keeper fed the last bird and shut the cage. Wiping his brow, he said to them, "There, all tucked in for the night."

They cooed a goodnight as he picked up his handlers gloves only to hear frantic flapping sailing toward him. He checked the window to see the scant shadow of a much larger hawk flying in an erratic pattern. Before he reacted, the bird dove through and tackled him to the ground. The hawks cawed in distress as the Keeper's voice gasped for air through gurgles of blood. Limbs flailed momentarily before going limp. The avian-like creature paused, then transformed into an Adami silhouette as Felthane coughed from the wounds he earned an hour prior.

"Damn mages!" Felthane spat as he lifted himself off of the dead body and looked around to see if anyone else had heard him enter the Aviary. The only company he had were the swarms of hawks crying warning sounds to those who would listen from their cages.

To this, Felthane snarled and whipped his hand out while shouting, "Quiet!"

A ring of shadow pulsed from his body, cascading through the bars rendering the birds unconscious. One-by-one they dropped to the ground as silence took hold. With a slow inhale, Felthane allowed the warm summer air to fill his lungs and clear his mind while he decided his next move.

He knew it was dangerous to return to Ysile Marden, but he was too close to achieving his goal to abandon the plan now. Fresh blood pooled around the Keeper's body and the warlock reached down and pressed both of his palms into the warm liquid. He got to work using it as ink to draw a circle and several runic symbols around the cadaver. This process required him to work fast since the blood started congealing while coating the stone surface.

After painting the summoning symbols, Felthane reached into his robes and pulled the reliquary he wrested from the ice mage. There was no way he could take back his kingdom with the power he possessed, now that the half-breed girl had the Sinefine Bible in her possession.

As much as Felthane hated to admit it, he needed That One's help again.

Foreign words slipped off of his tongue. Words that held meaning only to the one receiving the summons instead of the speaker. Felthane never wasted time trying to translate a language that no one knew. Those who did went mad and destroyed their work by fire before jumping into the flame themselves. All Felthane knew was that if he spoke these words, and offered a suitable sacrifice, One

Of Them would come. Who, and in what capacity, was always a gambit.

When Felthane finished, he lifted the reliquary high and went to throw it down, but hesitated. There was no guarantee that his offering would be accepted, and the last thing he wanted to do was destroy what little power he held. However, he snapped out of his cowardice and smashed the reliquary to the floor. The emerald green liquid splattered in all directions, coating the dead Keeper and the inner circle. Smoke spewed from the viscous remnants as the sound of souls cried all around him. Meanwhile, the bloody letters illuminated into a bright green color and slithered around the offering as another voice whispered around him. Felthane felt her presence, and he swallowed hard as he waited for the ritual to finish.

Her power prickled at his nerves as fits of giggles reverberated off of the Aviary walls, mocking him. The letters stopped, and all came to a pause. The only thing Felthane heard was the sound of his heart beating and the night calls of the wild animals beyond the castle. Seconds later, they leaped from the stone flooring and speared the fallen Keeper like long needles. The power brought the man back to life as his eyes widened and his body began to move on its own. Swirls of emerald smoke ebbed around and stood the body upright to face the warlock. Felthane straightened his posture to maintain a facade of bravery.

The corpse gave him a wry smirk as the deity clicked her borrowed tongue and said, "I haven't received a blood offering this lacking of quality since the first time we met. Did we run out of nobles to bequeath me?"

Felthane's lip twitched downward, but held his composure. "My apologies, My Goddess Nephiria. The next one will be of royal blood to make up for it."

"I certainly hope so."

While it displeased him to grovel before a higher being, Felthane took a deep breath and said, "Why didn't you tell me the Sinefine Bible can only be wielded by that half-breed commoner?"

"Did I not say that?" Nephiria mused as she reached up to touch her chin ever-so-delicately. "So sorry about that."

Her flippant attitude hit a nerve, and he growled, "You promised me the power to take back my kingdom!"

To that, she wagged her finger at him. "No, you asked me to lead you to great power. Then you showed me the scribblings of your mad ancestor and I helped nudge you along."

Felthane sucked in the air through his teeth as Nephiria tilted her head at him. "What's the matter? All you have to do is get the wielder to play your little warlord games."

"Taking back my birth rite is not a game."

"Oh?" However, Nephiria's tone lacked any surprise at his impassioned response. "Then what is it? Are you angry that you didn't pay attention to the details of our agreement before accepting? That is not my problem, mortal. You have no one to blame but yourself for your failings. I held up my end of the bargain, and luckily, so did you."

The warlock was about to refute her claim when the last words she spoke made him pause. Felthane had to pull every trick in the book to guide Siroun and the Vanis Aer to the Sinefine Bible's location since he could not find nor take possession of it on his own. He pondered why Nephiria didn't just grab the power for herself.

But before he wandered too far into those thoughts, she sighed, "If you have nothing further, I take my leave of you."

Smoke rose from the floor when Felthane shouted, "Wait!"

Her eyes narrowed. "What?"

"I wish to make a new pact."

She laughed. The jingling tone grated on Felthane's patience before she pretended to wipe a tear of mirth away and replied with, "Really?"

"Give me the power to overwhelm the forces of Ysile Marden and take back my throne."

Nephiria's expression shifted from amusement to contempt. "You have outgrown your welcome, mortal. I'm done humoring your fruitless ambitions."

Felthane was not about to let her go without having something in return for the reliquary he destroyed. He spat out, "I will pay you with the bodies you desire for your current projects. Many of them will be of great use to you."

The pause in her body language gave the warlock a sliver of hope as she took her time giving him an answer. He didn't have to wait long. Whispers danced along the stone walls as she glanced in their direction before the summoning circle glowed a putrid yellow, and a cylindrical vial rose and floated in front of her. Unlike the previous reliquary, this was cast in iron with the skeletons of multiple races clutching the vial as though their lives depended on it. The center radiated a hue of blood red and a fiery orange as though the essence of a volcano was imprisoned within. From it, the faint screams of over a thousand demonic voices pulsed in Felthane's mind, causing him to wince as the overbearing power cowed him.

Nephiria smirked as she offered it. "I have no further interest in you, but it appears my colleague wishes to make a pact instead."

As Felthane secured the powerful reliquary in his hands, she gave him a slight nod as though to send him off.

"Take this army and find suitable bodies for them," she commanded before the Keeper's upper lip curled into a sneer. "Enjoy a last hurrah while you cling to your pitiful dream."

When she turned away from him, Felthane sneered and replied in a saccharine voice, "Give your colleague my thanks."

"Hmpf."

With those last words the body hardened and turned black before falling into a pile of ash upon the floor. With the sacrificial body gone, Felthane confronted the frightened eyes of a youthful page who came to check on the Keeper.

As the young boy's breath quivered in fear, he turned and tried to bolt down the hall, shouting, "Help! Hel—!"

The page didn't make it five strides when Felthane held the youth's jugular in his left hand, and the twitching body in his right. White streams of smoke wafted off of it and Felthane breathed in the soul. Any damage rendered by the previous scuffle with the three Vanis Aer mages faded away. When he finished, he discarded the husk, grabbed one of the nearby sconce torches, and tossed it to the loose hay that littered the sides of the Aviary. While the flames consumed the kindling, it lapped up the blood and bones of boy and birds alike.

42

FLOWER PETALS RAINED upon the graves of those who had fallen in the conflict at the watchtower. Seven in total, with Colin placed in the center and decorated with top honors. The ceremony was serene, held in the private gardens of the castle where immediate friends and family of the dead could mourn their losses. Many of the gentry came to pay their respects, while Siroun stood with Zikky and Niamh within the crowd. Siroun's eyes were red and puffy from the endless tears shed the night prior.

As she sniffled and wept her way through the sermon, Zikky placed a palm on her shoulder and whispered in Vat'tu, *"It's okay, gel-gel."*

"Is it?" replied Siroun in the same language, to which Zikky nibbled at her lower lip and said nothing further.

The guild's council members took their places upon the podium to give their condolences and edicts on the courage of those who perished. Every word spoken made Siroun fight harder at curbing her tears. Meanwhile, Lord Valter, having an entourage of healers care for him the night before, appeared much better today. However, under the fancy clothing Siroun was told that the medics wrapped a support bandage around his chest. Felthane's attacks did internal damage more than anything else on the Duke. Zikky's wounds were cursory by comparison, and the bites she sustained healed under a cleric's care.

The priestess presiding over the funeral spoke her last prayer, and said, "You may now pay speak to the fallen."

One-by-one people approached the closed caskets and place their offerings. The brutality of the event made it impossible to show the bodies to the public. The mages were slaughtered like chattel and their souls siphoned from their bodies. Colin had no tangible body to put in a casket. Instead, one of his uniforms and guild badges remained inside as a symbol of what he represented within the guild. But that didn't ease the mourning process as Siroun, Zikky, and Niamh placed their hands upon the lacquered coffin and whispered their goodbyes into the wind.

Siroun dug her fingers into her chest, trying to stop her heart from aching. She watched Sebastian, whose brown eyes were crestfallen, as he stared at the box that held only mementos of his childhood friend. The councilman had not slept given the dark circles under his eyes and the disheveled state of his hair.

"I wonder," said Siroun, "what Sebastian must think right now."

Niamh didn't look up at him. Instead, she pressed her lips upon the casket and murmured back, "He thinks he's responsible."

As Siroun mimicked Niamh's gesture, the three women walked toward an unoccupied section of the gardens to chat further. While they processed everything that had happened, Siroun replied, "Why does he think he's responsible for this?"

"Sebastian taught Colin the spell."

Zikky raised a brow at Niamh, "The Kingman's Curse?"

She nodded, and silence befell the three of them. No one could replace the angst-ridden curmudgeon with a tender heart that was Colin. Siroun saw Niamh redirect her gaze toward the podium only to find Sebastian had vanished from sight.

Her eyes widened, and she turned to the others, "I must go find him."

"Do what ya gotta do," said Zikky, and the herbalist took off past the lingering noblemen, disappearing into the castle.

Siroun's eyes drifted over to Lord Valter chatting with his wife. The Duchess Ammeline maintained a stoic exterior, but Siroun noticed the lace accents of her hairpiece and sleeves trembling. Lord Valter, Zikky, and Siroun were the lucky ones to have survived. Her gaze drifted to the Vanis Aer council that remained stationed near the caskets. Grim expressions decorated every face as they conversed with the friends and family of the fallen.

With a long sigh, Zikky broke the silence between them with, "Guess we better head back to our rooms, eh? Want an escort?"

"Yes, please," said Siroun.

They walked side-by-side through the gardens and into the foyer that branched off into other hallways riddled throughout the castle. If it weren't for Zikky's impeccable sense of direction, Siroun would have gotten lost within the opulent corridors of Hjarta Castle. They went up the nearest set of stairs and made their way toward the guest wing without speaking a word to one another.

Siroun still couldn't believe that Colin had died. Despite all odds, she still maintained the hope that they would swoop in and save him at the last minute. When Felthane murdered Lilistraz and the others at the library, she felt responsible. But she didn't feel a sense of loss by similar comparison. In a matter of a few months, Siroun harbored a closer kinship to the Vanis Aer mages than toward most of the villagers she grew up with for the last twenty-four years. Even though Colin teased and berated her, there wasn't the same sense of malice. His behavior annoyed her in the same way a little brother picked on an older sibling. It was a strange bond, but a fond one in hindsight. A wistful smile tugged at her lips.

"We're here," said Zikky.

The words jarred Siroun out of her thoughts, and she blinked away a renegade tear before realizing they arrived at her room.

"Oh." Siroun replied, but didn't move.

Zikky observed her for a moment or two then pursed her lips. "Ya gonna be okay, gel-gel?"

It felt like a loaded question as Siroun realized that she would be in the room by herself. Though she had spent several evenings alone, recent events re-surged in her mind. The letter from Felthane, Colin's death, how the warlock infiltrated and moved around the castle with ease. Without realizing it, Siroun's breathing picked up and her body trembled.

Zikky's ears twitched as she asked, "Gel-gel… ya sure yer okay?"

To which a hand reached out and clutched Zikky's in response.

For a minute, all was still. Zikky's warm, dry hand intertwining with hers brought a sense of calm to the storm of anxiety in Siroun's heart. When Siroun found the words to speak, she whispered, "Don't leave me."

The Skivat's eyes widened before she replaced the surprise with a relaxed smile. "Don't worry, gel-gel."

"I can't be alone. I'm too afraid." The salty sting of Siroun's tears burned her eyes before running down her cheeks once more.

This time a thumb caressed them away. Leaning in, Zikky placed a soft kiss upon Siroun's brow then pressed foreheads and whispered back, "Then I'll stay here with you tonight."

43

Lord Valter hovered over his desk, thumbing the guild patch with Colin's surname embroidered into the fabric. Candle wax pooled around the base of the dimming firelight as his mind replayed the events from the day before, wondering what he could have done differently to save the young mage. With no living relatives, and no other personal belongings besides the clothes on his back, Colin was destined to disappear into the annals of time. They listed the Lockwood mage as a casualty after unsuccessfully thwarting Felthane, nothing more. That thought didn't sit well with Lord Valter. He, more than anyone, realized what Colin sacrificed in exchange for one chance at bringing the warlock to heel. The other guild members who fell in the fray had families to build memorials and honor their legacy. To think Colin only had a handful of colleagues to remember him felt disparaging.

His finger glided over the uneven threads of the patch as he heard his wife come up behind him. Lady Ammeline ran her hands along his shoulders, careful to avoid his injured arm, and gave him a gentle hug. "You have been awake most of the night, my love. Come to bed."

When that garnered no response, her gaze flicked toward the object in his hand. "It was nice for the King to have a sermon in their honor."

"Mm," he nodded, still fidgeting with the badge.

Lady Ammeline pulled away and positioned herself in a chair next to him. Her voice reposed as she asked, "What is wrong, husband?"

His wife always entrusted him to take care of these affairs without her involvement. But when he saw the look of concern in her eyes through the stoic exterior, he let out a drawn-out sigh.

Lord Valter set the patch aside and rubbed his right temple. "I realize that I am not the paragon of leadership with these field missions. My skills are better suited to matters of state."

She reached out and placed a hand upon his arm. "And your people love you for it."

Though simple, the words were comforting. Lord Valter forced a meager smile and placed his hand over hers. Together, they lingered in silence as his wife's eyes scrutinized him.

She tilted her head. "But?"

Lord Valter wrestled with burdening his wife too much on thoughts that lacked faith in their sovereign. On reflection, there were no other parties that were privy to his suspicions except her. They spent a lifetime building a home and country together. If anyone understood his frustration, it was her.

"I am concerned that His Majesty is hiding something of great importance behind this mission," he said.

"That is commonplace for a King, my dearest."

He felt silly for wording his concerns in such an obvious manner. "Yes, I agree that it is His Majesty's right to disclose what he sees fit. However, I have found it disconcerting that our target knows more about us than we do of him. Felthane navigates Anastas bureaucracies as though they were his own. He knows our every move, and how to infiltrate resources within Ysile Marden to his advantage. With the sequences of events being what they are, I have to wonder if the King knows him on a personal level. His Majesty is adamant about not disclosing those details with me."

Lady Ammeline leaned over and placed a kiss upon her husband's head before smiling at him, "Do not fret too much, husband. If Felthane is here, he cannot make a move without exposing himself. With both the royal army and the Vanis Aer Æther Guild, too many eyes and ears are within these walls to risk taking action."

He appreciated her optimism, but that didn't ease his mind any less. Those thoughts got interrupted when they both heard the fussing of their little boy. Donato padded his way into the room and buried his face into his mother's night shift.

She reached out and stroked the child's hair. "What's wrong, dear?"

Through sniffles the young heir stammered out, "Can't sleep."

In her soothing voice she replied, "Aww, I'm sorry, darling. Shall I fetch you something warm to drink?"

The child shook his head through her skirts, and Lord Valter realized it was one of Donato's usual nightmares. Glancing at his wife, he said, "I believe a walk to the kitchens for snack may be in order."

That perked the child right up as he looked over to his mother and nodded. It disheartened Lord Valter to know that his son preferred his mother to him, but he looked to Lady Ammeline and said, "You are the chosen one, My Lady."

She gave him an apologetic smile while picking Donato up into her arms and stood. "Maybe next time, my love."

That was always the response: Maybe next time. Lord Valter wondered how many times he had to endure before Donato chose him to pilfer the kitchen for nighttime snacks. As he followed her to the door, Lord Valter wrapped a heavy robe around the both of them to cover her state of dress. He exchanged a kiss and ruffled his son's hair before they made their way out.

"Be careful," he warned her.

She smiled as she gestured for the nearby guards to come to her side. "Get some sleep, my love. We won't be gone long."

Lady Ammeline placed one last kiss on his cheek before whispering instructions her guardsmen where to go. Soon, they rounded the corner together and disappeared. Lord Valter closed the door and ran his hands through his hair. Thoughts drifted back to the danger at hand. Time grew short for all of them, and he took the onus of uncovering Felthane's identity for the sake of his remaining team.

Lord Valter headed back to his desk, pushed aside Colin's patch, and pulled forth a weathered piece of parchment he kept on his person at all times. It was the original missive given to him by the King and carried the royal seal so that, in cases of dire need, he used it for acts of diplomacy. This document allowed his team into Niravad, albeit a short time. As he read through the orders once more, he tried to discern any clues to Felthane's identity that might have slipped past him. Nothing within the message stood out, except for: He is a danger to the crown.

That statement was too vague to extrapolate anything of value. Being an individual of esteem himself, Lord Valter thought of the many things that were a danger to his position. Things like assassination, war, political uprisings, and ambitious relatives were possibilities that endangered anyone with prominent wealth or titles.

But he paused on that last option.

Before he could think too hard on the King's relatives, he heard a wall open up within the room. The soft clanking of dishes made Lord Valter realize that a servant arrived to deliver something. A silver cart came out from around the dressing wall, and Lord Valter went to stand up when the servant gestured for him to sit.

"No need to get up on my account, Your Grace," she said with a mischievous smile.

He raised a brow at the woman as she carted her wares to the center of the bedroom and started setting up a small plate of cheese and fruit.

"You are here earlier than I expected," said Lord Valter, noticing that the time had to be well around three of four in the morning because of Donato's frequent stirrings.

"No earlier than usual, Your Grace."

While he knew the schedules of his servants back home

in Firenz, Ysile Marden had different operating schedules. Still, during his time in the palace, he remembered servants in the room setting up breakfast with the sun rising, not before.

Lord Valter furrowed his brows and said, "I do not recall having breakfast at the ready this soon."

She finished pouring tea into the cup. "The Duchess thought you could use a snack."

Upon hearing those words, Lord Valter relaxed, feeling silly for his guarded disposition. With a heavy sigh, he rubbed at his face to stimulate his sleep-deprived brain. "My apologies."

"No need, Your Grace," she replied as she offered him the tea. "It's been a hard few days for the lot of us given all that's happened. 'Tis expected you'd be on edge."

He took the cup with appreciation and sat back at the desk chair while she ripped a small hunk of bread from another plate and slathered some butter on it. He accepted the offered food and took a modest bite as he tried returning to his prior thoughts regarding Felthane's identity.

The servant girl spoke again to interrupt him. "Y'must be thinkin' 'bout somethin' very troublesome if you've been up this whole time."

Lord Valter's eyes narrowed when her accent changed. "Yes, you might say that."

The servant girl continued fussing with the snack cart by arranging things one way, only to change them up again, then several times more. From the looks of things, she appeared to be wasting time for no reason. She glanced up and caught eye contact with Lord Valter to give him a seductive smile. An uncomfortable flush came over him.

"You look tense, Milord," she sidled toward him as he leaned away.

The back of his chair pinned him in place, preventing his escape. He noticed the weight of her body slide onto his lap as she draped herself upon him and ran her fingers through his hair, whispering, "Allow me to help you relieve some stress."

It took several times of clearing his throat before Lord Valter lurched away with a stern, "You need to leave."

"Don't be like that, Your Grace," she cooed, running her fingers along his cheek. "I make sure everyone I service is satisfied. Even Lord Marcus."

Though most of the rulers of Anastas were not the most faithful of husbands, Lord Valter was in no mood to play this game with her. The mention of Marcus's name only added fuel to the fire of impropriety. As she snaked her hand toward his groin, Lord Valter grabbed her wrist to halt her.

He knew she was taking advantage of his fatigue, and mustered his remaining energy to steel both his gaze and his voice, "Get out. Now."

Lord Valter stood, shifting her weight off, when he felt a stabbing pain in his chest. Blood shot up his throat and into his mouth, and the excess dribbled down his chin. Though he tried to breathe, the foreign object that occupied his lungs prevented him from performing such a fundamental act of survival. Instead, he found the servant girl's arm jammed deep into his chest. The black discoloring of her skin, along with the familiar demonic form that mutated her hand into more of a claw made him realize he would never make that first trip to the kitchen with his son.

When he looked into the woman's eyes, she returned a satisfied smile while dropping the feminine voice. "Two dead, one more to go."

Smoke blanketed her form then vanished, revealing Felthane's devious smile. When he removed his claw, Lord Valter gave one last gasp for breath before falling back. However, the warlock grabbed him by the throat, holding him in mid-air. Though the Duke tried to struggle his body become frigid and limp. All he could do was watch Felthane open a free hand and cast a spell that tore at his skin as though it was being flayed.

"It's a pity the false King is losing his most loyal dog. Fear not, your skills are of use to me; and I'll send your lovely wife my regards."

Lord Valter's agonizing moans were not loud enough to alert anyone to come to his aid. As his life essence fell into an unknown abyss, his last thoughts were of the safety of his family as his mortal shell breathed out one last word, "… Ammeline."

44

THE RAYS OF the morning sun poured into the large window, rousing Siroun to waking. She turned over and smiled when she saw Zikky still passed out next to her in bed. Colin's death still weighed on her heart, but having Zikky with her to get through those dark emotions made it easier.

Zikky's yawn made the bed shake as the Skivat awoke to stretch her arms and legs before rubbing her eyes, mumbling, "Mornin'."

Through a yawn of her own, Siroun said, "Sleep well?"

"Oh yeah," Zikky grinned ear to ear, satisfied. "This bed's comfy. I should get one for my room."

"We can't afford such a luxury."

"Yeah, yer probably right." Zikky sat up and stretched again.

Siroun admired the subtle curvature of the Skivat's body. Somehow Zikky had no problem sleeping in the nude while Siroun preferred wearing a night shift. Even though she had seen Zikky naked before, things were different now. Siroun didn't have to act like someone she wasn't around the other woman, and Zikky was a fun person to be around even with the lack of decorum. Before Siroun got too lost in thought, she saw Zikky tense up, and her long ears twitch toward the door.

She tilted her head. "What's wrong?"

Zikky put a finger to her lips, and her ears twitched again. With careful listening, Siroun couldn't hear anything at first. As a few moments passed, however, the sounds of clanking metal fast approached their door. Not just any metal, but plated armor. Guardsmen.

Zikky pointed at the dressing curtain and whispered, "Go."

Before Siroun could slide out of bed, the door banged while a soldier barked on the other side, "By order of the King!"

Not a second later the guards barged into the room as Siroun scooted behind the dressing curtain. Zikky leaped out in front of them, and the soldiers halted in discomfort as the Skivat took a fighting stance in the buff. Their leader cleared his throat and stammered, "R-remove yourself, o-our business is w-with the h-half-breed."

"Half-breed?" Zikky narrowed her eyes at them. She opened up her hand and fire sprang from her palm. "She's an honored guest of the Rosario family."

By now the soldiers were staring at the ground while one tried sneaking around toward the curtain. They didn't get far as the ground lit up with an orange-colored rune and Zikky clicked her tongue at them. "I wouldn't do that if I were ya."

Siroun wiggled out of her shift and dressed as fast as

possible while the conversation continued between Zikky and the commander.

"She was a guest," he said, "until we found the Duke of Firenz murdered in his chambers earlier this morning."

The news caused Siroun to halt. Her breath hitched in her throat, and she felt a stabbing sensation in her chest. When she finished putting on her jacket, she clapped her hands over her mouth to remain silent through both the pain in her chest and in her heart. Tears welled up in her eyes, and as they rolled to the floor, they turned the carpet black where they landed. It took every ounce of willpower for Siroun to not have a mental breakdown.

Zikky's spell dissipated from her hand, her eyes wide in disbelief. "What? How? And what does this have to do with gel-gel?"

"That is none of your concern, Skivat."

"I beg to differ," Zikky replied as a series of new equations appeared around her right arm. "Gel-gel? Ya all right back there?"

The commander took a step forward. "Stand down, field agent."

Zikky balled her hand into a fist. "Don't move an armored plate, Tin Can."

Even though Siroun heard the words, she continued struggling to contain her rage. More tears rolled down her face in black streaks and her fingertips began to match in color as she dabbed at her eyes and realized something was wrong.

"Gel-gel?" Zikky called to her once more, this time with greater concern in her voice.

Siroun swallowed her grief and wiped at her eyes. The

tears stained a few spots on her clothes but she took a deep breath and carried onward. With Siroun dressed, she peeked around the corner and recognized the spell Zikky had on standby. The battle armor incantation had a particular series of symbols full of jagged numbers that danced in a double-helix formation whenever Zikky summoned it.

By the look on the commander's face, it appeared the guardsmen didn't expect Zikky to be here. Otherwise, they would have come equipped with a Vanis Aer mage to keep her busy. Zikky used this moment of surprised to her advantage and clenched her fist. The spell absorbed into her arm, creating rows of glowing tattoos upon her skin. In a split-second, Zikky leaped at the commander, clotheslined him in the throat, then slammed him to the ground. It was the only vulnerable spot against the neck-to-toe plate armor she had to work with. Her speed caught the rest of the soldiers off-guard, and when she dusted her hands off, they stood there dumbfounded. The commander writhed and coughed, trying to catch his breath.

Through the pain, he sputtered, "A-arrest them!"

The entourage snapped out of their surprise and descended upon Zikky while a couple broke off after Siroun.

Zikky reacted by sweeping the legs from underneath a guard. "Gel-gel, uniform!"

Time was of the essence as Siroun saw the oncoming guards. She yanked off the Vanis Aer uniform that hung over the dressing curtain, then kicked the screen forward. The large panels ricocheted off the soldiers' plate armor, disorienting them long enough for her to flee to the other side of the room. She separated Zikky's pants and tossed them in her direction, "Catch!"

The Skivat grabbed another guardsman by the shoulder armor and swung him around into the next. When the pants sailed in her direction, she plucked them mid-air and smiled. "Thanks!"

As more guards came to surround the fire mage, she tucked her feet into the pants before rolling onto her back and pinwheeled her legs over herself. The surrounding guards found themselves on the receiving end of a leg, striking them either at the knee, causing them to fall, or into their hip, knocking them into another colleague.

Zikky spun herself back to her feet and secured the straps of her pants in place, all the while grinning at the fallen soldiers. "Looks like y'all need more hand-to-hand combat practice. Captain Strait-Laced ain't gonna be pleased with ya."

While the groans within the room escalated, Siroun continued fleeing from the soldier that maintained pursuit of her. Siroun knew she couldn't take them on in hand-to-hand combat, so she aimed for an alternative approach. As the soldier chased her toward the front of the room, she grabbed a nearby sconce with one hand, turned around, and smashed it into the soldier's face, knocking them out cold.

"Ha!" Siroun gloated with pride. "Take that!"

Zikky saw the attack at the corner of her eye and said, "Nice work, gel-gel!"

Siroun's victory was short-lived as another guard noticed their colleague was out of commission and turned toward her. Her gloating switched to worry as she bounded toward the bed while the guard gave chase. With what little training she had, Siroun decided to use the surrounding furniture to gain an advantage. She leaped onto the mattress to gain some extra height and tossed Zikky's clothes in the other woman's direction before jumping off. When the pursuing soldier went around the foot of the bed, something swathed his face, and pulled him towards the floor. His head knocked sideways against the bedpost then fell to the ground. Standing over him was Zikky's smug grin as she gave her shirt a quick snap before putting it on. With that out of the way, the Skivat scrambled into her overcoat as the last guardsman tried making their escape.

"Alert the King!" the female guard shouted before the floor lit up with a burst of fire under her feet and blasted her backward. Siroun side-stepped when the female knight sailed by.

"Damn," Zikky muttered. "I was hopin' that wouldn't happen."

A high-pitched trill followed soon afterward, and Zikky plugged her ears as Siroun looked around to seek the source. Though annoying, Siroun couldn't help notice that Zikky's sensitive hearing took a beating. Through gritted teeth, the Skivat shouted, "Looks like some of my colleagues are in the area."

"Where is this noise coming from?" By now the two were almost shouting at each other.

"Magic detection wards," she said, making her way to the door and took a peek outside to see if others were coming. "They're great for trackin' rogue magic-users since anythin' arcane triggers them. I'm surprised it didn't activate durin' my first spell."

"Maybe they activated it when the guard alerted them?" Tears started welling up in Siroun's eyes as Lord Valter's death returned to her thoughts. She slapped her cheek to regain her composure, and said, "What do we do?"

"Run."

With no time to put on shoes, both of them ran barefoot through the hall. The ward that triggered earlier began hurting Zikky's ears, and she tried casting a counter-spell behind her to silence it only to end up triggering another ward ahead of them. Through the commotion, Zikky pulled Siroun along, bobbing and weaving into pockets of safety. The escape started going smoothly when a courtier they passed saw them and shouted, "Guards! She is here!"

The cry summoned forth a single Vanis Aer mage in a red-colored jacket, and Zikky clicked her tongue. "A fledglin'."

A distinct metal bracelet with glowing runes donned young mage's left wrist as they pulled their arms into an archer's position and conjured a series of equations as fast as he could muster. Bolts of ice formed, and he fired them in their direction, landing near Siroun's feet. Zikky pushed Siroun aside to escape the first shot. When the spell touched the floor, it spread out, freezing anything in a two-foot radius. More ice arrows rained upon them without further wards from going off, and Siroun realized the bracelet held the answer of why. Zikky came to a similar conclusion. Speeding toward the red-coated mage, she dodged left and right. When the Vanis Aer exhausted himself, Zikky closed in, landing a knee to his abdomen and knocking the wind out of him. He rolled several times before landing in a crumpled heap, coughing and sputtering from the strike.

"Sorry kid," Zikky said with a smirk as she reached down and removed the bracelet from his wrist to transition it to her own. She then snapped her fingers and the magic wards went silent. "Ah, quiet at last."

"We should go," said Siroun, then turned a corner only to bump into an approaching courtier. Her instincts kicked in, and she gave a respectful bow and replied, "Pardon me."

"Watch where you're—." The man locked eyes on Siroun, and both of them stood silent for a second to assess one another. It didn't take long before his eyes widened and he shouted, "Help! The strange one is on the loose! Guards!"

To that, Siroun cocked her head and narrowed her reptilian eyes at him. "Strange one?"

Zikky seized Siroun's wrist and tugged her along. "Not now, gel-gel."

Once again, they made another mad dash to find a different exit. Every time they attempted to avert one group, they collided into another. The loud clattering of boots on the marble floor closed in tighter around them until the two found themselves back-to-back.

Out of breath, Zikky glanced back. "Got any last second ideas?"

Siroun hunched over panting, lacking the stamina by comparison to her comrade. She brought a hand to her chest intending to summon the Sinefine Bible.

"Siroun," said a familiar voice that made her stop. For a moment she thought she had gone mad. However, the soldiers shifted to give room to a Dragomyr processing through the hall, confirming the voice she heard. His stern features never changed as he looked upon Siroun with disappointment.

"Cease this futile running," he said in the Drakish tongue.

A silver guard mage saw Siroun's moment of hesitation and seized the opportunity to act by speaking two words of power and flicked the summoned equations in her direction. The ground below both Zikky and Siroun lit up, and silver threads of light dove onto their legs, seizing any control they had over their bodies. As Siroun collapsed to her knees from the binding spell, she looked up at the one Dragomyr she never expected to be in Ysile Marden.

"… Brother?"

Wriggling his snout, Vasylvad turned his attention to a lieutenant, and said, "I believe my business here is finished."

When the Dragomyr turned away, Siroun reached out to him. *"Brother, wait! What's going on?"*

Her sight turned to darkness as both she and Zikky suffered blows to the head, rendering them unconscious.

45

WITHIN THE LAB Sebastian studied several pieces of crystal fragments pulled from the watchtower and placed them on a spell chart for analysis. They lit up under the enchanted ink drawn into several circles with a star pattern in the middle. He centered each piece, hovering his palm over the entire project. Next to him rested an old, massive book Sebastian drudged up from the guild library. The pages opened to a spell written in Arcandus' language titled the Kingman's Curse. Though Sebastian had studied this spell in the past, he took little interest in it, until now.

As the crystals glowed, they gave off a residual trace of magic that Sebastian's palm absorbed while feeling his way through the spell's remnants. The hope was that, somewhere in here, resided a clue on how Colin constructed the curse, and maybe find a loophole to break it. The chances of discovering such a thing were slim, but he felt compelled to try. Others took solace in mourning the dead, but Sebastian granted himself no such quarter. He knew

Colin's true fate of permanent entrapment in an abyss of magic that many believed could never be reversed. There was no way to bring his friend back to the living. Instead, what Sebastian sought for Colin was the release of his soul and a sense of peace.

He probed further into the residual magic trying not to break his concentration, when the door to his lab flew open and Niamh shouted, "Sebastian, trouble!"

The jarring of his focus caused him to reverse the spell on accident. Instead of pulling the Æther remnants out of the crystals with careful precision, he reversed the flow of the magic, causing an immediate overload. They gave off a high-pitched ring that triggered Sebastian to back away.

"Niamh, look out!" he tackled her to the ground and tucked them both behind his robes as the crystals exploded into smaller shards that splintered in every direction. A wave of frost blanketed the room, making the locations of the minuscule pieces that much harder to find. When the spell ended, the two of them exchanged glances before they scrambled away from one another.

Sebastian cleared his throat to gather his courage before saying, "You know it's dangerous when you burst in like that."

"I know, but this is important," Niamh replied with urgency in her voice.

Her tone abated his typical inability to speak. "What's wrong?"

"They found Lord Valter murdered in his guest chambers last night."

All color left Sebastian's face as he stammered out, "W-what? How?"

"I don't know," she said, shaking her head, "but the King accused Siroun of being connected to the crime, and the Royal Guard arrested both her and Zikky."

"Why Zikky?"

"Because she tried helping Siroun resist arrest."

His shoulders slumped. "Yeah, that'll do it."

The two of them shuffled to their feet before Sebastian opened his palm and cast out a quick burst of fire that purged the frost, returning the room to normalcy. Any research on Colin's magical cure would have to wait. Heading back to his table, he released another spell that coated the ground in arcane magic and caused the tiny crystal shards that littered the floor to glow.

"Watch your step," said Sebastian. "They stick to everything. By the way, how did you find this information?"

Niamh side-stepped the glowing pieces before making her way to the table with him. "My mentor, Maria, received an immediate summons when guards found Lord Valter. When I heard the details, I came here as soon as I could."

"I appreciate it," he said with a warm smile. Any remnants of Sebastian's work reduced to char and splintered pieces as he grabbed a small hand broom and dustpan and swept away the debris so that the table wasn't dangerous. The book he referenced during the project survived unscathed. He shut it and shoved it aside while continuing their conversation. "What I don't understand is why the King would think Siroun is a culpable party?"

"I'm not certain," said Niamh, "but it may have to do with Felthane and that bible that's now in her possession. There was a letter written to His Majesty with Felthane's signature left on Lord Valter's body. It threatened to give the crown back to its rightful heir using any means necessary. Perhaps the King is taking necessary precautions?"

"Sounds more to me like he's spooked. Siroun doesn't strike me as the type to help the likes of Felthane." Sebastian's brows knitted together as Niamh's recent information sparked a thought. "Wait a minute. Rightful heir?"

She watched as he stepped over to one of his bookshelves crammed with notebooks, avoiding the floor splinters. His fingers glided over several tomes as he tried recalling the exact information that linked the current events to a past project. One-by-one he pulled out the notebooks, flipped through the pages, and put them away.

As the minutes ticked away, Niamh spoke up, "Need help?"

"Nope!" Sebastian flustered, dithering faster through the journals. "N-no, I swear I'll find it."

"What are you looking for?"

Sebastian didn't respond to the question right away. Instead, he flipped through a few more research journals before his eyes lit up, "Aha! Found it!"

Tip-toeing through the shards, he turned it so that the both of them could skim through his notes. Unfortunately for Niamh, his handwriting looked jagged and smashed together. Many of the letters overlapped in such a way that she squinted only to give him a furtive glance and reply, "I'm afraid you will have to read this to me."

"Oh?" Sebastian blinked. He didn't recall writing the notes in an original language. Upon closer inspection he realized why she said that comment in the first place. "Oh. I'm sorry."

"It's okay," she smiled. "So, what's the connection?"

"Um, yes... well," Sebastian cleared his throat as he flushed from having Niamh's eyes upon him with great intent. "Before the King assigned the mission to Lord Valter, His Majesty had me identify an artifact they found while renovating an abandoned wing of the castle."

Sebastian flipped the page, pointing to a sketch he drew of a cylindrical vial framed with metalwork of two serpents wrapped around it on a linked chain.

Niamh's eyes widened. "A reliquary?"

"Correct."

"But, that... I mean, here?" she fumbled before putting a hand to her mouth and knitting her brows together.

Sebastian understood what Niamh was trying to say and followed up with, "The King claims ignorance on whom it belonged to since practicing the necrotic arts is illegal in Anastas. Still, reliquaries don't just get left behind. The renovators found it in a room that belonged to a member of the royal family from generations past. Which means someone in the family-."

"-was a warlock," Niamh finished for him and shook her head. "Who?"

Waving his finger, Sebastian flipped the page again. "By then the King told me my work was complete, and he confiscated the item to have destroyed; and it was, I saw a priestess purge the thing."

"You couldn't have just used your magic to trace an owner?"

"I had only a few seconds to look at it," said Sebastian. "The moment I identified it as a warlock's reliquary, he took it back and marched off. That is why I drew up a sketch once he left so I wouldn't forget the details. Any spare time I had between other projects I spent looking up old records or textbooks that might have helped me at least date the thing and pinpoint which generation of the Hanmel family to review."

"What does this connection have to do with the letter found on Lord Valter's body?"

The question gave Sebastian pause out of sympathy for the Duchess Ammeline's loss. Even Niamh seemed crestfallen as she fidgeted with the embroidery on her skirts.

Sebastian cleared his throat and ran his finger across the family tree he copied into his notes along with a few prison record entries. "In the 10,300's, during the height of the Finnean Rebellion, there was a cult called the Priory of Broken Tongues who worshiped Nephiria, goddess of lies and deceit. The signature design-work of her reliquaries at the time matches that of the double snake coils of the one we found."

"That's during King Leonel's time."

"Yes, I infiltrated the Heritage Vaults and did some digging."

"You did what?" Niamh couldn't believe it. "Only royalty accesses that place. How did you get in there?"

"I-uh... I have my ways." It wasn't the first time Sebastian broke into a forbidden room within Ysile Marden, and it wouldn't be the last. "Public records show that King Philip had an older sister who died just before his coronation, but that isn't true. He had a brother by the name of Llyr Leonel Tristram Alexander Hanmel."

"Wait a minute," said Niamh. "He has five name sequences. That means Llyr was to be the next successor, not Philip."

"Perhaps," replied Sebastian. "The only trace of Prince Llyr that I could find involved a prison entry, but no other details. Typically, the records enter a date of death, execution, or exoneration, but Prince Llyr only has an entrance date, no exit."

Niamh raised a brow. "Clerical error?"

"Not likely. The remaining prisoners recorded after him had exit dates before the book reached its maximum capacity. His name is the only entry that is the exception. The estimated creation date of that reliquary fits his timeline. If he was the true Crowned Prince of Anastas, then that means Philip isn't the true heir. Not only that, the royal family went to incredible lengths to scrub Prince Llyr from history."

"And the letter from Felthane states he intends to retake the crown to the rightful heir," Niamh murmured before looking over at Sebastian. "Does this mean that Felthane is Prince Llyr?"

"That would make him around seventy years old. Based on what little information I have, defying mortality is an easy feat for a Reaper Warlock as long as they're careful." Sebastian flipped back to the reliquary he sketched and stared at it longer before realizing that it shared similar qualities to the one given to Siroun. His lips transitioned into a grim frown. "The story fits."

"No wonder the King is so secretive," she said with equal candor. "He's been covering up his father's history for years. If this information got out to the public and other nobility, who knows what will happen to this kingdom."

"We need to help Siroun and Zikky escape," said Sebastian, shutting the book. "If Felthane plans to retake the throne, then the King is in danger and he'll need their experience on his side."

He navigated through the splinters and over to a set of cabinets that stored magical odds and ends. To the untrained eye, it looked like abandoned projects and heaps of junk. But Sebastian knew which items were functional between the mundane pieces of scraps.

"I'm not sure about Zikky," said Niamh as she watched him sift through the random scraps in his shelves, "but I overheard Maria tell me that the Vanis Aer Æther Guild detained Siroun in the 'special' cell."

Sebastian halted, and his jaw tightened. As he exhaled, static electricity consumed the room. Niamh watched his emotions change, and she touched the table only to receive a shock to her fingers. When Sebastian heard the snap of electricity bite at her, he calmed himself and shifted his search more to the left where a few spherical pieces of solid metal rested on individual stands.

He grabbed two and shut the cabinets, locking them with an arcane command and tossed one in Niamh's direction. "Catch."

The ball sailed into her hands, and she blinked at its simplicity before holding it up and pointing. "What's this?"

Sebastian returned to the table, tearing the last piece of blank parchment from the journal and grabbed a nearby quill. "I have a plan."

46

*T*IME WAS OF little consequence in this place. The bitter taste of the metal rod from a muzzle wrapped around her face continued to abuse her tongue while her body bemoaned the merciless pulling on her muscles and joints. She hung there, dangled by wrists in iron cuffs that encapsulated her hands. Most of the time, they chained her to a wall next to a cot and piss bucket. Today, however, they positioned her in the center of the room while her chains latched to a hook dangling over her head, forcing her hands toward the sky like a fisherman's catch-of-the-day. Though her feet touched the floor, the blood drained from her fingertips as her shackles kept her taut.

For clothing they gave her some basic linens that covered enough to keep her decent, but never warm. The small cell and shackles might have appeared mundane, but the Vanis Aer Guild mages coated every inch of the prison in enchantments designed to keep whatever unnatural abilities she had silent. They reserved these few specialized cells for the most dangerous of criminals, and Siroun garnered an invitation despite never having done anything to warrant such punishment. A few of the remaining Vanis Aer councilors took samples as though she were a research project. They ripped a few of her scales from her arms, and the linens stained red from the wounds that lacked bandaging.

Siroun could hear a conversation going on in the distance between a man and woman that sounded like Zikky, but it was hard to discern for certain. Her attention shifted back to the cell door with the sound of clicking metal locks and murmuring incantations. When the door opened, the first individual to come through was Vasylvad. Following behind him were several guild members of the Silver Guard who came over and removed the muzzle from her face, then placed themselves on each side of the entryway.

She didn't notice from her encounter with him in the hall that the quality of his robes had upgraded since she last departed Pustelia Crest. The rich embroidery and red colors showed promotion to a higher rank within their region of Libstravad. Seeing Vasylvad in good health felt reassuring. With any hope, he could help straighten things out so that the royal family would realize she was of no threat to anyone.

"Congratulations on your promotion," said Siroun in Drakish, trying to muster a smile with what little energy she had left.

"Thank you," the tone in the Dragomyr's voice sounded insincere.

Siroun picked up on the sarcasm after having spent so much time with Colin. Any hope she had of Vasylvad exonerating her disappeared as the Dragomyr paced around the cell and shook his head.

When he came face-to-face with her, he sighed and backed away a few paces. *"When our father took you in, I knew something was wrong. I was too young to understand what was going on back then. I couldn't believe my father took another lover so soon after losing my mother."*

Her eyes shifted to that of sympathy. Siroun understood that he endured just as many hardships as her these past years. The guards glanced at each other, not understanding the language Vasylvad spoke, but remained still.

"I spent years denying the truth," Vasylvad continued, *"and enduring the scorn from my friends and peers alike for accepting you as an equal. I endured it because I believed you were of my father's flesh and blood, and that family should stick together regardless of scorn or ridicule. However, the Regents gifted me with the truth after you fled home with Nikostraz and those mages, and I no longer feel the burdens of guilt and shame anymore. As you now see, I can pursue higher ranks among my people. My father can retire knowing that I can support our household on my own. I am now deemed ideal as a mate and a partner. For the first time in ages, I am treated favorably among my people. Without you, my father and I have been living the life we've always wanted."*

Siroun watched him pluck at the fabrics of his new tunic, emphasizing the promotion, likely because of her absence. An emotional piercing sensation ripped through her chest. *"I'm sorry to have brought you such hardships."*

Vasylvad's lip curled, then vanished. Instead, he changed the subject, *"I see that Nikostraz is not around to help you either. He might be a Dragomyr of the world, but he seemed more interested in your affections than aiding our village, and now I know why. He was part of the plan, wasn't he? It explains why he was so willing to sacrifice his work to protect you."*

Siroun shook her head in protest, and the chains that bound her clanked and jingled at her fervent reply. *"Nik was that intruder Felthane in disguise this whole time! He deceived me just as much as he did with you!"*

"Of course you have an excuse. Unfortunately for you, father and I are no longer your puppets to hide behind."

"What?" Siroun paled. *"Vas, what are you saying?"*

"Wise up, Siroun. You might be naïve, but you're not stupid. We know you're an abandoned experiment of the Immortal Ones. The council told me about the deal they made with Arcandus to hide you away so you wouldn't be of any trouble. I defended your honor at the cost of mine. Imagine my surprise to find out you're not related to us in the slightest. In fact, I doubt you're descended from either race your body portrays."

Siroun was too stunned to speak. All of this information was new to her, yet he seemed to assume that she had known about her past all along. She couldn't decide whether to protest his accusations or ask for further details.

He didn't give her time to act on either thought as he continued, *"I would be lying if I said I wouldn't miss you. It might take my father some time to adjust to your permanent absence but it won't be long before he realizes this is for the best."*

Her eyes ran hot with tears from both sorrow and anger. She never imagined her brother felt this way about her. The most frustrating part of this conversation was that he already had his mind made up.

"You've got this all wrong. Please, just listen to me for one second," she struggled against the chains once more. *"Brother, please!"*

Vasylvad wrinkled his snout as though he had smelled something foul in the air.

"Brother?" Vasylvad snorted at the word. *"We are not family. We share no blood, nor origin of kinship. Your existence is a taboo to The Great Three. You bring pain and hardship to everyone you meet. Even your mage friends paid the price. I hear that the Duchess of Firenz is inconsolable from the loss of her husband. No, you are no sister of mine. Never speak such blasphemous things again. Goodbye, Siroun."*

Turning around, he exited the cell with one of the guild members escorting him out while another forced the muzzle back onto Siroun's face and shut the door behind them. As the remaining Vanis Aer mages reinstalled the enchantments around the door, Vasylvad took one last look behind him before walking out of sight. Though the muzzle robbed her of speaking, they didn't steal the thoughts running through her head. The poem used to bring her comfort now summoned a different emotion.

Hear the words, but don't listen.

Acknowledge the action, but don't dwell on it.

Reject the pain and don't show it.

When all was silent, she took a deep breath and screamed. The prison echoed as she cried out her anger, her frustration, and the last shred of hope she had of ever seeing her family again. Going home was no longer a choice, for there was nothing to call home anymore.

47

ZIKKY HEARD HER cell door unlock, and she saw several familiar faces of the royal guard make their way in to surround the walls. That meant one thing, and as soon as the prominent figure stepped into the light, her suspicions were correct.

A wry smile twitched across her features. "Yer Majesty."

Close up, King Nathaniel's stocky build gave him an aura of intimidation compared to when Zikky saw him on a throne or across a meeting table. Though he was a healthy lad in his youth, age caught up with him, and she heard the small wheezing escape his lips as he approached. His bushy eyebrows furrowed as he looked down at her with contempt.

"The Sinefine Bible," he said, lacking humor in his voice. "How does it work?"

"Well, hello to ya too," Zikky replied, only to have the King not respond to her remark. She added, "Why do ya think I would know?"

"You are the only one still alive that knows anything

about that woman and the artifact. You also helped her try to escape."

"Oh yeah, that."

"Don't make me repeat myself," the King replied bitterly.

"Ya have an interestin' way of sweet-talkin' a woman. And here I thought we could be friends with some new connections."

Zikky felt bad that she wouldn't be able to hold up her end of the bargain with Pixie-Pop, but she didn't trust the King's intentions anymore. Guards unsheathed their swords, and Zikky found herself on the receiving end of two blades crossing against her throat. Running her tongue along the outer wall of her teeth, she made a regretful click of her tongue and leaned back. The blades followed.

"Ain't ya a little worried that Arcandus is gonna be angry with how yer treatin' his—," she took a moment to determine what might be the appropriate term she could call the relationship, "—daughter?"

"The Archmage has a habit of leaving his problems in our care before disappearing for generations at a time to address other matters."

"Yeah, that sound 'bout right," she sighed.

"Unfortunately for you," the King continued, "I take whatever steps are necessary to secure my kingdom and its people regardless of the Archmage's pet projects."

"Yer good at hidin' behind yer kingdom's safety as reasonin' for yer paranoia, but we both know it ain't the only thing that's makin' ya this aggressive toward Siroun."

King Nathaniel scrutinized the mage before replying, "Stick to the topic at hand. How do we use the artifact?"

Now Zikky leaned in, the blades followed, and she couldn't help but maintain a confident grin that itched at the King's insecurities. "Yer afraid Felthane might take somethin' from ya, ain't ya?"

King Nathaniel's eyes steeled, and he gestured to the rest of his guard. "Get out."

That didn't sit well with one of the Vanis Aer mages as they tried to interject with, "But Your Majesty—."

"I said out!"

The guards exchanged confused glances but complied with the order. They shuffled out of the cell but remained nearby as a precaution. People within earshot was about as much privacy a sovereign got, but it would suffice.

Closing the gap between them, he kept a free hand upon his blade just in case he needed it and kept his voice to a whisper, "How much do you know?"

This question caused the Skivat to tilt back a little and grin from ear to ear. "I'm startin' to put enough together to understand why ya tasked Lord Valter with this mission and dragged the poor Lockwood kid into the mix."

"The boy was an insurance policy, he wanted blood. It was a good match, given how precipitously he pressed, after that debacle with his parents happened."

"Stop tryin' to sell me that it was all a coincidence. Colin was a damn good mage, but he was still a kid. The Sinefine Bible ain't what Felthane truly wants; it's merely a means to an end. But ya already knew, didn't ya?"

Those words caused King Nathaniel's brow to twitch. "Which is why I need the artifact under my command."

The royal family had their unpleasantries, but this reaction from the King was new to her. He was afraid.

Felthane figured out a way to claim the throne, and the King's reactions verified those suspicions. Still, the taboo power of the necrotic arts Felthane wielded would never gain the support of the people. Unless he lied about having such abilities.

"Siroun is not an object ya can command at yer whim. But if ya weren't actin' like such a chickenshit, ya might've been able to convince her to help ya out."

"Speak to me like that again and you won't have a tongue to hold," the King straightened his stance before taking a step back. "If she believes your life holds any value, she will come to see things my way. Her power is a danger to the kingdom. I can have her executed, and then she'll be of no use to anyone."

Zikky's jaw tightened, and she held back the urge to make him eat those words. "Ya have that little faith in Siroun that she would use her powers to help that warlock? Ya have no idea what he's put her through, do ya?"

With a clang of his sheath against the metal bars, the guards returned to help escort him. His only reply to her question was, "My family hasn't kept our throne for ages out of random acts of mercy. I have little time to dally with you and the half-breed. Get her to cooperate, or I'll make sure you both take center stage upon the executioner's blade. Understood?"

"Are ya gonna give me the chance to talk to her before then?"

"Soon," the King turned and exited the cell as plated footsteps hurried toward the monarch.

As the Vanis Aer re-locked the cell door, the arriving soldier panted. "Forgive me, Your Majesty. Word comes from the outer gates of Ysile Marden, the dead are invading the city."

King Nathaniel sounded just as flabbergasted as the rest of the guards when he retorted with a bellowing, "What?"

"That necromancer from earlier," the messenger snapped his fingers several times before conjuring the name, "Felthane? He's somehow breeched the defenses with an army of demons and skeletons. Said they popped right out of the ground from the nearby cemeteries."

This information stunned the King for a moment before he cleared his throat and stormed toward the exit. "Get me my councilmen, and that Vanis Aer Magistrate right now!"

Divine province won this day for Zikky. Felthane was on the move to take the capital, which would give her the time she needed to find Siroun and escape prison. The downside was the warlock now had an army at his command. Regardless of her personal feelings toward the King, no kingdom deserved to fall at the hands of a psychopath.

Her ears then twitched as a cry of anger and melancholy echoed down the hall. She recognized that as Siroun's muffled sound and clenched her teeth. *"Hang in there, gel-gel,"* whispered Zikky in Vat'tu. *"I'll get us out of here."*

48

"WHAT DO YOU mean there's an army of undead outside the city?" King Nathaniel shouted as he stormed out of the dungeons and through the palace halls. A flock of advisers and councilmen from both the King's court and the Vanis Aer Æther Guild hurried themselves to keep up with him.

The Division Magistrate huffed and puffed next to the King. "We located him in the cemetery outside the northern wall, Your Majesty. I have dispatched all eligible agents within our ranks to your Captain's Royal Guard for added protection."

Sebastian heard the commotion down the hall and re-routed his path to follow the monarch's group from a parallel corridor. The booming roar of the King and his councilmen allowed him to understand the magnitude of the situation. With the King and his retinue occupied, Sebastian felt confident in infiltrating the prison to free Siroun and Zikky. Even though Sebastian was a councilman himself, he stayed out of sight to focus on more important affairs. He maintained a brisk pace to listen further.

"Your Majesty," cut in one of the other advisers, "Captain Gilchrist has alerted the troops and is mustering the Royal Order of the Sanguine Sword as we speak."

"I'm still waiting to understand how one warlock unearthed an entire city of dead at his command without us noticing! Where is that demigod you keep on a leash as your pet? Perhaps he can make sense of all of this."

"Uh, well," the man stumbled along. "We don't know, Your Majesty."

The King growled. "I'm surrounded by councilmen of every kind and caliber, yet not one of them can answer a question!"

"Y-Your Majesty," the Division Magistrate interjected, "the necrotic arts have been taboo for a while. We have put no funding toward that research in years."

"Well, that's all going to change after this is over. Muster your scouts to the front lines to assess the damages and get me answers, now!"

When the King and his entourage turned toward the war room, Sebastian slunk into the shadows to find Niamh.

49

THE PRISON WAS quiet as Zikky rested against the cell while her ears twitched. A small thump vibrated through the stones, and she placed her palm against the floor. For a while, there was nothing, and then she felt the vibration again. This time she pressed her ear against the wall and picked up the sounds of pain the stones carried into the depths of the cell. For once, it was not the underbelly of the prison that was the source of agony, but above its city steps. She got up and tried hovering near the bars without touching them. The containment runes poised to shock her if she got too close.

"Anyone out there?" Zikky paused and waited a few moments before calling out again, "Helloooooooo!"

A set of metal boots came clomping over to her cell and the guard grunted. "Hey, keep it quiet!"

"Aw, don't be such a mud bucket," she teased with a slight grin.

The guard snorted in disgust before returning to his post a few feet away. In the distance the echoes of more soldiers running through halls made its way along the dungeon's stairwell and through the prison. Though the guard shifted his gaze, he let the repetitive sounds slip past him.

Zikky needed to find Siroun. If Felthane was at their doorstep, it would only be a matter of time before the imperial forces would fall. The warlock had an insatiable need for revenge, paired with the ability to impersonate just about anyone to get through the front lines. Therefore, time was of the essence with escaping. She flicked her gaze to the guard who yelled at her earlier as she crept closer to the door and analyzed the lock enchantments. With so many spells embedded into the bars, she couldn't get a read on how to best approach them at the same time. Instead, Zikky chanted a series of equations while hovering her palm over the lock. The magic wards lit up in response, and before she broke through, the power behind her incantation negated, making her spell backfire.

When the loud pop echoed, the guard hurried over to the door. "What are you doing?"

Zikky sucked on her fingers a few times before she pretended to notice him and smiled. "Who me?" She gave him a blank stare, followed by a few blinks as though to feign ignorance. "Oh, I tripped."

The guard paused before replying, "Tripped?"

"Yeah!" By now, Zikky plastered a bright smile on her face while rubbing her injured fingers against her legs to mellow out the pain. "Yeah, I went to turn away, then my toe caught the stones. Ya should look into some new floorin'. Anyway, I tripped and did what any person would do and put my hands out to stop my fall, but I touched the wards, and it gave me a bad shock. I think I farted too—."

"Enough," he said, waving his hand. "Get back over to the cot and don't do that again."

"Yeah, sure Champ," she muttered as she turned away only to feel the vibrations from above get stronger. A chill crept down her spine as she sensed the twisted magic nearby.

While the guard appeared oblivious to it, something else caught his attention instead. He turned away from the cell door and clomped through the hall while calling out, "Hello?"

With the guard now out of the picture, Zikky was free to go back to her escape attempt.

"Very well," she murmured, cracking her knuckles and summoning forth a stronger series of incantations into her fist. Since hitting it with one spell didn't work, she decided to ramp up her efforts. *"Let's try this!"*

Putting every effort into one mighty punch, Zikky strung a series of explosive spells infused with a counter barrier that laced around her hand. With full force, she pounded the door with raw fire magic. When the spells came mere inches away from impact, the wards activated, and the spells dissolved. Her fist contacted the metal door, and bone-splintering pain jolted up her arm, rendering her mute. Only a squeak came from her lips as tears filled her eyes.

"The pain," she squealed, grasping the words in her native tongue. *"So much pain."*

"Hey!" The guard ran up to her cell door. "I thought I told you to knock it off!"

"I can't help it," she squeaked.

The sound of a glass shattering on the stone ground

near their feet resounded. Both glanced toward his feet to see smoke billowing up from the tiny puddle and clouding their vision. Zikky backed off while the gray plume obfuscated the guard from her view. Her ears twitched as she picked up on the sound of feet shuffling and the guard attempted to shout again. Only this time, his voice muffled, followed by armor clanging to the floor.

"Zikky?"

The female voice sounded unfamiliar at first. But when the smoke cleared and visibility returned, Zikky recognized the vine-pierced ears of the herbalist woman, Niamh. Not two paces behind her stepped forth Sebastian, who broke away in another direction, while she approached the cell door.

"Never thought I'd see either of ya here," the pitch in Zikky's voice still high from the splintering pain coursing through her hand.

"Felthane is attacking the city," said Niamh. "While the King is busy mustering all of his forces, we're getting you out of here."

"Took ya—," she cleared her throat to normalize her vocal pitch before continuing, "long enough. What kept ya?"

"Opportunity," Niamh replied. "The King is good at keeping his prison guarded until a few moments ago."

"Sounds about right."

Niamh started working on the door by pulling out a small orb that lit up when waved in front of the lock, and a piece of parchment with a series of codes. From there, various equations illuminated around the hand-held item as she manipulated the sequences with the gesturing of her fingers. She trembled while working her way through dismantling the ward.

Zikky eyed it before asking, "What's that nifty little thing?"

However, Niamh's focus remained on the orb. She murmured several equations to herself while practicing the sequence to the side. Once she had the pattern memorized, she keyed the final combinations into an orb-shaped contraption that sent strands of blue and silver Æther into the cell door. On the last sequence the orb twisted then clicked before transmitting a pulse of energy that spread along the entire barricade that stood between them. The magic wards keeping Zikky from touching the door reacted with a burning glow before vanishing.

A sigh of relief passed Niamh's lips. "That was close."

"What was that?"

"A prototype Sebastian invented," she said as she tucked it back into her satchel. "It allows me to cast the counter-spells one-by-one then negate them all at the same time."

"Well, I'll be damned."

"Had I messed up the equation Sebastian gave me, it's possible I could have blown up this entire prison."

The two stared at each other for a moment before Zikky said, "Ya couldn't have told me that before ya started wigglin' yer fingers at it?"

"Trust me, I had a similar response." Niamh's right eyelid twitched. "But if I told you ahead of time you would have made me nervous, and we'd both become a puddle of Æther dust." Niamh's hands plunged into her satchel once more, this time she ferreted out a lock pick, then continued with, "It's not an easy combination to remember. Our fellow mages wove multiple magic wards on this cell that require one person per ward to unlock in tandem, hence the notes."

A clicking noise came up, and Niamh twisted her fingers left to pop the lock. With Zikky free, her savior blinked at the fire mage's right hand. "What happened?"

"I lost a fight with this door," Zikky shook her hand a few times and winced. "Still smarts too."

"Shall I bandage it?"

"Not now, where's gel-gel?"

Niamh mouthed the words with confusion before saying, "You mean Siroun? Sebastian is working on unlocking her cell. That combination is way harder to brea—. Uh, Zikky?"

The fire mage already took off and left Niamh behind. Zikky remembered where Siroun's cell was since she herself had been there once before. Though prisoners hollered for their release, there was only one goal in mind as she turned the corner and descended along a small flight of stairs. The thrum of magic vibrations strengthening around her as Sebastian toiled over the spells that kept Siroun prisoner.

"Almost done?" Zikky asked with her arms folded and foot tapping.

Sebastian's focus remained resolute. Like Niamh, he spoke no words until he finished the last configuration of magical sequences. Only this time, the wards burst like firecrackers as they self-destructed. With the prison cell breached, Sebastian placed a palm upon the door and focused another spell that froze the hinges solid, followed by a burst of fire to crack them off of the frame. Up to this point, Zikky watched him work his magic and seemed impressed that the Councilman was so willing to defy guild law to save someone he barely knew. That admiration was short lived. When Sebastian went to break the door, he lunged into it with his upper body, smashing his shoulder against the sturdy barricade to no avail and groaned in pain. Zikky winced as she saw this play out, then burst out laughing afterward. Sebastian tried again, but the door didn't budge.

By now, Niamh had caught up and grimaced as she caught the last attempt by Sebastian and cleared her throat to stifle her amusement. "Maybe let the professional brawler do the honors?"

"Oh, yes. That might be best." Sebastian's cheeks flushed pink, and he shuffled back a few paces before gesturing for Zikky to try her hand at it.

"No, no, keep goin'. This is fantastic to watch," said Zikky with a wide grin plastered on her face.

They both gave her an arch of the brow in response to her goading to where she softened her chuckles, and replied, "Oh, yeah, I guess now's not the best time. Step aside."

Zikky approached the door and pressed her left palm to gauge the firmness. Then she backed up and recited a series of equations to tap upon both of her feet. The fire armor seared along her lower body, and she used its power to support the left leg within her stance. Shifting her weight back, she took in a deep, slow breath before moving in with a swift kick to the key-locked side. The brittle hinges snapped, and the door fell off with a hearty thud. The three of them stepped over it and made their way inside.

"*That Tyth'var-humping cur,*" Zikky cursed in Vat'tu as they closed in around Siroun to loosen the bindings that shackled her. The moment Niamh untethered the chains, Siroun descended to the floor only for Zikky to catch her in mid-air. Afterward, Sebastian leaned in and analyzed the metal gag intending to unlock it. But Zikky enchanted her hand with fire, gripped the lock, and melted it down just far enough to break it off without burning Siroun.

The researcher blinked and reacted with, "O-okay. That happened."

"Hey, gel-gel," Zikky whispered as she swept a stray lock of hair away from Siroun's face.

Niamh swooped in to finish removing the mouthpiece as Siroun's eyes fluttered open. When the shackles loosened and her freedom realized, Siroun flung her arms around Zikky and clung to her like a frightened animal. Zikky stroked her hair while Niamh got to work bandaging the wounds with ointments and linen strips. As Siroun let the herbalist tend to the lacerations the shackles left behind, her eyes darted around past the three of them and toward the door.

"Are they coming?" Siroun's voice trembled.

Zikky shook her head. "Felthane's keepin' their attention for the moment. Prison's abandoned, but it sounds like the Royal Army could use our help."

That suggestion made Siroun narrow her eyes and shift her glare sideways. Meanwhile, Niamh helped soothe the tenderness from Siroun's skin and scales rubbed raw by the shackles. As Niamh bandaged the wounds with antiseptic, she said, "Hopefully, the scales will grow back."

Even Niamh's somber expression told them everything

as she tended to Siroun and then moved onto Zikky's right hand.

Siroun murmured in a defeated tone, "Count me out."

"Gel-gel?"

"Everywhere I go, everything I do, bad things happen to the people I love. I'm hated because of things I have or haven't done, and I can't say I blame them. The Sinefine Bible is a curse. No wonder Felthane wants it."

"Summon the book," said Zikky.

Siroun's brow quirked. "Why?"

"Gel-gel, please. Summon the book."

Another thump reverberated down the stone walls, and dust snowed from the ceiling as the castle stones jostled. Siroun's gaze flicked sideways when she heard the noise, then sighed. She pressed a hand to her chest and the Sinefine Bible emerged from her body into her palm as though the process was second nature.

Satisfied, Zikky pulled away and cupped Siroun's hands into her own. "Good. Now try findin' an illumination spell."

Though Siroun opened her mouth to protest, Zikky followed up with a stern glare to silence her. Siroun took a deep breath and kept one hand in the cupped position while she tapped open the Sinefine Bible, letting the pages flip to the requested spell. Once the words appeared in the foreign language, she hesitated before placing her palm upon the text. Black ink crept along the surface of her skin and moved along her arms from the hand that rested on the Sinefine Bible, to the other. It then pooled in her free palm before sparking to life in an orb of black and purple flame. As it flickered, Siroun's fingers combed through the magic that gave off no light. Instead, it seemed to make their surroundings a touch darker, and Siroun stared at the spell with pain in her eyes.

Zikky saw this and forced a smile. "Let me tell ya a little somethin'. Everythin' carries the potential to do unpleasant things. It's the same with people. Just 'cause yer power stems from a weird school of magic we've never seen before doesn't make ya a bad person, and it doesn't make yer abilities some kinda curse. It's what ya do with them that counts. So far ya've only tried usin' it to help people, not hurt 'em."

By now Niamh had finished wrapping Zikky's hand and opened a different jar. The moment the lid lifted, a mentholated aroma wafted in the air. The strong scent burned Zikky's lungs, but Siroun appeared unaffected. Niamh coated her palms with the smooth gel then snaked her hands under Siroun's shirt and massaged it into her shoulders. At first, Siroun winced, but when Niamh's thumbs went to work in tandem with the penetrating effects of the salve, the pained expression softened.

Zikky hovered her palms over the black light, and recited a small incantation. Brilliant sparks of firelight leaped from the Skivat's hands and dove into the black flames. The two sources of magic coalesced, bursting with tiny cracks of power before stabilizing into a kaleidoscope of colors that danced to both of their magic. Siroun's eyes lit up as tears rolled down her cheeks. Zikky smiled at the beautiful combination of their magic and hoped Siroun realized it too. What few encounters Zikky had with the Sinefine Bible revealed that the artifact enjoyed bargaining with others. She hypothesized that something connected it to Siroun's emotions. It shared in it's master's triumphs and tribulations.

While Zikky mulled over these thoughts, Siroun interrupted by asking, "Zikky, what's it like to take a life?"

Zikky couldn't find the words to respond. For a while, she watched the flame of colors flicker and pop before the spell ended. She took a slow breath. "It feels conflictin' at first. Followed by regret and emptiness dependin' on the circumstance. Ya try to do everythin' in yer power to find another way. But sometimes ya gotta decide. Even if ya win the battle, ya still have to sleep at night knowin' what ya did."

Siroun acknowledged the words with a slow nod. Her gaze fixated on the floor. "I don't think I can do that, Zikky."

Zikky reached over and tucked another loose strand of hair behind Siroun's ear. "I know, gel-gel. I don't expect ya to. I'll be the one to make that call when the time comes."

"But I don't want you to either." Siroun reached for Zikky's hand and squeezed it. "I've already lost Colin and Valter, I can't lose you too."

Zikky looked at their hands intertwined and squeezed Siroun's in return. "I won't die, gel-gel. When this is over, we'll ride the Shot-Pipes 'till our feet give out. I promise."

"We'll help," said Sebastian, and Niamh nodded in affirmation.

Zikky smiled, welcoming the offer. "We know Felthane seeks the Sinefine Bible to carry out a vendetta against the King, but why?"

"Because he's the true heir to the throne," said Sebastian.

Zikky paused for a few seconds, letting the information sink in. "Well, that explains a lot. No wonder His Royal Sassiness freaked when I called his bluff earlier." The more Zikky reflected on Felthane's insane ramblings and uncanny countermeasures over the past few months, the more she pieced together that he was more than some incensed warlock with a vengeance kick. From there she asked, "So who is he, really? And how'd ya find that out?"

The walls trembled once more as Sebastian replied, "I believe his real identity is Llyr Leonel Tristram Alexander Hanmel, the original Crowned Prince of King Leonel, King Nathaniel's uncle."

"So Felthane sought the Sinefine Bible to take back his throne," Zikky's ears twitched in concern. "But now he's attackin' the city without it. What changed?"

"Hasn't he been searching for the Sinefine Bible for a while?" said Siroun. "There's no way he'd abandon it now. Why go through all of this trouble for so long only to give up?"

"More importantly," Niamh interjected, "if he doesn't have the Sinefine Bible, what is he using to raise an army of the undead?"

"A reliquary," said Sebastian. "He must have made a pact with a Dark God."

"He's done it before in Pustelia Crest," said Siroun.

A wave of screams echoed down the stone walls, followed by the guttural shrieking of other-worldly creatures. The group hushed to listen further, but the sounds had long faded away. Niamh's voice trembled, "W-what were those?"

Zikky heard the sounds before when Felthane

ambushed The Hive. From the steeled expression on Siroun's face, she must have remembered too.

"Demons," said Zikky and Siroun in unison.

Siroun looked over to Sebastian. "The reliquaries that warlocks have; how powerful are they?"

Sebastian blinked at the question. "D-depending on the terms of the pact, I can only assume there isn't a limit to their power. However, from the texts I've read, the greater the power, the steeper the price."

Siroun's face paled as she looked at Zikky. "You don't think murdering the city's populous counts as a debt paid, do you?"

Zikky's eyes steeled. "Unfortunately, gel-gel, I think it might. Probably got tired of waitin'. On top of that, the Sinefine Bible doesn't work without ya. If yer not gonna help him, I'd fathom he's takin' matters into his own hands."

Siroun's jaw tightened as the sounds of demons continued to echo from above. "The throne."

Zikky turned her attention toward the other two. "The guards are well-trained, but they'll struggle against a Reaper Warlock. As much as King Nathaniel pisses me off, this kingdom can't afford to have a regime change."

"Agreed," said Sebastian. "I believe he was heading to the War Room with his councilmen last I saw. That's just behind the throne."

"Then we head there." Zikky commanded before turning to Siroun, "Think ya can do this, gel-gel?"

"No." Siroun's gaze didn't soften. Instead, she took time to stretch her muscles as she ruminated on her initial hesitation from earlier.

The answer made Zikky purse her lips. While Siroun was more than entitled to abstain from getting involved, she worried that her abilities alone weren't enough to bring an end to Felthane's ambitions. Even if Sebastian backed her up, his experience with the Reaper Warlock was null, and Zikky wasn't sure what tricks the Councilman of Artifacts had at his disposal.

This introspection came to a halt when Siroun followed up with, "But I'm sick of running, and I'm tired of being blamed for things I didn't do. I want to finish this."

As Niamh finished up, Zikky saw a noticeable difference in Siroun's movement after the herbalist worked her magic. Siroun cracked a few joints in her hands before picking up the Sinefine Bible and absorbing it into her chest. Then she turned to Niamh and smiled. "Thank you so much for your help."

"You're most welcome," said Niamh.

With Siroun freed, the team made their way out of the cell with hurried footsteps. All the while, they scanned their surroundings to ensure that no one was coming to intercept them. When Zikky saw that the prison entrance was clear, she gestured the others to advance while saying, "We need to move fast if we want to make it to the King before Felthane."

To which Niamh took the lead and whispered, "Follow me, I know a shortcut."

50

THE GROUP MADE their way out of the dungeon and toward the main hall with only a smattering of guards defending the area. Niamh led them by creeping around pillars and corridors, inching their way closer to the Throne Room as the high-pitched shrieks and people screaming grew ever louder. The closer the sounds got, the faster the guardsmen abandoned their posts until none remained. While it made things easier to advance, Zikky's ears twitched around like crazy. Siroun expected her to explain what she heard, but the Skivat remained focused on their current task.

When Siroun could endure it no longer, she whispered, "What keeps making that noise?"

Not a second after asking, all went silent. Zikky stopped walking and held out her arms to halt the others. All of them sucked in their breaths as they waited and listened. Though Siroun lacked the pristine hearing of her Skivat companion, she watched where Zikky's ears pointed and sensed the most subtle of scuttling noises in the distance.

When the sounds stopped, Zikky said, "Run!"

They sprinted along the hall while a swarm of insect-looking demons burst through the walls behind them and commenced pursuit. Siroun glimpsed over her shoulder to see their six legs scurry after them with massive black pincers gnashing together. A black miasma billowed off of their glistening exoskeletons like smoke as they flooded the hallway and raced after the group. She screamed at their frightful appearance, motivating her to run faster while Sebastian and Niamh spared a glance and came to a similar conclusion.

"What are they?" Niamh shouted as she tried her best to not to lag.

"Demons," said Zikky.

"Yes, but what kind?"

"Ugly ones."

"How many forms do they come in?" Siroun shouted while still keeping pace.

"As many as Jethshir wants," the Skivat replied before muttering a series of equations into the palm of her hands.

"Who's Jethshir?" However, Siroun's question remained unanswered.

When the spell finished forming, Zikky veered to the side and slapped the ground, infusing the spot with magic. Several seconds later, an explosion emanated behind them, eliciting shrieks of pain from the demonic creatures. When Zikky glanced over her shoulder, she saw her spell only took out a handful while the rest persisted in chasing after them. She clicked her tongue in disappointment. "That didn't go as expected."

"Let me try," said Sebastian as he turned on his heels and flicked both hands toward the masses chasing them. The floor lit up several feet in front of him before a thick wall of ice shot toward the ceiling sealing off the hallway. Screeching emanated from the other side as the group stopped to catch their breaths.

Zikky sauntered over to Sebastian, patting him on the shoulder. "Nice work, Seb."

"Thanks."

They only had a few seconds of respite when Zikky's ears twitched again. The group looked ahead to find a small contingency of guardsmen rounding the corner with a Titanian woman among their ranks. Siroun had to do a double-take when she realized the tall individual was the same priestess betrothed to the Captain of the Royal Guard, Lyonesse. Instead of the billowy cloth fabrics the priestess sported before the King, and at the party, the woman donned skirts woven with chain mail, and plated regalia befitting a warrior. When Siroun locked eyes with the priestess, she took a step back out of an unspoken fear she couldn't pinpoint. Even Zikky and the others froze in their tracks, their muscles trembling as the Titanian priestess approached. Meanwhile, the demons trapped behind the barricade started burrowing through the ice.

Though time was of the essence, the stand-off began as the guards recognized Zikky and Siroun. As they reached for their swords, Lyonesse held out an arm to halt them.

"No time," she said.

Confused, one guard retorted with, "These are escaped prisoners! Well... two of them."

To this, Sebastian stepped forward. "They are in my custody. I need them to help me find the King and protect him from Felthane."

"Are you insane?" One of them replied, "That woman is his accomplice!"

"No, she is not," Sebastian protested, and Siroun glanced toward his hands to find them trembling.

She looked over to the priestess and sensed a strong magical aura radiating from her countenance. Lyonesse scrutinized the ice wall, and Siroun saw that a demon opened a large enough hole in the frozen barricade to squeeze its way through.

"They fight," the priestess replied with her heavy rhotic accent. "Worry about cage later."

Siroun admired Lyonesse's ability to command a small group of individuals not of her ilk in such a manner. Though the guardsmen didn't look thrilled to be letting prisoners escape, they gave Siroun and the rest of the group a passing nod. By now, the first demon cleared the barrier and leaped full-speed at them, its pincers opened wide. Lyonesse lunged forward and back-handed the creature in the face with her armored glove, sending it flying against the wall, and splattering the stones with its black blood. The other guardsmen lined up on each side of her, swords unsheathed and at the ready.

With a stomp of the priestess' foot, Siroun felt the once-intimidating aura shift into a sensation that made her feel like she could accomplish anything. Even Sebastian stopped trembling, and Zikky didn't seem as on edge as before. Something with Lyonesse's aura impacted the way people reacted to her, and Siroun wanted to figure out why. But with the onslaught of demons tearing through the barrier, she had to forgo that curiosity.

Zikky waved the team onward with an enthusiastic, "Let's go!"

The group ran toward the Throne Room, leaving the Titanian priestess and her retinue behind to face the demons alone. Sounds of battle and screeching echoed behind her as they pressed onward with Zikky leading this time. Winded, Siroun fell a few paces behind, with Sebastian and Niamh doing the same.

The Skivat glanced over her shoulder and slowed her pace. "Ya guys ain't used to runnin' this much, are ya?"

"I'm a researcher," Sebastian said through bouts of panting, "not a runner."

Niamh said nothing, but there was a flush in her cheeks to go with her rapid breaths. Another wave of screeching echoed from the halls and the arthropods came flooding into the area ahead. This time Niamh reached into her bag as they continued running and throttled a small vial into the demon masses. The glass shattered and a thin cloud of gas rose in the distance causing the nearby demons to lie down and sleep.

"Nice work!" said Siroun to Niamh.

She smiled back. "Since I didn't have to use these on the guards, I figured they might work on these creatures."

Though effective, the vials didn't impact all of them. Several stragglers made it through the dense sleeping fog despite the groggy nature in which they moved. As the cloud of sleeping smoke cleared, many of the demons that trailed far behind skittered over their fallen compatriots and pressed onward. The chittering that assailed Zikky's ears made her stop running and face the oncoming stampede. She rolled up her jacket sleeve as orange runes lit up along her arm. Through gritted teeth, she muttered, "Ya ain't gonna stop 'till I burn every one of ya to a crisp, eh?"

Sebastian interrupted her with a tap on the shoulder. "I've got this, be prepared to slide when I give the word."

"Slide?" Siroun said as the three women stopped running long enough to see Sebastian step forward and summon a large magic circle.

Static filled the air, causing everyone's stray hairs to float toward the ceiling. The demigod pulled back his hands as though he were pitching a ball, before leaning forward and slamming his palms to the floor. A net of electrical tendrils bolted along the floor, walls, and ceiling through the hallway in front of him, creating multiple nets of lightning. The magic danced through the air paralyzing the demons as they cried in agony.

When the lightning show ended, the creatures twitched and sizzled as their burnt scent wafted into the air. Siroun never saw a spell of that size come from the likes of Lord Valter before. However, the reason became clear when she saw Sebastian fall to his knees and pant in exhaustion. Niamh hurried to his side, but he waved his hand at her in reassurance before forcing himself to stand. Turning to Siroun and Zikky, Sebastian said, "Sprint, then jump."

Zikky blinked. "Ya sure yer gonna be able to continue, Seb?"

"I'll be fine," he replied as new equations began glowing around him.

"Good luck." She turned to Siroun and said, "C'mon, gel-gel."

Siroun followed her partner as fast as she could muster without asking why. Not every demon perished in the spell. Some avoided total annihilation as they emerged from the charred remains of their brethren and charged onward. As Zikky and Siroun jumped into the air, Sebastian stomped his foot, and a sheet of ice coated the floor of the hallway toward the Throne Room. Both women stuck their landing upon the slippery ice and slid down the hall toward the door.

Zikky raised her hands up in the air with a gleeful, "Wheee!"

Siroun wasn't surprised watching Zikky bob and weave through the frozen demons with ease due to her experience navigating the Shot-Pipes back home. She, however, wasn't as experienced. Her toe clipped off a creature's limb, making Siroun hit the ground, and slide on her hands and knees. Siroun shifted onto her butt to save her hands from frost burns, but her speed didn't diminish.

When they bypassed the swarm, Siroun rocketed toward the door and screamed, "Zikky, I can't stop!"

"No worries, gel-gel! I'll save ya!" Zikky braced her stance for impact in front of the door and reached out her arms to soften the collision.

Siroun saw what the mage was trying to do, and shouted, "No, no, no!"

"Yes, yes, yes!" she shouted back with a grin.

But the breakneck speed decimated Zikky's plan as they smashed into each other with a resounding series of thumps. Their bodies crumpling together in a pile of limbs before smashing against the Throne Room door and sliding to the floor. They laid there for several seconds as Siroun's eyes darted around.

"Are we still alive?" she groaned.

Zikky pulled herself to a sitting position. "I hope so. We've got too much to live for to die now."

It took some time to untangle themselves before Siroun tried to stand and failed. Instead, Zikky reached for the door and shoved it open, causing both of them to tumble their way inside. Siroun stood only to find King Nathaniel scrambling away as Felthane shifted his focus in her direction with a look of surprise on his face. She dared not take her eyes off of the man, but within her peripheral vision, she noticed the slain guards and councilors who littered the room to where only the King remained. The awkward pause that ensued made Siroun wonder if he was assessing what to do next. That decision revealed itself as Felthane lunged after the monarch with a growl of rage. The King made a narrow dodge as he skirted around the throne and attempted to push the cumbersome chair atop the warlock, but found it too heavy to move.

"Stop scurrying like a little rodent and face me!" Felthane seethed at the monarch through ragged breaths.

"This isn't possible," King Nathaniel said as he scurried side-to-side to avoid Felthane's grasp. "You are supposed to be dead."

"Yes, well, your father had a habit of not finishing what he started," he snarled back, and reached out to grab at the sovereign again with his demonic paw. When the King evaded the attempt, Felthane growled, "You're as gutless as the cur that sired you."

The King ignored the insults and pulled a nearby flag pole from its ground post to swing it in the warlock's direction. It didn't come close to striking its intended target, but it spooked Felthane enough to shield himself with an arm. By now Zikky was on her feet and, without incantation, throttled a wave of fire toward Felthane. The man transformed into his avian figure and flew out of the spell's path that set fire across the runway carpet before exploding against the throne. Splinters of wood and metal shot everywhere, forcing everyone to evade the flying debris.

"Will you watch what you're doing!" King Nathaniel roared at the Skivat before realizing it was Zikky. The King's eye twitched. "How did you escape?"

Felthane used this opportunity to make a break for the window, but Zikky bolted ahead and roundhouse-kicked the bird to the ground. With little time to think, Siroun placed a palm on her chest and summoned the Sinefine Bible into her hands. It floated open allowing her to flip through pages and found a spell in the middle of the book. Before she could activate the enchantment with her touch, Felthane turned to shadow and appeared behind the King. A clawed hand gripped the monarch's throat and squeezed.

"Ah, ah, ah," Felthane chided, forcing both Siroun and Zikky to stop what they were doing and wait for him to make the next move. Satisfied, he grinned. "I must admit, I'm surprised to see you here. I figured they would have thrown you into that special cell of theirs that nullifies people like us."

Siroun steeled her glare at him. "They did."

"Oh?" He quirked his brow. "Interesting."

"How do ya know about it?" Zikky interjected, taking

a step forward only to have Felthane squeeze harder on the King's throat. The monarch gasped while struggling to pry himself out of the warlock's claw to no avail.

"There is not a crevice in this castle that is unfamiliar to me," said Felthane. "What piques my curiosity is how you knaves escaped the intricate magic entrenched in those doors and walls. Who helped you?"

No sooner had he finished the question when the ground underneath him lit up with a soft blue light scribed with runes. Felthane grit his teeth as the Æther circle created a cylindrical wall around him, excluding the demonic hand that gripped at the King's throat. Felthane's entire body seized and pain radiated from his face as he held back every urge to scream. As the warlock struggled against the unknown magic, it weakened his grip, and King Nathaniel pulled himself free as Sebastian and Niamh rushed into the room. A bright sphere of arcane energy swirled in the demigod's right hand.

"Your Majesty," Sebastian shouted while assessing the bodies that littered the ground. Meanwhile, Niamh already descended upon the fallen, trying to find any signs of life to save.

"Don't... bother," Felthane hissed at Niamh through a clenched jaw. Through sheer determination, flecks of spittle ran down his lips as he said, "They're... mine. As are... you."

A Topaz-colored light radiated from the left side of his hip through the robes, and the room rumbled from a guttural roar.

"By The Great Three, not another one," Siroun muttered to herself.

She wasn't the only one who heard it either. King Nathaniel bolted out from behind one of the tall, velvet curtains toward their group. When he bypassed Sebastian, the wall behind the throne burst apart as a massive reptilian beast barreled through it, sending debris flying everywhere. With a vicious roar, the long-necked creature radiated the same shadow-like energy that the arthropods had in the halls. It balanced its massive body on four clawed legs, a long tail, and thickly scaled neck. How the thing got here was beyond Siroun's comprehension. The creature appeared to have been summoned from the other room since it left a trail of miasma in its wake and smelled of death. During the chaos of the demon's entrance, Siroun caught Felthane leaping out of the window. While Zikky and the others dodged the creature's onslaught, Siroun ran toward the window and saw his avian form gliding toward the outer city walls where the Royal Army and Vanis Aer mages engaged in battle with scores of undead and demons. Before she could blink, Felthane vanished into masses, leaving her in a frantic search to find him again.

But that got interrupted when Zikky called out, "Gel-gel!"

When Siroun turned around, she saw a massive tail sail in her direction. She felt the wind forced from her lungs as it slammed against her stomach and throttled her across the room. Tumbling along the stone floor hurt in more ways than she could imagine. Her skin burned as it scraped against the rough textures, and the sheer force of landing unceremoniously to the ground made it hard to take control of her bearings. She heard her name shouted several times through the ringing in her ears. When the world stopped spinning, she remained slumped face down for a minute or two. The chaos of battle rang in Siroun's ears as she struggled to push herself upright before shaking the dizziness from her head. From there she reached up and dabbed at her temples to make sure she wasn't bleeding. Despite the ache in her bones, Siroun stood long enough to see the Sinefine Bible laying on the floor a few feet away.

While Sebastian did his best to trap the beast with his arcane magic, Zikky kept it distracted by leaping and dodging its onslaught of attacks. By the time Siroun recovered, Niamh was at her side checking her pupils for any abnormal dilation.

"Are you all right?" she said, letting go of Siroun's face.

Siroun rubbed at her head one more time and diverted her gaze toward the Sinefine Bible. "Yeah."

"Careful with that tail whip. You could have gotten a concussion."

The ground shook from the monster rearing up again, and Niamh wasted no time helping Siroun to her feet before moving in to assist the others. Siroun ambled toward the book, barely jumping over the sweeping tail that came at her a second time, and scooped the tome into her hands. Her fingers tapped it open, and when the pages flipped to a binding spell, Siroun slammed her palm upon it and pointed her free hand in the demon's direction. Black energy seeped out from under her feet and writhed along the crevices in the stone flooring as it reached Sebastian's arcane imprisonment spell and merged forces with it. The creature elicited a horrible screeching noise in response to its inability to move. That gave the group time to assess the situation better as both she and Sebastian continued channeling their spells.

Through belabored breathing and flushed cheeks, Sebastian said to Siroun, "Thanks."

"Don't mention it," she replied. "You're not affected by the Hemophæther State?"

"It works differently on me," he panted. "Needless to say, I'll be taking quite a long nap after this."

Zikky made her way over. "Good work, guys. Niamh is with the King. Think we can vanquish this thing and move on?"

The sounds of mass screaming echoed in the distance, causing the Skivat to direct her attention to the window. The smile on her face transitioned to a frown.

"What's wrong?" said Siroun.

"We're outta time."

"What do you mean by that?"

The demon screeched again, and both Sebastian and Siroun winced. She felt it struggle against the bonds as a painful wave of energy pulsed into her hands and traveled through her nerves. Siroun clenched her free-casting hand into a fist, as a way of returning the pain threefold. Her patience for Felthane's antics reached its limits a long time ago, and she enjoyed taking her frustration out on his creations.

Zikky approached the window sill and appraised the situation outside. Several seconds later she said, "It's lookin' bad out there, gel-gel. The army's overwhelmed, and he's fightin' Captain Gilchrist."

"He barely escaped alive a moment ago," said Niamh

through pursed lips. "How is he taking on the Captain of the Royal Guard already?"

"Reaper Warlock, remember?" Zikky tapped the tip of her nose. "Kill a soul, take their life. Yer back on yer feet in seconds. And havin' an entire army around means it's an endless supply of energy."

Siroun knew nothing about Captain other than he ditched his own betrothal party a few nights back. Even if the Captain was a skilled soldier, she still worried for his safety. "Felthane will kill him for sure if we don't help."

They needed to aid the army, but Felthane's demonic creation in the Throne Room obligated them to stay. Meanwhile, the warlock was having his way with the kingdom's forces outside.

As Siroun tried piecing together a plan, she heard Sebastian say, "Go."

Both women blinked, and Zikky arched a brow. "Ya sure about this, Seb?"

"I can handle this one on my own. I'll make sure the King and his family are secure. You deal with Felthane. You're more familiar with his strategies than I."

Niamh gave the two women a nod of confidence and placed a palm upon her chest. "Don't worry, I'll make sure we're safe."

With Niamh's guarantee, Siroun pulled back on the spell, and absorbed the Sinefine Bible into her body. She watched as Sebastian took back the full responsibility of containing the creature. The look of strain reflected in his eyes as he worked to strengthen his grip on its movement.

Zikky tapped Siroun with the back of a hand. "C'mon, we need to go."

Siroun turned to follow when she realized a different issue. "The castle is enormous. Even if we ran, we'll never get there in time."

"Oh, that's an easy fix." Zikky smirked and hopped onto the ledge. "We take the same shortcut that Death Breath used."

"Wait. You mean we jump?" Siroun chuckled while tip-toeing toward Zikky to the window, and asked, "Have you gone mental?"

"Perhaps," she replied before looking over to the demi-god who was still struggling to contain the demon. "Think we can exert ya one more time, Seb?"

"One second," he grunted as he completed a series of new hand gestures which caused the arcane binding spell to shatter before an enormous ice spike shot up from under the creature, and impaled it in the shoulder. While the shriek of pain resounded from the Throne Room walls, Sebastian summoned a triangle of arcane light in mid-air then drew several quick mathematical equations with his finger and flicked it in Zikky's direction. The spell absorbed into her body, and two balls of light to burst from her back extending into giant ethereal wings.

When Zikky reached a hand out, Siroun swallowed hard and gathered her courage, putting her faith in Sebastian's spell. Zikky pulled Siroun up next to her and said, "Hold on."

A pink flush came to Siroun's cheeks as she wrapped her arms around Zikky's sturdy frame. When the Skivat jumped, Siroun shut her eyes expecting to plummet to the ground. Instead, the sensation of gliding caused her to open one eye, then the other. Though she didn't appreciate dangling in mid-air, the bird's-eye view she captured as they made their way toward the battlefield was thrilling. She saw up ahead where Captain Gilchrist and Felthane clashed in one-on-one combat. The warlock charged the Captain in the form of a massive equine beast with jagged antlers. Meanwhile, Captain Gilchrist took to his sword and shield and charged toward the animal in kind. When the two were within striking distance the Captain ducked low to avoid the massive antlers before backhanding the creature with his shield.

Siroun winced at the exchange while Zikky whistled. "Man, Cap'n sure knows how to hold his own in a fight! Must be that Titanian blood in him."

"Titanian blood?" Siroun blinked before remembering the last time she saw Captain Gilchrist in the royal court. He towered over everyone, except for the Priestess Lyonesse. "Is that why he's so tall?"

"Pure-blooded Titanians are much taller. I think he's got it from one of his grandparents if I recall correctly."

"You don't say," said Siroun as her attention shifted to the fight while continuing to glide high above the fray.

After several more exchanges on the battlefield, Felthane reverted to his Adami form and made gripping gestures with his hands. The ground below him flashed a bright yellow light as several creatures appeared from thin-air and launched in the Captain's direction. They were lanky except for their massive legs and long muzzles that revealed hundreds of teeth as they grinned. None of them had eyes. Instead, they relied on their huge snouts to sniff out their target and descend upon him. Their bony tails whipped side-to-side as they bolted across the battlefield and dog-piled the Captain. The first demon took a hard thwack to the jaw, while the second received a long sword in the belly. When Captain Gilchrist tried deflecting the third, fourth, and fifth, he met his match against the tall beasts.

As Siroun and Zikky descended closer to the battle, a lance of ice whizzed past them. Vanis Aer mages chased after them with spells in hand. When another sailed in their direction, Zikky countered it by fanning out her palm and muttering a few words under her breath. A small fire shield formed a few inches in front of them, shattering the lance.

"We need to make a quick landin'," said Zikky as she leaned forward, causing them to speed up their descent toward the ground.

At the same time, Siroun saw that Felthane backed away from his fight with Captain Gilchrist and began summoning large storm clouds over the soldier. Several more demons kept the man pinned down despite his struggling to free himself.

"What is he doing?" said Siroun.

Zikky squinted to get an unobstructed view before she replied, "Not good. I need to get to the Captain now. Tuck and roll when we land, gel-gel. This is gonna be rough."

Siroun could feel her pulse quickening as the gentle gliding transitioned to a death plummet. The roll of thunder echoed around them as flashes of light sparked within the ominous cloud formations. When they closed in on the Captain's location, Siroun let go of Zikky and landed, tumbling along the verdant terrain until she came to a stop. During that time, blinding light and loud cracks of thunder assailed her eyes and ears. Debris billowed, and Siroun heard ringing in her ears as she looked over to find the demons burnt to a crisp. Yet, Zikky stood over the soldier with her right arm in the air. Her enchanted battle armor glowed as the gem that absorbed part of the spell into Zikky's outfit radiated a white-gold light.

"Whew! That was a close one!" Zikky pulled her arm in and gave it a quick rub. "I always wondered what Fancy Britches could do at full throttle. Thanks to ya, I now know."

51

"WELL, WELL, WELL," Felthane pulled back his body into a relaxed position after he saw the lightning spell intercepted. Some residual energy struck the Captain, rendering him unconscious, but still breathing. Several of the guardsmen that broke free of the demonic entourage jumped in and collected the massive man to pull him to safety. While Zikky stood before Felthane readying for a fight, Siroun stepped out from the cloud of debris and faced the warlock.

"The weapon has escaped!" shouted one of the lower-ranked Vanis Aer mages as they ran through the flanks to fetch their commander. "Zikky is with them! Summon the Division Magistrate!"

Commands shouted back and forth to reassemble the line and prepare for any uncertainties. With the Captain out of commission, his lieutenants took this moment to shout countermeasures. Soldiers lined up per their commanding officers, staying at the ready for further instructions.

Felthane ignored the shuffling going on around them,

and raised a brow at Siroun. "You don't know when to admit defeat, do you? Or have you come to your senses and decided to join me?"

"You have nothing to offer that will reconcile everything you've done.

"Oh, really?" Felthane grinned as shadows wrapped around his body and changed his form into that of Lord Valter.

Siroun gasped while Zikky balled up her fists. "Ya got a lot of nerve showin' that face to us. If ya think that'll stop me from puttin' a first through yer skull, ya got another thing comin'."

The Duke's lip quirked into a smile before shifting back into the warlock's original form. "I can see that I still have one more distraction to take care of before I can convince you otherwise."

When Siroun noticed his glance flick over in Zikky's direction, she lunged toward the warlock only to have the mage stop her with an extended arm.

"He's goadin' ya," Zikky muttered.

"I know that."

Felthane clicked his tongue a few times. "Aww, no need to be protective. I'm just trying to have a little f—."

Zikky's lightning reflexes descended upon Felthane with an elbow to his face, and a look of surprise reflected in his eyes. Forced to his knees, he clutched at his already bruised face from his earlier altercation against Captain Gilchrist. Angrily, he sent a shock wave through the ground with his fist that everyone felt. Then slammed his clawed arm against Zikky, which sent her flying back.

Siroun caught her in the nick of time, both of them nearly tumbling to the ground.

"Thanks, gel-gel," Zikky rubbed the back of her hand against her chin and retook her fighting stance.

It wasn't a moment too soon as Felthane sent a barrage of lightning in their direction. Siroun felt herself get shoved out of the way, while the Skivat caught the tail-end of the spell. In a blink, Zikky descended upon Felthane and elbowed him in the chest. She then hooked his leg and twisted her hips, using her weight to push him to the ground. When Zikky went to strike again, Felthane's body turned to shadow and evaded. Her fist connected with nothing but dirt while he circled and shifted into his demonic cat form and bit into her right leg, puncturing the battle armor.

"By the sands, not again," Zikky cursed in Vat'tu.

Sizzling noises crackled and popped in Zikky's ears while her stance slumped the longer he held fast to her leg. She turned to connect a punch, but her speed slowed as he moved out of the way.

She limped back a few paces and Siroun noticed the battle armor changed back to its original state. Somehow, Felthane drained the lightning spell from her body. Now it was he who wielded the boost in speed, as he transitioned back into his Adami form having reclaimed the power.

"I swear, Reaper Warlocks are cheatin' bastards," Zikky spat through belabored breaths. "It's like swattin' at a pest ya can't catch."

Felthane pulled his reliquary out and called to it with a series of incantations. The remaining undead forces were almost obliterated, and the demons waned in number, but the warlock continued his onslaught. Despite the blood running down the side of his face, and his stance hunched from taking so many physical strikes, he beamed with confidence.

Siroun came up behind Zikky and analyzed the wound, but stopped when the mage said, "We can't take our eyes off of him. Somethin's up."

Both women looked on as the warlock chuckled. "Your methods are getting tedious with your punching and kicking. Don't you have anything else that's more entertaining?"

Zikky kept her fists up and said, "I dunno, seems to be workin'. I'd say a few more hits and yer done for the day."

Felthane spat again to remove the mouthful of blood that pooled along his gums after that atrocious bite he delivered to her. "Your confidence is astounding. Yet again, you fail to realize your limitations."

As the right side of his body tilted back, he wiped his mouth with his left sleeve. When a sea breeze passed through the battlefield, his stance swayed.

Zikky scrutinized his position before murmuring to Siroun, "Gel-gel, think ya can give me a boost like ya've done before?"

Siroun surveyed the rest of the army and the mages that occupied the battlefield. Commands from high-er-ranking officers bounced back and forth in the distance.

"Keep an eye on the three of them!"

"We need to build a stronger perimeter!"

"Where's the Magistrate? We need to find more re-enforcements."

It sounded like bees swarming. Siroun got the sense

the armies were holding off attacking just long enough to see if they considered the two friend or foe. For the moment, the warlock was proving to be the immediate threat, but who knew how long that would last.

"I believe I can," Siroun said, as produced the Sinefine Bible from her chest with her back turned toward the army. With luck, she hoped the soldiers didn't notice. "You'll need to end it quickly. The King's armies don't trust me to use this, and I can only channel one spell at a time. I can't predict their reactions once I start."

"Understood. I'll protect ya if anythin' funny happens with 'em. Felthane's only a few shots from a knock-out, but I can't be sure if he's legit hurt or feignin' it. Guess I'll find out."

Siroun flipped to the familiar spell she used on Zikky in the watchtower. There were other spells that she had yet to examine, but the uncertainty of their effects was not worth the risk when the slightest miscalculation could be the end of them. She placed her palm on the page and activated the text, putting her trust in Zikky's ability to bring closure to this fight.

The black lettering crawled down her body and crept over to Zikky. When Siroun's spell connected, the mage re-cast her battle armor spell. A few quick taps of her fingertips upon her shoulders, knees, and chest, and Zikky finished adding her spell-work as the bible's dark energy consumed her. The mages and soldiers of the front lines took notice of this new spell, and assembled themselves in a defensive position. When she emerged from the miasma, the scores of black tattoos that etched her body illuminated with power. The elaborate, onyx-plated armor crafted by the Sinefine Bible returned with a new design. Instead of lightning, it merged with the element of fire. Scores of small dragon scale plates coated her legs and arms while thick plate mail adorned the rest of her body. A rogue bolt of lightning shot across the battlefield from a nearby Vanis Aer mage, and Zikky caught the magic with a bare hand, and absorbed it into her flesh. An audible wave of gasps radiated from the front lines as they shuffled several steps back out of both caution and fear.

"Ready to end this, old man?" Zikky punched a fist into her palm as she eyed him like prey.

Felthane kept his right arm turned away as he hunched forward and waited for her attack. "I will not surrender the future of this great kingdom to the likes of you, little whelp."

She smirked. "Likewise."

Zikky dug her feet deep into the dirt before launching into a full-throttle assault. With such immense speed at her disposal, Zikky was on her target in a flash. Her fist pulled back while her body propelled forward. However, both she and Siroun heard the mutterings of his dark incantations again. To the surrounding demons, they screamed in agony before liquidating into dark pools of power and gathered around his silhouette. His physical form bubbled and mutated as the congealed souls melded together before solidifying into a bulkier amalgamation of demon parts and Adami flesh. The right half of his body bulged with muscle, while his shoulders and back unleashed rows of horns and spikes. Whatever beauty remained of his regal face twisted to exposed sinew, red eyes, and long teeth from a stretched jawline. His loose robes clung along disfigured body, torn by grotesque protrusions and soaked in oozing pustules.

His transformation completed just in time to have his claw reach out and catch Zikky's punch in mid-air. Though the mutated flesh of his hand sizzled once more, he didn't flinch. Zikky grit her teeth as the crushing grip halted her progression. Swinging her body around, she spat out an incantation that summoned blue fire around her left foot and kicked at his upper body to force her release. It worked. Enough to loosen his hold and wrench herself free. Felthane countered, and Zikky received a powerful kick to the chest, throttling her back with an unceremonious landing.

"I had a hunch I would see you again," he chuckled. "I saved a special spell just for you. Nephiria has been generous deity to me for so many years. It would be a waste of her gifts if I were to lose here."

"Nephiria?" Siroun tried to think if she recognized that name but lacked the time. In the distance she overheard a voice ringing clear as a bell among the armies.

"Evil has come to our doorsteps!" shouted a voice that made Siroun turn to the armies and see a priest standing before the front lines. "Demons surround us, but the greatest of terrors have shown themselves before us! If we do not purge it from this world, we shall be swallowed whole! I have seen our doom; she comes to murder us all!"

"What? No!" Siroun turned to the armies and saw the priest standing before the masses shouting his curses. "We're trying to help, please stand down!"

"Silence, do not listen to her lying tongue!" The priest

turned and pointed at her. "She'll bewitch us before she devourers our souls!"

Siroun now realized what was going on. "The cleric. Felthane is controlling him!"

Zikky cursed under her breath as she clutched her stomach and stood. The armies readied themselves and the Vanis Aer mages primed themselves to attack. Zikky growled at the warlock, "Ya coward, fight us fairly!"

The demand was met with laughter. "Fair? Do you take me for a fool?"

"No, I take ya for a cheat!"

"Why should I be obliged to play by the same rules?" With a flick of his hand, the remaining undead stopped their attacks upon the Ysile Marden forces and turned their attention toward Siroun and Zikky.

Those who were among the living looked confused at first, but the Vanis Aer used this opportunity to set up perimeter spells to protect the army and implement a counterattack. The archers didn't require much time to prepare by comparison. An arrow sailed toward Siroun, and she hesitated on what to do. Her arms lifted to cover her face with the book when she heard something splinter and opened an eye to find Zikky had snapped it in half after catching it with her hand.

Felthane capitalized on the moment by charging in and pinning Zikky to the ground. His gray saliva oozed off his fangs and landed on her shoulder, making a hiss as the acidity gnawed on the armor. Siroun's hand almost slipped off of the pages, but she maneuvered around the fight to continue supporting her companion. Zikky got up and throttled the warlock away from the rest of the troops. Blows exchanged back and forth while the armies and remaining mages prepared their attacks. A shield wall formed as the three elemental forces mustered from behind. Felthane's onslaught pushed Zikky toward them whenever he had the chance to position the two women between him and the army. Keeping both sides at bay wore Zikky out, and Siroun noticed blood trickling from her nose. The Hemophæther State was already upon the Skivat, but she wiped it away with her wrist and kept going. Meanwhile, the imperial forces launched their attack, raining a cascade of arrows that Siroun saw, and removed Zikky's enhancement powers to summon forth a curved obsidian wall just large enough to protect them both.

While taking time to recover, the screams of soldiers echoed across the battlefield. The women searched the front lines to find Felthane shouting at them with, "How dare you raise arms against your rightful King!"

Zikky quirked a brow and muttered, "He's really goin' off on this rightful heir bullshit, ain't he?"

"I guess fancy people don't enjoy having their stuff taken from them, and go on murder sprees to get it back," said Siroun, more out of sarcasm than literal interpretation.

Zikky chuckled. "Gel-gel, ya got no idea how accurate that statement is."

The tantrum didn't last long, and he turned his attention back to the women, while the armies closed in on them. Siroun juggled her spells between fending off her opponents and empowering Zikky. It was two against an army, undead, mages, demons, and a madman. Soon, the continuous spell-switching caught up with them.

Zikky fell to her knees as the power left her body again.

"Y'know, it's not a comfortable process to keep re-syncin' to yer book."

"I know, I'm sorry." When Siroun finished slinging a black fireball at a nearby demon, she reactivated the enhancement spell. "They won't quit interrupting me."

"S'all right, gel-gel."

But it wasn't, and the two of them knew it. A bolt of lightning crackled in Zikky's direction, and she leaned back to avoid it, letting it stray into the other mages. The wound on Zikky's leg where Felthane bit her earlier kept bleeding, and Siroun could see that the fire mage was struggling to walk.

In the distance a Vanis Aer commander shouted, "Fire at will!"

Siroun glanced at Zikky, but the mage seemed preoccupied with something else transpiring in the distance. She opened the Sinefine Bible to a new page and pressed her palm against it. With a swipe of her hand, the earth below the soldiers rolled underneath their feet, tumbling them to the ground. While they struggled to get back up, another contingency charged at her wielding spears. Flicking the pages once more, Siroun went to activate another spell when she heard Zikky's voice shout, "Gel-gel, look out!"

Siroun finished deflecting the oncoming spears with a wall of black ice and turned around afterward. A barrage of arcane-infused ice arrows whizzed through the battlefield in her direction like silent assassins. Siroun didn't see nor hear them as she glanced at Zikky with confusion while the Skivat ran up in front of her.

Tump-tump-tump.

Siroun's eyes widened, and her breath hitched. She reached out her arms to catch her companion as Zikky fell back, chest bloodied and unresponsive. The Sinefine Bible dropped to the ground. Siroun's knees gave out as she stumbled, cradling Zikky's body in her arms. "No, no! Zikky, open your eyes!"

All the joy and mischief that embodied the fire mage snuffed out in an instant. Tears welled in Siroun's eyes, and darkness lingered in the pit of her stomach. Frantic, Siroun gave Zikky's cheeks a few soft slaps in hopes the Skivat would awaken. "Please. Please, Zikky, don't leave me." Every muscle in Siroun's body trembled as she shook her lifeless friend, hoping it was nothing more than a bad dream.

"Please," she begged as she buried her face in Zikky's neck and rocked back and forth. "You're all I have left."

Armies closed in, all the while Felthane taunted her in the distance. As time marched on around her, Siroun's black tears stained her cheeks as she continued rocking Zikky's body in her arms and sobbed, "It's not fair. It's not fair!" Her voice warbled from swallowing her tears as she rambled more to herself than anyone else. "You promised me."

But promises became obsolete in the wake of Zikky's fall. When Siroun realized she was alone, she leaned in and pressed her lips upon Zikky's brow. She savored the rough skin of the Skivat mage through her kiss before clenching her teeth and screaming into the skies. Her agonized cries echoed throughout the battlefield and reverberated within the walls of the city.

In the back of her mind, something triggered her

thoughts in the written tongue of the Sinefine Bible. *"Kill them… kill every one of them."*

Setting the lifeless body upon the soft grass, Siroun stared into nothingness. The tears that dripped from her face turned the earth black where they fell. Though the armies were stunned silent from her cries of pain, the sounds of boots and hooves closed in on her from all fronts. Her gaze roamed the battlefield in a languid turn of her head, and she felt their fear and confusion. A sad smile cracked along her lips as Siroun decided that she had to end this madness. To make them come to heel. With a flick of her fingers, the Sinefine Bible floated over and ensconced itself into her hand. She rose to her feet and stepped past her beloved companion to face Felthane alone.

"This ends now," her voice deepened as it boomed over the battlefield, and vibrated into the very heart of every individual in and around Ysile Marden. With each step forward, Siroun's eyes turned black and her skin grayed. Her fingertips danced over the cover, and the Sinefine Bible opened to a series of pages long lost to the depths of time. It was a spell she did not read in this lifetime, yet hailed from a distant past within a forgotten memory. She raised her hand into the air as she spoke in the divine language of the book itself, *"You destroy everything I love. Now watch as I cleanse you all like the pestilence you are."*

Though they knew not the words, several soldiers lost their nerve and fled while shouts of panic echoed from others through the city. Her palm slammed down on the pages, enacting the spell, and triggering the black tattoos to race along her skin and sprawl out into a massive sephirot of runic gears, symbols, and branches along the ground.

The designs spun and intertwined as the twisted darkness dug deep into the earth and gripped pure terror into the hearts of those who were unfortunate to be caught within its design. Jagged wings shaped from gilded metal filigree jutted from her back. Her hands turned black as charcoal, and her body crackled with raw, unbridled power. Like watercolor paint on fresh parchment, darkness coated the sky and blotted out the sun. More screams echoed from within the city, while horses reared and fled with their riders still upon them.

"Yes!" Felthane chuckled, relishing in the chaos while calling to her. "Yes! This is the power that can reforge the kingdom anew! Cleanse the unworthy so I may take what belongs to me!"

"You are but a puppet to your wanton vices!" Her voice boomed with the vibration of a deity's power. *"You shall inherit no such kingdom. And when I'm done, you will beg for death!"*

When a contingency of Vanis Aer elites jumped in to cast a containment spell, Siroun placed her palm on a new page of the Sinefine Bible and flung her arm back. Though they were far beyond her physical reach, whatever invisible force she summoned slammed against the group, and sent them sailing into other troops. When she focused on Felthane again, he summoned the deceased into his command. She clicked her tongue in annoyance, and her fingers flicking at the pages. With her free hand, she made an X-shaped gesture, and two gashes carved into the earth, obliterating the bones of those long past. Next, she pressed her palm downward, which caused the land in that area to break into submission and cave. Many of the undead fell into the earthen abyss as the land swallowed them whole. Another flick of her fingers and it was on to the next page.

The sephirot underneath her expanded toward the capital city, the multiple wheels of its form spun and glowed as it crept across the ground and deep into the armies that surrounded Siroun. A wave of black spikes shot up underneath the feet of random people within those crowds. The puppet priest from earlier being among the casualties. Their bodies impaled for all to see. No blood spilled from their bodies, for they were dead long ago, animated by demon souls brought forth by Felthane's reliquary. Instead, they screamed as the black fire purged them to ashes. Then Siroun's fingers moved again, and the ocean trembled. Siroun crouched low, the Sinefine Bible followed the sway of her movements while the tide ebbed. When she stood tall, the waters rose as high as the palace and everyone scattered. Her gestures, large and fluid, commanded a riptide to bend to her whim. It mimicked her body language, leaping over the city and crashing down upon the battlefield sweeping away everything in its path. Felthane saw the rage in which she commanded such a force and changed forms to take to the skies.

"No!" He growled, watching his minions get flushed away by her power. "I've waited too long for this moment. I will not let it slip through my fingers again!"

52

WHILE CHAOS UNLEASHED its fury upon the kingdom, the heavy clop of a hoof along the mountainside marked the presence of another deity. Flowers bloomed and wilted as the equine snorted, pulling on the reins. The cloaked female rider atop the behemoth mount, who appeared as a beautiful woman one second, and the next her skin sloughed away into a skeleton, observed the spells at play.

When she saw the magnificent display of Siroun's sephirot come out into the open, her brow arched. "Someone meddled with the first seal."

She reflected on which deities could try such a feat. Only one name refreshed her memory. "So, the other is still alive."

At her left stood Arcandus, who watched with apathy. Revanine shifted her attention to him and said, "I believe your hand in this affair is ending."

The Archmage sneered. "I never wanted the job to begin with."

She excused his insolence for now. "It was my fault for leaving such a tremendous task in the hands of a pair of realm-bound servants with no more masters."

Arcandus scowled further, and Revanine hoped she had driven the point home that his place in this world was that of privilege since the Prime Architects were no longer keeping them in check.

She continued, "That doesn't mean one of you can't be redeemed."

"I'm regretting us having ever summoned your help."

Revanine reached to her waist and drew a sword from her hand. "You would not be here to regret had you not."

The Gothic blade looked otherworldly in both its design and the materials that forged its creation. Smoke wafted off of the metal as it, like its owner, shifted between a state of newly forged to rusted with each passing second. Revanine shifted her grip to where the blade faced toward the dirt before she let it drop into the ground where it dug itself into place.

She glanced to Arcandus, and said, "You know what to do. Perform my bidding, Champion."

The Archmage grunted in disgust as he slipped his hand into a single glove and looked upon Revanine's accursed tool with hesitation. He didn't waste much time as he gave an audible swallow before grasping the weapon. Tendrils of magic drifted up Arcandus's arm and through his body as he clenched his teeth in response to the raw power within the blade. Though fear gripped the deity's heart, he removed the sword from the earth and pulled it back behind his head. Its shape bent and stretched as it transfigured into a polearm to match the wielder's intent.

Arcandus locked his frame into a throwing position before launching the javelin weapon through the air. It rocketed toward the target over miles of terrain in seconds. From mountain to fields, the spear honed in on its destination. Past the waters and the torrential rage. Through magic and chaos, it flew. As Siroun turned to face the unknown force, the spear contacted her chest.

And everything went dark.

53

*S*IROUN'S EYES FLUTTERED open, coming face-to-face with the giant muzzle of an equine. She felt light-headed as she reached out to pat the animal on the nose while saying, "Hey horsey."

The moment she touched the creature, its hide faded away, and her palm pressed on decaying sinew and bone. When she looked into its sunken eyes she screamed and bolted upright into a sitting position as it recoiled its head. Siroun looked up to find the beast carrying a cloaked rider, whose billowing robes obscured their visage. Darkness also surrounded them. Only the soft glow from colorful streams of light dancing around them illuminated where she sat.

"Where am I?" said Siroun. "And who are you?"

At first, the rider said nothing, choosing only to stare at her from the nebulous space in the hood of their cloak. Siroun took this time to stand and brush her hands off. Streams of blue light swam past her mid-air, and she reached out to touch it, sensing the elemental power of frost as a cold sensation prickled her skin.

"My name is Revanine," the female-sounding rider said.

"Revanine," Siroun remembered reading that name before. When the Raven Knights book popped into her head, she gasped. "I've heard of you before! Wait, what are you doing here? Have you come to make me one of your champions?"

"No," she replied. "I have suspended your consciousness. You are witnessing the Astral Stream."

"Astral Stream?" Siroun reached out to another wave of orange light and it radiated the warmth of fire upon her fingertips.

"It is the unseen veil where all cosmic energies live when they are not manifesting in the tangible realms of existence."

Siroun stared at her for a few seconds before she said, "I'm sorry... what?"

Revanine sighed. "You are seeing another plane of existence in your sleep."

"Oh," she nodded. More silence ensued, then followed up with, "How?"

Now the horse snorted as though it were mocking her. She resisted the urge to stick her tongue out at it before turning her attention back to Revanine.

"You have a skill known as Origin's Sight. It is an ability that only higher deities possess."

"Higher deities? Like The Great Three?"

It took some time before Revanine responded with, "More or less."

Siroun got the impression that she annoyed the deity

with the constant questions, but she persisted, "Why do I have this ability? Is it this related to the Sinefine Bible?"

"Look behind you."

When Siroun turned around, her jaw dropped. An amorphous figure of pure shadow as big as a mountain loomed across the horizon. As it moved across the lands and wove through the mountain range, its form squashed and stretched before settling in front of an army of mortals from an ancient era. Siroun watched as they summoned magic and weaponry to fight against the darkness that sought to annihilate them. When individual efforts failed, they banded together to perform one last stand. They handed a blade blessed to a Titanian warrior who charged in and struck at the monster. Siroun shielded her eyes as a bright light obscured her sight. A piercing ring hit her eardrums, and when the sword splintered, the light faded. Siroun removed her hands to find the warrior dead within the maw of the giant creature. Nothing but a bloodied arm and leg dangled from between its teeth. Something about this gruesome act seemed familiar. A tightness formed in the pit of her stomach. Mortals fled as the creature finished its meal. Some casters remained behind, summoning whatever powers they had to delay the beast to buy the others time.

The scene transitioned to a black realm illuminated by a cornucopia of color streams. Siroun watched the streams flow in and out through the mortal casters as they summoned spirits, or invoked spells that altered their shape. Every caster used their own distinct elemental stream. It mimicked a rope that kept them connected to their abilities and allowed the energy that matched their color to move through this channel of power that bound them to that elemental force.

She watched the beauty of the colors push and pull through both the mortals and spirits to resist their foe. The vision played out while Siroun pondered its meaning. The beast changed form, and its mass shrunk. Unlike the casters, this creature radiated pure energy rather than pull from the streams of power manipulated by the mortals. Before Siroun blinked, the being zig-zagged past each caster. It stopped when it passed the entire blockade, taking the smaller form of a humanoid shadow with chromatic filigree wings identical to the ones that appeared on Siroun's back before entering this alternate dimension of consciousness. Its eyes were nothing more than slits of silver light as Siroun saw the Æther ropes of the casters break apart after the creature severed them. When the mortals realized they were powerless, the former casters fled away only to be slaughtered by the dozens. Blood soaked the soil as the shadow danced around them with gleeful laughter, annihilating anyone in its path. Stamping hooves echoed through the skies, and the creature turned to see a robed figure mounted upon an enormous black equine.

Revanine.

The woman's visage, along with her mount, danced between the living and the dead. With a hand on the hilt of her sword, the creature hissed and moved in to attack. Then everything went dark.

Siroun slowed her breathing. "Was that me?"

"Yes," said Revanine.

As much as she wanted to deny that the gruesome act had anything to do with her, Siroun knew that Revanine showed her this vision for a reason. She ruminated on the details until she realized how everything connected to her current plight.

Siroun looked up to the hooded rider. "I think I know how to stop Felthane."

"Do you?" the voice sounded unconvinced. "And what happens afterward? Will you lose control and kill everyone in your path like you have before?"

Siroun didn't plan on begging Revanine. Instead, she steeled her emotions. "Give me a chance to stop him."

"You are a creature born of Chaos. That is why I sealed your power, and my subordinates put you in that body."

Siroun's breath shortened, and she went silent. She thought of Colin, Valter, and Zikky, and how they sacrificed themselves for her safety. She had the key to stopping Felthane, and she would not let the rider stop her.

Looking the figure in the hooded void, she said, "If I'm such a danger, why not kill me?"

"Your permanent demise takes precision."

It was folly on Siroun's part to think Revanine would give her an answer that made any sense. "Then let me go."

"You dare to make demands of me?"

"If that's what it will take, then yes. Release me. Let me stop Felthane," she said, holding her head high. "After that, you and I can settle our differences."

"You will be alone."

A wistful smile crossed Siroun's lips. "That has never stopped me before."

She sucked in her breath and awaited an answer while Revanine deliberated. The rider grabbed the reins and turned her mount toward the darkness, fading away while her voice echoed, "Use precision, and harm none but your target."

The transition from the ethereal realm into the tangible wasn't as jarring, but it placed Siroun at the epicenter of her previous state. Purged of rage, the diagrams on the ground disappeared, and Siroun's body returned to normal. With the ocean retreating, and the remaining armies taking a moment to breathe, Siroun's eyes widened when she saw the marks her magic left in her wake. Patches of earth blackened littered the battleground from the spikes that purged the demons. Fault lines remained where she opened up the ground to swallow the undead. There was no ability to take back everything she had done. Instead, she kept her sights toward the task at hand. Siroun gestured to the Sinefine Bible, and the artifact returned to her possession as she pondered an effective strategy to use against the necromancer.

To beat him at his own game, she needed a weapon that could help her cut through his defenses and deliver a final blow. Though she had minimal combat experience, there were some farming tools she used back home that held potential. The pages flipped multiple times, while searching her memories for the right answer. The Sinefine Bible stopped and presented two spells on each page that she could combine to bypass her target. Without hesitation, her palm landed in the middle of both pages, and the book lit up. Its form mutated and stretched into a long pole-arm until one end of it jutted out into a bladed hook. When finished, Siroun grabbed the scythe and readied a defensive position.

The warlock sneered. "Do you think you have the skills to beat me with that primitive thing?"

"We'll find out." Pointing the weapon in his direction, she commanded, "Release Lord Valter and the other souls you imprisoned."

Felthane clutched his belly and bellowed with laughter. "My dear, you haven't the ability to enforce such a request."

There would be no negotiating with the man, but she had to try. Siroun ran a finger down the pole, and a line of text lit up. She sprang toward him, swinging the scythe hastily only to have him deflect it. Twisting her body in the other direction, she came in from the side where he side-stepped the sweeping attack. He used this moment of vulnerability to swipe at her face. The quick strike of his claw created a searing sting across her left eye, and she reached up to feel the warmth of her blood running down her cheek.

"Is this the best you can do?" He clicked his tongue in feigned pity. "Come now, stop this nonsense and surrender already."

Siroun dabbed at her face a few times and slowly opened her eye. The gash just avoided blinding her. It was clear that her skill was lacking, but the speed in which she attacked made for decent compensation given her opponent's reaction time. Still, she had to keep her wits through his goading. The Sinefine Bible held untold levels of power that she had yet to understand. Within its infinite possibilities there had to have been a solution that outmaneuvered someone like him. With that in mind, she planted her stance and prepared another attempt. When her scythe came down again, and Felthane deflected her by releasing a surge of electricity that made every muscle seize.

Felthane shook his head in disdain. "Look at you. You spent all that energy ravaging the city with your nonsense, and then you fizzle out at the final hour."

His gloating allowed her the recovery time she needed to pull the scythe back. "Release them."

"Or what? What will you do? I would like to see you try something that mattered." Felthane cocked his head to the side and scoffed. "I have spent decades trying to find that artifact. Imagine my disappointment when I realized that only you could wield its power. What a cruel irony."

Siroun's brows knitted together. "What makes you think you'll be able to keep the throne once you steal it back, Prince Llyr?"

There was a twinge of insanity in Felthane's chuckle that made her skin crawl.

"I see that someone's done their homework," said Felthane. "I've waited long enough to reclaim my rightful place on the throne. All of my pieces are in place within its walls. Once I dispose of you, the kingdom is mine to take."

Felthane shifted into a defensive stance, and Siroun waited for him to make the first move. Thousands of spells raced through her memories until she found something that gave her an idea. With a deep breath, she closed her eyes and made a single stroke with her thumb along the snath of her weapon and then back up to enact a second spell. Strings of words lit up along the handle, and when Siroun opened her eyes, she saw the threads of energy that tethered him to three souls: An Archdruid, another warlock, and Lord Valter. At the base of his feet resided a single link of energy tethered to the ground: The source of his power.

The warlock used the time she took to cast her spells as an opportunity to conjure another bolt from the heavens. When they both moved in to clash, her blade came down just as lightning struck the back of her leg. Felthane grinned at Siroun's cries of pain as the spell tore through her body. But the warlock's confidence faded when her physical form vanished in front of him.

"What?" He snarled, head whipping side-to-side in search of her. "What is this?"

By the time he looked over his shoulder and found her, it was too late. Siroun jammed the scythe into the ground under his feet, slicing through the gray stream of energy that connected him to his abilities. Tendrils of power flitted away into the atmosphere as Felthane clawed at his chest. He must have known something was slipping away from the panic etched on his face.

"How——!" He seethed through his teeth. "You were right there!"

While remaining power drained from his body, Siroun looked up and the last remnants of Lord Valter's soul dissipated from view. Tears trickled down her cheeks as he vanished from sight. Siroun knew she could not save him, but at least he was free.

"Goodbye," she whispered into the air. When she heard Felthane's body hit the ground, she slammed a boot against his back and pinned the curve of the blade against his neck. "Yield."

He didn't speak. Only the sound of his heavy breathing caressed her eardrums. Those who surrounded her stood there, stunned, and unable to decide what to do next.

Felthane spoke up, "Why don't you kill me?"

The taunt made her press her foot harder against his ribcage, and she smiled when he groaned in agony. "I want to kill you," she seethed. "I wish I had some way to make you pay for everything you've done to Colin, to Lord Valter, to Zikky, and to me."

Her foot pushed harder upon his chest, and she could hear him gasping for air. She wanted nothing more than to give in to impulse and seal his fate. However, she pulled herself back from the precipice of desire and lifted some pressure. His gulp for air was like music to her ears, yet she felt no satisfaction from it.

"But no matter what I do to you, I already know you'll never be sorry for the choices you've made. And I'm not the only one who needs closure. You've tormented others far longer than me. So, I'll let them have you instead," she nodded toward the approaching soldiers.

Pulling back, she turned the blade away and struck him in the head with the blunted side. His unconscious body fell limp under her foot, and she wept tears of relief while looking back up to the skies above. She wondered if Zikky was proud of her. If Colin was at peace. If Lord Valter forgave her for leaving his son fatherless. She fell to her knees and wept. The remaining armies of Ysile Marden and the Vanis Aer Æther Guild closed in around her. Chatter started among the higher-ups, whoever was still conscious, on what to do with their savior and herald of damnation.

Soon they approached Siroun, and one of the generals belted at her in their gruff voice, "By the order of the King, we are to take you into custody."

Her eyes drifted in their direction, knowing what those

stern expressions on their faces meant. She was to return to that damned cell for crimes she did not commit. Just as the mages that came to apprehend her, an unnatural force flew past their noses. One minute Siroun sat there, awaiting her apprehension. The next she vanished. Nothing but a pile of wilted flowers remained upon the ground where she once stood.

54

*G*ULLS AND OCEAN waves roused Siroun to waking. She didn't recall passing out or fainting after the battle, but as she sat up she tried to recall what transpired. She brushed the dirt from her hands and took a look around to gain her bearings. From the lull of the ocean waves, she had to be near a beach. The wind slapped her in the face with her own hair, and she struggled to see as she got to her feet.

Siroun looked out over the stone wall and discovered that she was standing on an old tower rooftop about three stories tall. Not too terrible of a height, but Siroun wasn't about to escape by jumping. Upon further inspection, she found the weathered structure tilting a skosh. As surmised, the beach was only a few hundred feet away from where miles of sandy banks resided to the left, and craggy mountains kept watch along the right. On the opposite side a few miles inland, a small town went about its daily business all the while avoiding the stretch of abandoned buildings that resided between the village and the ocean.

It seemed strange that the villagers made no path through the wreckage to reach the ocean. In fact, the destroyed buildings gave the impression that this town used to be part of a larger port city not long ago. Most of the damage looked recent, and new makeshift barricades marked the active part of the town from the ruins left behind.

"Ah, I see you're awake," the gravelly voice chimed in, causing Siroun to shriek and clutch her heart before facing the person who just spoke.

Her breath slowed once she visually assessed the individual in front of her. It was hard to tell who, or what, she was addressing. Though the entity was giving her a pleasant smile, it was off-putting against the stout, hunchback form with thinning hair, ragged clothing, and a plethora of skin anomalies. Siroun had seen many things in the past several months of her travels but never had she encountered a creature this grotesque. Words escaped her as she pressed herself against the wall, realizing that certain death was right behind her if she fell. "W-who—wh—."

"Who am I?" they said, and Siroun picked up on the more predominant male tones in their weathered voice.

She nodded.

"Mortals used to call me Xacnak."

She tilted her head in reaction to the peculiar name. "And now?"

He chuckled before transitioning into a fit of coughing, the phlegm reverberating as he breathed. When he managed to clear his lungs, he replied, "As far as anyone's concerned, I don't exist. Well, everyone except for Arcandus, Revanine, and now you. If you don't mind, I'd like to keep it that way."

"Uh, sure," she said. His voice tickled the back of her memory before her eyes widened. "Wait, I know you! I've heard your voice before— the map! You're the voice from the map!"

It was hard to tell if he was grinning or not, but she assumed he was when he stood a bit taller. "That, I am."

While the wind continued whipping up her hair, her brows furrowed. "I'm sorry, I'm really confused right now. Where am I? Why am I here?"

Xacnak wobbled over to her, grunting every step of the way. Not sure if she should be calm or repulsed, Siroun stepped aside when the tiny man-creature shuffled next to her and plopped down to sit. His body slightly bounced when he landed. Afterward, he patted the stones with his knobby hand and waited for her to do the same. She didn't want to be rude and refuse, but his appearance was so unnerving that she lacked the desire to comply. Instead, she sat across from him with a couple of feet of distance between them.

That satisfied the old man, and he said with a raspy breath, "You're in Caspia, a former port city within the continent of Finnlock."

"Finnlock?" Siroun remembered Nikostraz mentioning bringing her here. Whether it was true or not was a different story.

"Yes, many ancient wars once started in these lands."

Vast mountain ranges stretched along the north and south, while in the west resided Caspia. Beyond that were swaths of fields before she saw the never-ending stretches of forest. The lands appeared idyllic and fertile, unlike the rocky slopes of Pustelia Crest.

"The reason you're here is that I am to be your mentor," said Xacnak.

She raised a brow at him. "My mentor? Why you?"

"I helped create you," his face contorted momentarily, and he made a brief screeching noise through his mouth before shaking it off. "Actually, I didn't create you, I re-engineered you. Because of my shortcomings, Revanine has brought you here under my tutelage."

"Shortcomings?" She quirked a brow at him. "What do you mean by that?"

"I diverted from Revanine's original instructions, and she's fairly upset that I put half of a destructive space god's soul into a mortal body. Honestly, she has no idea how hard it was for me to—."

"Hold on, hold on!" Siroun gestured for him to stop, now regretting that she wanted him to elaborate. "Are you serious right now?"

"Yes. Why would I lie about something like that?" Xacnak said without irony before giving a loud sniffle.

Siroun lacked the appropriate words to respond. She concluded that the explanation was too ridiculous to believe, it had to be. Her thoughts traveled to Zikky, and she felt a tightness in her chest when the losses resurfaced. Her face must have given her emotions away because Xacnak spoke up again.

"Is something the matter?" Tilting his head, he watched Siroun rub at her temples and groan.

She fought back the urge to shed more tears over the matter. She had cried enough on this journey. The final battle left her numb mentally, physically, and emotionally.

"Every time I feel I have control over my life, something else always comes up."

"Mm, I see." He tapped his fingers against the ground in contemplation. "Unfortunately for you, the only constant in this universe is that there is no constant. Change is inevitable."

"That might be true, but I don't find any joy having my friends and family taken from me by murder or deception."

That gave the old man pause. Every facial expression, always transitioned to contemplation whenever he was thinking of an appropriate response. Eventually, he said, "There was a time when I experienced similar situations that put my life in flux. I no longer remember those emotions. The memories are a constant reminder to those of us that survived that life is not an infallible state. I keep telling my colleagues that even gods die. You've experienced a mortal's existence for the last twenty-four years. Given all you have been through, I expected that you would fall into a state of despair. However, you're not mortal; you have never been. Today you are given a choice. What you make of it depends on you."

Siroun got to her feet and set to work inspecting the walls of the rooftop.

Xacnak pursed his lips to the side and grumbled, "What are you doing?"

"I'm searching for a way off of this thing," said Siroun. "I don't want a choice. I don't want a destiny or any other path that you and those so-called gods have in mind for me."

"Didn't you make a deal with Revanine?"

She stopped and reflected on that sentence before

saying, "I don't care. I'm tired of being led around by others simply because I'm ignorant of the world."

"The Lady of Ravens takes promises very seriously."

Siroun turned to face the little goblin of a man. "You don't understand, I thought I was hallucinating."

"Yes, that is typically the reaction others have with her." He paused before saying, "I think it's the horse. It's a bit too spooky for them."

A twitch came to Siroun's eye. "I'm sorry, but I'm not hanging around this dilapidated tower waiting for Revanine to figure out what to do with me."

A female voice spoke up this time, "Even if the alternative is your demise?"

Siroun turned to see who spoke and nearly collided into a behemoth of a dark horse. It snorted into her hair, adding to the unruliness from the wind. Her gasp of surprise garnered no reaction from the rider. Where before Revanine's face was shrouded in a black void, now it displayed the beauty and horror of both life and death as she moved.

"Oh no." Siroun groaned. "How did you get up here with the horse?"

"I believe a re-introduction is in order," the cloaked rider replied.

"Uh, no. That's okay, I—."

"I am Revanine, one of the twenty-one deities of this world's current pantheon. I was the one who entrusted you to Arcandus and Xacnak to hide you away so that mortals could not try and harness your power. Perhaps that trust was misplaced," her gaze traveled slowly to the old figure who appeared ambivalent to the snide remark.

Siroun took a step back. "Well, that's certainly enlightening, but I thought I was a god. Gods can't die, can they?"

The rider did not answer Siroun's question. Instead, Revanine's gaze steeled upon Siroun with eyes that shifted from a hetero-chromatic green and blue to a white-gray cloudiness. Her unflinching countenance made Siroun fidget with the hems of her sleeves in silence.

Satisfied, Revanine continued, "I realize you have questions, and that is why you are under Xacnak's care and counsel. He is to mentor you while I deal with the multiple anomalies have arisen in this world. Though I never intended to have you crafted into a conscious form, Xacnak believes there may be some use of you in the future. Since events with that meddling Hanmel Prince being as they were, you are to remain here until such a time that your talents might be of use to me."

Siroun's brows knitted together. "How long will that be?"

"Indefinitely."

"What? You can't keep me here forever!"

Xacnak waved a finger in the air. "On the contrary, we can."

Siroun was about to retort when Revanine cut her off. "Your abilities are unhinged and dangerous. You must wield your power with precision, and not lash out in bouts of fury as you demonstrated earlier. Ysile Marden has a long road to recovery from the damages you have rendered to their lands. However, your interactions with the Vanis Aer mages showed me something that has piqued my curiosity."

"Gee, lucky me," Siroun muttered, folding her arms.

"I offer you a choice: Agree to be trained by the Keeper of Infinite Knowledge. With him, you will understand the true nature of who you are and the power you wield. You will also understand the burden of responsibility that being an immortal of this world entails. Refuse, and I shall finish what I started ages ago when you first came to this planet with your counterpart."

It was probably unheard of to roll one's eyes at a Death God, but Siroun couldn't help herself. More importantly, the word that stood out the most in Revanine's last statement gave her pause as she said, "Counterpart?"

"Do we have a deal?" asked Revanine without skipping a beat.

Once again, Siroun found herself in another situation where she had no choice but to follow a path she never wanted. Despite the desire to tell Revanine off, she knew better. She would never go back to yesterday with her comfortable room, her father telling stories, or scribing books for the library. Never would she hear Lord Valter's soothing words of comfort, or experience the passion of love with Zikky. Even Colin's endless sass left some fond memories behind. They gave up everything for her, and she refused to desecrate that sacrifice.

"May I—," she hesitated. "May I have a bit of time to think it over before I give my answer?"

Revanine nudged her steed forward with the movement of her body. "I will return when the sun touches the sea. If you cannot decide by then, I will do it for you."

The enormous hooves clomped upon the stones. Flourishes of flora sprouted before wilting to death with each step. Watching Revanine was a spectacle all unto her own. She was a fearsome looking wraith when death took over her visage, only to look like a figure of flawless beauty when the flesh returned to her bones. She shimmered and decayed with such repetitive elegance that it was hard for Siroun to take her eyes off of the imposing goddess. The moment she blinked, Revanine was gone, and she wondered what kind of grand tales people told whenever they faced her. So enraptured she had been, that Siroun didn't hear Xacnak ambling up behind her. When he patted her on the back of the leg, since that was as far as he could reach, Siroun hopped sideways and cringed.

"Come along," he instructed, hobbling forward.

She wondered where he planned to go. "How are we getting down?"

Xacnak chuckled and stationed himself in the center of the roof. With a gesture beckoning her to follow, Siroun relented to the silent request even though she was still wary.

"This is a tower of illusion," he happily replied. "Nothing is what it seems."

With a stomp of his foot, the stones came to life, radiating a burst of power before a bright flash followed. In the blink of an eye, they disappeared.

55

*S*CORES OF PEOPLE gathered around the scaffold and filled the streets in anticipation of the execution. Conversations buzzed, townsfolk shared stories, and rumors circulated about the true origins of the warlock's history. King Nathaniel's arrival came with the trumpeting fanfare one came to expect from the monarch. Being the eldest female of the royal family, Princess Antoinette was on her father's arm as she walked with him to the staging area before taking her place among her other siblings. Captain Gilchrist, along with the other prominent members of the Vanis Aer Æther Guild, were present to witness the execution. Sebastian was not among them.

The King's fingers twitched and fidgeted while his eyes darted about the grand display. Almost every citizen of Ysile Marden came to witness this spectacle of justice unfold. When he raised his arm to the crowd, an immediate hush befell the city. Mages had their spells and tricks, but real power came from that one gesture. When the crowd submitted to silence, the King nodded to both the executioner and judge who were waiting at the ready.

The judge's voice resounded over the crowd, "Bring forth the prisoner."

Cheers erupted as a steel-barred carriage, pulled by two Elderhorns, trotted into view along with an array of guards and guild agents. Though Felthane was bereft of any magical abilities, they spared no expense in using the nullifying shackles and mouthpiece that once held Siroun. The prisoner slammed the shackles against the bars as his muffled screams got drowned out by the jeers of the people. Rotten food rained upon the cage, and one of the guild members erected a barrier to prevent the spoils from further striking them.

Everyone wanted to see this beacon of terror brought to justice, including the Dowager Duchess Ammeline, who arrived dressed in black with the new Duke of Firenz, in her arms. Her eyes were red and puffy despite multiple attempts to hide such displays of mourning with make-up.

When the carriage reached the scaffold, the guards dragged Felthane out of the cage screaming and struggling against his metal bonds. They restrained him before inching up the steps toward the block. The judge unfurled the parchment that listed the crimes and spoke, "Felthane, you stand convicted of the following atrocities: The acquisition and subsequent practice of the necrotic arts as founded by the Dark Gods of corruption…"

As the judge continued, a Sylvani-born executioner stood over the former warlock, a merciless gaze reflecting in her eyes. Wisps of frost billowed off her bluish skin despite the warm summer weather. At her side was a long, black blade, imbued with the soul of an ice elemental, and crafted with the precision of a master sword-smith.

After several minutes of struggling, the guards tethered and bound Felthane to the block. Unlike other regions, the executioners of Seda never asked for forgiveness before doling out the sentence. There was no sense of sympathy as she pulled the blade from its sheath and inspected its sharpness while the judge finished reading the conviction.

"... for these crimes, we have found you guilty, and the sentence: Death." The judge rolled the parchment up and looked to Felthane's quivering visage. "Have you any last words?"

The guards removed the metal gag, and Felthane spat the foul taste out of his mouth before looking over to the King and his children. "You have the wrong man! I am innocent!"

A roar of jeers and boos erupted from the crowd, while the rest of the gentry looked upon him with contempt. That no one believed him brought further terror to his eyes.

"I am the true King of Anastas!" he cried. "This man that stands before you is an impostor, I swear it! Please!"

Seeing that he was garnering no attention from the nobility, Felthane leaned toward the eldest of the daughters, and the guards grabbed him by the arms to restrain him. "Antoinette, my dear. My little bird—."

A nearby guard slapped him across the face, "You will address the Princess as Her Highness, knave!"

But Felthane remained desperate to catch her attention. And catch it, he did.

Princess Antoinette glared at him at first, but muted

her expression afterward. Though she made no motion to halt the procession, that there was no show of disdain when addressed so informally caused Princess Claudette to stare at her sister.

King Nathaniel's chest heaved as he stood and steeled his stare at the man who called him a fake in front of the crowd. The youngest of Nathaniel's children, Princess Lisette, hooked her fingers into Princess Claudette's armored skirts and hid behind her sister.

Princess Claudette rubbed a hand along her back in comfort and whispered, "It will be over soon."

Among the nobility that stood with the King in solidarity was the Duke of Vasile, Lord Marcus Rovani. Though an important member of the royal court, Lord Marcus found himself relegated to the rear of the aristocratic party in attendance. While most considered it an affront, the Duke of Vasile didn't mind as it permitted him the opportunity to observe others without being heavily scrutinized himself. It was in this moment that a person in clanking plate armor sidled up behind him. The Duke watched the executioner's procession while noting the proximity of the knight.

He tilted back and spoke over his shoulder while remaining attentive of the impending execution. "A bit close, aren't we?"

Bored by the cries of insanity, the executioner shifted her eyes to the King who gave the nod to finish the job. With a firm grasp on the hilt, she widened her stance to prep the swing. The blade's song lulled every spectator into a sense of awe as it struck true through the neck of its unwilling sacrifice. Those who could not stomach such a sight shut their eyes or turned away. Children buried their faces in their parent's clothes, or flinched at the moment of impact. As a testament to both the sharpness of the blade and the wielder's swordsmanship, there was no need for a second swing. When the head thumped into the basket, she released her stance. A sharp flick of the sword helped loosen the blood before she wiped the blade clean and sheathed it.

Meanwhile, the strange breathing behind Lord Marcus stopped. "I've come from the Lady of Ravens to give warning that you are not to interfere in her work."

The Duke couldn't help but chuckle when he recognized the voice. "Dressing up as a messenger, are we? I didn't know you enjoyed playing Revanine's lapdog, Arcandus."

The plate-wearing knight stood in silence at first, but when Lord Marcus spared a moment to glance over his shoulder and raise a brow, a disgusted scoff echoed from the armor. "She's not pleased to know you're still alive."

With a smirk, the Duke murmured to ensure no other ears perked. "I wondered how many eons it might take for her to notice."

"Such arrogance," Arcandus muttered. "You stir the ire of a power you do not comprehend."

"Trust me when I say I am well-versed in what the Lady of Ravens is capable of doing," said Lord Marcus. "But that is negligible to me when you turn my beloved partner into a biology experiment, thus forcing my hand to get involved. Be careful how you rebuild her destiny, for we buck the laws of order at whim."

There was little more than a snort of distaste before

Arcandus melded away into the crowd. Meanwhile, the executioner held up Felthane's severed head to show everyone within Ysile Marden of the completed deed. King Nathaniel steeled his gaze at the face that had haunted the family lineage for two generations. When the gruesome token of victory paraded the stage long enough, the King stepped forward and raised his hand to quiet the crowd. A gleam of excitement flickered in his eyes. Princess Claudette raised a brow at her older sister once more, but Princess Antoinette paid the glance no mind.

King Nathaniel took his position before the people and projected his voice, "Today we bear witness to the dawning of our revelation in these trying times. We shall never forget the sacrifices made to emerge victorious from the horrors of battle. Let this event be a reminder to every Anastian that our greatest triumphs are a testament to our indomitable strength as a kingdom and a country. Hold your heads high, for we were tested and found worthy against a mighty foe. His death is my tribute to you as King, and I give my solemn vow that we will reach new heights. This day begins our Golden Era!"

A roar of elation resounded throughout the city. Never had the King given such a speech that stirred the hearts of the people like this. As the nobles and his children clapped in adulation to the riveting words, King Nathaniel turned around, signaling the end of the event.

"I never knew you had that in you, father," said Prince Anthony, eliciting a roll of the eyes from Princess Antoinette.

"Thank you, son," the disingenuous words rolled off of the King's tongue.

The monarch processed back into the castle halls surrounded in a flurry of conversation and gossip among the gentry. Meanwhile, Princess Antoinette slowed her gait to make eye contact with Lord Marcus and flicked a gaze upon her arm waiting for him to catch up.

The Duke wasted no time bidding a colleague farewell and sidle up next to the Princess, tucking her arm under his own. "That was quite the speech His Majesty gave. It makes me wonder where he procured such confidence."

"Yes, well, my father is not himself as of late," she replied without the same humor in her voice. They both slowed their steps further, allowing the crowds to pass. Princess Antoinette pulled out her fan to hide her lips and whispered, "What have you done?"

Lord Marcus kept smiling despite the Princess looking anything but amused. "Helping you keep your plans on course."

"This was not part of the agreement. What did you promise him?"

"Nothing that you can't handle, my dear. Trust me."

She narrowed her ice-blue eyes at him. "I love my family, but—."

"I thought you loved the crown more?"

Her steps shortened at the bold interjection, but she picked up the pace and held her head high despite the accusation. "I have never spoken such words."

"You might not have said it," said Lord Marcus, "but I know it fills your thoughts every waking moment. So, when I say it is for your benefit, then I expect a modicum of trust to follow suit. Agreed?"

Once again, she glared at him before giving a tittering laugh. "Oh my, how our true nature shines."

With that, he took a moment to place a chaste kiss upon her knuckle. "Don't worry, Your Highness. This slight doesn't ruin our friendship."

He could tell she was forcing a smile which he mirrored in jest toward her anger. Eventually, her Ladies in Waiting came flocking to fill her in on the recent gossip now that the execution was over, and it was business as usual in the royal courts of Ysile Marden.

56

THUNDER ROLLED IN the distance as Siroun put the final touches on the memorials to her friends. Stones and seashells laid in an array of patterns indicative of their elements, giving homage to each mage. Siroun found a stray animal tooth to add to a fourth placement meant for Nikostraz. Even though she never knew the real Dragomyr, she felt it prudent to honor him if there were no others that mourned his death. These grave markers rested along the base of the tower facing away from the beach and toward the town. In the several hours she mulled over her decision, not a single resident of Caspia approached the beach.

She took this time to meditate on everything that had happened, and to give her friends thanks for coming into her life. Despite the hardships, she did not regret the journey nor the lessons learned along the way. However, those fond memories wrought unspeakable pain, and Siroun wasn't sure if she could continue to face those trials of the heart if everyone she met slipped away. Revanine's offer didn't hold back the message that Siroun's current existence was by complete accident. She knew that Revanine and Xacnak dangled information about her past if she shackled herself to a lifetime of servitude to Revanine's plans. Not just an average lifetime, an immortal's lifetime. She spent the hours flipping back and forth, questioning herself, and pretending to converse with each of her friends as though they were there. Their wisdom fabricated by memories of what she believed each would say to her. Tears cropped up throughout the process, and she found it hard even pretending to have a conversation with them.

None of it brought her to a final decision, and the sun was getting close to the water's horizon. With a heavy sigh, Siroun continued to meditate next to the grave markers until she heard a strange sound of magic warbling behind her, followed by a fall and the grunting of a male voice. She turned around to find someone dressed in Vanis Aer clothing, facedown in the sand. The familiar entity pushed himself to stand, then brushed off the dirt. Now she recognized him.

"Sebastian?" She shuffled him close against the tower so that no one from the town in the distance could see him and said, "What are you doing here?"

He looked terrible, with his disheveled hair and dark circles under his eyes. Though she wanted to ask him why he looked so sleep-deprived, she stuck to her main concern. "If anyone sees you, they will throw a fit."

"I know," he grinned from ear-to-ear, as though the act of getting into trouble was the exciting part of this whole adventure. He then gave a large yawn and followed up with, "But Niamh and I had to see for ourselves that you were safe. I pestered Arcandus until I pulled a stunt he couldn't ignore."

"Why are you so tired?" She then eyed him. "And what did you do?"

"To answer your first question: I have yet to get any sleep since that battle we had yesterday." He yawned again before continuing, "As to your other question: I rerouted a leyline and blew up part of the guild hall."

Siroun paused and recalled him mentioning that the Hemophæther State affected him differently. The second answer caused her to shout back, "Are you nuts? Why did you do that? You could have killed someone!"

His face drooped into a childish frown. "I made sure it was empty."

She smacked at her face with a hand and let it slide down her cheek. His presence here was a significant risk on multiple fronts. "As much as I'm upset with you for risking your life, and others, to come find me, I have to admit it's appreciated. Although, how did you get here without using one of those Orpheum Compasses? And how are you going to get back?"

"Trade secret, but don't worry, I have a way to get back. Niamh wanted to tag along, but she's indisposed with the injured." He snapped his fingers and pulled a small book bag out. "That reminds me, I brought a few things for you."

He took time rifling through his satchel before pulling out a book and a small jar. "I found it when I was cleaning out an old storage unit the other day. Being that you are part Dragomyr, I figured you would appreciate it. The salve is from Niamh. She made to help your scars heal better." He pointed to the gash near her eye. "Did Felthane do that?"

"Yeah," said Siroun, then lifted her arm where the guild researchers removed a scale and saw that the bandage had long fallen off and needed attention. Even though Niamh barely knew her, she was still thinking of Siroun's well-being. It was easy to see why Sebastian harbored affections for the woman. She collected the gifts from him and flipped through a few pages of the book. It was an old tome on the history of The Great Three, and research on the plausibility of their existence.

It brought a huge smile to her face, and she hugged both of the items to her chest. "Thank you, Sebastian. Your friendship means a lot to me."

He smiled at her through another yawn before another portal started opening up behind him. Siroun blinked while Sebastian peeked over his shoulder. "I have one more gift. I think you'll enjoy this the most."

The portal flashed and pulsed, leaving Siroun on bated breath to see what it could be. With one last flash, she shielded her eyes as a figure came through the rift of magic before everything closed.

"Ah-ta-ta," the female voice griped as she ruffled her frock of colored hair before giving Siroun a wide grin. "Hiya, gel-gel!"

Siroun stared in disbelief as she reached up to pinch herself. When the pain registered in her face, tears welled up in her eyes, and she flung herself at the Skivat. "Zikky!"

"Whoa!" Zikky caught the sobbing Siroun while grimacing in pain.

At first, Siroun paid no attention to the sounds while squeezing her girlfriend as hard as she could muster. But when Zikky let out a pleading gasp, she let go. "Oh! I'm sorry! I mean, you're alive! How are you alive?"

The Skivat coughed a few times when the air became available to her again. She lifted the top of her shirt to reveal a large bandage around her chest. "I never died."

"But…" Siroun tried to wrap her head around that response. "But I saw you take the hit. I tried to wake you up. You weren't breathing."

"Oh, I was unconscious and almost died, but I never crossed that final threshold, thanks to Seb's healer friend." Zikky turned to Sebastian only to see the man leaning against the tower, snoring. Reaching over, she flicked the tip of his nose which startled him back to waking.

"What? What'd I do?" Sebastian grunted and looked around in a daze while both women giggled at him.

Once again, Niamh's help made a monumental impact, and now Siroun wished the other woman had been here so she could thank her. However, that needed to wait for another day. Joy overwhelmed Siroun as she wrapped her arms around Zikky one more time, careful not to hurt her.

After a few seconds Zikky tapped her on the shoulder and she backed up and pointed to Siroun's face. "What happened to yer eye?"

"Oh, this?" Siroun reached up and ran her fingers along the wound that ran across her brow and upper cheek. "It's Felthane's fault."

The Skivat sucked in the air between her teeth as she pawed at it to get a better look. "That's gonna leave a scar, gel-gel. Ya got too close when he was swipin', eh?"

"It was a rookie mistake, I know."

"Nah," Zikky gave her a light pat on the arm and

beamed with pride. "It's a badge of honor for beatin' that turd into the ground!"

A flush of heat radiated from Siroun's cheeks as she touched the gash once more. She wanted to take every second in the world to absorb this moment, but she noticed something odd about Zikky's attire. Taking a step back, she stared at the mage's leather pants and linen shirt before asking, "Where's your guild uniform?"

"Ah, that," Zikky grinned sheepishly. "Let's just say my bravery didn't exonerate me in Mister High-and-Mighty's eyes."

Sebastian rubbed at this face with his fingers to stay awake as he replied, "They tried to imprison her again, and the guild stripped her rank."

Siroun's eyes widened. "What?"

Zikky waved her hand, dismissing the concern. "Psh, no biggie. Besides, the King and I ain't fond acquaintances anymore. He's branded me a fugitive and put a bounty on my head."

"What!" Siroun gaped.

"Don't be jealous, gel-gel. Ya've got one too!" She grinned despite the grim news. Pointing in Sebastian's direction, she said, "Our demigod gets a pass because he protected the King and his family after we moved in on Felthane. Must be nice gettin' a royal pardon."

With Siroun speechless, Sebastian shook his head. "Anastas is hostile territory to the both of you. Niamh patched Zikky up enough to survive the teleportation."

"And survive, I did!" Zikky patted her chest before her cheerful mood sobered. "In all seriousness though, it's for the better. If I had to choose between the Vanis Aer, The Hive, or my gel-gel; I'm gonna choose you every time."

Those words warmed Siroun's heart. The journey with Felthane might have been over, but she wasn't alone. Zikky then looked at Sebastian and said, "Give Herbalist Girl my thanks. She's got real talent."

Sebastian smiled and nodded before turning his attention back to Siroun. "Why are you out here, anyway?"

The question made sense. Siroun vanished on the battlefield, and she already picked up on the fact that these gods weren't keen on divulging information to others. Sebastian probably learned that lesson long before her, and it explained why he went to the lengths he did to garner a scrap of attention. Had he been mortal, and not Arcandus's son, she doubted the Archmage would have replied at all.

"They brought me here to train," said Siroun.

"Train?" Sebastian said while trying to fight off another yawn. "For what?"

"My actions in Ysile Marden got a lot of unwanted attention, so Revanine has me staying here until she says otherwise."

Zikky's eyes widened. "Wow! The Death Goddess herself is keepin' an eye on ya? Color me impressed!"

Sebastian's face contorted in confusion. "That's extreme."

"Yeah, well, when you obliterate half of Ysile Marden's forces and reshape part of its geography, someone's bound to notice," she said, glancing in Zikky's direction only to be greeted by a clueless grin.

"Wait, that was you?" Sebastian furrowed his brows. "I thought that was Felthane's handiwork."

To that, Siroun remarked, "Didn't you hear? I read books and break worlds."

"Ha!" Zikky guffawed. "That's a good one, gel-gel."

Sebastian was not amused by that little quip, but he put on a brave face for posterity's sake. "Part of the land is carved up. I guess I should be grateful that the damage remained predominantly outside of the city walls. But Ysile Marden's forces took heavy losses, which impacts the deal he made with that Titanian priestess since there was a promise to aid them in Balforem. Now they lack the resources to fulfill their end of the bargain."

Siroun hadn't put too much thought into the ramifications of going berserk until now. Revanine's words made sense once Sebastian put it into perspective. She knew she didn't have full control over the Sinefine Bible. There were only notions based on reactions Siroun witnessed while using it. However, there was another side to the artifact that reared its ugly head; that tipping point where she delved into the greatest recesses of rage. She remembered the satisfaction as she unleashed her anger upon the masses. Even now, she felt justified. Remorseless. Therein resided the issue, and it was understandable that Revanine wasn't going to let someone like her wander freely without additional terms associated with them.

With a sigh, Siroun said, "I have no idea how long I will be here. My mentor is educating me for something specific, but I have only a vague understanding."

"That's ominous and oddly similar to my situation," said Sebastian as he averted his gaze. Siroun and Zikky waited to see if he planned on elaborating further, but didn't.

Zikky changed the subject with, "So yer stuck here until yer warden says otherwise?"

Siroun nodded. "Revanine said forever, but maybe there's a reduced sentence for good behavior?"

The silence that followed afterwards turned into a series of giggles between the three of them, then escalated to laughter. In truth, the suggestion wasn't meant to be a joke.

After wiping a tear of mirth from her eye, Zikky said, "We'll figure somethin' out. We always do." She then reached out and took Siroun's hand to give a squeeze.

"I hope you consider Niamh and me your allies in this endeavor," said Sebastian. "I might not provide much support at the moment, but if you need me, I will help."

Zikky gave him a playful punch in the shoulder. "Ya got bigger things to worry about like chasin' that dream to escape."

Siroun's interest piqued. "Escape?"

The demigod grinned with his sleep-deprived eyes. "I think you're right."

Siroun remained lost on what he was talking about. But when she asked, "Where are you planning to go?"

Sebastian answered with, "When I figure that out, I'll let you know."

It wasn't the answer Siroun hoped for, but let it go.

"So, where ya stayin'?" said Zikky. "Is it another luxurious guest room so we can sleep the days away together? I mean, bein' imprisoned for eternity could have benefits with the bedroom exploits and whatnot."

While Sebastian pretended not to hear that last part, Siroun blushed and replied, "That sounds like a great proposal."

Xacnak's silent and sudden appearance within their circle caused Sebastian to leap away out of instinct. Unfortunately, he couldn't stick the landing, and toppled backward into the ground, dirtying his uniform further. Even Siroun skirted back several paces since she still wasn't used to his creepy features. Zikky was the only one who appeared unfazed, and even commented with, "Well ain't ya the apple of yer mother's eye."

Xacnak adjusted the thick-rimmed glasses on his stout-hooked nose, then looked at them before grunting at the lad, "Who are you, Vanis Aer?"

"U-uh, S-S-Sebastian Di M-Mercurio, sir," said Sebastian.

"Ah, Arcandus' whelp. He told me you might show up. Mentioned you were a precocious little git." He then turned to Zikky and looked her up and down. "I can already tell you will be a pain in my ass."

"Hello to ya too," Zikky replied with a smirk.

Sebastian conjured up his courage to ask, "A-and you are?"

Siroun opened her mouth to state his name, but Xacnak cut her off, "Her mentor. Now, have you settled your visit with her?"

Sebastian gulped. "Who, me? Um, I guess?"

"Good. I assume you can make your way back without being seen by the locals, yes? We can't be starting another war between Anastas and Finnlock over a misunderstanding."

Sebastian nodded, overwhelmed by the man's bluntness. Meanwhile, Xacnak's eye traveled back to Siroun and noticed what she was holding. He plucked the tome from her grasp while muttering, "What is this about, I wonder? Let me see."

His thumb bent the pages, forcing them to flip at a rapid pace, and his eyes twitched side-to-side. He skimmed the book in a matter of seconds and Siroun recognized the identical technique of her speed-reading process. He snapped the book shut, and gave it back to her, "Yes, that's acceptable. Can't have you taking on any more spellbooks for now."

Hobbling a few more paces forward, Xacnak shook his finger at Sebastian. "No more books, understood?"

"U-understood, sir. May I at least write to her?"

"Yes, yes, but keep your research findings to yourself. You have a solid foundation of magical principles as part of your education. Beskonerynth does not. Don't go filling her head with your theoretical nonsense until I've instilled the basics."

"Y-yes sir, understood."

"Good. Also, get some rest before your magic hurts someone." Xacnak looked back at Zikky and pointed a knobby finger at her, "Now, as for you. You're leaving with the boy."

"Nah," the Skivat replied with nonchalance. "I'm gonna hang around a while and check this place out."

Xacnak stared at her long and hard before saying, "No."

Siroun protested with, "That's not fair!"

"Nothing's fair," he retorted. "I'm not running an inn for your friends. Do you not understand the meaning of discreet?"

"No, but I know the meanin' of persistence," replied Zikky with an ear-to-ear grin.

Once again, a long pause came over the group. Nothing but the sound of gulls and crashing waves echoed while Xacnak tried to hold his ground against the stalwart Skivat. The staring match didn't last long before he gave in. "You're never going to leave, are you?"

"Don't underestimate my ability to annoy you to the brink of insanity," she said with confidence, then pointed in Siroun's direction. "Besides, we can train her together."

An incoherent curse slipped from his lips before grumbling, "Fine, but you stay in the village."

"Will ya let gel-gel out to play if I do?"

"Yes, yes! As long as you say nothing to the simpletons on the real purpose of your residence."

Zikky took a moment to consider the terms before saying, "Sounds good."

With an impatient sigh, Xacnak pointed to Sebastian and belted out, "You, leave already."

"Y-yes, sir," said Sebastian as he saluted.

Xacnak waddled over near a side of the tower that did not show a door or opening and stared at Siroun while making audible taps with his stubby foot. She realized she needed to wrap things up.

When he straightened himself up, Sebastian said, "Don't forget to write."

"You too," said Siroun, then wiggled the jar of salve at him. "And thank Niamh for me. Her kindness means a lot, and yours."

There was a knowing smile between the two of them that Xacnak interrupted by an endless fit of coughing. Several times the little gremlin of a deity banged on his chest before he ceased, grumbling, "Damn sea air."

Siroun couldn't help but sigh as she looked over to Zikky while twisting her finger around a ringlet of silver hair. "Are you sure you will be all right?"

"Yeah, I got it covered," said Zikky as she reached over and pulled Siroun's hand away from the endless fidgeting. "From the looks of things, the village could use some muscle, and I heal quick." She leaned in and whispered in Vat'tu, *"I'll figure out a way for you to escape this place."*

"I can speak your language, Skivat." Xacnak said through a wheezing fit.

"Oh," she chuckled while scratching her cheek with a forefinger. "Whoops."

Though Siroun remained unconvinced that everything would be fine, she still trusted Zikky. "Come find me if something is wrong."

"Gel-gel, I'm a big girl," Zikky reached up and stroked Siroun's cheek before leaning in to kiss her. Zikky tasted of herbs and flowers, likely from the healing tonics Niamh administered to help her recover faster. Siroun didn't want her to leave after learning that Zikky survived the injury.

When their lips parted, Zikky tilted her head and said to Xacnak. "Don't forget yer promise."

The troll-ish looking deity grunted and waved his hand dismissively at her.

"Work hard, and learn lots," said Zikky, giving Siroun a gentle smack on the butt. "I'll be waitin' for ya in town when he lets ya out to play."

Siroun squeaked along with a smile as she meandered over to her new mentor. Xacnak didn't spare her the chance to wave a final goodbye as they teleported into the tower. Her footing shifted, and a light whoosh of air caressed her face before finding herself in a large, cylindrical, pseudo-lit room where the walls were bookshelves as far as the eye could see. Siroun gasped as her eyes scoured the crammed rows of an endless ocean of books, maps, and other wonders. In the middle of the room sat a large desk and several small tables full of parchment, knick-knacks, and other supplies. Wonder took over, and Xacnak grinned before snapping his fingers to pull her out of a trance.

"Yes, yes. I realize you've reached your happy place. In due time you will have your fill. Under my tutelage, you will read only the books that pertain to the topics at hand and nothing more until you've advanced to the next subject. Are we clear?"

"That seems," she paused, "limiting."

"Trust me when I say, you won't be bored. Books won't be the only methods of instruction I have planned for you. To understand yourself, you need to understand the world you live in," his face contorted again, and he clarified. "The world in which you decided to stay. Before I impart this knowledge, I need your agreement as set by Revanine's command. Otherwise, I'm afraid our time together ends now."

Siroun considered the recent string of events. Her fingers rubbed against the jar of handmade salve, and she took another look at the deluge of knowledge that encircled her. When she met Xacnak's gaze, a new purpose filled her eyes. "I agree to the terms. Please teach me."

"Good, that's what I wanted to hear," he gestured for her to make herself comfortable as he waved his hand a few more times and a giant board pulled into view as chalk danced across its surface. Notes started scrawling across the board for Siroun to read while he gave his first lecture. Once Siroun settled in, her eyes honed in on the board. She absorbed every written word, forever locked in her memories, same as the books read in the past. When she appeared to be engaged, he began Xacnak lecture, "I'll get right to the point. You are a god, a mighty one at that."

"The only thing I don't understand is if I'm so powerful, why can't I do anything without the Sinefine Bible?"

"Ah, yes. That's because of our re-engineering efforts. There was a hiccup in execution when we went to design a suitable shell for you. We're not experts on the matter."

Xacnak glanced Siroun's way and saw her glaring at him. The deity delivered every new piece of information in such a crass fashion that she wanted to boot him off of the rooftop. It might not have mattered much to him, but to her this was a major rewriting of everything she knew or ever believed. While it was easy for him to act flippant over 'trivial mortal affairs', Siroun did not view it that way.

He must have noticed the annoyance on her face and cleared his throat. "I apologize if this is a lot to digest, but I know what Revanine is up to and I believe she'll need your help more than she realizes."

When she heard that last sentiment, Siroun set aside her anger. "Why do you think she needs my help?"

"Your abilities might be as powerful as hers, and that is why my mischievous immortal colleagues nudged Prince Llyr to seek you out. My theory is if the world will dive into chaos, then I say we fight fire with fire. Revanine needs time to realize that I'm right. Her issue is that she's stubborn. Thinks she knows better just because she's older than the lot of us, except you, maybe."

"You don't lack confidence in your convictions, that much is certain," Siroun quipped. She didn't want to become an immortal weapon for another deity after she had fought so hard to avoid becoming one for Felthane. "If it makes Revanine feel better, I have no intention on being swept up in her problems. I'm happy to oblige staying out of her way."

"If that's what you wish once you're free, so be it. But Clayne needs you, and I intend to arm you with the knowledge to thrive on your own, and I'm guessing the Skivat intends to improve your fighting prowess. To do that, we'll use the issues cropping up in Caspia as your training grounds to achieve both goals at the same time."

"Wait," she looked up at him, now worried for Zikky's safety. "What's going on in Caspia?"

"Lots of things." Xacnak didn't feel compelled to enlighten her further, but followed up with, "It's nothing your girlfriend can't handle, I'm sure."

"Won't Revanine get angry?"

He waved away the concern. "Feh! She's too busy doing other things to pay attention to you anymore. Right now, she's molding her Chosen One to pay you any mind, as long as you're in my care."

Siroun remembered this same situation in the Raven Knights book. Revanine was selecting someone to be her Champion and bestow great powers upon that person to enact a cause in her name. Siroun didn't envy this new Chosen One. Xacnak might have looked like a little gremlin, but he seemed pleasant enough, and the tower appeared to provide all the comforts of home for now. It saddened her that someone was going to be plucked from their life and thrust into a mission of immense burden for the sake of Revanine's purpose.

"Why doesn't she just handle the problem herself?" she said.

"You've seen what your abilities can do to the world when you lose control, yes?" When Siroun nodded, Xacnak continued, "Your powers are still broken. Yet, even in such a state, you have rendered a great deal of damage. When Revanine wields her abilities, it is said that worlds exist no more. Therefore, she must entrust others to do her bidding."

"Wield your power with precision," she murmured to herself, realizing the advice Revanine gave her earlier.

"Yes."

"Who did she choose?"

"One whose fate was woven by Revanine's hand since the day they were born. A Titanian priestess by the name of Lyonesse."

ACKNOWLEDGEMENTS

I want to thank all of my BETA readers who went through the tireless process of providing me some great critique. Your honesty means the world to me!

Amanda
Andrew
Bryan
Crow
Jamie
Jeff
Jesseca
Kris
Lara
Maria

ABOUT THE AUTHOR

Lauren Sefchik is an Arizona native who avoids the sun by day, and conquers raid bosses by night. Her love for geek culture started with a video game system from the 70's, a set of polyhedral dice, and a team of heroines in sailor suits. She seeks an army of adventurers willing to journey with her to the furthest reaches of their imaginations with love, laughter, and a lot of mead!

CPSIA information can be obtained
at www.ICGtesting.com
Printed in the USA
LVHW011734201120
672131LV00001B/8